To Pat from

Love
Peter

Black Coffee

Edited by
Andrew MacRae

DARKHOUSE
BOOKS

Anthology copyright © 2016 by Darkhouse Books
ISBN 978-0-9961828-9-8
Published May, 2016
Published in the United States of America

Darkhouse Books
160 J Street, #2223
Niles, California 94539

Black Coffee

Introduction

by Andrew MacRae

Noir is a slippery genre to define. The meaning swirls and drifts like fog under flickering streetlights, and it sneaks up from behind like a junkie in search of a fix. Noir schemes like a unfaithful wife, and lands a sucker punch when your back is turned.

As definitions of noir split and splinter like cracks in a bullet-scarred window, the three hundred-plus pages of our anthology would be consumed were we to attempt transcribe them all. Accordingly, we will not. Rather, we will let the following twenty-three stories do the defining for us.

Some of the authors will be familiar to readers of previous Darkhouse Books anthologies, others are new to our pages. Some are long-time authors, and some only recently published, but all demonstrate wicked writing chops.

Hustlers and harlots, cops and robbers, philandering husbands and wayward wives, gangsters and priests and dames who know how to use a gun; they take us on a murderous journey across the country, around the world, and back through time. We rub up against sin and deceit, sacrifice and sensuality, shimmering evening gowns and blue jeans and white blouses—and yes, the requisite cats. And, while these tales tell of death and despair, wrack and ruin, they also offer the possibility of redemption. After all, what are noir stories, if not modern takes on cautionary tales of old?

Now it is time to settle back with a tumbler of your favorite beverage, perhaps a cat on your lap, or a dog at your feet. Outside, rain falls in fitful bursts and car tires hiss on wet pavement. A door slams in the distance and soon after a motorcycle roars into life and speeds away, its gears whining in protest.

It's a noir world after all.

Andrew MacRae
May, 2016
Niles, California

We begin our anthology with a tale of deceit, danger, and death by Peter H. Denton. Set in a sultry clime, his story examines the Eternal Triangle – and the emotional forces it engenders and eventually unleashes.

Mr. Denton has led a remarkable life, including sailing a sixty foot gaff-rigged schooner across the Pacific and around the South Seas until his boat was lost in a hurricane. He has a PhD from the University of North Carolina at Chapel Hill, and now devotes himself to writing full-time.

Diving for Dollars

by Peter Denton

NOUMEA NEW CALEDONIA

The sun set like thunder on the surging reef across the bay.

Five couples sat with Jake and Maggie on cushions in the comfortable cockpit of *Searene*. Simon stood and hung a lantern from the boom. It was bright enough that we could see each other and dim enough that I could sneak glances at Jake. We had finished eating and I clattered the dirty dishes to the sink below. I slipped off my sandals, quickly, quietly, returned to the deck, stood outside the umbrella of light, and watched Jake. He never moved, obsessively stroked his beard, offered an opinion on which anchor held the best, or spoke unless he was spoken to. His hands lay quietly on his thighs or clasped across his chest.

All the other women scrounged for an excuse to say something, anything to capture Jake's fleeting attention. I searched for a tactic to approach him with dignity and to say something without blushing or stuttering. At 10 o'clock, heading back to their own boats, our circle of friends clambered into their skiffs, which were tied off to *Searene*, a corny name, but since the seventy-foot sailing yacht was a wedding gift, I had laughed and hugged my newly minted father-in-law, Saul, and said, "Dad, it's beautiful beyond my dreams, and the name is so deliciously cute."

That had been three years ago, and Simon and I had argued in every port from Nassau to Noumea. Seawater washes away the surface and lays bare the truth. I had lost all respect for him. *En route* to the South Pacific, marinas were scarce and *Searene*, like all cruising yachts, normally anchored out. If a stiff breeze piped up, while all the other skippers in the anchorage slept, Simon jumped out of bed and ran forward to reassure himself that the anchor still held. In the tropics, the easterly trade winds prevail, so most anchorages are on the west side of the islands. On our first night in Martinique, the wind shifted to the west and *Searene* swung around up into it. Simon sent out an SOS. Many skippers rushed to rescue us, saw our boat happily bobbing in the westerly breeze, and turned back in silence to re-anchor their boats.

First thing the next morning, Betty rowed over and said, "Honey, don't feel bad. Any of us could've made the same mistake." Except that no one they knew had made such a blunder, and no one, especially me, would forget it.

In port, life proceeded at a slow, predictable pace. By nine o'clock in the morning, the boys had gone into Noumea to buy the wherewithal for the unending repairs yachts require, and the girls assembled on *Searene* for our morning coffee klatch. Addressing no one in particular, I asked, "What's the deal with Jake?"

One of the younger women answered, "Do you mean is he screwing Maggie? Nobody seems to know for sure, but he's not screwing any of us."

Betty said, "More's the pity."

I laughed with the others.

More's the pity, I thought. B*ut don't pity me. I'm going to be the exception to the rule.*

Money was a safe topic. I asked casually, "How does Jake get by?"

Betty, always poised to talk about Jake, said, "I thought everyone knew. He runs an under-the-table dive charter to where the action is. John and I don't see eye-to-eye about much anymore, but we agree that diving with Jake is the best. You and Simon ought to give him a try. You won't be disappointed." Betty hesitated. "Besides, from the look of *Searene*, I'm sure you can afford it."

I never apologized for my wealth, the result of hard work at the Yeshiva and my ascent to Vassar, an excellent vantage point from which to survey the field. I had known where the boys weren't: Queens, Brooklyn, and especially, the Bronx; and where they were: Yale, Duke, and especially, Harvard.

I took a sip of coffee and with a smile said, "You've got that right, Betty. Money's not much good if you don't spend it."

My mom, who bored her friends with talk of my accomplishments, bored me with the wisdom that it is just as easy to fall in love with a rich man as with a poor man. Racing in Vassar's sailing club, I met relaxed young men who came from good (meaning, to my mother, wealthy) families, and what's more, because they were satisfied with the gentleman's C, could adjust their schedule to fit mine. Mom was willing to relinquish me during vacations so I could accept invitations to the elegant homes of suitable suitors.

Even though Betty had asked for it, she put her coffee cup down on the cockpit, rose and said, "Look at the time. I need to get to Le Magasin before they close for their lunch break."

When Simon came back for lunch with a generator gasket to replace one that had blown, I said, "Betty says Jake takes out dive charters to the best places on the ocean side of the reef."

Simon and I had eagerly taken up diving in Provenciales. We never dove unless we could find a native to take us to the reef in his skiff. Even where he might have done so safely, Simon avoided the reefs as if they were wild animals that could jump out and bite him. Jake intimidated him, and Simon reacted as I'd hoped he might. "Sounds terrific. But I've gotta work on this pump. Why don't you see if you can arrange a weekend dive?"

As in the past, I said, "Why the hell don't you go over and talk to him yourself?"

"Because if I don't fix the generator, no AC tonight."

I stormed below even though I wasn't angry, far from it. Simon's timidity had given me a chance to talk to Jake without sacrificing my dignity. Half an hour later, I returned to the deck in a beautifully embroidered, gauzy top that unsuccessfully hid my breasts. Simon didn't notice the change or the faint smell of perfume. I pulled the Zodiac to the side of the boat, stepped into it and said, "Once again, I do my master's bidding."

The rubber Zodiac was fast and I gunned her. Jake's boat, *Reliant*, was on the other side of the anchorage. I didn't throttle down quickly enough and clumsily bumped into *Reliant*. Jake looked over the side and motioned me aboard without saying hello. "I'm right in the middle of splicing an eye into a piece of wire rope. Hard as marlinspike work gets."

I didn't know whether to talk or shut up. Talking seemed better than fidgeting. "What are you making?"

He held up a piece of wire rope and showed me the small loop he had spliced in. "The tether has an eye on both ends. For a dive, we lower the tank and its backpack into the water. Makes getting into the gear easier. None of this jumping off backwards from the deck with sixty pounds of gear on your back. At the end of a dive we reverse the process."

"Well, diving is what I wanted to talk about."

He smiled, put the finished tether on the deck, and said, "Is that a fact?"

He motioned me forward, turned on a spigot, and handed me the hose. I sprayed the sweat off him.

He said, "Now you."

I pulled my shift over my head, wiggled out of my shorts, and placed my clothes carefully on the top of a locker. He hosed me down, dried me off, and pointed to the entrance of the cabin. I picked up my clothes and went below.

His bunk was at the end of the cabin and I climbed in. No foreplay, no fancy dancing. He knew when to speed up or go slow.

We fit as if we had been lovers for years. His body went rigid for the last time and slumped on top of me. "So, Clarice, what was your excuse for coming over to talk to me?"

I slid out from under him, sat on the edge of the bed, and put my clothes back on. "I'm not going to pretend I didn't get what I wanted. But sex aside, Simon and I want to charter."

The sun was high in the sky and we had turned his cabin into a steamy sauna. I followed him back on deck. We sat in the protection of a shade he had hung from the boom.

"I charge what the trade will bear. You pay for the food. Bring your own equipment. I provide the weight belts and guarantee the best dive of your life. Does two thousand a day sound fair?"

I might be a pushover, but I wasn't a patsy. "No."

Jake smiled, "For you, a valued customer, how does sixteen hundred sound?"

"Not good, but good enough. When do you want the money?"

He extended his hand to shake mine. "Whenever it's convenient."

"It would be most convenient tomorrow, before the dew dries on the deck. Today's Wednesday. We'd like to start out early on Friday."

"Fine, but when your husband's aboard, not an eyelash out of place."

"Jake, did you just have it on with a teenage girl? If there's one thing I've never needed, it's advice on how to manage men in general, and my husband in particular."

Jake smiled. "Okay, okay. Don't get sore. You're always welcome back, and the sooner the better."

I said nothing. I turned toward the boarding ladder and let myself down to the Zodiac. Cheating on my husband was a brave new world for me. I appreciated Jake's compliment and didn't want to ruin it with idle chatter, not even a goodbye. I motored back across the bay. As soon as I had tied up to *Searene*, I dove into the water. The sting of the salt was a sweet souvenir of Jake. I climbed aboard, and Simon looked up from his Clive Cussler thriller, stood, and threw me a towel. He sat back down, pushing behind himself the bag with the pump gasket still in it.

I stepped into the cockpit. When a serious prospective buyer stepped aboard a luxury yacht, the first thing they saw was the cockpit, which could make or break the deal. *Searene's* cockpit was U-shaped and twelve feet wide. A settee curved around a U, topped by a stainless steel rail. The back of the settee was polished African mahogany, and the deck was teak inlaid with an elaborate compass rose.

"Hey babe, how'd it go?"

I sat down on the settee across from Simon and waited a few beats before I answered, "It didn't go. The man's impossible. We went back and forth for almost an hour, and he wouldn't budge. Sixteen hundred a day for the boat and an extra four hundred for a mate. He's just trying to scam us because he thinks we're rich."

Simon came and sat beside me. He held me by the shoulders and said, "Clarice, you dodo bird. We are rich and everyone says he's the best."

"Simon, the man's impertinent, doesn't know his place. You ought to see the inside of his boat. It's got all the charm of a broom closet. We'd be sleeping on bunks as big as ironing boards."

I took Simon's hands from my shoulders. "It's his brass. Jake said to me, and he smirked when he said it. 'Bring me the money before the dew dries on the deck tomorrow.'"

"That's just an expression. He needs the money to hold our place, and you know what? Dad makes ten times that money before lunch."

He shook my shoulders, "Dammit Clarice. The New Caledonian reef wall is the ultimate, but it's too dangerous for us to go out there on our own."

I pried Simon's hands from my shoulders. "Well, if you've got your heart set on it. For your sake, I suppose I can put up with anything for a few days."

Simon relaxed and leaned back on the settee. I had given him permission. "Clarice, sometimes you are so dim. Look at his boat: rust bleeding from the chain plates. Varnish flaking from the mast.

Now look around you, one point five million dollars' worth of a boat that could hold its own in the America's Cup. Don't you get it? The dude is burning with envy. I've got the best boat and the best broad in the anchorage, maybe in the South Pacific. And he'll never get his hands on either one of them."

I snuggled up to Simon and said, "That's so sweet of you to say. And I have the best husband in the world, who satisfies my every need. But anyway, I told him I couldn't make the decision. You need to call him on the VHF and confirm. I penciled in Wednesday."

Simon reached under my top and gave a nipple a twiddle "Well, let's see if you can satisfy my every need after the gang goes home tonight."

I wanted to be on my game in the morning, so I said, "I can satisfy some of your needs, but my you-know-what has started. Oops, look at the time. If you want to give the shyster his money, you have to hurry before the banks close so I can bring it to him 'before the dew dries on the deck.'"

Simon said, "I've got a lot more than that in the safe."

When I came out onto the deck the next morning, Jake was waiting for me in his skiff. "No need to get the neighbors wondering why your Zodiac is tied off to *Reliant* at six in the morning," he said, helping me climb in. "If Simon wonders why I came over, tell him I was hungry for the money and you wanted to look *Reliant* over to be sure it was safe enough. I hope you have time for a cup of coffee."

"How kind of you to ask. I take mine black, no cream or sugar."

By Thursday afternoon, the *Reliant* was provisioned with the finest gourmet food available in Noumea, which, because it was the capital of a French possession, had plenty.

When Simon and I arrived early Wednesday morning, I was annoyed to see Maggie aboard. Maggie, freckled from too much time in the sun, helped us bring the diving gear onto the boat and said simply, "I'm the cook and the crew."

Couldn't the woman lose the dreadlocks? Bugs could be infesting them.
I blurted, "You live on *Reliant?*"

Maggie was a big woman, but decidedly a woman. She held a dive tank in each hand, lowered them with ease to the deck, and bent over the railing so her face was close to mine. "Spit it out. Are you asking if Jake is fucking me? Even though it's none of your business, no, Jake and I were an item a long time ago, but now it's strictly platonic. I hope I don't know why you're asking."

She held the high ground. I had to hang onto the side of the big boat to stay erect. "I am here because my husband has paid Jake a good deal of money to go diving. I don't appreciate the crude insinuation."

With a little lilt in her voice, Maggie said, "'Insinuation,' now that's a word I don't hear often. Here, Mrs. Green, give me your bag. We got off on the wrong foot. Let's start over."

"Good idea. You can start by calling me Clarice."

"Welcome aboard, Clarice."

A continuous palisade of coral surrounded New Caledonia. On its inside was a ten-meter-deep lagoon, and on its outside, a plunge of a thousand meters. Cognoscenti rated it as superior to Australia's Great Barrier Reef.

The trip from the shallow anchorage to the outside of the reef took a bit over an hour. When we entered the cobalt blue ocean, Jake motored along the arc of the reef until he yelled to Maggie, "This is the spot!"

Maggie motioned him forward until we were only a few feet from the reef. Simon gripped the rail and looked out over the ocean behind us. Maggie threw over a small anchor designed so Jake could rev the engine in reverse, if the wind changed, and be certain he could easily pull away from the reef. Maggie let out a lot of chain and *Reliant* streamed out into the deep water.

Maggie stayed forward to keep watch while Jake put the engine in neutral. He walked the stern, where Simon and I were sitting on the lockers. Jake said, "Simon, you don't look too good. Are you sure you're good to go?"

Simon nodded yes. "Let's go over the dive plan again," he said. Jake did.

Holding our masks, we jumped into the water and wrestled into our backpacks, which Jake had lowered into the water on the tethers. Simon turned on my air and then I did the same for him. He looked down and swam a few strokes back to the boat and grabbed onto the tether. I looked down and saw the same thing. Nothing. We were suspended in air, like standing on the edge of a hundred-story building. From a hundred feet, the intense ultraviolet rays of the noonday sun illuminated a mural of shapes and colors created by an artist gone mad. We swam over to the anchor chain, and then hand over hand, travelled down to the anchor. First thing, we checked the anchor, which had fallen safely behind a brain coral, a five-meter sphere whose surface was a labyrinth of green and silver-blue cranial folds. As we approached, the silver-blue exploded from the coral head's surface into a cloud of tiny fish that, like a flock of swallows, swam as one. Scintillating in the light, the ball shapeshifted, floated toward the surface, coalesced, and disappeared. Beauty stole the time. Simon tapped my tank and pointed to the gauge. Way below red.

We ascended at the speed of our bubbles, ate a light lunch, and dove back again.

———••———

Before Jake, I had never used the freedom Simon's predictable jaunts provided, but instead, spent those *Searene* afternoons in paradise doing power laps around the boat, reading Virginia Woolf, and shopping at the sophisticated French boutiques in Noumea. The hurly-burly, the demeaning mendacity, and the dull fair of adultery were not for me. Simon had excellent staying power, and had mastered the technical aspects of the art of sex, so I got what I wanted when I wanted, which wasn't often. In a single morning, Jake had given me more than Simon ever had. Artifice was no substitute for animal energy. In bed, the two men were as different as ping-pong and jai alai.

A year on a yacht is equal to a decade on dry land. I was sick of mothering Simon. I wanted out, but I was hooked on the money, the prestige, and never having to look at a price tag. The prenup was unbreakable. I was locked into an arranged marriage, arranged by me. *The secret to winning a wealthy, Jewish, young man's heart in an age of healthy eating is not through his stomach, but via an alliance with his mother. During Hanukah, Simon proposed and slipped a five-carat ruby ring on my finger. His mother, Esther, had said to him then, "Don't forget that Clarice is worth more than rubies."*

Although the sea had been bumpy, Simon and I had sailed on an even keel, but now a storm was brewing and cargo was shifting down below.

On Monday morning after the dive trip, I motored to *Reliant* for a cup of coffee. As had become our habit, at my arrival, we went straight to his bunk. Lying on his pillow, I said, "You didn't have much trouble ignoring me."

Jake sat up. "Uh oh. I thought we had an understanding."

I hid my breasts behind my arms and said, "Maybe, but you don't seem to understand that there's a person attached to my pussy."

I jumped up and pulled my clothes on. "Jake, I'm sorry. I don't know why I said that. Things are fine between us just as they are."

I stayed away until I couldn't stay way. When I came aboard on Thursday, Jake said, "Maybe we should cool things off."

His words terrified me. I grabbed his hand and led him below. "No way, Jake. I was completely out of line the other day."

How could anybody lift me so high without even a little bit of love? My job now was to help him discover that he loved me. I needed to rearrange my arrangements. If you look at it from the right angle, something that might be true is true. The next day Jake met me at the dive store to help me choose a new mask. All above board. Before we went our separate ways, I suggested some real coffee in the nearby café. He helped me with my chair and I whispered, "I've something real important to tell you."

A handsome, perpetually confirmed bachelor, Jake had little appetite for important disclosures, but I soldiered on. "Simon is planning to divorce me when we go back to the States for the holidays."

Jake said, with little conviction, "I'm sad to hear that."

"Not as sad as I am. Simon and I are seriously rich. I should say Simon's family is seriously rich. I'd lose it all. The prenup is bomb-proof. No more swanning around the oceans, and no more you."

Simon, who could keep his cool, at least on land, walked into the café escorting a nineteen-year-old hardbody. He didn't skip a beat, walked over to our table, and introduced us to Denise, who was in serious need of advice about buying diving gear. How good of Simon to dot the i's on my lies.

When I arrived at *Reliant* the next morning for a cuppa, Jake sat me down on the aft locker, went below, and brought up a pot of coffee and two cups. "We need to talk. You know I'm not a touchy-feely kind of guy, but you have become very important to me."

Hooray. He loved me, but he was a tough guy, too embarrassed to admit it.

Jake continued, "What would happen if Simon had an accident?"

"Then I'd be a merry widow. Sounds like you have a plan."

He stood up and walked across the deck. "Like all good plans, it's simple. At each stage, we can walk away and be in the clear."

I pretended I was playing for time, trying to decide what I'd already decided. I pointed to the windsurfers leaping across the waves on the beach south of the Hilton resort.

He had given me time to say no and I hadn't. He sat beside me. "Step one is the hardest and will cost you big time."

I said, "It takes money to make money."

Finding a bent French official was easy. He signed a document addressed to the American consul in Samoa. A passport with Simon's name and Jake's picture arrived at Post Restante in less than three weeks.

Jake and I had put that time to good advantage. He was a certified PADI instructor and I invited Simon to join me in a class to get an Open Water Certification. Simon said, "I need an advanced class in diving about as much as I need an advanced class in fucking." I waved goodbye to Jake, motored over to *Reliant*, and received advanced instruction in both disciplines.

The diving lessons focused on dangerous situations one might encounter on a night dive.

———••———

Step two was also risk-free.

I motored over to Betty's boat. She asked me aboard, but I said, "I'm in a little bit of a rush. I have to fix a candlelight dinner and then spend some quality marital time. Tell the gang no potluck tonight."

She said, "Quality time is just what I don't have enough of."

After the quality time, we snuggled on the pillow and I said, "Guess whose birthday is next Monday."

Simon said, "Out here, you don't know one day from the next. I guess it's mine."

I twirled the hair on his chest, "It's hard to buy a present for the man who has everything, but I thought of something and I've got to give it to you now."

"If you mean another roll in the sack, I'll take a rain check."

"No, no. Something more exciting than that. A night dive."

Simon gave me a hug and said, "Baby, that's terrific, but…"

"I've got everything arranged. We can use *Searene* with Jake at the helm. We've got the forward scanning sonar. Should be a piece of cake. Just keep it a secret, and if there's a last-minute problem, then nobody needs to know."

Simon jumped up and paced around our king-sized bed. "Hell yes. We've got the experience. I'm up for it."

I said, in a Sharon Stone kind of voice, "Get back in bed, and I'll get you up for something else."

———••———

On Thursday, Jake called Simon on the VHF. "Simon, could I borrow Clarice and the Zodiac. My regulator's got a problem. I called Alain at the dive store and he says he'll stay open and fix it for me."

Simon spoke into the mic and said, "I've got a spare. Why not just use mine?"

"No offense, Simon, but I never borrow dive gear."

"A-OK. Over and out."

The sun was below the horizon but there was still enough light so that I could see *Reliant* at anchor. I needed to buy us some time. "Well, Simon, I guess I'm going to be the chauffeur again. But I'll tell you what… I'm not going into Noumea looking like a rat bag. Jake will just have to wait until I look presentable."

By the time I had I finished putting on makeup and choosing just the right ensemble, *Reliant* was masked in darkness. Simon had pulled the Zodiac up to the side of the boat. Careful not to get my dress wet, I climbed in. I punched on the outboard and headed for *Reliant* at fifteen knots without turning on the running lights. When I reached *Reliant*, I pulled the Zodiac alongside and handed up the line to secure it. As he cleated off the line, he asked, "Have you got the handheld GPS?"

"Jake, you couldn't possibly think I wouldn't."

Jake ignored the comment and said, "We have about two hours before Simon gets restless."

As soon as I was aboard, Jake told me to take the helm. I put the diesel in gear and, as I had many times on *Searene*, I inched the boat forward as Jake winched in the anchor. He returned to the helm and brought *Reliant* around on a course to the pass where the reef opened out onto the ocean. We motored through the pass and continued a half a mile directly away from the reef into deep water.

I put an arm around Jake's shoulder. "We're really going to do this, aren't we?"

A voice from the companionway said, "Was there ever any doubt?"

Maggie stepped out onto the deck. I said, "What the fuck?"

Maggie was a lot taller than me. She came to the helm and put her arm around my shoulders. "I guess my husband hasn't been completely frank with you."

"That's a goddamn understatement."

"What differences does it make?" Maggie said. "It's not like you love Jake and vice versa. We have a plan going. When we take *Searene* on the night dive, Jake's going to need help."

I said, "And then what?"

"Simple. We go back to *Searene*. You open the safe, and I go back to my boat, Spray, ten grand richer."

Jake went below and opened all the seacocks. He returned to the deck and said, "The bilges are flooding even faster than I thought. You two, can the catfight. We need to get away from *Reliant*. She's got a heavy, lead keel and will go down fast. If we're not far enough away, she'll suck us down with her."

The three of us jumped into the Zodiac.

With the handheld GPS, it was easy to find our way back to *Searene*. Jake handed his dive bag up to Simon, who said, "Maggie? What are you doing here?"

"Jake asked me to come along to back him up when we get to the reef."

Simon said, "Fine with me."

Jake said, "I've picked out a really exciting spot."

When we arrived at the spot Jake had chosen, the wind had picked up a little from the east. Jake said, "The wind is perfect, the boat will stream away from the reef wall."

Jake brought *Searene* slowly forward. Maggie stood on the bow with the spotlight and guided Jake to within ten feet of the reef. Jake put the engine in neutral and Maggie released the anchor, which almost immediately caught.

The four of us huddled in the cockpit. Simon took hold of my hand. Jake said, "Here's the dive plan. Rule one: hold onto the anchor chain and don't let go until you snap your tethers onto it. Sometimes strong currents run parallel to the reef wall. If you get swept away, well, you know what."

Simon squeezed my hand harder and Jake continued, "Before you descend from the surface, let all the air out of your buoyancy compensator. Adjust it to neutral buoyancy when you arrive at the bottom. The tether is long enough so you can move around and check things out. When your tank is half-empty, start back up. Most important of all, before you start back up the chain, let the air out of the buoyancy compensator."

Simon was gripping my hand so tight it hurt. I pulled my hand free. We walked over to the side of the boat and let ourselves down on the ladder into the water. Simon came beside me and opened the valve on my dive tank. It took three turns to open it fully. I swam beside him and open his valve a quarter of a turn. At five thousand pounds per square inch, it made no difference if the valve was cracked or fully opened.

As we moved down the chain, the dive light's bright beam illuminated the coralline wall, which was iridescent, far brighter than it was during the day. Simon excitedly pointed out exotic creatures on the reef wall. I had pressing matters on my mind and paid no attention to the unfolding spectacle. A few feet from the anchor, Simon snapped his carabineers onto the chain and I mimed attaching mine. We adjusted our buoyancy compensators so we floated at that depth without effort. Simon's dive light was bright enough that I could shut mine off and hang it from my weight belt.

Simon peeked into a small crevice, where a parrotfish was sleeping. He hovered only inches away from the fish, which didn't awaken. I pointed to a lavender sea anemone from which a tiny clown fish, broadly striped in orange, white and black, attacked us to protect the tendrils of its home. I nearly choked from laughing at this tiny, but purposeful, guardian.

As Simon moved to get a better look, I moved back from the wall and let him pass in front of me. As Jake and I had practiced many times, I threw a scissors lock around Simon's waist, swept his dive mask off his face, and turned his air valve off. Simon dropped his light and struggled to reach the valve, but it was in the middle of his back and impossible to get to. He bucked with all the strength of a panicked beast, threw me off and grabbed my mouthpiece and sucked in some precious air.

My dive knife, which Jake had sharpened to a surgical edge, was ready in hand. I slashed the hose connecting my tank to the mouthpiece clamped down hard in Simon's mouth. The arc of the knife cut through the hose completely and inadvertently gashed Simon's shoulder. Now neither Simon nor I had air, and we were in a blinding billow of blood mixed with bubbles jetting from the cut hose. Simon tried to rip my mask off, but I pushed him away with my legs. He grabbed one of my ankles. I concentrated on not exhaling the small amount of air in my lungs. Simon thrashed in panic and used up his air immediately. I pulled my ankle free.

Go and blow was the maneuver Jake had made me rehearse over and over. At any depth, there's enough compressed air in your lungs to get you to the surface easily, if you rise at the same speed as the bubbles that come out of your lungs. If you freak out and race to the surface, the compressed air will burst your lungs. Jake had hung a dive light over the side of *Reliant*. As I diagonaled up, I came out of the cloud of blood and made it to the surface in a couple of minutes. Discipline. My success depended on my discipline.

I threw off my backpack and tanks and climbed up onto the deck. Maggie went forward and turned on the electric winch. The anchor didn't budge. Jake inched the boat up toward the reef wall and put the diesel into full reverse. The anchor came clean and Maggie pulled it in with the winch. Jake put the engine in neutral and let the wind blow us farther away from the reef. He left the cockpit and came up to the forward deck where Maggie and I were standing.

Maggie said, "Bitch, if you don't want to get cut up into tiny pieces and fed to the sharks, give me the combination to the safe."

I turned to Jake, who was leaning against the mast. "What's she talking about?"

Maggie grabbed my arm. "Two's company, three's a crowd. Go on, explain to Miss fancy-pants here, who's going to Australia on this yacht, and who's going nowhere."

Jake walked slowly across the deck to Maggie. He spoke softly to her. "Maggie, as usual, you're a little confused. Clarice has a valid passport. She is officially the owner of *Searene*, and a whole lot more. What do you bring to the table?"

Maggie shrieked, "What about the plan?"

Even more softly, Jake said, "Plans change."

Maggie didn't see the left-hand roundhouse coming. She fell to the deck, still screaming, despite her dislocated jaw. Jake bent down to her. "I'm truly sorry, Maggie. We've had some good times together, but I'm afraid Clarice holds the aces."

He grabbed Maggie's dreadlocks, she choked, "No, Jake, no."

She grabbed onto the winch and held tight. I picked up my weight belt and smashed it against her fingers. She let go and Jake flung her, still howling, into the water.

I followed Jake back to the cockpit and slumped onto a cushion. First Simon and then Maggie. Things are always worse in Technicolor. Jake and I didn't talk on the way back. We dropped the anchor, went below, and slept in different cabins.

In the morning, I cooked up an all-American breakfast of eggs over easy, bacon, and sourdough pancakes. We were both very hungry. Jake said, "What choice did we have?"

I heard the thrum of a diesel, looked up and saw the water taxi pulling up beside us. Saul and Esther were standing up and waving. Esther said, "We wanted to surprise you. Tell the birthday boy to come on deck and hug his mother."

From the Pacific South Seas we travel next to the dry land of Texas with Michael Bracken. Rowdy Boyette lives alone, a long way from anywhere. That changes the day he spots a long-legged blonde with car trouble. As fine an example of Country-Noir as we've seen.

Mr. Bracken never stops writing, or so it seems. He has published eleven books and well over a thousand stories, in numerous genres, and counts Alfred Hitchcock, Ellery Queen, and Mike Shayne mystery magazines among his publishing credits.

Deep in the Heart of Texas

By Michael Bracken

Rowdy Boyette stared hard at the photograph he had removed from his wallet and placed on the worn wood of the bar before he'd begun downing longnecks. Though the edges were frayed and one corner sported a stain, nothing diminished the beauty of the dark-haired woman staring back at him. The photograph had been taken shortly after they first met, when mutual lust was the driving force in their relationship, and in the photograph she wore his shantung straw Stetson and leaned against his then-new F-250. A year earlier, almost five years after posing for the only photograph of her that Rowdy ever possessed, the dark-haired woman had walked out of his mobile home and out of his life. Though she was long gone, he still wore the Stetson and still drove the pick-up truck.

"You still hung up on Stella?"

Rowdy looked up to see Red leaning against the other side of the bar. Whatever drinking he didn't do in the privacy of his own home, Rowdy did at the roadhouse on the state highway west of town. He had been drinking at Red's for so many years that the owner knew him by name and let him run a tab that often stretched weeks before being brought up-to-date.

"Not any more." Rowdy tore the photograph into tiny pieces and swept the pieces onto the sawdust floor. "She ain't coming back."

"Sometimes life sucks," Red said. "Then somebody dies. Don't let it be you. You've had enough to drink. Go home and sleep it off."

Rowdy stared at the older man and considered arguing. He'd not had enough to drink during the entire year Stella had been gone because no amount of alcohol had been enough to dull the pain of her absence. After watching Red fold his thick arms across his chest, Rowdy finished his beer and staggered outside to his truck.

As he rounded a blind curve five miles from the roadhouse, his truck's headlights swept across a black Mustang convertible with New Jersey license plates that was half-on the road. The car's lights were off, smoke billowed from under the hood, and a long-legged blonde stood beside it waving her arms. Rowdy slammed on the brakes and swerved to avoid hitting the car or the woman. His truck fishtailed down the highway until he wrestled it to a stop.

Rowdy shifted into reverse, slung his right arm over the back of the seat, and watched through the open beer window as he backed his truck along the narrow shoulder, careful not to let the truck slip down the embankment. He stopped well short of the smoking car, fearful that some drunk might round the corner, plow into the Mustang, and drive it into the back of his uninsured truck if he parked too close.

He climbed down to the road and approached the blonde. She looked to be in her thirties, but Rowdy had never been a good judge of a woman's age. Her blouse was too tight, her skirt too short, and her heels too tall.

"You all right?"

"I've been better," she said.

"You called anyone yet?"

"I don't have a cellphone."

Rowdy had one clipped to his belt and he reached for it. "I can call someone for you."

"Don't."

Rowdy hesitated. "What about a ride, then?" he suggested. "I can take you back to town."

"Back? I'm not going back. I'm going the same direction you are," she said. "Take me with you."

"What about your car?"

She glanced at the smoking Mustang. "It isn't mine."

Rowdy thought about that a moment. "We'll need to push it off the road first."

"Let me get my things."

The blonde retrieved her purse from the passenger seat and he removed two suitcases from the rear seat. They carried everything to his truck, but when he tried to put the suitcases in the bed with his collection of empty beer cans, she stopped him. "Put the blue one inside with us."

He did, and then they returned to the Mustang. She slipped into the driver's seat, turned the ignition key to unlock the steering wheel, and released the parking brake.

Rowdy put his back against the rear of the Mustang, grabbed the bumper, and dug the heels of his Justin ropers into the loose gravel as he began pushing. He didn't feel the blonde step out of the car, and he fell on his haunches when the Mustang rolled over the edge of the embankment and suddenly gained speed on its way down to the scrub below.

He stood up and brushed Texas off the back of his Wrangler's. "Thought you'd steer it to a safe spot."

"It's off the road, isn't it?"

Rowdy looked down at the still-smoking Mustang, shrugged, and walked with the blonde to his truck.

After ten miles of silence, he slowed the truck to a crawl, turned off the state highway onto a county road that was more gravel than asphalt, and brought the truck to a halt. "You can get out here and maybe catch a ride."

They had not seen another car the entire time they'd been together. She asked, "Where am I?"

He told her the name of the nearest town but his answer meant nothing to her. "West Texas," he elaborated. "Every direction you go from here is nowhere."

"And we're in the middle of it?"

Rowdy nodded. "If you don't want to get out here, I can take you to my place for the night and figure out what to do with you in the morning."

"You live alone?"

He nodded again.

"Ever get visitors?"

"Out here?" he replied. "Never."

She looked him over. "You got a name?"

"Rowdy," he said. "You?"

"Andrea," the blonde said. "Call me Andy."

Rowdy glanced at Andy. Her blue suitcase lay on the floorboard in front of the passenger seat and she rested her feet on top of it. Her knees thrust upward, causing her already too-short skirt to hike far up her thighs, and he forgot all about the woman who had broken his heart a year earlier.

"Okay," he said as he returned his attention to the road. "I will."

He lifted his boot from the brake and eased his tuck on down the road. After several miles, he turned onto a private drive that was little more than twin ruts in the dirt. He followed it over the crest of a low rise and down into a shallow valley. At the end of the private drive sat a singlewide mobile home that rested on concrete blocks. He stopped the truck a few feet from the steps that led up to the mobile home's front door, silenced the engine, and said, "This is home."

Before he could get to her side of the truck, Andy had opened her door and climbed out. She held her purse in one hand and the blue suitcase in the other. Rowdy retrieved her other suitcase from the bed of his truck and led her up the stairs.

He held the door while Andy stopped and looked back up the drive. They couldn't see the county road from where they stood, which meant the mobile home couldn't be seen from the road.

Rowdy let Andy sleep in his bedroom and he slept on the couch. He woke first the next morning and, despite a hangover that made his head throb, he put on a pot of coffee, fried bacon, and scrambled eggs. The smell woke his guest and she joined him in the kitchen.

Andy wore one of Rowdy's long-sleeved blue work shirts, the sleeves rolled above her elbows and only the bottom few buttons fastened. As best he could tell without staring or asking, she wore nothing beneath the shirt.

She carried her purse with her and, after she sat, she emptied the contents—which included a Ruger LCP, a pill bottle, and a cell phone charger—on the table and began pawing through everything.

Rowdy placed two plates of bacon and eggs on the kitchen table, one in front of Andy and the other in front of the chair where he settled. "I thought you said you didn't have a phone."

"I don't."

Rowdy pointed his fork at the charger. "What happened to it?"

"I mailed it to Florida."

"Why?"

"If anyone tracks its location via GPS, they won't find me. They'll be chasing the phone through the postal system to a non-existent address in Miami."

"Who would do that?"

"My boyfriend." Andy separated the pill bottle from the detritus covering his table and then she shoveled everything else back into her purse.

"Why would your boyfriend try to track you?"

"Because it's his money in the suitcase."

A forkful of eggs stopped halfway to Rowdy's mouth. "You took money from your boyfriend?"

"He owed me."

Stella had broken Rowdy's heart when she'd driven away, but she hadn't left with anything that wasn't hers.

Andy shook a pill from the bottle, washed it down with black coffee, and tossed the bottle back into her purse. Then she ate everything on her plate, finished her coffee, and leaned back in her chair. "That was good," she said. "Where'd you learn to cook like that?"

"I spent two years working the grill at a Waffle House," Rowdy said. He'd been working the overnight shift when he met Stella. She had come in bruised and teary-eyed after her boyfriend had hit her one too many times, and he'd offered her a shoulder to cry on. One thing had led to another and she had moved in with him not long after.

"And now?" she asked.

Rowdy shrugged. "I ain't worked in six months."

"How are you getting by?"

"Partial disability," he explained. He'd used the settlement from an accident—a woman driving a utility company vehicle had rear-ended his truck—to buy the mobile home, the land it sat on, and the truck he drove. "I get a check every month."

Her gaze traveled over him. "You don't look disabled to me."

"It's my back."

Rowdy didn't elaborate and she didn't ask him to.

"What are we going to do with you?" he asked.

"You mind if I stay here a few days?"

Rowdy shrugged. That's how things had started with Stella. She had asked to stay with him a few days while deciding what to do about her boyfriend. A few days had turned into a few weeks, then a few months, and then five years had passed and he was standing in the bedroom doorway watching her pack her things.

He shook the memory out of his head as he stood in the open bedroom doorway and watched Andy unpack one of the suitcases and put her things in the drawers Stella had emptied a year earlier. Other than underwear, Andy had packed little more than too-tight blouses, too-short skirts, and too-high heels. Rowdy offered her a pair of Stella's Wrangler's that had been buried at the bottom of the clothes hamper when she drove away, and he let Andy choose a shirt from his closet to replace the one she wore. While she showered, he rooted around the bottom of the closet for footwear. Doubling up on socks kept an old pair of his boots from being too loose for his guest, and when Andy finished dressing she didn't look much like the woman he'd picked up on the side of the road.

"If you don't work," Andy asked after Rowdy showered and dressed, "what do you do all day?"

Drank beer. Watched television. Shot hogs. No woman liked to hear that a man was hung up on his ex, so he didn't mention all the time he'd spent moping after Stella, and when he'd torn up Stella's photo at the roadhouse the previous evening he'd pretty much decided to get on with his life.

"You a good shot?"

"Fair to middlin'," Rowdy said.

"Show me."

He kept his hunting rifles in what should have been the mobile home's second bedroom, and from there he retrieved his Winchester Model 94 and pocketed a box of 30-30 shells. After he settled his Stetson on his head, he led Andy outside and around to the back of the mobile home.

He loaded the rifle, used the lever action to jack the first round into the chamber, and then pointed at a prickly pear cactus downwind about ninety yards. "Watch the second pad from the top."

He brought the rifle to his shoulder, sighted carefully, and squeezed the trigger. The cactus shook and daylight peeked through the hole he'd punctured slightly high and left of center in the second pad from the top.

Three more times he directed her attention to a specific pad on the five-foot-tall cactus, and each time he shot a hole through the pad. He was about to point to a fifth pad when she asked, "You ever shot anyone?"

Only once. Rowdy lowered the Winchester and glared at Andy. "Why would you ask that?"

"Just making conversation."

He turned the question back on her. "What about you?" he asked. "You ever use that peashooter in your purse?"

"Not yet," she said. "If I ever do, though, the man I use it on is going to be close enough that I can't miss."

Rowdy slept on the couch again that night, prepared breakfast for them again the following morning, and watched while Andy washed down her morning pill with black coffee. After they showered and dressed, Rowdy grabbed his Winchester for protection against feral hogs and took her for a walk around the rolling hills of his and the surrounding property. They passed the fire pit where he burned all of the household trash and, by sticking to established trails that led through waist-high grassland, an abundance of prickly pear, and a fair bit of juniper, mesquite, and live oak, they avoided the burned-out Nissan in the wash.

As they walked, they startled a doe that went bounding away, watched a roadrunner race down the trail, and saw scat from several different animals. During the trip out Rowdy kept up a running commentary, identifying everything. On the return trip he didn't talk as much.

"Whose jeans are these?" Andy asked as they crested a low rise and could see Rowdy's mobile home in the distance. The jeans were loose in the seat but long in the leg and she'd had to roll cuffs to keep the legs from dragging in the dirt.

"Stella's."

"How long's she been gone?"

"She's never really left," he said, "but I ain't seen her in a year."

"That's a long time to be without."

Rowdy glanced at Andy. "Yes," he said, "it is."

"Any hope of rekindling that spark?"

He smiled at the unintended irony and shook his head.

Andy stepped closer and hooked her arm in his. They walked the rest of the way without talking.

After they returned to Rowdy's mobile home, Andy opened the blue suitcase and showed him the banded stacks of one-hundred-dollar bills that filled it. Rowdy had no idea how much money was in the suitcase, but he was damn certain it was more cash than he had ever seen before or was ever likely to see again.

As he reached out to touch the banded hundreds, Andy stopped him. "Don't." She glared at him. "Don't ever touch my money."

Rowdy drew his hand back and wondered why Andy's boyfriend would have that much cash. "What does your boyfriend do?"

"He kills people."

"For a living or for fun?"

"Both," she said. "If he finds me, we'll have to kill him before he can kill us."

"You don't have to sleep on the couch every night."

Rowdy looked up to see Andy standing at the end of the hall wearing his blue work shirt. This time it was completely unbuttoned and he was certain she wore nothing beneath it.

"Come keep me company."

Rowdy pushed himself off the couch and followed her to the bedroom, where she took off the shirt and helped him remove his clothes. They made the bedsprings squeak and made each other sweat, and they fell asleep without any further discussion.

The next several days were much the same. They ate. They drank. They watched television. They hiked around Rowdy's property. They made the bedsprings squeak. One day he shot a feral hog that had gotten too close to the house. He gutted it, butchered it, and packed the meat in his deep freeze.

He finally asked, "What are you going to do with all that money?"

"Disappear," Andy said.

Rowdy suspected that she already had. No one knew she was living with him, and no one likely ever would know, not like they'd known about Stella.

One morning a week later Andy called to him from the bathroom.

He stood in the hallway outside the door, and he could hear the water running for the shower. "What's wrong?"

"I'm early."

Rowdy had not lived with a woman for an entire year and had forgotten many things. "For what?"

She told him, and she told him what she needed. "You'll have to go to town."

He had three dollars in his pocket and his disability check wasn't due until the first of the month. Rowdy opened the blue suitcase and removed two one-hundred-dollar bills. He tucked them into his wallet, grabbed his Stetson and an ice chest, and was gone before Andy finished her shower.

Rowdy drove all the way to the lone grocery store in town. He purchased beer, feminine products, and groceries, spending most of the first hundred. He filled the ice chest with frozen food and dairy products for the long drive in the heat, and he covered it all with a bag of ice.

On the way out of town, he checked his Post Office box, finding only bills and junk mail. Then he stopped at Red's.

As Rowdy settled onto his usual stool, Red opened a longneck and slid it across the bar to him. "I ain't seen you in weeks."

"I been busy." Rowdy handed the roadhouse's owner the second hundred-dollar-bill he'd taken from the blue suitcase. "This pay off my tab?"

Red snapped the bill, examined it carefully, and said, "And then some."

As Red slipped the hundred-dollar-bill into the bottom of his cash drawer, Rowdy lifted the longneck to his lips and drained half the bottle.

"You want another?"

"Not today," Rowdy said. He finished the beer and slid the empty bottle across the bar to Red. "I got things to do."

Partway home, Rowdy stopped on the shoulder of the blind curve where he first met his houseguest and stared down into the scrub. The Mustang was gone. He pondered that for a moment and then drove the rest of the way.

Andy burst out of the mobile home as soon as his truck crested the hill and headed down into the yard. When he opened the door, she asked, "What took so long?"

He didn't mention stopping at Red's or looking for the Mustang she'd been driving the night they met. "I did a little shopping," he said as he took two grocery sacks from the passenger side of the cab and headed up the steps to her. "We were out of lots of things."

Andy saw what she needed, grabbed it from him, and hurried down the hall to the bathroom.

Rowdy unloaded the truck by himself and put away all the groceries without help. He finished before Andy rejoined him.

"I'm sorry I snapped," she said. He could see the bulge of the Ruger in her front pocket and couldn't remember noticing it before. "You left without saying goodbye and I was worried about you."

"Why?"

"I thought you might be with her."

"Her?"

"Stella," Andy said. "I thought you might be with Stella."

"That can't happen," Rowdy said. "I'm with you, now."

Three days later Rowdy carried the household trash to the fire pit several yards behind the mobile home. He emptied the kitchen trash and then the bathroom wastebasket. Andy's empty pill bottle had been at the bottom of the wastebasket and it landed on top of the trash pile. Rowdy picked up the bottle and looked at it. He couldn't remember the last time she had taken a pill and the prescription meant nothing to him. He dropped the bottle back amid the soiled tissues and other household waste. Then he squirted charcoal starter fluid over the pile, tossed a lit match atop it, and watched it burn.

As soon as he returned to the mobile home, Andy confronted him. She stood in the middle of the living room with her arms folded under her breasts. "Where were you just now?"

"Outside, burning the trash."

"You weren't planning to leave me, were you?"

"I was just burning the trash," Rowdy repeated.

"Don't leave me alone," Andy said. "I don't want to be alone."

After Rowdy assured Andy that he would never leave her alone, she relaxed. As he gathered her into his arms and held her, Rowdy wondered how he was going to get to town to collect his disability check and other mail from the Post Office.

Rescuing the blonde from the side of the road had been exciting, making Rowdy feel more alive than he had felt since the day Stella almost reached the end of the drive. Discovering Andy's suitcase full of banded hundred dollar bills had only added to her appeal, but they had little in common beyond her desire to disappear and the secluded location of his home. Even time spent making the bedsprings squeak had begun to wear thin. Andy's increasing fear of being alone made Rowdy wonder what had caused her previous relationship to implode. He knew he couldn't ask, just as he knew he could never tell her what had happened to Stella.

They were in the bedroom when Rowdy heard a car coming down the drive, and a quick glance through the curtain revealed a black sedan slowing to a halt in the yard.

Rowdy grabbed his Winchester from the second bedroom. By the time he stepped onto the porch a dark-haired man in a suit had stepped out of the car and stood beside it looking around. Rowdy used the lever action to jack a round into the Winchester's chamber and he aimed his rifle at the man. "That's far enough."

Andy stepped onto the porch behind Rowdy and called to the man. "How'd you find me?"

The man jerked his chin toward Rowdy. "Lover boy spent some of your money in town."

Andy turned on Rowdy. "You took money from the suitcase?"

"Only a couple of hundreds," he replied without shifting his attention from the man standing in the yard.

"I told you not to touch it!"

"I didn't think you'd miss one or two."

The man in the yard asked, "Andy tell you where she got the money?"

"She said it was yours."

The man in the yard laughed. "Robbery in Boston," he said. "She killed her partners when she went off her meds and thought they were conspiring against her. Shot them in the back, took the money, and left. One of them lived long enough to tell me what happened, but I had to clean up the mess before I could start looking for her." He shifted his attention. "Mailing your phone to Miami was a nice trick, Andy. I tracked it to the Mail Recovery Center in Atlanta before I realized what you had done."

"You need to leave," Rowdy told the man in the yard.

"I can't do that." He reached under his jacket.

"Kill him," Andy said.

Rowdy squeezed the Winchester's trigger. A single shot penetrated the man's forehead and erupted though the back of his skull. Even at close range it was a touch high and to the left.

He descended the porch and crossed the yard, for the first time noticing the sedan's government license plates. Andy followed him.

"Is he dead?" Andy asked from behind Rowdy.

He nudged the body with the toe of his boot. "Yeah."

"You sure?"

He squatted and lifted the flap of the dead man's jacket. He saw the Glock 22 in the shoulder holster. He also saw the badge hanging from the dead man's belt.

Over his shoulder he asked, "Your boyfriend's a cop?"

Andy didn't answer with words. She had her Ruger LCP in her fist and jerked the trigger twice without aiming. As she had promised, she was so close to Rowdy that she couldn't miss.

He fell face-first into the dirt next to the dead federal agent.

As Andy rooted through his pockets for the keys to his truck, she said, "I told you not to touch my money."

Rowdy didn't think about Andy, about her lies, or about the reason she had shot him. Instead, he thought about Stella, about the bullet he'd put in the back of her head as she'd driven up the drive toward the county road, and about burning her Nissan in the wash.

Then his final thoughts shredded like the photo he had torn apart at the roadhouse. He never saw Andy drive away.

Let's slip back in time to the Roaring Twenties, when gangsters ran booze down from Canada to the thirsty citizens of Chicago and Detroit. Bootleggers weren't the kind of customers hotels preferred, but Hotel Hateras in the Michigan woods welcomed them – as long as they followed the house rules.

Michael Chandos is the pen name of a retired intelligence officer with a degree in criminal investigations. His story is a result of his research of hotels and resorts in the '20s and '30s for "criminals on their best behavior", particularly in the upper Midwest. He is a member of MWA, SinC, RWA/KOD.

Hotel Hate

by Michael Chandos

Hotel Hatteras was a three story, solid brick building deep in the Michigan woods. One train a day. One road in and out too, but I could show you another if you needed it.

We catered to Midwest "businessmen" and their women who needed a vacation away from public view for a few weeks. Or a month. Room and board were reasonable, the booze was too. Everything ran by strict St. Paul Layover rules, the so-called O'Connor system. Mind your manners, pay your bills. Simple as that. Even gangster rivals behaved themselves in Hotel Hatteras, or it's me they answered to. I meant what I said.

My husband Al hated everything about Hotel Hatteras. Everything: the hotel, the speakeasy, the clients and, especially, me. A classy hotel for the criminal classes was my dream and I called it Hatteras to lend a holiday flavor, but he always called it Hate-Her-

Ass or Hotel Hate just to offend me. He said it looked like a three story shithouse.

I tried to please him and do things his way. I hired a new bartender and I bought better booze. I hired a cute girl, named Hannah, as a waitress. Yeah, he liked the waitress. Too much. I even built a hidden entrance in the trees out back so his gangster buddies could come and go without being seen.

He eventually abandoned it and me. If he ever comes back, I have a nice, warm place reserved for him: the furnace.

That morning, the County Sheriff was in the lounge leafing through wanted posters; he liked to make my clients nervous. There were no major towns in this rural County so there was just the Sheriff and three Deputies. The Sheriff and I were good friends and kinda like business partners. He drank here for free.

"Hinky, what are you drinkin', Honey?" I leaned across the bar to the Sheriff.

"Hi, Miss Rose. Mostly ice cubes with a tiny splash of rye for flavor. Enough for now, thanks. A Sheriff needs to mind his breath during the day. You never can tell. President Hoover may stop by at any moment."

"Honey, he'd have to be a spirit medium to find this place."

"No residents around this morning?"

"Most of them are still sleeping it off, but the smell of lunch will bring them down soon."

"New gentlemen on this morning's train, Miss Rose. From Detroit, I think. I acquainted them with the rules and accepted their entrance fee. They're over at the steakhouse for a quick lunch. Should be along shortly."

"We've been lucky with Detroit clients, so far," I said. "Well-behaved and quiet. Much more class than the independent gangs and Chicago hoods."

"Not like Al, huh?" He quickly glanced at me. He knew his joke had just fallen flat.

I steamed for a second. "He used me, Hinky. Screwed me, both ways. And I loved him too, even though I wished I hadn't."

"Well, uh, sorry. I'll keep an eye out." He gathered up his papers and drained his glass. "Be mindful of the four Illinois bank robbers that came in real late yesterday. The worst of the worst. Pure scum. Deputy Anders says they knock their women around too. May have killed a couple guards in the heists. Be careful of them, Miss Rose."

"I always have my Baby Browning with me and I know how to shoot it. See you later, Hinky."

"Yes, M'am. You are the boss." He tipped his hat and went out the polished-wood and glass front door.

I went into the dining room. Fritz, the front desk man, was setting up the lunch tables.

"Fritz, the Sheriff says we got some bad boys in from Illinois. Probably be good to keep them separate from the other clients." I looked around for a good idea.

"The big-time poker game is still running in the back party room, Miss Rose; I can't put them in there." Fritz picked up a *Reserved* sign. "I'll put them at the large round table in the alcove near the porch door."

"That'll work." I went to the front desk to see what name they used in the register.

⸻

The Illinois gang stumbled noisily down the stairs about half past twelve. Four men in their late 30's at least, and two women who looked very tired. Obvious lowlifes, pomade thick on their hair and a hostile sneer to everyone, on a high after a couple small-town bank robberies. And a couple killings. They all smelled like cigarettes and days of sweat, and their clothes were wrinkled like they'd slept in them. As long as they bought their booze and smokes here.

Hannah, the cute waitress, started to lead them to the round table, but she stopped suddenly and backed up a little.

"Hi ya, Sweet Meat. Long time no see. Miss me?" I was behind the front desk, but my stomach knotted anyway. I knew that voice: Al, my bastard husband.

I walked over to the round table. "Hello, Alphonso," I said, staring at him directly in the eye.

"Alphonso, Boss?" "Holy shit, that's your name?" "What a pussy name." Smooth talkers, these hoods.

"Yeah? Tell that to Capone then. I like Al, same as Capone. You sloppy crappers keep your big traps shut, or I'll shut 'em myself! You hear me?"

"OK, Boss. Geez."

"We're here for grub," said Al. "This is a nice place and we gotta be nice too. Ain't that right, Rosey?"

I took a deep breath. "Good Morning, gentlemen… and ladies. Lunch today is navy bean soup with ham, beef stew, ham or beef sandwiches, and all the fixins."

"Listen, ya saggy bag a' guts, we don't need no pig today," said Al. He was wearing an expensive suit that was starting to wear on the elbows. "I want sweets and tea for the ladies, beef and beer for us. Got that?"

He had a silver revolver jammed under his belt. He stood up and pulled a small bottle of brandy from his hip pocket; the brandy wasn't purchased here. He took a slurpy sip and passed the brandy to the next man, a permanent five o'clock shadow guy. "Get to it, Sweet Meat." Hannah didn't move.

"Fellas, let me explain the Layover Rules to you since you got in so late. To stay here…" I started to say.

Bang! Al pulled his revolver and shot into the ceiling.

People dove under tables.

"I don't take no crap from no ugly woman! Now, you get our—" Al stopped shouting.

My bartender Ernst was there in a flash. He's a very solid six foot three. He was a machine gunner in the Great War, for the other side, and he's still good with machine guns. He cocked his Tommy gun and aimed at Al's face. His boys were frozen in their chairs. A tall, muscular man with a machine gun inches from your face tends to stop the action pretty quick.

I stood against the round table opposite Al and shoved it back hard, trapping him in the corner. I pointed my little automatic at his big pink nose. "As I was saying, we operate by St. Paul Layover Rules," I commanded like a pissed off Sunday school teacher. "You report to the Sheriff when you arrive. You commit no crimes while you are here, cause no trouble, shoot no guns. And you pay your bills and all appropriate fees. The rooms are safe, the food is good and the Sheriff will deflect any State Troopers or FBI trying to find you. There's gambling in the back, and booze and jazz in the front."

I glared at each one. "Bother people or commit crimes, and I'll either turn you over to the Sheriff myself, or Ernst will walk you into the woods, one-way. I mean what I say, fellas."

As I expected in moments like these, Al and his gang were silent. Al's arm slowly lowered and he slipped the pistol into an inner coat pocket. He snickered.

"That gunshot will cost you a hundred dollars for damage to the ceiling," I said. "It'll be added to your bill." I stood up straight, hands folded, the little Browning back in my skirt pocket. "Now. Sweets and tea for the ladies. Beef and beer for the men." I spun on my heel and walked back to my office. Hannah went into the kitchen to place their order.

Deputy Anders dropped off the Detroit gentlemen at the front desk at about 2 o'clock. They were a huge step above most of my clients. They were clean, very well dressed and courteous. The Detroit Partnership was a stable business enterprise compared to most other Midwest organized crime groups, white collar criminals in a dirty blue collar line of work.

"Miss Rose, I'd like to introduce Mister Tuco and Mister Mozano from Detroit. They are registered with the Sheriff and have paid their tickets," said Anders.

"Thank you, Deputy, and good afternoon gentlemen," I said.

"Ma'am," said Tuco.

With that, Deputy Anders turned to walk out the front door. One of the Illinois gang stood up and gave him a wet raspberry and a hand gesture.

"Fuckin' screw. Come over here and get some."

Al laughed and made a one-fingered gesture himself. All his boys thought that was hilarious. The Deputy stopped, his right hand moving toward his pistol.

"Enough!" I said. "We've heard too much from you boys today. Why don't you check out the poker game or go into the lounge?" Ernst was instantly in the doorway again.

Al stared at me, then smiled and shrugged. "Just being happy at Hotel Hate, Rosey. Relax, relax." He and the guy with the heavy shadow went into the back. The other two men went upstairs with the women, who looked like they'd much rather stay downstairs.

The Deputy grinned, tipped his hat brim and left by the front door.

I turned to the Detroit gentlemen and gave them my most inviting smile. "We see small gangs like that in here. They always want to prove they're tougher than everyone else. Please pay them no mind. It's so pleasant to have you men up from Detroit. Please sit with me," I said with a royal gesture toward my office.

We adjourned to my office and closed the door. "How can I help you?"

"We are looking for a quiet location for an important conference," said Tuco. He was the only talker. Maybe Mozano, taller and wide-shouldered, was protective muscle, a heavy. "Tony Jack, the Detroit Partnership Chairman, wants to have a sit-down with his Family Capos concerning business plans and personnel changes. We've been to Cicero and St. Paul in the past, but thought we'd stay in-state for a change. We need quiet and solitude, and room for twelve, plus a few soldiers, for two days, two evenings, starting next Friday night."

"We operate by strict St. Paul rules here," I said, "and my relationship with the Sheriff is excellent. I'll clear the top floor of the Hotel's main building for the Chairman's meeting. There's an excellent suite there and enough apartments for everyone, and a Board Room with a large table, leather chairs and a bar."

"The Chairman doesn't want your other patrons to know he's here."

"There's a private entrance in the back and I'll give you the key to the private elevator that services the top floor only," I said.

"Excellent," said Tuco. "The Chairman is very particular about his accommodations and meals. Day after tomorrow, two trucks will arrive from Detroit. The first truck will have food for the conference, including live lobsters, French cheeses, fresh fruit and vegetables, bread and the usual additions. The second truck will carry sheets, blankets and pillows, and the drinks, including fresh beer from St. Louis and Canadian Club whiskey we bring in from Windsor. You can keep all leftovers, if any. His personal chef and sous-chef will arrive with the trucks."

"How very exciting!" I said. "My chef was trained in five-star Chicago hotels and can assist. I'll make sure the Sheriff is invisible. He'll be busy keeping the town quiet anyway. Let's go up to the top floor and I'll show you around."

As we left my office I noticed Al and his buddy were standing just outside my office door. Did they hear about the deal I had just made? They tried to look innocent and wandered off into the lounge. The Detroit gentlemen noticed them also.

As the Detroit clients headed upstairs with Ernst I started for the kitchen to talk briefly to the chef.

"Hey, hag."

I stopped. The world closed in on me and I instantly felt hot and cold at the same time. I turned around. "Why'd you come back, Al? You suddenly love this place?"

"My gang is on the lam, Honey. We needed a place to let things cool. Why not the best hotel in Michigan?"

"I hear you killed a few people in your bank-robbing spree."

"Small town nobodies and a couple bank security guys. No one who will be missed."

"Thirty days from now you'll still be too hot. Cops take a long, dim view of the killing of innocents, Al. I'd appreciate it if you and your little gang leave tomorrow morning. We don't need your kind of heat."

"Little gang? Do six successful bank robberies in three weeks sound little, bitch? We give this place notoriety." He was slowly getting closer. I wasn't going to let him back me down again.

"You abandoned me, Al. And you stole all my savings. For two years I had to clean all the bathrooms myself because I couldn't afford to hire anyone else." My hand was in my pocket gripping the 25 automatic. "Do me a big favor, Al. Leave, forever, leave the hotel and leave my life. Things are better with you gone."

"I'll pay you back, Rosey. What was it? Five hundred bucks?"

"More like fifteen thousand."

"Now you're the damn liar, you old cow. Moo. Moooo." He made horns with his fingers on his head. "That's the only language you understand."

"Leave."

"Do they know you used to work in the Chicago jail? You were part of the police. A matron to all the common whores. They liked you 'cause you were one of them." He smiled. I didn't. My employees and the sheriff knew my history.

"You should be happy to have me back. Let me warm you up tonight, Rosey. Huh? You'll change your mind when you get another taste of me." He reached for my hand. I pulled it away.

"Don't mess with me, Al. I still have the 44 you gave me. I'll use it if you give me a reason." I spun on my heel and went into the kitchen.

———

That night and all the next day I had maids and repairmen making sure the top floor was in tip top condition. The three groups I had to move didn't complain. I apologized endlessly and gave them better rooms on another floor, and free booze and dinner.

The following Thursday morning I was at the front desk when the Detroit gentlemen came down. "Good morning Mister Tuco, Mister Mozano. Tomorrow's the day. After lunch, perhaps we can look over the preparations upstairs," I said.

The Sheriff burst through the front door, which made most of my clients reach for guns and to look for escape routes. He was agitated and didn't pay them any attention at all. Mozano reached inside his jacket and stepped in front of Tuco. The Sheriff hurried up to my group, his hat in his hand like he had been caught stealing lemon drops at the candy store.

"My God, Miss Rose! The State Troopers have just called us out to a hijacking and multiple murder. Two trucks, ambushed not far from town. And I'm afraid both drivers and their four passengers were killed."

No one in the lobby made a sound. I was careful to not advertise the Detroit business, but news travels fast in the hotel. "This is not good for anyone, Hinky," I whispered. "The Chairman's personal Chefs, too?"

"So it appears. The State Police said the ambushers ransacked the trucks. Food, broken bottles and stuff are all over the place. Looks like they mostly stole whiskey since that was the easiest to heist."

Mister Tuco ran to the phone booth while Mozano took up a defensive position in front of the booth door. Two 45 automatics appeared in his hands.

"Now, I can't cover this up, but I can deflect any attempt to connect it to the Hotel Hatteras," said the Sheriff. He knew the danger here.

"Thank you, Sheriff," I said. "I'll tell my clients this might be a good time to relocate. Please check with the station master and ask him to signal the next train to stop."

"You bet." With a glance at Mozano, he turned and went out the front door.

I signaled to Ernst. He came over to me, a Luger already under his belt. Clients started for their rooms, to pack, presumably. We both went over to the phone booth as Mr. Tuco came out.

"I'm sorry, Miss Rose, I must go out to…" he said.

"Mister Tuco, please don't jump to any conclusions and let the Sheriff handle this," I said.

"Miss Rose, understand my position. These were Tony Jack's personal men. He doesn't care about the goods so much. It's about the dead men and the audacity of those vulgar, homespun Illinois hoods," he said.

"Wait, we don't know it was them."

He looked around the lobby. "Then where are they? Not in the Hotel Hate today?"

I winced at the term. "Please, do what you must, but give me some time too. The Sheriff will tell me who they suspect and why. Let's wait a few hours. Please, don't start a battle. If it's the Illinois gang, the Sheriff will hand them over to the State Police."

"I must go make certain preparations and it will take a few hours to do them. Good day, Miss." He and Mozano went upstairs, Tuco talking quietly and intently to his Heavy.

"Ernst, take a look at Fritz's Tommy gun at the front desk and make sure it's good. Bring him an extra drum of ammunition too. I'll go get my 44. Be ready."

"Ja, Miss Rose. Right away." He went to the front desk. A man and a woman were already there with baggage to check out.

I've never seen my town so quiet. Except around the bus and train stations, it was becoming a ghost town. Several men in suits and without luggage came in on the afternoon train and disappeared into the town. The deputies kept everyone departing in line. A few residents didn't leave; nowhere to go perhaps. The two Illinois women stayed in their rooms.

Early in the evening, Al and his Illinois hoods came downstairs to their reserved round table. I didn't know they were back in my hotel. The gang was obviously celebrating. They had bottles of whiskey and two new girls I didn't recognize. They were noisy, calling for glasses and dinner. There was only one other group for them to bother: two men sitting at the back of the lounge. Ernst watched them intently.

I walked over to Ernst. "Who are those men, Ernst? Why aren't they drinking?"

"They just asked for black coffee, Miss Rose, and they haven't even touched that. They haven't said a word to anyone otherwise. They noticed the Illinois gang when they came down." Ernst spoke softly into my ear. "Did you see what that gang is drinking? Canadian Club, Miss Rose."

"How stupid. Ernst, send one of the boys to notify the Sheriff. Tell him this gang of fools is here, but, please, no shooting in my hotel. I'm going upstairs."

———••———

Mozano opened Mister Tuco's door an inch. A gun barrel poked out of the gap. We said nothing to each other. He opened the door further when he recognized me and I went in. Tuco was sitting at the small desk using the telephone. He looked stern and dark. He hung up and turned to me. "Miss Rose, do you have news for me?"

"The Illinois gang is downstairs and they appear to be drinking Canadian Club they brought in themselves," I said carefully. "I think two of your soldiers are in the lounge also. I have sent for the Sheriff. He may bring the State Police, so I recommend you stay up here."

"Miss Rose, I knew the chefs. They made the cake for my daughter's sixteenth birthday party." He got up from the desk and whispered to Mozano, who immediately left. "We must confront them. Perhaps we will convince them to run into the arms of the law."

"I'll tell my men to lay back." I left and went to the lobby.

———••———

"Fritz, whatever happens, stay behind the counter. Don't use your gun unless you have to. Tell everyone else to stay out of the lobby, the dining room and the lounge."

I went to the lounge, passing by the celebrating gang. Food had been served and the table was a mess. Al sneered at me and grinned like a dead catfish.

The two Mafia soldiers were now sitting at a table where they could watch the gang from the dimness of the lounge.

"Ernst, don't shoot unless you must. Hopefully, this will be brief," I said.

I went back to the lobby and got behind the registration desk with Fritz. I mentally rehearsed my plan on where and when to duck. My 44-caliber revolver was resting on a shelf under the counter.

About five minutes later, Mozano slowly came down the stairs, stopping halfway where he had a visual advantage over the Illinois gang. He had his jacket draped over one arm and nothing in his visible hand. Mr. Tuco silently came down just behind him. The two boys in the lounge also stood up and arranged themselves so they'd have good shot-lines to the round table. Ernst moved out of the line of possible return fire.

The four Detroit men said nothing. One of the girls finally noticed them.

"Hey, buddy, join the party. There's enough booze here for everyone," she said.

The Illinois boys were almost too drunk to stand. They laughed and hooted since everything was hilarious. "Hey, Sluggo, have a drink. More upstairs too," said Al. He was too blind-drunk to notice Mozano on the stairs.

Mr. Shadow Face still had a brain cell that worked, apparently. His eyes got very wide and he reached for the pistol in his belt.

I started to duck behind the registration desk. Mozano's 45 roared like an artillery piece. I felt the concussion on my face and the roar hurt my ears. The shot hit Shadow Face in the shoulder. He spun around and fired several shots wildly. Al tipped the table on end, scattering the food, bottles and dishes in a crash nearly as loud as the gunshot.

The two soldiers pulled their automatics but this was Mozano's lead, and they each fired one shot into the upturned table. Tuco was right behind his heavy, also firing into the table.

The women screamed. The redhead tried to escape into the lounge and ran into Tusco's men . One of them bitch-slapped her to the ground.

Aware they were out-gunned, Al and his buddy made a run for the front door. Shadow Face held one arm close and wasn't firing; Al fired wildly behind himself. I felt one round hit the registration desk. The other woman was screaming and crying on the floor. The last two Illinois boys clumsily got up and ran for the door.

I braced myself on the registration desk and drilled Al in the back with the 44, a Michigan quickie divorce. Al slapped into the front door, shattering the glass. He turned to see who had shot him. I think he was astonished that it was me. A deep red flower bloomed on his shirt. He stumbled out the door, but he wasn't in control any more. Shadow Face shouldered the door wide open and ran into the night and the other two followed. The Detroit men had stopped firing.

A second after the gang went out the front doors, lights came on outside, State Police car headlights, I guessed. I heard several pistol shots and lots of shouting, then the unmistakable rattle of several Tommy guns. Just as suddenly, everything went quiet. I stashed the 44 back on the shelf and came out from behind the registration counter.

Tuco and Mozano were already back upstairs and out of sight. Ernst came into the lobby and nodded his head. I think he had let the two soldiers out the back. He helped the woman under the table into a chair and checked on the other, who looked unconscious to me. "Put your guns away, boys," I said to Ernst and Fritz, "and try to look as innocent as you can."

"Miss Rose, are you ok?" It was the Sheriff calling from outside.

"Yes, Sheriff, we're all ok," I yelled back. "Two women might need a little care. No more shooters in here. They all ran out the front door."

"Ok. Things are all done out here too. I'll be in in a minute."

The porch alcove looked like a tornado had gone through. The table was upside down, food and drink were everywhere. Dishes were broken. Smoke from the guns hung in the air. Hotel Hatteras looked like Hotel Hell. The sheriff came in with Deputy Anders and a state trooper. They went to the round table.

"Some sort of gun fight break out, Miss?" asked the trooper.

"They were partying wildly and started to argue. I don't know who shot first. We were all ducking for cover," I said. "Do you think these were the hijackers?"

"That's what it looks like. There's more bootleg whiskey and fancy food in a stolen car out front. They might be the bank robbers from Illinois also," said the trooper. He holstered his pistol. "We can close the book on this one, Sheriff. Thanks for the support. We need more sheriffs like you." The trooper left with Deputy Anders.

"Oh my, what a mess!" I said. Fritz and Ernst started to sweep up. "Break up that table and throw it in the furnace. Account for all the brass casings and see what we need to do about any bullet holes, boys."

The Sheriff pulled me aside. "Sorry, Miss Rose," said the Sheriff, "I didn't mean to have the battle in your hotel."

"That's okay, Hinky. Glad to have them out of here. For a minute, it really was Hotel Hate." I grinned and took a deep breath and smoothed my blouse. "Well, back to Hatteras."

"Yes, Ma'am," he said. The sheriff went out the front and propped up the broken door. "I'll ask the carpenter to come over right away."

"Any clients still in the train station, Hinky?"

"I'll check and tell them it's ok, just as soon as the State Police leave."

"Thank you. I'm going upstairs, boys, and recover what I can with the Detroit gentlemen. Let's get ready to welcome clients back. Hotel Hatteras is open for business!"

A modern-day folktale from Karen Gough is next. Set on a ranch, this story harkens back to an earlier time, when spirits lived in the trees and deep magic swirled with the mist.

Ms. Gough is a writer and photographer and lives with her family in Silicon Valley.

The Cat

by Karen Gough

It wasn't till after I bludgeoned her that I noticed the cat. The moon had not yet risen and the night swept over the dry fields and up to the open window until it merged with the cat and you could hardly tell which was which.

"Get out!" I snarled.

The cat didn't blink.

It was my wife's cat, the stray she'd adopted, huge and black, with great green eyes. She was the only one who could touch him; I tried once and got my hand scratched. But he followed her like a dog—around the house, about the ranch, even riding in the truck when she was making her rounds.

"You've got no one to follow now," I laughed.

The cat only stared at me from his perch in the barn window.

I turned back to my wife, who lay as she fell, face down among the machinery. Blood was already matting in her copper dyed hair.

She wasn't moving. I knelt down to make sure her cell phone was still in the back pocket of her jeans, then I got an old blanket, spread it out next to her and rolled her onto it. I put a hand to her wrist. The pulse was weak.

I should hit her again, I thought. But the sound of the crowbar against her head was too terrible to hear a second time. Besides, she'd be dead soon enough.

I wrapped her up in the blanket, and then examined the ground for blood. There was none. The only blood was a bit on the crowbar; I scrubbed it off and put it back with the other tools. Glancing over at the barn window, I saw the cat still watching my every move. I wondered if he'd seen the whole thing.

"Why did you call me out here?" she had asked.

I pointed toward a shadowy area of buckets and tools. "I wanted to show you the fox I surprised." She was always a sucker for wildlife.

"A fox?" She stepped closer to get a better look.

It was then that I clubbed her, and she crumpled without a sound.

———

The truck we shared was parked just outside the barn door. I put my wife's blanketed body into the truck bed and covered it with a tarp. Then I walked over to the house. We were the only ones who lived there so I wasn't worried about being seen. Using an old shirt to pick up my wife's purse and overnight bag, I walked back to the truck and placed them on the passenger seat. Then I turned out the barn lights, and drove off.

I drove with the dimmers on, so had to go slowly through the brown grass, watching for the occasional ruts and rocks. There was a prickly feeling in the back of my neck, like I was being watched, but the only creatures around were an occasional cow and calf. I drove down to the creek and bumped along its dry bed, but the feeling grew stronger. Stepping on the brake, I turned to look behind me.

"Shit!"

That cat, with its great green eyes, was crouched in the back seat, staring up at me. It must have jumped through the open window when I was loading the truck. I reached back and tried to grab it, but the cat backed into a corner where I couldn't reach it.

"What the hell, you wanna go for one last truck ride? Be my guest."

I resumed driving, eventually leaving the dry creek, and parked in a thick stand of trees. I got a headlamp out of the glove compartment and put it on, then lifted my wife's wrapped body out of the truck. Out of the corner of my eye, I noticed the cat jump out the window. He followed me as I trudged up the hill, carrying my heavy burden.

I picked my way through oak trees and scrub, looking for the funnel shaped hole of the abandoned mine shaft. There were many in this area of Amador County, most of them unmapped, and this one had no protective barriers or signs to mark what I estimated was a two-hundred foot drop. I'd almost fallen into it one day, out looking for a stray cow.

It wasn't long till my headlamp lit up the rock cairn I'd made to mark the hole. I lowered my wife to the ground and began to remove her blanket. There was a muffled groan. For one second I froze. Then I reached out with shaking hands and unwrapped her.

I saw her chest rise and fall, her eyelids began to flutter and she moaned again.

Quickly, I cradled her to me. "There's been an accident, honey, but you'll be alright. I have you." I lifted her up like a baby and took a step closer to the mineshaft.

"My head... what happened?"

Two more steps and I was standing at the edge of the funnel, as close as I dared to the hole.

She worked a hand free and squeezed my left bicep.

"Mike."

I could feel her looking at me, and when I looked back, she winced.

"The light..."

I tensed, preparing to throw her and felt her grip tighten around my arm. I heaved her toward the hole, but she clamped on with both hands, and together we fell to the ground.

When I opened my eyes, my skewed headlamp revealed the glint of her bracelet, lying in the dirt. I noticed her hands clutching my arm, then I lifted my head and we were staring at each other, face-to-face. Her legs were dangling in the hole and I saw her eyes widen as she kicked at empty space. She was sliding into the mine shaft and pulling me down with her.

"Mike! Help me!"

I didn't answer, just concentrated on peeling back her fingers, trying to break the vice-like grip she had on my arm; but as quickly as I'd unhook one hand and go for the other, she'd grab on again. It was a game children might have played, only this one was deadly. I was conscious of her gasping, and the feel of her clammy skin before I finally twisted free. Then she dropped—and there was nothing. I stared into a black hole of silence.

———————

On my hands and knees, I backed away from the sloping ground and rolled over onto my back. God, that was close. I breathed heavily, staring up at nothing. Gradually, the moon came into focus and I heard the sound of crickets chirping. But then I heard another sound, the rise and fall of a piercing howl.

I sat up.

Crouching near the hole, the cat was panting in distress, and then he yowled again.

"Goddamned cat!" I lunged at him, but he sprang into the trees. At least he won't be bothering me again, I thought. I kicked over the rock cairn, picked up the headlamp and blanket, and began the long trek back to the ranch.

At home, I had a well-deserved drink, showered and went to bed. The next morning, I washed the blanket, and then went out back to do the usual chores, almost stepping on a dead mouse laying on the doormat. Its head had been crunched. I didn't think much of it, just picked it up by the tail and flung it into the fields.

After breakfast, I got in my jeep and drove into town. On the way, I stopped at the local animal shelter and donated the blanket and some old towels. The young receptionist smiled and said they'd put them to use right away. Then I drove to the feed store, ordered some supplemental hay and corn, did a few more errands and got home about 2pm. It was time to call my wife's cell.

"Hey Honey! Guess I was still sleeping when you got up, sorry I missed you. So, were you able to account for all the calves this morning? Guess so, or I would've heard from you. I had a good day, just finished some errands in town. Not much else going on, just wanted to see how your conference was going. Anyway, give me a call tonight if you can. Love ya!"

That done, I went to the kitchen, made myself a sandwich, got some chips and a beer, and settled down in front of the TV. A couple hours later I was asleep on the couch.

Glimmer of light—my hands are scratching, clawing uselessly at dirt and rock. Her hands are on my ankles, dragging me slowly, but relentlessly, down the mineshaft. I'm falling…

I opened my eyes, and for a moment, didn't know where I was. It was dark outside and I realized with relief that I was lying on the couch. I rubbed my face and sat up.

There was a scratching sound coming from the front door. I walked over. The scratching stopped for a moment, then started up again, more insistent than ever. I turned on the porch light and slowly opened the door, afraid of what I would see.

No one was there. I looked down. On the door mat lay a dead rat, a trickle of blood oozing from its head. I grimaced. First a mouse, now a rat, both with their heads crunched. The cat was back and I didn't think he was leaving me presents.

"Here, kitty kitty!"

No answer.

I picked the rat up by the tail and threw it into the dark. It was too quiet around here, I decided. I'd go into the city.

I didn't get home till after 1am. I entered the house and was glad to see the cat hadn't left me another dead rat. Just to be sure, I checked the back door step as well. All clear.

I ran a hand through my hair and laughed, why should I be so nervous about a damn cat? It was ridiculous.

I went to the kitchen and opened the fridge. There was some leftover apple pie Linda had made. I got it out, poured myself a glass of milk and ate directly from the pie tin. I didn't bother to clean up afterward, just turned out the lights before going to bed.

It was another hot night, so I opened my bedroom window, but it didn't help much. Not a single breeze stirred the leaves on the tree outside. I crashed on top of the covers and fell asleep instantly. It seemed only a minute later that I was awakened by a shrill screech.

I jerked upright. I could hear a hideous caterwauling outside. I leapt out of bed and leaned out the window. "Shut up!" I yelled, "Shut up, you damn cat!"

The yowling stopped, and I waited, breathing hard. Finally, the cat emerged from the branches of the tree. He leapt down and walked toward me—a panther on the prowl—and all the time, he stared at me with those green, green eyes.

I ran to get my gun, banging into the dresser in my haste to get back, but he had gone. I listened to the silence, then slammed the window shut and went back to bed, unable to sleep, and sweating in the dark.

———————

I didn't report my wife missing until 11p.m. the next night. They took an initial report over the phone and assured me they'd check with the CHP to see if she'd been in a traffic accident.

They sent an officer out who arrived about 20 minutes later. He seemed pleasant enough, shook my hand and told me the department would do everything they could to help me. We went into the kitchen and I offered him a seat at the table.

"Can I get you something to drink?" I asked.

"No thanks."

I got myself a glass of water and sat down opposite him.

"You don't mind if I use a tape recorder, do you, Mr. Reid?" he asked. "It would help with my notes."

"Go ahead, and please, call me Mike."

"Alright Mike. I'd like to start by asking you some standard questions," he said. "Your wife's name, description, things like that."

"Sure. I can get you a photo of her too."

He went through his questions then asked, "Where do you think your wife is right now?"

"Well if I knew that, I wouldn't have called you out here."

The officer stared at me.

"Look, she told me she was going to do a quick check on the cattle, then leave for the conference, so I assumed that's where she went. I don't know where she is now."

"Which conference was that?"

"The California Cattle Women's Conference. It's in Sparks, Nevada. She was just going for the last two days; it's a three day conference."

"What time did you expect her to be home?"

"She told me the conference ended before noon, so assuming she went out for lunch, and then with the drive home, I was expecting her around 5 at the latest."

"Did you see Linda before she left for the conference?"

"No, she usually gets up early and tries not to wake me so I can sleep in a little longer."

He smiled, "I didn't think a rancher could ever sleep in."

I shrugged.

"How do you know she actually went to the conference?"

"Her overnight bag was no longer on the chair where she'd left it the night before."

"Did you try calling the hotel to see if she'd checked in?"

"I did, although, it didn't occur to me to call the hotel until this evening. I'm so used to texting her."

"Did she answer any of her texts?"

"No, but sometimes she has her phone on silent and doesn't notice her texts until later."

"Had she checked in at the hotel?"

"They wouldn't tell me whether she'd checked in or not. They said they no longer give that information out over the phone. I'd have to go through the police, file a missing person report."

"Is that when you called us?"

"I waited an hour or two. I didn't want to overreact. If Linda showed up and found that I'd called the police, well…" I shook my head and chuckled, "I'd never hear the end of it."

"Okay, our department will contact the hotel. How about the people running the conference, did you try them?"

"That did occur to me, but by then the conference was over and I figured everyone would have gone home. Will you be able to check that out for me as well?"

"Yes, but we probably won't be able to reach the organizers until business hours tomorrow." He wrote something down, and then asked, "Do you think it's a possibility that she never made it off the ranch?"

"I don't think so. Earlier this evening, I drove around the ranch looking for her. If she'd been on the grounds, I would have seen her truck."

"And you tried texting her. Did you call her too?"

"Oh sure, I called her around 5 p.m. today and left a message. I was getting worried because I hadn't heard from her, even though I'd left a message the day before, too."

"Can you think of anywhere she may have gone?"

"Originally, I told myself she may have gone out with some friends, made a long day of it. Then it would still be a three-hour drive back. But now," I shook my head and frowned, "it's just not like her to stay away from the ranch so long, especially with the fall calving season."

"How long have you been raising cattle?"

"Only three years. I'm more a corporate sales guy, computer hardware. That's how we met, Linda and I."

"You worked together?"

"Not really. She was a VP of business development. We used to run into each other at the water cooler. I asked her out for a few drinks, and it continued from there. We got married a year later."

"She's quite a bit older than you, did that cause any gossip?"

"Maybe, but it didn't affect us. Linda was able to retire early and she wanted to chase her dream, so we came to this ranch."

"Was it your dream too?"

"I just went along for the ride." I smiled.

He scribbled a few notes, then nodded his head toward the window, "This is a big property you have."

"Yeah."

"How large is it?"

"About 700 acres."

He waited for me to say more.

"It's mostly Linda's property. She made good money from a previous startup and did well as a VP."

"So the ranch is under her name?"

"Mine too, I contributed a bit."

There was a pause, and I tried to turn the conversation. "I wondered if maybe Linda was visiting her mother in Sacramento. She's got Alzheimer's and lives in a home; but when I called to check, they said Linda hadn't been there, and they hadn't heard from her either."

"Okay. Is there anything else you want to tell me, Mike?"

"No, I just really want you to find her. I'm getting worried.."

"We want to find her too. We'll move as fast as we can. It would help if you gave me a list of everyone she may have been in contact with—friends, relatives, ranchers, past co-workers—and of course, the hotel and conference numbers too."

"I can get most of that for you now."

"Thank you. I'll need to collect some other things as well—personal items, electronic devices, online information—we can go over that when we're done talking here."

"No problem."

"And if you don't mind, I'd like to take a look around your house and barn. Would that be okay with you?"

"Sure, that'd be fine."

Ninety minutes later we were done and I was on the front porch, watching the officer drive off in his cruiser. I walked down the steps and gazed out.

There was a full moon, and a warm breeze rippled across the fields. The quiet didn't bother me tonight; it was a relief to be alone. I turned to go back inside, but my hand froze on the railing at the sound of a rolling growl.

I looked behind me. A moment before, the path had been empty, but now the cat was there. Moonlight illuminated him as he sat and stared at me, swishing his tail back and forth. He continued to growl as I stared back. Then he hissed and a chill went up my spine.

I hurried inside and shut the door.

Shortly after, I went to bed and lay there with my hands behind my head, staring at the ceiling. The interview with the cop had gone well, although I didn't like his remarks about Linda being older than me, and the size of our ranch. Tomorrow he'd be back, and I would play the part of a worried husband who still hadn't heard from his wife. The police would initiate a more thorough search of the ranch. They would find her truck in the thicket of trees, and from there, the mineshaft and her body.

That's what I wanted; you can't collect insurance without a body. The whole thing would be easily explained. "She must have been looking for a stray cow and fell into the mine shaft. Linda and I had no idea there were abandoned mines on our property, this is a total shock."

I tried to picture the kind of camera they'd use, to drop into the shaft. How would they light up the bottom of the hole? It would be interesting to watch. And what would she look like? Would her body be contorted? Bloody? I grimaced and wiped the image from my mind. Who cared anyway? The important thing was her money, my money. I'd have quite a bit—money from her will, from the future sale of the ranch, from her life insurance policy… I began to drift off, dreaming of what I would do with my new wealth.

Suddenly, I got an image of her silver medical bracelet, lying in the dirt. I felt a rush of panic and opened my eyes. The bracelet had broken off her wrist during our struggle. Had I remembered to pick it up?

I tried to relax and picture exactly what I had done before walking away from the hole. That damn cat had freaked me out, yowling like a banshee. I could see why people used to believe black cats were evil. What the hell did that cat want with me anyway? I pressed the palms of my hands against my eyes and tried to concentrate.

I remembered chasing the cat into the trees, then what? I saw myself kicking over the rocks, picking up the blanket and walking down the hill, back toward the ranch. I had not picked up the bracelet. Shit. I would have to go back there, tonight. If the police found her bracelet, they'd know there had been a struggle and would suspect me at once.

I threw the covers back and got dressed. I had a flashlight and was about to grab the keys to my jeep, when I thought better of it. The officer had just left. But what if he was hanging around, watching the ranch from a distance? I couldn't take a chance that he would see the lights of my jeep, leading him straight to her. It would be safer to walk.

I kept my flashlight off and walked fast. Crickets were chirping and an owl hooted in the dark.

It was easy to see in the moonlight, easy to see the shadow that flickered in and out, running alongside, crossing my path, or waiting for me to catch up. The cat was leading me, I realized with a shudder, anticipating my every step. He was no longer following me, I was following him.

I wasn't sure if I could find the mineshaft without the rock cairn, but the cat led me right to it. He looked back at me once, as if to be sure I was following him, then disappeared into the brush.

It made me nervous to think of him hiding near the mineshaft, watching my every move, so I picked up a large rock and heaved it in his direction. There was no answering scuffle. He wasn't there.

I took a deep breath and let it out slowly. The moonlight shone down on the sloping ground around the mineshaft and on the sparse coyote brush that seemed determined to grow in its dry earth. The hole itself was black, too deep and deadly for any light to shine through.

Carefully, I directed my flashlight around the funnel of the hole, working out in a concentric pattern. Just to the left of the funnel, I caught a sparkle of silver. I strode over, picked it up, and examined the bracelet with my flashlight. Only the clasp was broken. I grinned, and tossed this last bit of evidence into the mineshaft. Home free.

I turned my back to the hole, took a step and the cat leapt at my face. A flurry of claws raked my nose and cheeks and I screamed. I lurched back, my arms windmilling as I tried to stop the fall, but I fell anyway, landing on my side and sliding, feet first, toward the hole.

Frantically, I scrabbled at the sloping walls of the funnel, and with one hand, managed to grab onto the coyote brush. But it was flimsy, and my weight was too much. I watched the dirt crumble and the roots slowly pull away, and I looked up toward the full moon, hoping for a miracle.

But instead, a shadow crossed the moon. It was the black face of the cat, staring down at me. And I swear, his green eyes glowed.

Now for another trip back in time, to the early days of the cold war. A man awakens in a hospital in East Berlin with only fleeting memories of how he got there.

Craig Faustus Buck is unemployable in any field except writing. He has been a journalist, nonfiction book author, TV writer, screenwriter and novelist. His short stories have won a Macavity Award and been nominated for two Anthony Awards and a Derringer Award. His debut novel, the noir romp Go Down Hard, *was published by Brash Books in 2015. Learn more at CraigFaustusBuck.com.*

Blank Shot

by Craig Faustus Buck

His face hit the pavement hard. He tried to recall what just happened, but his thoughts wouldn't sync. His head felt like he'd been whacked by the claw end of a hammer. Blood flowed into his field of vision, expanding on the ground before him. Must be his. Bad sign. He closed his eyes against a stab of afternoon sun reflecting off the crimson pool.

The relentless pounding in his head accelerated like the sound of a train starting up from a dead stop. The insides of his eyelids darkened. Something was blocking the sun. He opened his eyes to see polished black boots standing in his blood. Like Stasi boots. He was too weak to lift his eyes to see who wore them. He waited for his life to flash before him but all he saw were black boots in red blood. The world was running in slo-mo. If this was death, it was taking its fucking time.

Something new moved into his sightline. A small brindle mutt sniffed the boots. The dog seemed familiar. He realized she was his. He couldn't remember her name. He watched her wade through the ooze and start lapping up his lifeblood like she was in doggy heaven.

Next time he opened his eyes he was on his back with rows of lights rushing past. No. The lights were fixed. He was rushing. It dawned on him: he was alive.

He saw "Operationstrakt" painted over the swinging doors as his gurney crashed through them. Women in white caps grabbed his arm and slid a needle into a vein. He tried lifting his head but hit a brick wall of agony.

"Kannst du mich hören?" asked one of the nurses.

He understood she was asking if he could hear her but he didn't answer. He didn't want to move until the pain was under control. Not even his lips. He felt his eyes flag.

He woke up in a hospital room feeling a weight on his brow. Something shading his eyes. He inched his arm toward his head, trailing a tube attached to his hand. He felt a semi-hard surface cradling his head.

Another bed in the room was mostly hidden by a drape. He could see feet. Yellow toenails, cracked and furrowed. His roommate was old.

A man walked in, short and skinny, lab coat hanging open to reveal a navy bow tie and a blood smear on his white shirt.

"Ich bin Doktor Hermann." The doctor's baritone seemed deep for his size. "Wie heißen Sie?"

What should have been a slam-dunk question brought nothing to mind.

"I don't know my name."

"You speak English."

"I understood your German, but English seems easier." His words flowed slower than sap.

"You sound like an American."

The label fit like a pair of old jeans but he noted a sudden mistrust in the doctor's voice. He shrugged.

"At least you can speak," said Dr. Herrman. "That is a good sign. You are a lucky man."

"…don't feel so damn lucky."

"Do you know what year it is?"

He started to shake his head but movement hurt too much so he stopped.

"Nineteen-sixty," said the doctor. "You're in East Berlin."

"How the hell did I get here?"

"Most people from the Western Sectors take the U-Bahn."

"I meant…." He realized he didn't know what he meant.

"Sorry," said the doctor. "Bad joke. Do you know who shot you?"

"I got shot?"

"Yes."

"In the head." He tapped his bandage. None of this made sense to him.

"Do you remember where you live?"

A few bits and pieces came to mind. A narrow concrete-block row house. An iron gate. A black door. But that was it.

"Should be some ID in my wallet," he said.

"You had no wallet when they brought you."

"Where's my dog? She had a tag."

"Nobody mentioned a dog."

Shit. No papers, no memory, no mutt.

———————

His head X-ray revealed that the gunman who tried to put a slug in his skull did a half-assed job, but the X-ray was useless as a prognosticator. Doktor Herrman had no clue when or if his memory would come back or whether he might suffer potentially lethal brain swelling, a threat that only a seizure would reveal.

He was wired to a monitor in case he launched into some kind of crisis but after a while he must have passed a stability benchmark because the nurse allowed a Volkspolizei cop to come in.

Just under six feet, translucent aquamarine eyes, the VoPo removed her grey felt pillbox hat with its metal emblem to reveal red glossy hair cropped short like a Kabarett singer from the Weimar years.

"I'm Leutnant Fleischer," she said. "The doktor told me you are American."

Her German accent was crisp, like her skirted semi-dress uniform.

"That's what he tells me, too."

He was glad she was just a People's Police instead of a Stasi interrogator, but he had no idea how he knew this was fortunate.

"What is your name?"

"I don't know."

Her lips curled into a knowing grin, making her look sexy even in her somber grey-green uniform with jade green necktie.

"Everyone knows his name," she said. "It won't help you to make me spend weeks leafing through fingerprint cards to find it."

"What makes you think I've got a card?"

"It is written all over your torso. This is not the first time you have been shot. You have been stabbed, as well. If you are not in the Volkspolizei files, I am sure the Stasi has you somewhere."

The mention of the Stasi rattled him. He had no reply.

She ran her fingers over her ear like she was brushing back long hair. He wondered if she'd just recently cropped it. Maybe to look more like a man. Despite the Party line, he suspected women still struggled for equality in the People's Police.

"After all," she said, "it was the Stasi who brought you here. Any idea how or where they found you?"

"No. Didn't they say?"

She ignored the question. He assumed the elite Secret Police hadn't deigned to brief a lowly People's Police Lieutenant.

"You have a tattoo that reads 'Slade,'" she said. "Does that sound familiar?"

"No."

"You are sure?"

"Why would I lie?"

"Because you have something to hide."

"If I do, I don't know what it is."

She toyed nervously with the caliper and hammer insignia on her cap.

"Unless you are a homosexual with a tattoo of his lover's name, I am going to assume Slade is your own."

Her mention of a lover sparked a faint memory of the back seat of a car, a woman's tongue in his ear, her hand in his crotch. He couldn't picture her face but he vividly recalled his passion. He wasn't homosexual. On the other hand, it seemed odd that he'd have a tattoo of his own name. He supposed "Slade" could be a nickname. At any rate, it was something to latch onto.

"Where are your papers?"

"Whoever took my wallet has my papers."

He watched her ice-cold eyes study his face for signs of deception.

"What do you remember about the person who shot you?"

"Nothing."

Fleischer squeezed her brow as if tormented, as if the memory problem were hers, not his.

"I know you are lying," she said. "I know who you are."

"Maybe you could let me in on the secret."

"You are a biergarten brawler. A provoker of violence. And this wasn't the first time by the look of your scars. Hardly the marks of a paragon of Socialism."

Slade was surprised that she trotted out the word "paragon." She must have a daily-English-word calendar taped to her fridge.

"What's your point?" he asked.

"This memory loss. I find it a bit too convenient."

"Not for me."

Fleischer looked disappointed, as if she'd been expecting Slade to dissolve into tears and confess to something. Slade couldn't imagine what.

The lieutenant stomped her boot as if trying to get at an itch on the sole of her foot. The gesture prompted another fragment of memory.

"I remember boots," said Slade. "Black, glossy boots."

"And? Was he tall? Short? Fat? Thin?"

"I don't know."

"A man shot you and all you remember is the shine of his boots?"

Slade threw a glare so harsh Fleischer winced.

"I was kind of busy gushing blood."

Slade spent the night trying to sleep through flushing toilets, clattering bedpans and a groaning roommate. By morning he was ready to get the hell out of there. He tried sitting up. It seemed like a good idea while he was lying down but when he swiveled his legs off the bed, his opinion changed. As he waited for the room to stop swinging, a stout nurse walked in.

"Look who's sitting up." She spoke in a thick Bavarian accent that stirred a memory of an old woman. Why did this regional accent ring a bell? Was he remembering his mother?

The nurse steadied him as he cautiously stood. The room slowed to a gentle sway but he was still afraid to lift his foot, afraid he'd have trouble replacing it on the moving floor.

The Bavarian helped him shuffle into the bathroom with his IV stand. At six-one, Slade had to bend down to stare into the mirror. His hazel eyes looked familiar, if slightly dilated. The rest of his face looked like Black Forest roadkill. The rough pavement had not been kind.

Half his head was covered with a thick plaster bandage, augmented with surgical tape. It reeked of sulfa powder. He turned his head but the makeshift helmet hid any hair he might have. He thought he remembered it being black.

He lifted the sleeve of his worn cotton hospital gown to reveal "Slade" tattooed across his bicep in graceful blue cursive.

As the nurse helped him shuffle back to bed, Dr. Hermann walked in. "How's the patient?"

"You tell me."

Hermann pushed his wire-rimmed glasses up his nose, took Slade's chart from a pinewood pocket on the door and leafed through it.

"You should be well enough to go home in no time."

"If I can remember where it is."

An orderly wheeled Slade's wheelchair into a community room. A one-legged man sat deep in concentration, playing chess by himself. A young woman was slumped on a couch in a drug-stupor, her arms spotted like leopard skin from cigarette burns.

On the far side of the room, Slade recognized Dr. Kohl, the psychiatrist who had done his mental evaluation after his interview with Leutnant Fleischer. The trim, silver-haired man wore a thick wool suit and leaned against the windowsill, tapping his foot as if *The Flight of the Bumblebee* were playing in his head.

"Glad to see you again, Herr Slade," he said.

"That's Slade."

"As I said."

"Not Herr Slade. Just Slade. I don't know if it's a first name, last name, nickname or what."

Dr. Kohl smiled unconvincingly. "I see."

Slade thought psychiatry was a masturbatory joke but Dr. Hermann had insisted he see Dr. Kohl. Apparatchiks work in mysterious ways. Slade guessed he needed a shrink to sign off before Dr. Hermann could release him, so he decided to play it safe and keep a civil tongue.

"My job is to help you get to the root of your problems," said Dr. Kohl.

"I already know the root of my problems," said Slade. "I got shot in the fucking head."

The first words out of his mouth and his inner censor was already failing him. He wondered if impulse control had been a problem before the shooting or whether this was another symptom.

Dr. Kohl spent an hour grilling Slade about the shooting, about his identity and about his past. Slade remembered the dog, the black boots, the car sex and a few things from his childhood, but that was it. As Dr. Kohl took his leave, he told Slade an orderly would collect him shortly to take him back to his room.

While Slade waited, a stranger strolled in. He was tall, maybe six-five, with weathered skin and yellowish-gray coyote eyes. He had a gap between his stained front teeth where a toothpick would look right at home. He wore Levis, a sweat-stained cowboy hat and snakeskin shit-kicker boots. Slade suspected the man spent more time astride a barstool than a saddle and the phrase "dustbowl cowboy" popped into his mind, origin unknown. Another tidbit for Dr. Kohl, should Slade have to see him again.

"I been lookin' for you," said the man. Slade was encouraged that this man seemed to know him, but the cowboy didn't feel familiar. His dress marked him as a visitor from the Western sectors.

"Do I know you?" asked Slade.

"You sayin' you don't recollect?"

Slade pegged the twang to Tennessee. Apparently, he recognized regional accents in both German and English, but English felt like his native tongue. His thoughts were all in English and, as far as he could tell, so were his dreams.

"I don't remember much of anything," he said.

The cowboy absorbed this for a moment. "How 'bout a cup of java?"

Slade envisioned the orderly finding him gone. "Why not?" he said.

"Name's Rommy."

The elevator doors slid open and Rommy pushed the wheelchair straight in, leaving Slade facing the back. Cargo blankets covered the walls. It felt like a padded cell.

"Looks like they was expecting us," said Rommy. Slade heard the doors close to confine them and it struck him that the cowboy could very well be the man who shot him.

The cafeteria was fluorescent, cold and depressing. Soviet-style minimalism at its worst. Dented metal trays, scarred wooden tables, hard chairs and the smell of canned sauerkraut. Rommy parked Slade at a table as far as possible from the few other diners.

"Coffee comin' up, blond with sand," said Rommy, mimicking words Slade remembered himself saying. Rommy smirked as he swaggered off, leaving Slade to wonder how the cowboy knew how he ordered his coffee. What else did this stranger know about him?

When Rommy returned with two mugs, Slade asked, "How do you know me?"

"You and me used to be tight."

Slade couldn't imagine being friends with this man. There was nothing about him that Slade liked.

"Then who am I?" asked Slade.

Rommy grinned, revealing a gold-capped canine. "Not that tight. You call yourself Slade, what sounds about as real as a hooker's sob story, if you catch my grift, but I never heard no last name."

"Do you know where I live?"

"That, amigo, I do not the fuck know. We hung at the same saloon is all. Das Kocktail off Kurfuerstendamm."

Rommy licked a drip from the side of his mug.

"How did you find me?"

"A little birdie."

———————

The next day was a whirlwind of tests. Doktor Hermann showed Slade his X-ray, explaining how the bullet had grazed above his right ear and drilled a trough through his skull just deep enough to skim the surface of his brain, searing a four-centimeter burn across his frontal lobe.

By the end of the day Slade was exhausted from all the prodding. There was nothing but propaganda on the radio so he amused himself by poking some Marxist excuse for red Jello to watch it jiggle.

Rommy walked in. "Remember me?"

"New memories aren't a problem," said Slade.

Rommy picked up a limp Spreewald pickle chip from Slade's dirty lunch tray. "You gonna eat that?" He stuck it in his mouth before Slade could answer. Slade waved his belated permission.

"I asked around Das Kocktail," said Rommy. "Nobody knows nothin'. You're a fuckin' mystery man."

"Somebody must know something."

Rommy flopped into the visitor's chair. "I'm takin' the Fifth 'til you're out of this slaughterhouse. You got VoPos nosin' around here like roaches in a sewer and with you bein' all doped up, who knows what you might say? It's a wonder the Stasi ain't come callin'."

"The Stasi brought me here."

"What?"

"That's what the doctors told me."

"I wondered how you ended up on the wrong side of the tracks."

Rommy foraged for another pickle and slipped it in his mouth.

"Fucking Stasi," Rommy said, still chewing. "That's all I need."

"Did I walk to Das Kocktail?" asked Slade. "Maybe I live nearby."

"You had a Volkswagen and a midget dog. That's all I know. You and me, we never got too personal. We was more like... associates."

He adjusted his hat. Slade saw it as a tell, like in poker, only he didn't know what it signified.

"So if we weren't that tight, why are you here?"

"I'm the only friend you got, seems to me. I may be rough-grained, but I ain't heartless."

"And I may have amnesia but I'm not stupid," said Slade. "You came here looking for me." Slade tapped his protective helmet with his index finger. "You want something from me."

"Just tryin' to help a pal saddle up."

"Bullshit."

Rommy flashed another glint of gold tooth. "Tell you one thing, my friend. You didn't used to be such a doubtin' fuckin' Thomas."

———————

Slade found physical therapy more punishing than healing.

"You lack stamina," said Dr. Hermann. "Your physical thera-pist cannot find any problems that she can trace to your injuries, so I am guessing it is the cigarettes."

"I smoke?"

"If you don't remember, this would be a good time to stop."

"What about releasing my photo to the papers?" asked Slade. "Someone is bound to recognize me."

Slade tapped his helmet. This was getting to be a nervous habit, like tonguing a loose tooth.

"Leutnant Fleischer does not want the gunman to know you are alive. He might try to correct his bad aim before she catches him."

Slade grunted, seeing the obvious logic but lamenting the result.

"Dr. Kohl thinks you are ready to go home," continued Dr. Hermann.

"What do you think?"

"Physically you're progressing well, assuming you don't get infected. We have no medical reason to keep you here more than another day or two. But I am concerned that you still suffer amnesia with no place to go and no money that we know of. If you stay here, the expense will be on your head."

"What's left of it," said Slade.

Dr. Hermann smiled. "Perhaps the Volkspolizist can arrange a place for you to go."

The thought of being locked in an East German jail or, even worse, a workhouse with the "asocials," gave Slade the shivers.

"I have a friend in the West," he said. "Maybe he'll put me up."

"You will need permission from the lieutenant to leave East Berlin. You are the only one who can identify your attempted murderer."

"But I can't."

"That may just be a matter of time."

"You will not leave," said Leutnant Fleischer. "Your case is not closed."

"Everyone knows Krushchev won't seal off East Berlin," said Slade. "At least not while Eisenhower's still President. If you need me, I'll jump on the U-Bahn and be here in ten minutes, not counting the hour it takes your border guards to check papers."

"Danke, Herr Slade. You are too considerate." Her sarcasm was as close as she'd come to a joke since he'd met her. "And if you do not come? I cannot very well cross the border and drag you back."

"Do you really think you have more interest than I do in finding out who I am and who shot me?"

She considered. "I will check with the Stasi."

This jolted Slade's nerves. He wished he knew why.

———————

"Leutnant Fleischer approved your release to the care of your friend," Dr. Hermann said the following morning. "She gave no explanation. I made it no secret that we were short on beds but somehow I do not think that was a deciding factor."

The four blocks from the hospital to the U-Bahn station seemed endless. Slade felt dizzy on the station stairs and Rommy had to hold him up as they descended to the bleak platform. But once they were on the train, Slade felt better. The car was almost full but silent as they rumbled under the city toward the border.

When the loudspeaker announced they were now entering the American Sector, a wave of relief washed through the passengers. The tension yielded to animated talk and laughter.

The train stopped for a border check. An American soldier came through to spot check papers. The G.I. frowned at the DDR stamp on Slade's hospital discharge and asked him to name last year's American League champions. Slade couldn't remember his own name, but he knew the White Sox won the pennant for the first time since the Black Sox scandal in 1919. And he knew they went on to lose to the Dodgers in the first World Series ever played on the West Coast. He marveled at the detail he recalled and wondered if this was a sign of improvement.

The soldier welcomed him to West Berlin.

———————

The faded couch had more stains than a butcher's smock and smelled even worse.

"She ain't much, but she's all I got," said Rommy.

The ragged brown davenport was a good ten inches shorter than Slade but he said it was fine.

Rommy grabbed two beers from a dented Frigidaire and tossed a can to Slade.

"Your tab is now open," he said. "When you're making some scratch you'll pay it all back, including that there Schlitz." He opened his can, then tossed the churchkey to Slade.

Slade sat on the couch and felt it sag along with his spirits. How did he wind up in the clutches of a man who lived in the Shangri-la of beer and chose to drink Schlitz from the PX?

The walls of the small, one-bedroom apartment were darkened by years of smoke and poor ventilation, making the place feel doubly claustrophobic. The only window was blacked out and barred like a prison cell. The bolt on the front door was keyed both outside and in. If there were a fire, Slade would be fried.

But at least he had a place to live.

"What else can you tell me?" he asked.

Rommy sat down on an old wooden chair that creaked in protest.

"Das Kocktail is what you might call my office," said Rommy. "You and me, we'd meet at DK, have some beers. Sometimes I'd need a runner, you'd need some cash, we'd work somethin' out."

"What kind of runner?"

"Morphine, sometimes a little Moroccan kif."

"I'm a dealer?"

"You're a fucking patriot. I know an East German Army Major, happens to be addicted to morphine. This Ossie sends me a drop box location; you deliver the dope and bring back classified documents; I sell 'em to the CIA for a pretty pfennig and we've both served our country."

Something about trading drugs to a Communist for secrets didn't seem right to Slade, yet it felt somehow familiar.

"I reckon whoever tried to kill you was trying to move in on my action," said Rommy. "It's bad for business to let that kinda shit slide. That's why I sprang you out of that pinko klinik in the Soviet Sector. Somewhere in that head of yours, you know who shot you. And when you remember that asshole's name, I guaran-fuckintee I'll make him pay for what he done to you."

"Hey, Rommy." The woman's voice startled Slade. He turned to see her in the doorway to the hall, banding her long, honey hair into a ponytail. Standing about five-three, she wore only a white slip, short enough to give him an eyeful of the garter clips that gripped her nylons near the tops of her thighs, but she didn't seem self-conscious.

"Is this our new roommate?" she asked.

"Fuckin' A," said Rommy.

She could stand to lose fifteen pounds but Slade still found her riveting. Was it her sexy lingerie? Or was she triggering a memory?

"Have we met?" he asked.

She broke into a smoky laugh. "Just barely, darlin'. I've seen you at DK a few times, but we've never been properly introduced." She spoke with a gentle drawl.

"Charlene, this here's Slade," said Rommy.

"Pleased to make your acquaintance," said Charlene.

Rommy's coyote eyes turned on Slade. "She ticklin' your memory? You look like you seen a ghost."

Slade shook his head.

"I'll go find you a towel," said Charlene. "And don't you be leaving the toilet seat standing at attention."

She turned and walked down the hall. Slade couldn't keep his eyes off those thighs.

"You follow through on that sweet ass," said Rommy," and I'll put another hole in your head."

Slade wondered if he had put the first one there.

———

Slade slept like a drunken dog, but in the morning his back felt like he'd been hauling bricks all night. Charlene insisted they go to Cafe Kranzler on the Ku-damm for coffee and strudel with lots of whipped cream.

When they got back to the apartment, Rommy retrieved a battered leather briefcase and headed back out. Slade saw a bulge beneath his jacket. Armed and concealing, he thought. Yet again, Slade wondered if Rommy had shot him, but the notion seemed absurd. If Rommy had, or planned to shoot him again, why invite the attention of the VoPos by taking Slade into his home?

Charlene went to change out of the sundress she'd worn to breakfast. When she came back she was wearing a pair of Rommy's boxer shorts and one of his flannel shirts. The top three of six buttons were undone.

"He's off on his rounds," she said. "He'll be gone most of the day." She looked at a dirty ashtray on the wooden crate they used as a coffee table and added, "That man is such a pig." She leaned over to retrieve the ashtray and her shirt drooped open. Slade stared at her breasts.

"Whoops," she said without embarrassment. Slade felt a twinge in his crotch even as he thought about the gun in Rommy's belt. Charlene disappeared into the kitchen to dump the ashtray.

When she returned, she'd buttoned a fourth button and put on a short black skirt making her somewhat less likely to breach public decency laws.

"Let's get out of this dump," she said.

Charlene kick-started her German Army-surplus reconnaissance motorcycle. It was loud. She told Slade her father wired her the money for the DKW bike on her twenty-fifth birthday. Slade hopped on behind her and they rode to the Wannsee Lakes to take a walk.

The sky was clear, the water unruffled. They strolled across the bridge between the two lakes and when a chill breeze arose she took his arm and huddled close. He liked the feel of her.

She led him along a path by the Kleiner Wannsee, through the yews, to some steps down to a small neglected incline bordered on three sides by a short wrought-iron fence. He kneeled with her before two headstones.

"Ever hear of Heinrich von Kleist?" she asked.

He shook his head as he read the name on the larger stone.

"Nineteenth century poet," she said. "His lover was dying so he brought her here and shot her, then shot himself so they could spend eternity together by this lake. Do you think that's romantic?"

"I'm not a big fan of people getting shot."

She looked at him for a moment, trying to parse his meaning, then picked a small flower and placed it before the headstone of the poet's lover.

"I think it's romantic," she said.

She led him back to the path and they walked along the lake. Her silence felt ominous, like a storm cloud about to burst. When she finally spoke it was almost in a whisper.

"I lied to you," she said. "We have met."

"We have?"

She stopped and turned to face him. He heard the S-Bahn train pass not far away.

"We've more than met."

Her green eyes seemed to peer right into his broken skull, as if searching for his memories of her.

"Tell me," he said.

"One night the Landespolizei came through DK and took Rommy in for questioning on some trumped-up drug charge. We started talking and you introduced me to a good many shots of rye and we wound up in your car, scorching the backseat."

"I think I have a vague memory," he said.

"That's because we did it more than once. Your little dog used to go nuts. I couldn't take you back to Rommy's and you said your landlord didn't allow guests, so your car became our secret love nest. It was getting a lot deeper than just sex. We were falling hard."

"Sounds like something I wish I remembered better."

"Maybe I can help you." She clasped her hands behind his neck. A nanny pushing a pram down the path tsk-tsked as Charlene stood on tiptoe and kissed him. He felt transfixed. Was this déjà vu? Or was it just lust? Her soft tongue parted his lips, leaving no doubt it was both.

Rommy was waiting when they got back. "Where the fuck you been?"

"I took Slade to von Kleist's grave," said Charlene. "Do you expect us to stay cooped up in this luxury palace all day?"

"I expect you to do what I fuckin' tell you to do."

"Who the hell do you think you are, giving orders like the high and mighty King of Sheeba? If I want to take him to the lake, I'll take him to the damn lake!"

"The man has an open hole in his skull, Charlene. What the hell you doin' putting him on the back of a bike with a fuckin' diaper for a hat?"

"He's a grown man, Rommy! He can make his own decisions!"

"It's okay, Charlene," said Slade trying to smother her fuse.

"No it's not!" she said. "He thinks I'm just some goddamned piece of ass!"

"You're whatever I fuckin' tell you to be," said Rommy.

She slapped him. A red handprint bloomed on his cheek. His expression hardened.

"I oughta rip your goddamned hand off."

"Hey," said Slade. "Let's all just calm…"

"Shut up," said Rommy.

"Or what, big man," said Charlene. "You going to pull out your shiny steel dick and shoot him all over again?"

Rommy backhanded her fast and hard, sending her tumbling across the coffee table. Slade jumped up to intervene but Rommy raised a semi-automatic pistol.

"Don't you fuckin' move," he said.

Slade froze. He recognized the standard-issue Soviet Makarov and wondered if that meant he'd been in the Army.

Charlene was drooling blood. "I swear to God I'll cut your dick off in your sleep."

"Don't you make me hit you again, you won't be gettin' up," said Rommy.

"Is it true?" said Slade. "Did you shoot me?"

Rommy smirked. "If I wanted you dead that's what you'd be. Don't you go believing nothin' that lying bitch has to say."

"You wouldn't know the truth if it kicked you in the balls," she said, starting to push herself up. Rommy shoved her back down with a snakeskin boot.

"Why would she lie about that?" said Slade.

"To stir the fuckin' pot like she always does. I'd be a rich man, I had a nickel bag for every damn bar fight she's lit off. She just loves to watch me bleed."

That night Slade tossed for hours, kept awake by the din of his own thoughts. He wondered if there were really women out there who'd pit men against each other for the sport of it. He wondered if it was a common practice. He supposed he once knew more about women, but now he was at a loss, unable to summon memories of the ones he'd known.

He shot awake at the clack of the front door bolt being thrown. He was surprised that he'd fallen asleep.

Rommy flung open the door to flood the room with the light of the morning gloom. "No more fuckin' daytrips, Charlene!"

Briefcase in hand, Rommy stepped outside, kicking the door shut behind him. A moment later, Charlene came into the room, tying her robe.

"Asshole," she said, sitting on the crate, her pink robe draped over her knees just inches from Slade's face. She ran her fingertips gently down his cheek. "How are you feeling this morning, Sugar?"

Her brief touch made him hunger for more.

"Do you know what really happened to me?" he asked.

"Some of it," she said. "The night before you got shot, you and me were out making honey in your car. Alex came out to dump some trash, heard your dog barking, caught us at it."

"Alex?"

"Bartender at DK. You gave him fifty Deutschmarks to keep his mouth shut. But I'm sure he told Rommy anyways because, when Rommy came home the next day, he had blood all over his shirt."

Slade flashed on his own blood pooling. "Does he have some black boots?"

"He's got a lot of boots."

She led him into the bedroom. It stank of cigarettes and spilt whisky. The bed was unmade, the sheets stained by years of night sweats and drunken sex. Two small closets faced each other across the room. His and hers. Hers was closed; his open, the floor a cramped jumble of dirty clothes and three pair of boots, none of them black.

"Maybe they got stained by your blood," she said. "He would have tossed them; he's not stupid."

Slade stared at the boots. "Why would Rommy risk taking me in if he was worried enough to destroy evidence? And why would he leave me alone with you if he was jealous enough to shoot me?"

Slade's mind felt like a hamster on a wheel.

"You need to give your brain a rest," she said.

He turned to find her lying on the bed, robe splayed wide like angel wings, transforming the sullied sheets into a field of dreams. A recollection almost arrived but never quite made it.

"Come to me, Sugar," she said. She grabbed his belt and pulled him closer. "Make up for lost time." She unzipped his pants and threaded her fingers through his fly. He was hers.

They lay slick and spent in the dark, fetid room. He felt at peace for the first time since he woke up in the hospital. Charlene blew a perfect smoke ring then gave him a deep kiss that tasted of Pall Mall. He didn't mind.

He wanted to clean the sheets before Rommy returned but she assured him Rommy would never notice as long as they were dry. She used her hair dryer to speed up the process.

Later, they walked to Cafe Einstein.

"Coffee," he ordered. "Blond with sand." The waitress was mystified.

"Cream and sugar, Fräulein," said Charlene.

They sat side-by-side watching an ant drag a crystal of sugar across the counter.

"We talked a lot about running away," she said. "Get out of Berlin. Just you and me."

"We could still do it," he said.

"He'd find us. That night we got caught I told him I was going to leave him. I'm sure that's why he shot you. That's why he'll do it again." She leaned over and whispered in his ear, the warmth of her breath spreading through him. "He keeps his spare gun in his nightstand."

———•••———

Slade was watching Charlene slice chicken for schnitzel when Rommy came home.

"I'm starvin'," he said.

Charlene stabbed a piece of raw chicken and held it out to him.

He gave her the finger. "Gimme a goddamned beer."

Charlene pulled two beers from the fridge and smacked them onto the dining nook table for Rommy and Slade.

"Another on your tab," said Rommy, puncturing his with a church key. Beer sprayed on his shirt. He paid no attention. "About time you earned your keep. Think you can drive?"

"He's not ready for runs," said Charlene, leaning against the counter.

"The man can speak for his own self."

"I can drive," said Slade.

"See?" said Rommy.

"Bullshit," she said. "He's just acting big, strutting around defending his manliness like you all do, leaving what little common sense you might have in your tracks."

"Who went and appointed you Dear Abby?" said Rommy.

"I'm entitled to my opinion."

"The hell you are. The man's gotta earn his keep, so shut your fuckin' yap or I'll shut it for you."

"Leave her alone," said Slade.

Rommy turned in mock astonishment. "Since when is my bitch any of your goddamned business?"

"I don't like to see girls pushed around."

Rommy rose so fast his chair flew over.

"Who gives a shit what you like, you fuckin' freak. I'll treat you any way I goddamned want to!"

To emphasize his point, he sucker-punched Charlene. Blood sprayed from her nose tracing her path across the room before she smashed into the wall.

Rommy turned back at the loud click of his spare gun being cocked. Slade aimed at Rommy's glittering canine. Everyone froze.

"You touch her again I'll kill you," said Slade. Then, to Charlene, "You okay?"

"Almost." She spat out a tooth and dragged herself up to lean against a cabinet.

"I don't know what the hell she told you," said Rommy, "but she's playing you."

Slade eyed the revolver. "This the thirty-eight you shot me with?"

"I wasn't even here the day you was shot. I was in Munich scorin' morphine at the Army…"

He lurched forward. Slade fired, realizing too late that Rommy was falling not lunging. The slug missed but Rommy still dropped like deadweight. The chef's knife in his back must have pierced his heart. Charlene's hand glistened with Rommy's blood as she stared wide-eyed at her handiwork.

Slade stood immobile, the sound of his shot having blasted shards of memory through his mind like multicolored shrapnel. Yellow flash. Powder blue sky. Crimson pool. Black boots. Brindle dog.

Charlene was trembling so hard she couldn't stand. She crumpled to the floor, wrapped her arms around her shoulders and proceeded to rock back and forth.

"What do we do?" she asked.

Slade knelt to check Rommy's pulse but they both knew he was dead.

"Call the VoPos," he said.

"Are you crazy?"

"If we don't, there's no chance they'll believe us. Either way, they'll be here soon. Someone must have heard that shot."

"What are we going to say?"

"It was self-defense. He beat you. I grabbed the gun to make him stop. When I missed, you stabbed him. And that's all we remember. It happened so fast."

"You make it sound so easy. But you're not the one who killed him, are you."

He eyed the revolver.

"Go get a towel," he said.

She left the room.

Charlene returned with a towel.

"Put it over his head," said Slade. "So we don't have to look at him."

She didn't seem happy about approaching the body but she did as he asked. Slade headed down the hall toward the bedroom. He was in Charlene's closet when she came in. He held up a pair of black patent leather boots.

"I remember my little dog standing next to these boots. They were no bigger than she was. Too small for Rommy. But not for you."

Charlene blanched and ran out. He followed her into the kitchen. She raised the revolver.

"I really did love you," she said.

"But you shot me anyway."

"I was afraid I'd go down as an accessory to Rommy."

"What do you mean?"

"That night behind DK, while you were paying Alex off, I had to fix my smeared lipstick before going back inside. I dropped the tube on the floor of your car. While I was fishing around for it, I found your Polizei ID pin under the seat."

It took him a moment to fathom her meaning. The answer seemed absurd.

"I'm a cop?"

"Slade," her eyes locked on his, "you're Stasi."

His stomach pitched at the thought of belonging to the Secret Police.

"That's why they took you to East Berlin for treatment," she said. "Your comrades found you first."

"If I'm Stasi, they'd have my fingerprints on file."

"I'm sure they do. But they'd never blow your cover to a lowly VoPo."

"But I'm an American."

"So were the Rosenbergs."

It felt wrong. If he was a Stasi agent, he'd know it, wouldn't he? On the other hand, if the Stasi was trying to identify an East German Army officer who was trading state secrets for drugs, it would make sense to start with the traitor's drug connection, which would explain Slade's relationship with a scumbag like Rommy.

"I was in love with you," said Charlene, "while you were lying to my face." Twin tears striped her cheeks.

She cocked the revolver. The sound triggered his memory of being shot. And of loving the woman who shot him.

"I remember loving you," he said.

"You remember because we had something rare. We still do. I know you felt it this morning when we made love."

He nodded. She lowered the gun.

"I felt it, too," she said, reaching out to touch his cheek. "We can start over. Run away to Paris, the States, anywhere. We could be so good together."

He kissed her, tasting salty tears on her lips. "I do still love you," he said, "but I'll never trust you."

"Then it's goodbye." She raised the gun and pulled the trigger.

Nothing happened.

He opened his hand and, one by one, let the bullets fall to the floor.

"Aufmachen! Polizei!" The police pounded on the door.

Her eyes begged for mercy.

He said, "I'd be a fool to give you another shot."

Our next story is a study of two men—one about to die—the other, the man who will escort him to his death. Death Row is prison guard Manny Rodriguez's beat. We explore their unique relationship in Herschel Cozine's story.

Mr. Cozine is the authors of numerous stories published in such markets as Alfred Hitchcock, Ellery Queen, and Mysterical-E. His latest story, A Private Hanging, was a finalist for The Derringer Award. A collection of his stories, The Osgood Casebook, is published by Untreed Reads.

Today You Die

by Herschel Cozine

If anyone deserved to die, it was Hack Jensen. Convicted of the brutal murder of a child, Hack had shown no remorse. Indeed, he had no conscience. It showed in his eyes—soulless, cold, cruel eyes that looked out at the world with hatred and contempt. The man was truly a monster.

Manny wouldn't throw the switch that sent the fatal surge of electricity through the condemned man's body. Nonetheless he would be a participant in the death of Hack Jensen by his mere presence. As a result, he would be vilified by many and thanked by no one. He had long ago accepted the unpleasant—some would say barbaric—duty. As a guard at the State Penitentiary, it was part of his job.

And today was Hack's day to die.

Putting a man to death, even a man as evil as Hack, was not a task Manny looked forward to. However deserving of death, Hack was still a human being. And somehow that made the task that much more distasteful. Manny would never get used to it.

These thoughts tumbled around his head as he walked down the hall toward Hack's cell, accompanied by another guard and a priest. He squared his shoulders and mentally prepared himself for the next hour. It never got any easier.

Manny unlocked the door of Hack's cell and stepped inside.

"It's time," he said softly.

Hack grunted at the guard, looked past him at the small man by the cell door.

"Get him outta here," he said.

"That's Father Terrence," Manny said.

"I don't care if he's Jesus Christ. Get him outta here."

"Hack…" Manny started.

Hack swung around. "I don't want no weepy eyed Bible thumper prayin' over me." He spoke directly to the priest. "Get the hell outta here!"

The sad eyed priest studied Hack for a moment. Then, with a slight bow, he crossed himself and left. Hack glared after him, cursing under his breath.

"Goddamn preachers."

Manny shook his head. "Hack," he said. "Today of all days, couldn't you show a spark of humanity?"

Hack snorted. "Today I die," he said. "Why the hell should I care how some sawed off religious jerk feels?"

"Father Terrence is not a 'religious jerk'. You could…" Manny stopped in mid sentence. Shaking his head again, he glanced at his watch. "It's ten-thirty," he said.

"Yeah," Hack replied. "Time to get ready for the big event."

Manny nodded mutely. He motioned to the bunk in a silent order for Hack to sit. Hack sat down heavily and eyed Manny with a hint of a sneer.

"How many guys have you seen fry, Manny?" He said.

Manny shook his head. "Too many, Hack."

"You like watchin' 'em?"

"No," Manny said. "Not at all."

Hack snorted. "The hell you don't. Why would you take this job if you didn't like what you do?"

"I like what I do," Manny said. "Most of it, anyway. But I'm not sadistic. I don't enjoy this part of my job. Not a bit."

Hack snorted again. The second guard was shaving the top of Hack's head. Hack swore and stood up. He grabbed the guard's wrist and twisted it savagely. "Watch what you're doing for Chrissake!" he said. "Just because I'm a dead man don't give you the right to mangle my head."

The guard winced in pain and pulled free from Hack's grasp. Manny put his hands on Hack's shoulders and pushed him back down on the cot.

"Take it easy, Hack. He didn't mean it."

"How do you know?" Hack growled.

Turning back to Manny, Hack appraised him with a scowl. "What's so great about what you do? Do you like ordering us cons around like we're dogs? Does that make you feel like a big man?"

"Is that what you think this job is all about, Hack?"

"Yeah," Hack said in a growl. "That's what it's all about. Little assholes with big guns and power over guys like me. Pricks like you who would never make it on the streets. But in here, you're God."

"If you say so, Hack," Manny said. He turned away from the condemned man and stared out the barred window to the yard below. It was deserted now. A spotlight bathed it with an eerie glow as it swept over the blacktop. The scene matched the mood of the moment. Desolate, lonely, depressing. The high walls, topped with barbed wire, stood foreboding in the cold dark night. Beyond the walls Manny could see a small crowd carrying signs and singing. They appeared like clockwork on days such as this. The gathering, mostly women, but a few men and one or two children, walked in a tight circle by the prison gate.

Another, smaller crowd, those who wanted Hack dead, stood a short distance from the others, watching in silent disapproval. It would stay that way until the execution was over. Manny had seen it many times. There was seldom any violence among them. He wasn't sure which group he would join if he were out there. He didn't allow himself to think about it. Whether it was right or wrong, it wasn't a pleasant thing to watch. The groups outside, though philosophically opposed, had one thing in common. They were not required to watch the execution. Manny envied them that. He always found it difficult to sleep afterward. Tonight, he knew, would be no different.

"You guys are as bad as the cons you're guardin'," Hack was saying. "You beat us for no reason, steal from us. But you got the uniform, so that makes it all right."

"No. It doesn't," Manny said.

Hack waved a hand impatiently. "The hell it don't." He eyed Manny for a moment, then gave another wave of the hand. "Never mind. You ain't one of them."

"Who beat you, Hack?"

"It don't matter. After today it will be all over. Nobody can touch me."

"It does matter. There are the others here. Think of them."

"Why should I? What did they ever do for me?" He shrugged a shoulder and looked to Manny. "You got a cigarette?"

Manny reached into his shirt pocket and took out a pack of cigarettes. Although a nonsmoker, he had learned to carry them on occasions such as this. He handed one to Hack, struck a match and held it to the cigarette.

Hack inhaled and let out a stream of smoke. His glower slowly softened. Taking another drag on the cigarette, he leaned forward.

"Guess what I had for dinner," he said. "My last meal."

"What?" Manny asked.

"Lobster. Ain't that great? I never had lobster in my life."

"Did you like it?"

Hack shrugged. "It's OK. But I wouldn't pay no fifty bucks for one in a restaurant. Crab's just as good and a helluva lot cheaper."

Hack smiled. "I guess you're right, Hack." He checked his watch.

The second guard turned off the electric shears and stepped away. Hack ran his hand over his freshly shaven head.

"Hair gets in the way, huh?" he said.

Manny raised an eyebrow. "What are you talking about?"

"The thingamajigs that you put on a guy's head. You know. To fry him. They don't work if the guy's got hair?"

Manny frowned and looked away. "I don't know."

Hack snorted. "You don't want me to talk about it. Well ain't that too bad?" He stood up and crossed to the window. "It's my funeral, pal. If I want to talk about it I guess you just have to listen."

"Hack, I…" Manny started. "Make it easy on yourself."

"Easy, hell. I been on the row for eight years now. I got used to it. Y'know?"

Manny nodded. "That's a long time."

Hack grunted and looked around the cell. "I sure won't miss this place. I'm glad I'm gettin' outta here. Let some other poor bastard have it."

He nodded to the window. "Get a load of those people out there. Bleedin' hearts. They don't want me to die." He grunted. "I'm all choked up." He laughed a hollow, coarse laugh. "Hell, I coulda killed one of *their* kids. Then I bet they wouldn't be out there wavin' signs and singin' hymns. Nope. They'd be with that other group of vultures, callin' for my head. What a bunch of hypocrites!"

Manny started to say something, thought better of it, and looked away.

Hack looked at Manny and frowned. "I know what you're thinkin', Rodriguez. You wanna know what makes guys like me tick. Ain't that right?"

Manny didn't answer.

"Do we gotta have a reason to do the things we do? Maybe we just like it."

Manny shrugged. He had seen condemned cons before on the day of their execution. Each one had his way to deal with it. Hack was no different. Today, execution day, the condemned man should be allowed to cope with it however he wanted. If he wanted to talk, let him talk. If he wanted to cry, let him. Manny kept silent.

"Yeah," Hack went on. "Maybe we like seein' them die. Y'know? Guys kill every day. Hunters. They take their guns out into the woods and shoot them defenseless animals. Then they come home and brag about it to their friends. They *like* it. Right?"

Manny nodded. "Yeah."

"But guys like me are different. We kill people. We're bad." He studied Manny with a sardonic grin. "C'mon, Rodriguez. Tell me what a bad guy I am."

"I'm not here to lecture, Hack. That's not my job. It's a good thing, too. I'm not very good at it."

"Hah!" Hack snorted. "You're a punk, Rodriguez. I could wipe my feet on you if we were on the outside."

"You're right, Hack. You're right." Manny agreed. He thought back to his own childhood in the inner city with hoodlums and addicts. Hardly a day went by when he wasn't beaten up by a bigger kid. He fought back, of course, and even came out on top occasionally. But he never looked for trouble. Thugs like Hack were a dime a dozen where he grew up.

"Yeah," Hack said. "You're a piece of shit, Rodriguez. You'd be sliced up like a chunk of dog meat where I come from." Hack's cold laugh echoed down the hall.

Manny remained silent. Hack was baiting him. It wasn't the first time. Others in the past had tried fighting with him on their execution day. He supposed it was their final act of defiance at a world they never understood. He would probably do the same thing if he were in their place. They had nothing to lose.

"Did you hear me, Rodriguez?"

"I heard you, Hack."

Hack glared at Manny for several seconds, fists clenched, eyes hard with hatred. Then he relaxed and motioned to the cell door.

"Who's comin' to the big event?" Hack asked.

Manny shook his head. "I don't know."

"Mama, I bet. What's-er-name. Betty." He let a low chuckle escape. "She wouldn't miss this for the world. Watch Hack the Butcher fry. Watch him squirm. Watch the good guys send his soul to Hell. Yeah, Betty'll be there for sure." He grunted and rubbed his chin. "I killed her kid. Yeah, I croaked him and got my kicks watchin' him die. Now little old Betty's gonna get her kicks watchin' *me* die."

Manny exchanged glances with the other guard. They shook their heads in unison but said nothing. This wasn't the time.

"Y'see that's different," Hack went on. "It's OK for her to get off watchin' a man die. But it's not OK for me. Y'know what I mean?"

Manny listened to the twisted logic and wondered if Hack believed what he was saying. He probably did. How could a man like Hack live with himself if he felt any other way?

At the sound of footsteps in the hall Hack tensed. His steely eyes narrowed as he saw Warden Haines and a distinguished, well-dressed man approach the cell.

"The warden," Hack said in a disdainful voice. "Now I *know* I'm gonna die."

The two men entered the cell. The warden looked past the prisoner to Manny.

"Is he ready?'

Before Manny could answer, Hack let out a snort. "Hey. I'm still alive. I can answer for myself."

Warden Haines ignored Hack. His eyes on Manny, he waited.

Manny nodded. "Ready, Sir."

Warden Haines turned toward the man next to him. This time addressing Hack directly, he said, "this is Mister Grayburn. He is from the Governor's office and is here to decide if the execution proceeds or not. As you know, it is scheduled for 11:30 tonight. It can be cancelled at any time if the Governor should so decide. There is a phone in the…"

"I know all that shit, Warden," Hack interrupted. "Let's get it over with. To hell with the governor and cancellations and appeals. I'm tired of all that."

""Understood," Haines said. "But it's the law. It's out of my control."

"The Governor ain't gonna call this shindig off," Hack said. "He wants me outta his hair. Hell, there's more votes for him with me dead. Y'know?"

Haines didn't respond. He turned to Manny. "Let's go," he said.

Manny stood on one side of Hack while the other guard took his position on the other side. Haines and Grayburn fell in behind. They started out the cell door and down the bare, cement walled hallway. Two guards stood by an iron door at the end of the hall. Seeing the small group approaching, they opened the doors and stood back.

The clock struck eleven.

Manny sighed inwardly. Looking around the small room, he tried to avert his eyes from the plain ugly chair. But there was no avoiding it. Manny knew the ritual too well. The condemned man would be strapped into the chair, fitted with wires to monitor his vital signs, and offered a hood to put over his head. Many of them refused the hood. Manny would be surprised if Hack didn't refuse it. Through the years he became pretty good at this guessing game.

He peered through the window to the small room outside. There were only a few people seated in the hardback chairs that faced the execution room. Most of them were regulars: a policeman, reporters, prison officials who were required to attend and, like Manny, only doing their duty.

Manny looked at the woman in the first row. Dressed in muted clothes with a scarf around her neck, she sat with her hands folded in her lap. Her eyes were riveted on Hack as he was strapped into the chair. It was too dark for Manny to see her clearly, but he knew who she was. Elizabeth Martin, mother of the boy who had been brutally murdered by Hack Jensen. Jimmy had been his name. Manny remembered that from somewhere. He wondered if Jimmy had ever tasted lobster.

The minutes passed slowly. The executioner, a small middle-aged man who Manny only knew by his last name—Harkins—checked the straps holding Hack's arms and legs and placed the metal cap on his head. Then he stood back. There was nothing more to do until 11:30.

Hack was hoodless. Manny had been right about that. He watched as the condemned man lifted his eyes and squinted at the window. The chair was situated so that it was bathed in light while the witness room was almost dark. Manny knew that Hack could not see who was out there. It was designed that way.

Hack said something to the executioner. Harkins shook his head. Hack's voice rose, but Manny could not make out what he was saying. Reluctantly Harkins crossed over to Manny.

"He wants to talk to you," he said.

"Me?"

"Yes."

Manny looked to the warden in silent appeal. The warden nodded. Manny approached Hack slowly.

"You wanted to talk to me?"

"Is she out there?"

"Who?"

"You know who," Hack growled. "Mama."

"I don't know. I think so."

"Where?"

"First row. Middle chair."

Hack squinted at the window. His cold malevolent eyes took on an evil glow.

"Tell the bitch I'll see her in Hell," he said.

Manny said nothing.

"Did you hear me, Rodriguez?"

"I heard you."

"Tell her."

Manny stepped away and returned to his position against the far wall.

The hands on the clock above the chair moved steadily toward the appointed time. Manny's eyes fell on the telephone on the wall next to Grayburn. It would not ring tonight. Everyone knew that. Still, they would wait.

11:30. An air of expectancy filled the room. Manny tensed as he watched Haines cross slowly to stand next to Grayburn. The two exchanged words. Haines nodded to the clock on the wall. Grayburn, grimfaced, returned the warden's nod.

Haines walked over and stood facing Hack. Manny was familiar with the routine. State law required that the sentence imposed on the condemned man be read at this time. The warden read from a paper in his hand, ending with the obligatory line: "May God have mercy on your soul."

Warden Haines stepped away from the chair and looked to Harkins who was standing by the switch. He gave an almost imperceptible signal.

The lights flickered, and a hum filled the room. It was over in a matter of seconds. The prison doctor pronounced Hack dead, noted the time on the certificate, and left.

Manny breathed a sigh of relief. Hack's last words to him had made the execution a little easier. As unpleasant as it was to witness, Manny felt nothing for the man he had just watched die. Hack deserved what he got. Manny would save his sympathy for Elizabeth Martin and her son.

While two attendants removed Hack's body from the chair, Manny walked into the witness room. Elizabeth was weeping quietly. Manny wanted to console her. He wanted to say something that would make her feel better. But there were no words. What could he possibly say that would ease her suffering?

Nothing. Nothing at all.

The clock struck twelve. Manny's day was over. It had been a long, stressful day. He walked across the room, pausing briefly by Elizabeth Martin's chair. He felt an overwhelming sympathy for the woman, sharing in her loss; knowing that the scene she had just witnessed brought back painful memories along with the feeling that justice, however inadequate, had been served. But it was a hollow act. Perhaps it provided closure for her. If so, Manny felt the depressing experience had served a purpose.

As he started to walk away, she reached out and touched his arm.

"Excuse me, officer," she said.

Manny turned to face her.

"What did he say to you?"

Manny winced at the question. He shuffled his feet and looked at the floor.

"He wanted me to give a message to one of the other inmates," Manny lied. "Nothing important."

Elizabeth studied Manny's face for several moments, deciding whether or not to accept his story. Then she looked away.

"Can I do anything for you, Ma'am?" he asked.

She shook her head. "No. Thank you. I'm fine." She dabbed at her eyes and smiled wanly.

Manny left the room. He didn't say his usual goodnight to the guard who relieved him. Nor did he stop to visit with his fellow workers. He would never get used to these executions, no matter how deserving of them a man might be. And, he guessed, that was a good thing. Otherwise he was no better than they were.

Manny crossed the gloomy parking lot and got into his car. Ellie would be waiting up for him. She always did on days like today, knowing he needed her there even though he would not talk about it. She accepted his silence, or, if he chose to talk about—whatever—she would listen. He loved her for that.

As he drove through the prison gate, a woman carrying a sign made a fist and shouted, "murderer!". Manny drove slowly by the woman, eyes straight ahead. He wondered if she would shout at Elizabeth Martin as well.

Hack's sullen face danced in Manny's thoughts as he drove the deserted street toward home. He had paid the supreme penalty for his crime. The scales of justice had been balanced. Hadn't they? Manny shook his head and sighed. Some questions didn't have answers. Perhaps the woman at the prison gate was right. There was a fine line between a state sponsored execution and a wanton murder. Was "an eye for an eye" true justice, or was it mean spirited vengeance? Manny had never come down on one side or the other. Both philosophies had their virtues and weaknesses.

Meanwhile life goes on; at least some lives do. And there would be more Hack Jensens and more Elizabeth Martins. That was as certain as sunrise. The human condition. It was a damning reality that he faced every execution day.

Manny had a difficult time getting to sleep.

A kindly old minister with a remarkable talent at giving eulogies is featured in this next story, written by the prolific Warren Bull. Previously published in Killer Eulogy and Other Stories, Untreed Reads

Mr. Bull recently retired from a long career as a clinical psychologist, perhaps explaining the satisfying complexity of his characters. Regarding the verisimilitude of the hospital scene in this story, Mr. Bull comes by it honestly, as a survivor of bone marrow cancer.

Killer Eulogy

by Warren Bull

"We are here to celebrate the life of Kenneth David Nelson. He's no longer with us. He has passed on. There's reason to grieve, but no reason to be afraid. It's not the end of his story. He has gone ahead to where all of us will follow at our appointed times. He has gone from the present to the eternal. However, he remains with us in spirit and in memory. Whenever we think about him, he lives on through us."

The Reverend L. Davis White, with his white hair, baritone voice, and distinguished appearance, could have been cast as a clergyman in a Hollywood movie. He noticed the deceased's granddaughter squeak twice, squirm out of her mother's arms, totter over to her grandmother, and climb up into her lap.

"As little Katie just reminded me, Ken also lives on through his descendants. And Ken remains, as always, with God. As the Apostle Paul tells us in his letter to the Romans, 'For I am convinced that neither death nor life, nor angels nor rulers, nor things present nor things to come, nor powers, nor height, nor depth, nor anything in all creation, will be able to separate us from the love of God in Christ Jesus our Lord.'"

Dr. White's face showed only concern and sympathy, but a few of the more irreverent members of the church who had seen his practiced expression at funerals before referred to it as the minister's "funeral face." They claimed White performed eulogies on autopilot, directing his attention toward an internal debate about the meal to follow the service. Triple fudge brownies, cherry cheesecake, or apple crisp a la mode?

"What was it like when Councilor Nelson attended services here?" asked the minister. "He was a frequent visitor and true friend of this church family long before I arrived, which, by the way, he was never shy about mentioning. Like our letter-writing Apostle, Ken was not overly deferential to those in authority."

White paused in response to chuckles from the pews.

"On Sunday mornings about eleven fifteen he'd start to look at his watch. The closer it got to eleven thirty the more obvious he was about it. At eleven thirty on the dot he would start talking to his neighbor or stand up and walk out. It didn't matter if we were in the middle of a song or prayer. It was eleven thirty and the service was over—for him."

People laughed.

"A public servant is always on call. Ken had more to do than he could possibly get done. Maybe that's why he didn't stay with us past the time he had allotted. He wanted to do as much as he could in the time God allotted him. Ken had the hardest head and softest heart of anyone I know. Another way he reminded me of the Apostle Paul is that he never expressed opinions. He only stated facts. How do I know? He told me, as a matter of fact."

Many in the congregation nodded and smiled. White smiled back at them.

"I see I wasn't the only one he told. I can remember one time…."

White's voice rose and fell. His cadence was like poetry.

Bishop Darby looked over his glasses at Evelyn Ingram, the short, round-faced blond woman sitting on the other side of his desk. He frowned and sipped his coffee before speaking.

"Thank you for coming in, Associate Pastor Ingram. What is your complaint this time?"

"How do you know it's a complaint?" she asked in an unpleasant tone.

"Oh, have you come in to tell me about something you're especially pleased with?"

She shifted in her chair and did not speak.

"I assumed this would be another of your criticisms of the Reverend Davis White. Of course you don't ever confront to him in person. You always bring your grievances to me."

"He's a scary man. You're his boss. You're the one who should do something about him."

"As I recall, you first complained about his treatment of you in seminary. In fact, I've looked at the records since we last spoke."

The bishop picked up a folder from his desk. "From your rating of Dr. White as his student, it seems you enjoyed his teaching and sought out his classes until he recommended that you not be accepted into the ministry due to, in his words, your 'emotional immaturity.' We accepted you anyway, thinking you would mature."

Ingram sat up straight, forcing her shoulders back. "I think I've demonstrated my level of maturity since then," she said.

"I agree," said the bishop. Another set of papers on his desk revealed her story. Three church assignments in four years and none of the churches were willing to extend her contract. Two of the three asked her to leave before the contract expired. One even agreed to pay the last two months of her salary as long as she stayed away from the church during that time. There were already angry rumblings from the congregation at her current assignment.

"Next you objected that he was too 'old fashioned' to appeal to younger members of the church. Never mind that he has an energetic youth minister and has backed that young woman to the hilt. We never had any complaints about him from young members of his church."

She said, "You know how young churchgoers act. Would you really expect them to whine to a bishop about problems in their local church?"

Darby shook his head. "Probably not, Ms. Ingram. Some people complain frequently about everything imaginable. I know one member of that church who repainted the church office on his own because he didn't like the grayish brown beige it had just been painted. He painted it grayish yellow beige. Usually we learn that someone doesn't like something about a church only after he or she leaves one congregation to join another. The people who attend Dr. White's church usually stay there. I once raised the question of appealing to younger members with him and he's been asking me for suggestions about how to do it ever since."

"Which just shows he doesn't have a clue about how to increase the attendance of children and adolescents," Ingram said.

"Not beyond the many and varied strategies he has already tried with some success."

"I'm glad we agree about that at least," she said.

Darby sighed. "Then you griped about his choice of liturgical music, a service with liturgical dance, his use of the lectionary, and his interpretation of doctrine."

"Not in that order," she insisted. "You let him off on each one. But I've got him this time. Even you will have to admit that he does far more than his share of funerals." She looked intently at the bishop and leaned forward. The chair creaked.

"I'm not certain that funeral services could or should be partitioned out among clergy," said Darby cautiously. "Usually the individual or the family chooses the minister they want to conduct the service. If they don't have a church or if they don't know a clergyperson on their own, funeral homes offer the names of clergy from different faith communities. They also have a rotating list of clergy who offer services to the unchurched."

"The list is supposed to rotate," said Ingram. "I think the funeral home staff plays favorites. We both know who their favorite is."

Darby shrugged. "Possibly. Of course if the family attends a church, they may want the service done by the minister at their church—"

"Even then he horns in," interrupted Ingram. "Members of my church often ask for Dr. White rather than me or the senior pastor. Of course he always asks for permission. He invariably suggests that we do a joint service. He wouldn't dare do anything else. Somehow the families always want him to present the oration. Not long ago he did a eulogy for City Councilor Nelson. The councilman wasn't officially a member of any church at all."

"Sadly, these days church membership is sometimes used against politicians," said Darby. "I suppose Davis does do an unusually large number of funeral services. He's really very good at them. I've thought about asking if he would speak at mine when the time comes. Megan, who volunteers in my office, attended the councilman's funeral. She said the Reverend White gave a 'killer eulogy.'"

Darby smiled. Ingram did not.

"I'm not clear, Ms. Ingram, on how this is a problem or how it affects you. We don't take collections at funerals. Even if Davis gets extra referrals from funeral homes, some families don't have much money. I know he does a good number of memorial services for free. He always takes the time to learn something about the deceased that he can use in his service."

"It's customary to pay the minister," said Ingram. "Most people do. Often the clergyperson will get quite a bit. Even when mourners are asked to support a charity, the minister's church still gets donations in memory of the deceased. That makes budgeting less of a headache. Funerals present an opportunity to be heard by people who usually don't go to church, maybe by someone has been thinking about starting to attend a church. If they hear a minister who has something to offer, they may consider his church. It's a good way to get noticed."

Ingram counted on her thick fingers, breathing heavily, "Direct income, donations, new members, recognition, and don't forget about the free positive newspaper coverage. Why should White keep all that for himself? Why shouldn't he share with others?"

"Dr. White to you, Ms. Ingram. If you think that I am going to ask him to go against the wishes of a dying person or that person's family by refusing the comfort of delivering a eulogy, you are either sadly mistaken or actively delusional. If you want to conduct more funerals, I suggest you work to become the kind of clergyperson that church members trust and turn to in moments of crisis and despair. You might start by becoming someone they can trust in good times."

Ingram flinched as if she'd been slapped. "I don't suppose you've noticed that lots of the people who ask him to do their funerals die shortly after they meet with him. What does that tell us?" she asked. Her tone was caustic.

"Maybe that healthy young people rarely think about who will give their eulogies. It seems to me that fragile, elderly, and unhealthy people are the ones who think about their funerals. They're also the ones most likely to die in the near future."

"It tells me Dr. White hurries them along. I believe he kills them."

Darby stared at her. "You can't be serious."

"Look at how many of them die. I agree with you they're frail and decrepit. But too many of the Alzheimer's generation pass away right after they meet with the good doctor. Just after they plan for their overblown tributes—"

Darby's face reddened. The veins in his temple throbbed. "How many exactly? Have you done a statistical analysis and found an anomaly? Give me one reason to believe you beyond your obsessive dislike of the man. Do you have one fact? One iota of evidence?"

Ingram gulped. She shook her head. "No, but still...."

Darby rose from his chair and glowered at the woman sitting on the other side of his desk. "I have listened to you with forbearance for entirely too long. I see why you're too cowardly to approach Dr. White directly. Understand one thing. If so much as a whisper of this vicious and slanderous accusation comes to my ear, I will assume that you spread the poison. I will act accordingly."

"Wh—What will you do?"

"Honestly I don't know," said Darby. "I most strongly suggest that you do absolutely nothing to put me in a position where I have to do anything. We bishops assign clergy to churches. We remove them, too. If I'm forced to act, you could wait a very long time for another church position. I also strongly suggest that you pray for guidance before you speak out against a fellow clergyperson again. You may leave now."

Ingram took a moment to gather herself, stood up, and hurried toward the door. She didn't hear Darby's muttered prayer.

"Thank you, God, for being more forgiving than I am."

———————

L. Davis White stood in the corridor in front of Massachusetts General Hospital's Ellison 14, the bone marrow transplant unit. The doors swung back on each side. He noticed that there was a short hallway, followed by a second closed interior door that led directly to the unit. He entered the short hallway. The doors behind him closed. As instructed by bold red lettering on signs affixed to the walls, he stepped up to a sink and washed his hands thoroughly with antibacterial soap and warm water. He dried his clean hands on a paper towel that he threw into a receptacle. Then he approached the second door, pushed a button on the wall, and waited. Because the outside door was now completely closed, the inner door swung open. White entered the unit.

At the nursing station an attractive young woman with a no-nonsense demeanor quizzed him: "Did you wash your hands thoroughly with soap and warm water when you entered?"

"Yes, I did."

"Have you had the flu in the past two weeks or been around anyone who has the flu during the past week?"

"No."

"Do you have a cold, sniffles, runny nose, or sore throat? An illness of any sort?"

"No."

"An infection of any sort?"

"No."

"Have you been vaccinated for shingles or had shingles during the last six months?"

"I have not."

"Good." She relaxed slightly. "A bone marrow transplant wipes out a person's immune system entirely. When we send people home, we give them a long list of who and what to avoid. But our patients are most vulnerable while they're here right after the transplant."

White asked, "How dangerous is the procedure?"

"We have a five percent fatality rate here. Nationally it's around eight percent. There are lots of serious but less-than-fatal potential side effects."

"May I see Daniel Howard? I'm his minister, Davis White."

The nurse checked his record. "Yes, you're on the visitor list. Daniel is in room 412. You can see him but his transplant was yesterday. He's miserable, napping on and off. If he's asleep, please don't wake him. He probably won't be able to carry on a conversation. Even if he can, he won't remember that you were here. Patients who go through transplants lose their memories for up to a week following the procedures. You just missed his wife. Nancy left about twenty minutes ago to get some dinner."

The nurse pursed her lips and narrowed her eyes. "Reverend White, I might be out of line telling you this, but I wish you could do something about Pastor Ingram. She hangs out here a lot, upsetting Mrs. Howard by her constant chattering. I don't believe she's really concerned about Daniel. I think she's lonely and she's found a captive audience."

"Thank you, Miss. Let me think about it. I might be able to do something to get her to stop. Can I see Daniel now?"

"Of course."

"Thank you. I won't stay long." White pressed a touch plate by the door. A chime sounded and the door swung inward slowly. He entered the room and looked down at the pale, sweating man on the bed. The door swung back automatically at the same leisurely pace before settling with a thud into a rubber gasket around the frame. White noticed that, with the door closed, noise from outside the room virtually ceased.

Daniel's breathing was shallow. He didn't open his eyes. An intravenous line dripped saline into a small catheter in his chest from a half-empty bag hanging from a pole.

"Hello, old friend," said White. Daniel did not stir. "I hear you're miserable. First cancer, then chemo, and now this. You told me it was too much."

White walked closer to the bed. "You said you'd suffered enough. Remember how you worried that Nancy would spend everything on your recovery? Your insurance will run out. You won't be able to work, even part-time, for months. Nancy's already worn out from worrying about you. Taking care of you might put her into the hospital. You said you'd rather die than have all that happen. She's a beautiful, vivacious woman, but she's getting old before her time. You were very definite you didn't want your illness to ruin her life. You told me over and over again. You know I wouldn't do this otherwise."

White carefully pulled a syringe out of his pocket. "In Isaiah Chapter 57 verses 1 and 2 we are told, 'The righteous perish and no one ponders it in his heart; devout men are taken away and no one understands that the righteous are taken away to be spared from evil. Those who walk uprightly enter into peace. They find rest as they lie in death.'"

White paused. "I hope you will find rest and peace, Dan. I also hope God will forgive me for what I'm about to do."

White pointed the syringe upward and squirted a few drops of liquid from the tip of the needle.

"It's amazing what you can pick up in hospitals when they're used to seeing you around. Did you know you can just walk into the hospital lab if you get to know the people who work there? Of course it helps that I used to work here as a chaplain. Chatter at them while they're busy and they stop paying attention to what you're doing. All the biohazards are clearly labeled, including drug-resistant staph. Even the best hospitals have trouble with staph infections."

He pushed the needle into the top of the bag containing saline and pressed the plunger all the way down. Then he pulled the needle out and inspected the bag. "Just a pinprick. I can barely see it and I know just where to look. Nobody will notice. There are places all over the hospital to dispose of used syringes. They really need to beef up their security."

White headed toward the door. "If there is a heaven, old friend, I'm sure you'll go there. Don't look for me, though. I'll never make it."

He stopped at the door. "I'll come back the day after tomorrow if you're still here, Dan." He paused before touching the pad. "You know, I'm sorry you'll never hear your eulogy. It'll be one of my very best."

*You can find hair salons like the Black Orchid Salon in
strip malls across America. What you probably won't find
is a hair stylist with the peculiar skill set as the protagonist
The Cleaner, and perhaps that is for the best.*

*Wenda Morrone's writing has appeared in several
Darkhouse Books anthologies and it is a pleasure to include
her latest story. About writing it, Ms. Morrone says the plot
occurred to her when having her own hair done, in a church
turned salon.*

The Cleaner

By Wenda Morrone

She pulled the windowshades of Black Orchid Salon down to the
floor and walked outside to check for chinks of light. Back inside
to twitch the middle shade down an inch on the left side, then
on to the rest of her routine: floor swept clean of the day's hair
clippings, cape (her own) over a chair, new towel (also her own)
folded over a chair-arm. Pop rock, low, on the sound system to
make the salon seem less empty.

The bells on the front door chimed at ten minutes past eight.
About average. She opened the door to a man little taller than she
was. Twenty-five pounds overweight, maybe thirty, a bored face.
Pouty. Not a car salesman, the guy at a desk in the back who does
the paperwork. Not a bank teller, but not a vice-president, either.
The middle guy who checked on the tellers.

He turned his back for her to take his coat. "You the lone
ranger tonight?"

"Usually the cleaner stays, but she asked if I'd sweep up." She hung up his coat and waved him to the chair. "Sick kid."

"And you are?"

"Didn't they tell you?" She pressed the nameplate on her pink smock that said *Mirabelle*. He peered instead at the breast behind it. Better her boobs than her face.

"So how'd I end up with you, Mirabelle?"

"We draw straws for the late ones," she said.

"And you got lucky?"

"I guess we'll see."

She had jacked the chair up earlier just so she'd have to pump it lower after he sat down. "Always have to adjust for you big guys."

He preened in the mirror.

She folded the towel close against his neck and swirled the cape around him. "Let's see what we're working with, shall we?"

Standing behind the chair, she cupped his face in her hands and tilted it left and right. He got serious, watching her as she studied him in the mirror like a painting and smoothed the arch in his eyebrows with her thumbs. Several seconds into it he cleared his throat nervously.

Her cue. "Okay, I'll try to be fair here," she said. "Whoever you go to, they haven't done a bad job. What I call everyday hair. I just don't think they have the right take on you. Not, you know, executive enough."

He preened again. "What makes you think I'm an executive?"

"Part of my job to notice things like that. You're an executive, you need expensive hair."

He came back fast. "But this cut's free, right?"

"All the purple coupon cuts are free, right."

If he could get down to business, so could she. "Here's the thing about everyday hair. It's always too square." She held her hands out from his head to demonstrate. "Maybe they're trying to hide bald spots. Nobody cares how much hair an exec has, it's all about how expensive it looks. You know, powerful. Executive hair, you emphasize the shape of the head." She turned the chair so he could see the back of his head in the mirror. "See? You got a good shape. Not flat. It'll take a closer clip."

"Go for it, Mirabelle."

"I should warn you, it'll take a while. If there's somebody you should call, maybe outside waiting—"

"I'm on my own."

As if she didn't know.

"Good." She took scissors off the tray and snipped with care.

"How many people show up for this coupon gig?" he asked.

She kept her gaze vague. "You'd have to ask Rosemary about that." Of the eight—now nine—coupons she had slipped into the mail along with Rosemary's? Every one. Her assignments had so far all been greedy. "I think she plans to do it again."

"Then it must be working. Where'd Rosemary get the idea?"

She clicked her scissors. "I think it came from a cleaner, actually. Maybe not this one, the one before. That's the second time you've smiled when I mentioned her."

"You do notice stuff. We have cleaners in my business, too. A little different from yours."

"Is that a fact."

"Most women would ask me what my business was."

Like he was miffed. Go figure.

"That's another thing about executives," she said. "They want to tell you, they tell you. Questions get on their nerves."

Every time she said *executive* he seemed to get a little fatter.

"What does Rosemary do when she needs a cleaner?" he asked.

"Puts a sign in the window in the morning. She always has somebody by night. You're smiling again. I guess you can't do that." Careful to make it not a question.

His smile broadened. "Too bad we can't. Finding a good cleaner is the hardest part of my business. A want ad wouldn't work any better than a sign in a window."

Pity she couldn't ask him what did work. Could she sidestep? "Maybe your cleaners are more like hairdressers. We keep a book. Shows what we can do."

"Yeah, we work something like that."

She added tentatively, "Plus I try to get references from my last place, if we parted friends." She turned the chair so he faced her. "I need to work on your hairline. You might want to close your eyes."

"I can handle it." Like he didn't want to stop watching her. "We don't give references. No need. Once we have a cleaner, he stays."

"Really? I swear, sometimes Rosemary's cleaners leave before I know their names. Maybe it's easy come, easy go. Or maybe you're a better boss than Rosemary."

He got fatter again. "You have to figure out what's in it for them, is all. Make them see why it's better to stay."

She snorted. "That's easy. More money."

His smile seemed stuck on for good. Though it went back and forth from secretive to—now—smug.

"God, is that ever a woman talking. One reason we never use them. Money's just a treadmill you never get off. A man knows to weigh risks." Under the cape his hands seesawed up, down, like two sides of a scale. "Leaving. Staying."

She finger-combed his hair to the left.

"I always wear it to the right," he said.

"I can tell. Always do it the same, it gets flat. You have to change it up every few months. It sounds like you have it better than Rosemary. No worries about staff. She has that plus finding customers."

He laughed outright. If his bosses—the real bosses—knew how careless he was, they'd send a cleaner after *him*.

"Yeah, we can't advertise for our customers," he said. "But word gets around, people start to find you."

She shaped his hairline, then spun the chair back to face the mirror. "So like Rosemary's coupons, in a way—your reputation gets you return business."

He chuckled. Not a good sound. "Not exactly. Most of our customers are one-timers."

"Is that a fact?" She let lack of interest show. "Speaking of return business, if you decide to come back, I'd like to see your sideburns a quarter-inch longer." She put down her scissors and laid her hands against his cheekbones, palms up. "See what I'm saying?"

He met her gaze in the mirror. This time his was puzzled. Like something wasn't what he expected. Like *she* wasn't what he expected.

A warning bell clanged. What if he hadn't come for the haircut? What if he knew who she was, he'd been playing cat and mouse this whole time? Her hands were at the back of his head, he couldn't see whether or not they shook, but he could feel. She held them away a few inches.

He had no reason to come here expecting anything but a hairdresser. Damn it, she *was* a hairdresser. He was getting a hundred-dollar haircut, easy.

"I'll think about the sideburns," he said, gaze still locked with hers in the mirror. Then, abruptly, "You got a boyfriend, Mirabelle?"

For a split second she forgot he meant her. She made it a pause for thought, which she needed. That look at her breast when he arrived—maybe he came expecting a hooker?

She picked her words. "Not to say boyfriend."

"What do you say?"

She shrugged. "Maybe ships that pass in the night."

"I'm interested in a particular ship. Passes at least once a month."

His eyes in the mirror weren't puzzled now, they looked dull and hard as rocks. Which was a mistake, because now she could see where he was headed.

"Oh, that one," she said. "I don't keep track. When he shows, he shows."

"He doesn't live in town?"

"Maybe he has a wife somewhere. I don't ask. We don't actually spend much time talking."

His eyes softened. Not with lust. Bastard was experimenting: first threat, now sympathy. See what worked. Good cop/bad cop under one skin. Only not a cop.

"I wasn't entirely truthful with you earlier, Mirabelle," he said. "When I told you our cleaners always stay."

"Oh?" By now he'd probably like to see her hands shake. She let him.

Yes, he liked it. He went back to preening. "See, sometimes *we* decide it's time to change things with a cleaner. He gets careless. Maybe he's bored, maybe his girlfriend is pushing him to get more money, I don't know. It's his problem."

So open. Clearly he thought he knew who she was. So that much was good.

"You're saying Teddy got careless?"

"Teddy. Is that the name he told you? I'm saying we're worried about him. He's good, don't get me wrong. But he's a little too mysterious. Just sends us word the job is over, plus enough ID for the customer. Never lets us know time or place or method. Like I said, mysterious. The way he is with you."

"I didn't say that." She gave a panicky look around the salon and raised her voice. "Teddy baby, I did not say that."

He was out of the chair faster than she would have believed possible, hands groping under the cape. "He's here? Where?"

"Of course, he's not here. He trusts me." Pause. "I'm not saying he doesn't keep ears here."

"Because he trusts you?"

"It's like with you," she said sullenly. "He's mysterious."

"The thing for you to think about, Mirabelle, is that we found you." Now he sounded like an uncle. She'd never had much luck with uncles. "It's only a matter of time till we find Teddy. I don't recommend him waiting for us to do that. The best thing for him—and you—is for you to talk him into being a little more open with us."

"I don't even know when I'll see him again."

"Don't tell stupid lies, Mirabelle." His eyes went stony again. "You know it'll be soon. His last job was a month ago. He's due a new assignment. This time we want to give it to him face to face."

She nodded, a little too fast. "I'll tell him. As soon as I see him, I'll tell him."

"Good." He made to get up.

"Wait! Wait. I haven't given you your neck trim yet."

"Say what?"

"It's the final touch. You see a celebrity or a big-time athlete, look at the back of their necks. Like a line drawn. Perfect. I don't think whoever does your hair now has ever bothered."

He looked at her as if she were crazy.

No. As though she were desperate to please.

She made sure she had panic in her voice when she said, "If I don't do a good job, why would you come back?"

To find out if she'd talked to Teddy, obviously. But she was a woman, so automatically stupid. And they didn't want to alienate Teddy, just control him.

"Mirabelle, you know I'll be back."

She showed him the electric razor, in case he needed reassurance. He nodded and sat back down. She tipped his head forward. Her hands weren't shaking any more, she shaved a perfect line from the middle to each side. Paused for just a second. She didn't think he ever knew when she slid her Smith and Wesson out of her forearm holster and down her sleeve, put it against the nape of his neck in place of the razor, and pressed the trigger. Twice.

Her first assignment she had expected to hear *bang bang*. Now she knew it was more like *chunk chunk*.

His grunt was almost as loud. He slumped forward.

The man who sold her the Smith and Wesson said it was too small to do much damage unless she actually pressed the muzzle against what she wanted to hit. He laughed so she did, too. But that's why she always shot twice. Let two tiny bullets bounce around inside a head. They rarely exited, so there wasn't much blood—another advantage of a small pistol. What the towel didn't catch, the cape did.

For a few seconds she contemplated leaving him there, as a way of getting word out about how good she was. Because if he was being straight about how hard it was to find cleaners, she could have told him it was at least that hard for a cleaner to find a paymaster.

But after her first job she had vowed, never improvise. Never. Adrenaline kept you from knowing the difference between clever and stupid, even from knowing you were high on it.

She unfolded the bag she always used—designed for Christmas trees—and eased it up over him as she lowered him to the floor. She hadn't realized in the beginning how fit she'd have to be, but she'd learned. Moving him wasn't a problem, her shopping cart was just outside the back door. She tipped him up and in.

Shit. His car keys. See? Adrenaline.

She had to reopen the bag and paw through his pockets. Another reason she preferred women, pocketbooks were easy.

She added his coat to the shopping cart before she huddled into her own shabby coat and hole-y gloves and her wool hat—her prize possession, there were straggly locks of gray hair sewn inside it—and wheeled the cart down the alley. Instant homeless.

Three blocks and a right turn. She stopped at the next dumpster and heaved him up and in. This was a different route from the garbage truck that picked up from Black Orchid. Harder to make a connection. Another block and she dropped the coat. Two more to leave the shopping cart at the Piggly-Wiggly parking lot where she'd taken it a few days ago. She walked back through alleys to Black Orchid, dropping her coat and smock and nameplate in separate dumpsters along the way, and used his panic button to light up his car. A Lincoln, why was she not surprised? She drove it several blocks in the opposite direction of the dumpster, near where she'd parked her own. She left it locked. With luck, cops would tow it, hiding it better than she ever could. She'd drop her gloves in another dumpster, his keys in the next town.

Adrenaline showed again in her ragged driving, but it was late enough not to matter, plus she always picked back roads—she knew from experience she was about to be sick. She barely made it out of town before she had to pull over and make a dash for the side of the road.

It made no sense. She had known what she was meant to do since the afternoon she shaped the nape of a super-chatty client and it occurred to her how easy it would have been to press a gun against that neck instead of a razor and end the yammering forever. The world seemed to slide and catch hold at a different angle. Its brightness dialed up. She never looked back. Only her stomach still refused to sign on.

Tonight wave after wave of nausea rocked her, the worst ever. Because it was a man? No. She had had a couple of male assignments. She didn't like them, but she managed.

No, it was because she'd almost been caught. The phone calls had been too full of questions for weeks. That was how she understood she had to kill him—how else could she handle him? But she hadn't once guessed how close to her he had come. She had planned how to stay hidden with such care, she hadn't realized invisibility would be a threat to a paymaster.

Her nausea finally ebbed. When she tried a few crackers, they stayed down. She climbed back in her car and drove on, hands still shaky on the wheel.

She had to do better next time. Maybe work out an alternate kill method?

No. Her problem wasn't her skills. What she had to do was give her next paymaster somebody to watch. A man.

Teddy.

She'd made up a man and hidden behind him to add another layer of invisibility. Now he had to get real.

Short man? Tall?

Definitely a short fuse, quick to blow up if somebody asked too many questions.

Why did he only communicate through his girlfriend?

She'd have to work on that.

We head across the Atlantic to a quaint town in the English hinterlands, but fans of English Cottage Cozies take warning – exploding cows lurk ahead.

Ross Baxter writes primarily in the realms of science fiction and horror. We hope he continues his visits to our side of the bookshelves.

Beefed Up

by Ross Baxter

Detective Sergeant John Asher lolled on his chair, idly relieving the boredom by cleaning the remains of his stubby fingernails with a steel letter-opener. He had been at his new post for only four weeks, and his nails had never been so clean in his whole life.

"Anything for me?" Asher asked hopefully as a constable dropped mail on some of the desks in the open-plan office.

"Err, no," the constable mumbled. "Sorry."

Asher shook his head in disgust. After fifteen years of working the mean streets of London he had been forcibly seconded to a small market town in rural Rutland. It was meant as a punishment; his aggressive methods of investigation not sitting well with the new chief. His Superintendant told him he had six months to become 'a more rounded officer', and hoped that the slower pace of a rural force would blunt his belligerence and soften him. Four weeks into the secondment, and all Asher's assignments had been either minor misdemeanours or petty theft. No assault, no murder, no serious drugs; the place was driving him mad. Yesterday he had even been asked to investigate a stolen bicycle. It was the worst kind of punishment he could have been given, a living hell for cop like Asher.

He idly inspected his battered knuckles, worried they would soften as he had not hit anyone for over a month. As he absent-mindedly traced the scars and scabs, the telephone on his empty desk started to ring. Even the phones were soft in the country; it was a gentle ringing, musical even, politely asking for his attention. What he really wanted was the opposite; the joy of listening to the shrill non-stop shrieking of the phones in the police stations back in the city.

"Yeah?" Asher answered harshly.

"Is that Detective Sergeant Asher?"

"Yeah," said Asher.

"It's Mickey Taylor here."

Asher remained silent, a trick he often used to unease people.

"We did some work together last year on that big drugs bust you did in the east end," offered Taylor after an uncomfortable pause. "It was sometime back in the summer."

"Work together?" Asher asked dismissively.

"Yeah, well, I supplied you some information that helped you do the bust. You said then that you owed me one."

"If I remember rightly, I helped ensure you didn't end up doing time at Her Majesty's pleasure in Wandsworth. In my book that makes you owe me one," Asher replied gruffly.

"Well, yeah. But I was hoping you could help me and help yourself out at the same time. I've got some info that might lead to another big bust for you."

"I don't work in London anymore. I've been seconded to clean up the badlands of Rutland, so I can't help you," spat Asher, bitterness dripping from every word.

"I know, that's why I'm calling. I had to get out of town after the bust and I live here now. The bust would come under your jurisdiction in Rutland."

"Would the crime require me to exercise extreme prejudice, use excessive force, and include a significant amount of violence and grievous bodily harm?" Asher asked hopefully.

"Yeah."

"How much violence and bodily harm?" Asher growled.

"Possibly lots."

"Then I'm up for it," Asher mused. "Where do you want to meet?"

"Do you know the Queen's Arms near Oakham?"

"No, but I'm a big boy and I'm sure I can find it," said Asher. "What about four o'clock this afternoon?"

"Great," said Taylor with surprise. "I'll meet you in the car park."

"You will," snapped Asher, putting the receiver down.

He cracked his knuckles loudly and drained the remnants of his black coffee, hoping that things might finally be looking up.

Asher screeched to a halt in the car park of the Queen's Arms, sending a shower of gravel over the diminutive Mickey Taylor, who instinctively ducked for cover. Slamming the door hard he strode up to Taylor, who was vainly trying to brush himself down.

"Mr Taylor," Asher warned, "whatever you've got it had better be worth dragging me all the way here!"

"It is worth it, Mr Asher," Taylor said with deference, trying desperately not to be too intimidated by the hulking detective. "It's probably best if I show you, it's just in the field over there."

"In the field?"

"Yeah," said Taylor, leading the way. "What happened to the Jag you used to drive?"

"The rural police just don't have the same sense of style we have in the city," Asher snorted, casting a derisive glance at the small, unmarked Ford Fiesta.

"So, how come you've ended up here?" Taylor asked.

"I'm teaching the yokels here how to be real coppers," Asher spat.

Taylor nodded and trudged up the small country lane. After a few minutes he stopped at a hawthorn hedge.

"This had better be good," chided Asher.

"Take a look for yourself," offered Taylor, pointing over the chest-high hedge.

Asher looked and saw three dead cows. All appeared to have been disembowelled, their dark intestines, offal and blood spread in a gory wide arc around each body. Swarms of flies buzzed hungrily in the afternoon sun whilst a couple of crows sated themselves on the eyes and abundant carrion.

"Dead cows!" Asher demanded. "I'm a detective, not a bloody vet!"

"It's not the cows," Taylor replied, "but they do give a clue as to what it's all about."

"And what exactly is it all about?" pushed Asher.

"When I left London I turned legit," Taylor explained. "I'm now head of security for a small pharmaceutical manufacturing company based just down the road. We produce animal steroids, used mainly by farmers for fattening livestock. Cattle are our speciality, although we are starting to work on high-end steroids for racehorses."

"How interesting," drawled Asher in a sarcasm-laced voice.

"A few weeks ago we discovered that small batches of products were going missing. Not many, but enough to be worried about."

"Are you having a laugh?" Asher cut in angrily. "Surely you're not suggesting this is something for me to investigate?"

"Wait," said Taylor quickly. "The product is worth an absolute fortune to farmers, but it can also be distilled down into a form that can be used by humans. The drug is derived from cocoa beans, and so when it's taken orally it tastes like chocolate. It's impossible to detect in doping tests but massively increases muscle growth and anaerobic performance, which means its worth more than gold."

Asher yawned loudly.

"Anyway," Taylor continued, "my security team did some investigation and found out who was stealing it. It's an employee named Blythe who works in despatch. We were going to pounce but then we realised he must have also stolen samples of a new version the company has been developing."

"So what?" demanded Asher, trying to control his frustration. "At best, this is just a job for the local plod!"

"The trouble is, the company doesn't have the correct licences to produce the new product. If the local police do get involved and the stuff is analysed, the business is likely to be closed down. I'd lose my legit job, and over a hundred people would be put out of work. I was hoping that you could do the bust and make sure the samples disappear, to save the company," explained Taylor.

"Come on, Taylor!" growled Asher. "This is just minor stuff. What's in it for me?"

"It's more serious than you think. The test samples are in massively concentrated quantities. If taken by an animal the steroids react aggressively with the acids in the gut with a lethal and explosive result," Taylor nodded towards the dead cows. "Our man must've sold a batch to this farmer."

"I'll ask again," said Asher menacingly. "What's in it for me?"

"We know he's recently joined a muscle gym. If Blythe sells any of this stuff there then whoever takes it will end up the same way as the cows. Worse in fact, I don't think the stomach and intestines of a human are as robust as those of a cow. You'd be preventing a few very nasty deaths," Taylor offered.

"And?" hissed Asher.

"Because of its cocoa base the drug smells, looks and tastes a little like chocolate. Just think what would happen if a kid found some! Surely taking this off the streets would get you some brownie points?"

"I don't need chocolate brownie points," Asher lied.

"You'll get to check out the gym, might be something there that takes your fancy?" Taylor ventured.

"What else do I get?"

"Well," Taylor continued, "he's a big bloke, a muscle-man who thinks he's hard. He won't come quietly; it might be the sort of arrest you like?"

Asher smiled, cracking his knuckles. "That sounds more like it. Let's go and pay this Blythe a visit then."

"Don't you need a warrant or something?" asked Taylor.

"Don't worry about that," Asher sneered. "But just remember you will owe me."

"Just like old times then," Taylor sighed sadly.

"Exactly," Asher agreed, starting to feel much happier.

***

They waited in the cramped car outside Blythe's empty house for almost two hours before he came back. Asher spent the time reading a newspaper after tasking Taylor to keep watch.

"He's here!" Taylor hissed, sliding down in the seat.

"About bloody time," Asher grumbled, peering down the street to where a large figure swaggered towards them. "You were right about him being big."

"Are you sure you're alright on your own?" Taylor said, his voice devoid of any enthusiasm to help.

"Yeah, but just make sure no one else comes along," Asher instructed. "And remember, he hit me first."

"He only took one phial of the experimental steroids, but they were concentrated enough to treat a dozen herds of cattle. It's a clear bottle with a purple label on, you've got to retrieve it," Taylor reminded him again.

Asher watched silently as Blythe drew closer, walking on the other side of the road. As the bulky figure turned up his driveway Asher shot out of the car, identity badge in his left hand.

"Blythe, I want a word with you!" Asher shouted.

Blythe stared at him dumbly for a moment, confusion written over his broad face. He then spotted the identity card in Asher's hand and that seemed to instantly clear his head. He turned and started to run but Asher was on him in an instant. Asher tried to wrestle him to the ground but Blythe fought back, breaking Asher's grip and flinging him off. Asher ran at him again but this time Blythe knocked him over with a blow from his tree-like arm. The big man then bolted for the door, getting inside the house and locking it before Asher could get back to his feet.

"Shit!" Asher cursed, angry and winded.

Moving to the locked door he aimed a well-placed kick next to the latch. The flimsy frame splinted on the second kick and he rushed in. Hearing a noise from upstairs he bounded up the narrow stairs two at a time, kicking open the nearest door at the top. The untidy bedroom beyond was empty. He ducked back out and stepped up to the next closed door, still breathing hard after his winding.

"Give it up Blythe!" he shouted, rapping his truncheon on the door. "We know about the drugs."

He waited just a second before kicking the bathroom door so hard that it came off its hinges. Blythe stood by the sink, taking large gulps from a bottle of vodka.

"You're nicked!" Asher roared, brandishing the truncheon.

"You've no evidence, copper," Blythe snorted with contempt. "I've just taken all the steroids. Not only do they taste like chocolate but they're invisible to any toxicology report once swallowed. All you've got is an empty glass container, which proves nothing!"

Asher saw the purple label. He then thought back to the dead cows earlier in the afternoon, and how far their guts had travelled from the force of their exploding stomachs. In a flash he turned and ran for cover, pursued by a blood-curdling scream and the sound of rending flesh.

———

The paperwork had been a nightmare, as had his dry-cleaning bill. Exploding criminals were a step too far for the Rutland Constabulary and they had wasted little time in terminating Asher's secondment and presenting him with a one-way rail ticket back to London.

He whistled happily as he collected the few things from his desk. Whether he had become a more rounded officer during his short time in the rural force he was unsure, but at least it had cured his occasional penchant for taking unlicensed bodybuilding pills.

Paul Rosen, the protagonist of our next story, has but one goal, to escape the murderous forces arrayed against him. He's a PI who learned too much about a powerful client and now he's on the run. But who can he trust?.

Steve Shrott has a fondness for this story as it captured well the turmoil that can consume one's life. It was originally published in 2007 in Great Mystery and Suspense Magazine.

Escape

by Steve Shrott

Paul Rosen took a deep breath as he stood in the darkness of the alley. He was safe now, but for how long? The other side of the street seemed a mile away. At least the police hadn't seen him yet. He knew if caught, he'd be thrown in jail on trumped up charges. Or worse.

Paul carefully leaned forward, and peered around the corner. He saw the two officers exchanging words. It appeared as if one of them glared at him. He prayed he was wrong. Maybe the officer was looking at something else. But then he started sprinting toward Paul. Paul's muscles locked: his heart pounded.

There was nowhere for him to run.

A moment later, Paul watched as the shadow of the uniformed officer passed by. He relaxed for a moment and then surveyed the street again. It was dead. No policemen, no one out for a stroll.

Now was the time to make his move. He sauntered out onto the sidewalk. For a moment it felt as if things were back to the way they were before. Before his life had turned ugly. Paul would never have believed that a successful, smart private eye like himself could have gotten mixed up in this mess.

The freedom felt good, but would it last? With each step, Paul's confidence began to return. He stopped at a tavern to get something to eat.

Paul looked up at the sign and sighed. Wally's Bar and Grill. It used to light up the street. Now, most of the bulbs were burnt out or broken. But it didn't matter; the place was still crowded with desperate people who needed a drink and a little hope in their lives.

He sat down at a table in the corner and ordered a club sandwich. When the food arrived, Paul realized how hungry he had been. He tore into it while keeping an eye outside, wondering how long things would be safe here.

"You Paul?"

He heard a woman's voice behind him and every muscle in his body froze. He'd chosen this place because no one knew him. Yet here was someone using his name. Slowly, he turned and saw her—a stunning blonde wearing a smile that could make a man forget all of his troubles.

"This fell out of your pocket." She handed him a stack of business cards.

"Thanks." His exhaustion must have made him sloppy. He'd have to watch that.

"My name's Cherie. Mind if I sit down?" The woman sat without waiting for an answer.

"So you're a private eye eh?"

Paul hesitated a moment. "Yeah."

"You don't look like one. I'd say you were an airline pilot or something like that."

"Sometimes you don't wanna look like what you do."

Cherie nodded. "I do a little palm reading. Want me to tell your fortune?"

"I don't believe in that stuff." But the woman had already picked up his hand.

"This crease here, in the Plain of Mars," she said, pointing to the padded area beside his thumb, "indicates courage. The looped whirl shows your mind is always working, analyzing things. Maybe, right now, you're analyzing me." She giggled. She looked again at his hand, paused a moment, and touched the area under his little finger. "You're in some kind of trouble, aren't you?"

Paul jerked his hand away and stood up. "I should get going."

The women wrote something down on a napkin, folded it, and tucked it into his pocket.

"Don't worry, everything will work out." She kissed him on the cheek, then walked over to another table.

A little shaken, Paul left the bar and headed out to see an old buddy of his, Randal Winters. Along the way he noticed a few cops, but lowered his head and kept walking.

Randal and Paul used to be partners in Arrow Private Investigations, but Randal had left months ago, deciding that he didn't have the stamina to work the nine-to-five grind anymore. He started his own agency and took cases when he needed the dough. He didn't have an office, but Paul knew where to find him—race track, second row from the back.

He looked the same as always, tall, thin, with the scar on his left cheek from a knife fight when he was a teen.

"Hey, Pauley, good to see you." Randal put his arm on his friend's shoulder, whispered in his ear. "I got a nag in the second race, gonna win for sure. Just don't ask too many questions, okay?"

"Not today, Randal. I just need to talk."

"Sure, sure. What's on your mind?"

"I've opened up a can of worms, working a case for Senator Dixon."

"The Senator. Bet that paid top dollar."

"His daughter went missing. He called it a kidnapping, turned out she eloped with her boyfriend. Found them in a Motel 6 in Van Nuys. Brought her back safe and sound, but a few days later, Dixon wanted me to take care of the boy."

"Murder?"

Paul pursed his lips, nodded.

"Why?"

"Boyfriend was upset with Dixon 'cause he made the daughter break up with him. So he started nosing around his financial affairs. Found out he'd been involved in a money-laundering scheme. He was gonna go public. The senator couldn't have that, not in an election year. He offered me fifty grand to whack the kid. But you know me, Randal...couldn't do it."

"A lotta guys woulda."

"Spose so. The next day, cops find the boy's body and now they're after me for murder. Dixon musta planned for me to take the fall."

"Dirty business."

"Normally, I could handle it, but he's got the police chief in his pocket."

"You got a mess of trouble, Pauley. How can I help?"

Paul spread his hands. "Don't think you can, Randal. Just needed to know you're in my corner."

"Always got your back, Pauley. You just gotta call and I'll—"

"I know."

Paul said goodbye to Randal and promised to keep in touch. Outside the track, he hailed a taxi and had the driver take him through the side streets to Figaros, his favorite piano bar. He entered and grabbed a table way in the back. He ordered a beer and relaxed as much as he could, listening to Maurice Hampton's magic fingers fly across the keyboard. In between songs, he heard police sirens echoing distantly in the night.

He reached into his pocket for a tip and found the napkin Cherie had left. He opened it up and saw that she had written down her phone number. Paul thought a moment. He needed a place to stay the next few days, and Randal lived in a tiny one-room walk up. He had to trust someone. He took out his phone. "Cherie? It's Paul, I met you at Wally's. I wondered if you knew a place I could stay for a—"

"Where are you now?"

"Eighty–seven Churchill, the piano bar."

"I'll pick you up."

Moments later he sat beside Cherie in a blue Chevy with a dented fender. They were driving down Balboa.

"I figured you for something sporty," said Paul, tapping the dashboard.

"Me too. Unfortunately, my paychecks didn't"

"I guess you're not gonna get rich reading palms."

Cherie nodded. "Actually, I'm trying to finish a business degree."

"Whatch you gonna do?"

"Don't know. I like to help people." As she turned the corner, she pointed to a brown-bricked house with a large bay window. "That's it over there."

"Cozy."

"I got the house and my ex got his stupid girlfriend. But I'm not bitter." A mischievous smile played on her lips.

Cherie took Paul up the stairs to a dimly-lit room. There was a single bed with a multi-colored quilt on top and a wooden table beside it. Across from the bed was a bookcase that almost reached the ceiling. Cherie pointed to the books filling it. "As you can tell, my ex was a reader."

Paul pulled a book from the shelf and examined the cover. *Laws of Aerodynamics* by Henry Wilson. "Your ex must have been one smart guy."

"Yeah, that he was." Cherie checked her watch. "I gotta turn in. If you need anything, come and knock on my door. I'm just down the hall." She smiled and left.

Paul lay down on the bed with the book. A moment later, he was asleep. Strange dreams drifted in and out of his mind, awakening him, then sending him back into a coma-like slumber. Late morning, he got out of bed, sweat dripping down his face. He washed up and headed downstairs to the kitchen, where Cherie stood in front of the stove, cooking.

"Morning," Cherie said. "Have a good night?"

"Had better."

"I'm sorry, this is all I've got," she said, handing him a plate of pancakes.

As Paul sat down and ate, he studied Cherie's face. She seemed even more radiant than the previous evening. Her ocean-blue eyes sparkled, almost glowed. He'd never seen eyes before like that, yet somehow they seemed familiar.

She joined him at the table. "If you don't want to talk, it's okay. But I just wondered…what kind of trouble are you in?"

Paul explained his situation and waited to see how she'd react.

She didn't say anything for a moment, and then stroked his palm. "Someone with hands like yours couldn't kill anyone."

"My only solution is to get out of town. You know, go to Florida maybe. I have some friends there. Unfortunately, at the moment, I'm tapped out."

"I'll get you money."

"You've already done enough."

Cherie picked up her purse. "I told you, I like to help people. I'll go to the bank, you relax."

Paul sipped a drink while waiting for Cherie. A half hour later, she returned. She plopped down onto the couch beside Paul, and handed him an envelope.

He opened it and spread the bills inside. "I appreciate this. I'll send it back as soon as I'm settled."

She stared at Paul for a moment, moving her face near his.

Suddenly her phone rang.

Cherie's shoulders tightened. She took out her phone, holding it in a death grip.

"Yes…uh huh, right…that would be good," said Cherie.

Paul could hear some kind of commotion outside and drew the curtains apart. Police cars and uniforms were all over the front yard. One cop, a cell phone to his ear began edging toward the door.

Paul looked back at Cherie. He now realized the terrible truth. When she had gone to the bank, she must have contacted the police. But why? And why had she given him the money? There was no time to think about those thingsnow. He dashed for the back door.

"Paul, wait, wait. It's not what you—" But he was gone.

Paul heard police dogs yelping as he raced through the adjoining yards. He knew now that he couldn't trust anyone. Everyone was an enemy.

He was alone.

He poured every ounce of energy he had into running but soon felt himself gasping for air, slowing down. He couldn't hold on much longer. His only solution was to hide.

But where?

He ran out onto the street, chest heaving, and looked around wildly. Finally, he spotted a small variety store on the corner. He pushed his body forward with his last ounce of strength.

He rushed inside the store. The grey-haired owner looked him over. " Cold night eh?"

Out of breath, Paul could only nod. He hunched his shoulders and ducked down an aisle.

He stood by the magazine rack, about to pick up a paperback when he stopped cold. On the cover was his name.

Paul Rosen.

What the…?

He read the title: *The Case of the Crooked Senator*. Puzzled, he picked up the book, opened it to the middle and began reading:

"Not today, Randal. I just need to talk."

"Sure, sure. What's on your mind?"

"I've opened up a can of worms, working a case for Senator Dixon."

"The Senator. Bet that paid top dollar."

"His daughter went missing. He called it a kidnapping, turned out she eloped with her boyfriend. Found them in a Motel 6 in Van Nuys. Brought her back safe and sound. but a few days later, Dixon wanted me to take care of the boy."

Paul's hands shook. He dropped the book. The door of the variety store flew open and he heard a man say, "Police!"

It was all over.

The stocky officer walked up to him. A second thinner man followed, dressed in a suit and tie.

"Is he the one, doctor?"asked the officer.

"Yes, yes, that's him."

The policeman began to handcuff, Paul, but the doctor interrupted. "No cuffs, he's not dangerous."

"What's going on?" Paul asked.

"We need to talk with you down at the hospital."

———

Paul sat on a chair in an all-white room with a bed. The doctor stared at him. "Do you understand?"

Paul shook his head. "You're wrong."

"Let me go over it again. Your real name is Lou. Lou Hanson. In your family there is a history of Affective Schizophrenia. Sometimes, it's there from birth, other times it doesn't appear until some incident precipitates it. You were an airline pilot. There was an accident, people were killed. You blamed yourself, even though the plane malfunctioned. The trauma seemed to cause you to go into a fugue state where you forgot who you were."

"I'm Paul Rosen."

"At the time of the accident, you had been reading this mystery novel." The doctor held up a copy of the paperback Paul had picked up at the variety store. "From that moment on, you started to assume the identity of the lead character. I believe your subconscious was trying to shield you from the pain. I tried many different therapies, but nothing worked. Then two days ago, you went missing.

When we found you, I knew I had to try something different. I put together an experimental procedure where we role played, *The Case of the Crooked Senator*, using your brother as Randal and your wife as Cherie. I hoped you would eventually make the connection between your imaginary world and the real one."

Paul stood up. "I have to go."

At that moment,the door swung open and Lou's wife entered. She hugged and kissed Paul. "The police aren't after you, honey, they've been trying to help." She let loose the tears she'd been holding in for so long. "Please let us help you, Paul. Please."

Later, while he was being admitted to the hospital, he escaped once more.

The next day, Paul Rosen took a deep breath as he stood in the darkness of the alley. He was safe now, but for how long? The other side of the street seemed a mile away. At least the police hadn't seen him yet. He knew if he caught, he'd be thrown in jail on trumped up charges. Or worse…

Our next story shows us the high-roller world of Las Vegas, as seen through the eyes of a seasoned nightclub bouncer.

Timothy O'Leary is nominee this year for a Pushcart Prize and The Nivalis Prize, and in 2015 he won the Aestas Short Story Award, as well as being a finalist for numerous other prizes, including the Mark Twain Award for Humor Writing. His collection of short stories, Dick Cheney Shot Me in the Face, and Other Tales of Men in Pain, will be published in early 2017.

Bouncing

by Timothy O'Leary

I was working the rope at Tao when Assholio broke through the line. I love the place, but Vegas is ground central for dicks, a town constructed on cleavage and free booze, where morons decked out in Ed Hardy pay five hundred bucks to see circus acts performed to old Beatles tunes. You want to see idiots in hyper drive? Spend an evening doing my job, corralling drunks into any of the hot clubs. Everyone's a big shot in Vegas, a plumber from Oxnard suddenly channeling Tony Montana.

At least a dozen times a night some dude tries to impress his girlfriend by laying down a line of bullshit to get past me. "I'm a friend of Donny's," they say, as if I know who the fuck Donny is. Or, "hey, I'm on the high roller list, just talk to my casino host." When that doesn't work they flash a twenty, like I'm going to disrupt the fragile dance club ecosystem for twenty dollars. They don't understand that a genuine master of the universe never has to demean himself that way. A real high roller discretely passes me a rolled-up Benjamin or two in a hand shake like we're old war buddies, then confidently strolls to his table to pound back a fifteen hundred dollar bottle of Cristal.

But the jerk pushing his way through the line was not that guy. He looked to have a little Hajji in him, greasy hair and decked out in something from the Men's Warehouse sale rack. Now I don't want to sound prejudiced against our Arab brothers, even though I wasted two years of my life dodging their IUD's in Iraq. When I say Hajji, that's my code for any swarthy type. Iranians, Greeks, hell, even Italians tend to get on my nerves; pushy and talking fast without saying anything. My guess was that Assholio was from the Valley, the mixed-race descendant of a hardworking, olive-oil eating immigrant who owns a dry cleaner or convenience store, and the ditzy blonde he knocked up. Junior was probably taking a break from his job working for daddy to blow off steam with his goombah brethren.

But you had to admire his moxie. He was right in my face, all five and a half feet of him, crowding my six-foot-four frame, spouting some nonsense about his friends being in the club. "See, they sent me a text. They're waiting for us inside," he says, pointing at his phone, like that makes any difference. His buddies are of the same lineage; zit-faced nerds dressed in Lakers jackets or suits a size too large.

I'm a trained professional, which meant I couldn't tell these boys the sad truth; there was no chance in hell *they* were getting into Tao on a weekend. Hey, I know it's not fair, but we only populate our dance floor with pretty girls size four or smaller, and guys that are either handsome or rich enough to take them home.

If it were up to me I'd be happy to admit a few average Americans into the hallowed halls of Tao, but management is strict about their brand. Unfortunately, these dudes belonged downtown at a low-rent strip club, where hookers flirting with retirement might throw them a little love. "Sorry pal," I say holding up a hand, "back of the line, but my advice, you should find another club, because we're booked-up for at least the next couple hours. Don't want to see you waste your night standing in line."

But this guy, drunk or flying on some kind of party powder, gets on me. "Listen, I told you my group is already in there, spending a shit load of money, and they're waiting for us," he yells with too much attitude. Then he tries to shove past me.

Stupid move. I'm not a guy that gets shoved. Ever. I clock-in at two twenty, and I guarantee you'd need to pinch hard to find even a hint of fat. I've put down coked-up NFL linebackers when they got rambunctious, so this guy was not a problem. I grabbed him by his six dollar tie, his arms windmilling, and escorted him outside the rope. "You're gone," I say, "and don't come back."

And believe it or not, Assholio freaks and takes a swing. I intercept his skinny arm, stretch it around his back, and drop him calf-roper style to the floor, placing a knee dead center on his spine. I'm not pissed, it's part of the job, and since I know at least a dozen people are filming us for their "what happens in Vegas video," I'm as gentle as possible. But he goes nuts, hollering like I was vice-gripping his cahones. Once he's on the deck and under control I tap my ear bud to request security, and within sixty seconds backup arrives, two guys in red blazers to escort him and his friends outside.

"I'm going to fuck you up," he spits at me as they lead him away. "You won't even see it coming. You're dead. You're fucking dead." He's wearing a pit-bull face, and even though he's a plebe, it's a little disturbing.

"Yeah, right," I say. "You guys have a real good night, and I better not see you in here again." And then I forget about it, and I'm back to surveying a giggling group of pretties to decide who gets the golden ticket.

Twenty minutes later I get a text. *Care to help babysit a couple whales tonight after your shift?* It's from Lizzy, the head of hotel security. Lizzy's the reason I'm here, Semper Fi and all that, and the truth is I owe her my life. We did our basic together at Parris and became friends over a few hundred beers. Nothing hinky, though Lizzy's a looker if you're into big Swedes with walnut-cracking thighs, but we've never gone there. We had similar backgrounds that drew us to the Corps, and spent many nights commiserating our miserable childhoods. I shipped off to Iraq, and since the Marines didn't put women in combat—even though Lizzy is one of the scariest motherfuckers I've ever met—we didn't see each other for almost four years.

I was a mess after my tours, close to becoming one of those guys you see mumbling to imaginary friends while living out of a shopping cart. Lizzy had risen the ranks through intelligence in the Corps, and afterwards got a big job running security at The Tivoli. "Come to Vegas," she said, "I'll give you a job, sort out your shit, and you can bang cocktail bunnies." It was supposed to be temporary, but three years later I'm still here. I substituted weight lifting and martial arts for the booze and drugs that had soothed my disturbed personality. I read self-help books and eat a lot of kale. I'm eighteen credits towards a business degree at UNLV. One day a week I go to the VA to help some of my equally screwed-up brothers try to assimilate. I still have nightmares, but they're tolerable, and for the first time I have big plans for my life. But right now I'm happy bouncing the lounges, and occasionally providing security for some of the high rollers that come to the hotel.

In fact, if I'm seducing some beauty, my stated profession is bodyguard, as the ladies find it more alluring than being a bouncer. But the job isn't as exciting as Kevin Costner would have you believe. Mainly I'm clearing a path through crowded clubs and restaurants for rich dudes who get a kick out of having security, sometimes getting them cocktails or bringing girls to the table. But the extra pay is fantastic—it keeps my closet stocked with black Tom Ford suits—and you meet a lot of interesting people.

I buzz Lizzy, and she tells me that she and I will relieve another security detail at midnight. Our client is some dot-com billionaire and his girlfriend. He's been playing cards in the big-boy room, is up almost a million dollars, and now wants to party with the commoners, as long as Lizzy and I can make sure the little people don't get too close. I smell an obscene tip.

At 11:00 p.m. I'm done at Tao, which leaves enough time to rush home and change into a fresh shirt, and strap-on a little .38 that snugs into the low of my back. I've never had to draw a weapon on one of these gigs, but the client wants to know I'm carrying. It completes the fantasy.

Lizzy's waiting for me outside the poker room, looking like a Nordic princess warrior in her sleek silver pantsuit. She reminds me of a Bond girl, especially knowing there's a sexy little chrome Beretta tucked in an ankle holster under those bell-bottom pants. The team we're replacing, Patty and Phil, give us the briefing. We run a male / female detail when we're covering a couple, so our woman client is always covered, even in the bathroom. "So far so good," Phil nods at the couple. Phil's craggy old-school Vegas, with a pit boss's demeanor. He's somewhere around sixty, though he's the kind of guy that probably always looked old; a retired cop goosing his pension. "Easy one. He's been playing cards all day, and starting a few hours ago he really began kicking ass. He's some kind of Einstein, counts cards, that kind of thing. Wish I could bet with him. Sarah, his girlfriend, just watches and sips Cosmopolitans. Sometimes she gets up to pee and walks around the shops. Patty says she dropped five large just on lingerie. He drinks Diet Coke with a lime, and just stares at his cards, probably running mathematical calculations like some kind of human IBM computer."

Lizzy and I hover in the corners for the next twenty minutes, and suddenly our guy, Mr. Demorest, signals he's done. I notice he tips the dealers ten thousand each, and the cocktail waitress a grand, which makes me feel all warm and fuzzy inside. I've had my eye on a Ducati Scrambler to take on midnight rides through the desert when the demons refuse to let me sleep, and Demorest might be my patron.

He says he wants to have a drink and wind-down, then hit a dance club. I suggest the Emperor's Room at the top of the Nero's, and we rush Demorest and Sarah through the casino and into a stretch parked outside a private entry. My man Bobbie G. is covering the door at the club. Bobbie's ex-Ranger with two Afghan tours. I met him at the VA a year ago, made a few calls to get him into the trade, and now we spend some time together at the gym. I reach out, and he has a nice set-up at the back of the room, a table with walls on two sides, making it easy to establish a perimeter. Demorest seems to be coming out of his card-counting fog, perking-up and turning out to be a friendly guy. He orders a Stoli martini, extra-dirty, and we actually have a bit of a conversation, with him asking the same questions clients always ask: "What's it like being a bodyguard? Who's the most famous person you've ever guarded? (I always answer Johnny Depp even though it isn't true.) Are you carrying a gun?" I let him pat the little lump on my back, which produces a wide smile.

Demorest tells me he started several app companies. I know most of the names, and use one of them to buy movie tickets. Lizzy asks if there's any particular threat we should be aware of. Most of the time clients just say, "No, a guy in my position just needs to be careful," which is code for "I think it's cool to have a bodyguard."

But he gets serious and drops his voice. "There could be an issue." He doesn't want Sarah to hear. "We bought a website from some Russians, and the deal didn't go down very well. I had a pretty tense meeting with the owners yesterday, and they weren't happy. Made a few threats. These guys tend to take things personally. That's why I thought it might be a good idea to have you around until they have a chance to cool off."

I have a hard time believing Russian mobsters would come to Nevada to whack an American billionaire, but it did sharpen me up a bit. When you bounce, the scariest dudes to confront are the Russians, Serbs, and Chechens. Especially the ones built like rhinos, with shaved heads and tattoos covering the back of their hands. They have dead eyes, like they've spent an afternoon or two stacking bodies. In Iraq you learn there are two kinds of human beings; the kind that only kill because they absolutely have to, and those that do it because they think it's so damn much fun. I'm always careful around the latter.

So Lizzy and I scan the crowd more carefully, keeping watch for anyone that looks like he might be pals with Putin. Demorest slams another cocktail, and he's in high spirits and ready to do some clubbing. We end up at The Ocean Club, parked in a raised private booth with a great view of the dance floor. I like the fact we're against a wall so Lizzy and I can control access.

Demorest might be a geek, but once he's buzzed the man parties like Kid Rock, switching from vodka to champagne, amped-up and smiling. He even pulls out a fancy little vape pipe, cupping it in his right hand, toking-up all discrete-like. "Just between you and me," he leans in, "I took your casino for $1.2 mill today."

I give him a surprised grin, even though I already knew the number, and we attempt an awkward high-five. "Great job Mr. Demorest. They can afford it, but I gotta to tell you, it's a rare man that takes their money. You really got some game." Demorest eats it up. Something I've noticed, no matter how old, rich, and powerful a man becomes, he still seeks the approval of two people; his dad and the high school quarterback, and everyone assumes I wore the main jersey. I could hear that Ducati-purr grow louder.

Demorest and Sarah get up to dance. I anticipated he'd hit the floor like a spastic monkey, but the man actually had a groove. They're blaring this trance crap that does nothing for me—I'm more a rock and roll guy—but the two of them looked great, probably warming up for the lingerie show Sarah had planned for later. Not that I'd know, but I suspect winning a million dollars is a pretty good aphrodisiac.

A dance floor is a tough place to cover, and Lizzy and I get as close as we can without blowing the fun. All of a sudden I see three Pravda-types take a table to the left of the floor. Demorest spots them too, and his happy-stoned-fucked-up-face gets pasty, like he's about to heave. We escort them back to the table. "They're here," he says in a shaky voice.

Lizzy and I both know who he's referring to. "Who are they?" she asks.

"The Russians. The guys I told you about. They must've followed me from San Francisco. It's too much of a coincidence that we both just happen in Vegas at this club."

"Alright," Lizzy says. "We're out of here. We'll take the service entrance at the back. I'll have the car waiting."

Demorest looks at his drink for a minute, then shakes his head. "No, no... this is bullshit. I did a perfectly legal deal with them. This isn't Moscow, and I'm not going to be intimidated. What are they going to do, beat me up in front of two hundred people? They're just here to scare me. If I leave they win."

Suddenly I really do love this guy, and not just for the monster tip I see on the horizon. You've got to admire a geek that stands up to the Russian mob. "Mr. Demorest, are you sure? I'm not comfortable with the risk," Lizzy says.

"I'm positive." Demorest swigs a glass of Dom. "And I want to dance." And with that we follow them back out to the floor. Lizzy takes a position ten feet to the right of the Russian's table, and I see her reach into her jacket pocket and ball-up her fist. I know she keeps a sweet little ball-bearing sap in there that leaves a big dent when applied to a man's forehead, and I think *God help the Russians if they make a move on our clients*.

The crowd is surging. They've switched from the techno-crap to some kind of Eminem set, and the floor is crowded. I stay within a few feet of Demorest and Sarah, shuffling my feet to blend-in. I know I look silly; one of those big sad lugs dancing by himself. There's a group of seven or eight partiers in the midst of some kind of ecstasy-groove-love-fest that surround me. Two of the girls start rubbing up and down my legs, like cats scratching a pole. The blonde moves behind me, tracing her hands down my shoulders and all the way to my ass. I worry she might encounter the metal lump in my waistband, but her fingers go straight to my glutes. This would be a dream situation if I wasn't working, but I start to slide past them to keep a straight line to the clients.

One of the Russians rises from his table, and Lizzy prepares to intercept him. The truth is, these guys don't concern me. Pudgy and stern—one sporting Breshnev's eyebrows—they don't look particularly tough. If something goes down I'm confident Lizzy will neutralize them, and I'll cover the clients and hustle them out the back. Plus, the head bouncer, a stocky brother named Teddy, is twenty feet away. He and I make eye contact for a second, and

I roll my head towards the Russians so he knows something's up. Teddy's not a man that tolerates bad behavior in his club.

I move a few more steps, but one of the stoned girls pulls at my arm, trying to get me to dance. And then I'm on my knees and falling forward, not clear what's happening. Initially there's no pain, I just lose my ability to move, and I'm on the ground, the girl rushing past me. I reach around the back of my leg, and my hand is coated with oil. *No, not oil*, I realize, *blood*, the kind of black blood that pumps out an artery. I yell, and Demorest and Lizzy turn towards me.

Then I'm in total disbelief when I see Assholio, the little jerk from earlier, move out of a crowd of dancers towards Demorest. He's not wearing his shitty suit, so at first I don't recognize him. He's dressed in a trim black leather jacket, but I recognize the smirk, as he glances at me and mouths "told you," his right arm swinging wide as he jams something into Demorest's neck before disappearing back into the crowd. Lizzy is rushing at me and doesn't see it happen. Demorest is as shocked as I am, reaching to his leaking throat before he collapses.

The girl has sliced my femoral artery, probably with a box cutter or razor, and it dawns on me how truly screwed I am. Lizzy's ripped off her belt to fashion a tourniquet, lynching up my thigh to slow the blood flow, but I know from experience that I've got anywhere from another thirty seconds to a couple minutes to live if the life keeps leaking out of me at this rate. I'd seen it in Iraq; guys with their legs blown off, amazed look on their faces, as they watched their entire blood supply blow out in a pile underneath them.

People are screaming and running as the dance floor floods red. Lizzy doesn't realize what happened to Demorest because her eyes are on me, urging me to relax, purring that everything will be fine in a voice that says it won't. I can see the Russians watching and I wish I had the energy to reach around and pull my gun so I could blow the smug looks off their faces.

But more than anything, I feel foolish. Lizzy and I were amateurs, allowing them to get at Demorest. We should've known better. I'd forgotten the big lesson I learned overseas; that the ten-year-old kid sidling up to you might shoot your balls off or be wearing a suicide vest. Expect the unexpected. Lizzy's shaking me now, and I'm trying to apologize. I know how much flak she'll take for this. But I'm not sure she can hear me.

Sex worker Diana Andrews lands in trouble once again in our next story. What should have been a simple noontime tryst gets complicated.

Albert Tucher is the creator of prostitute Diana Andrews, featured in more than seventy short stories, including one in The Best American Mystery Stories 2010. Untreed Reads published a novella, The Same Mistake Twice, in 2013. This story first appeared in somewhat different form in Thug Lit in 2009.

The Full Hour

by Albert Tucher

"Nice ass, Wolverton."

Diana froze. With Wolverton on top of her, her modesty was preserved for the moment.

But then Wolverton raised himself to a praying position. He tried to pull his pants up, but he had trapped them under his knees. After a couple of yanks he realized his mistake and tried to stand, but his waistband hobbled him. He toppled to his right and landed on the wall-to-wall carpet.

"Why don't you try that again?" said the same female voice. "Nice and slow this time. Focus. Oh, and I don't need to mention that you're fired, do I?"

Diana could see the woman now—forty-something, blonde, attractive. Her power suit spelled "realtor." The desperation lines in her forehead said, "realtor in the middle of a recession."

The woman hadn't come alone. A sixty-ish couple stood behind her in the doorway. They wore mismatched expressions—horror on her face, and glee on his.

The man aimed his gaze at Diana's crotch. She pressed her knees together and turned them to the side. It was time to get up, but she felt too stiff to move. The client had spent a good twenty minutes on top of her, hammering her tailbone into the floor.

Wolverton finally managed to stand and buckle his belt. His mouth worked, as if he hoped to find words that would fix the damage he had done, but he soon gave up the effort. He started toward the doorway, picking up speed as he went. The older couple barely made it out of the way as he bulled his way between them.

"Could I ask you to give me a moment?" said the realtor. "Until I straighten this out?"

The older woman nodded and grabbed her husband by the elbow. She pulled him from the room with enough momentum to suggest that they would keep going until they reached their own living room.

The realtor watched them go. Diana made it to her feet and used the distraction to go to the corner of the room, where Wolverton had thrown her panties in a frenzied moment. She stepped into them. As she pulled her T-shirt down and smoothed her short denim skirt, she turned around and found the realtor confronting her.

"You dressed down for this job. Smart."

"Dressed down?"

"I hope you got paid up front."

Diana wondered why this woman wanted to know. Did she think she was entitled to Wolverton's money? Or did she plan to go to the cops and try to make an issue?

"I just got carried away."

"Maybe I'm missing something, but I can't imagine someone like you getting carried away with Wolverton."

"We both think beds are boring."

"And you thought it would be hot to let him wipe the floor with you? Please."

Diana shrugged.

"Why don't you run along now?" said the realtor.

Her expression mixed anger and amusement. Diana thought she understood, but it was none of her business. She picked up her bag, stepped around the woman, and left without wasting more words.

By the next morning she had almost forgotten her date with Wolverton, but then she opened the Newark *Star-Ledger*.

"Realtor Shot Dead in Lakeview Office."

She started reading. Beverly Angelone, forty-two, had died while working late in her office. Angelone had started her own real estate agency just over a year earlier. The business had not prospered, and she had decided to cut one sales agent. Other employees didn't know what Francis Wolverton, forty-four, had done, but he had made her choice for her. Lakeview police were looking for him as "a person of interest."

Diana decided that it was intriguing to have inside knowledge of a story like this. She picked up the phone and punched in a number that she had memorized over the years. Detective Tillotson's extension went to voice mail. She left him a message and got up from the kitchen table to pour more coffee. Twenty minutes later the phone rang.

"Let me guess," said Tillotson. "You want to do my job for me again."

"Is the Beverly Angelone case yours?"

"I thought that sounded like you."

"You talked to the older couple?"

"Apparently you weren't introduced, but they gave a good description. She did, anyway."

"I know where he was looking."

"Why do you do stuff like that?" said Tillotson.

His voice had taken on a fatherly, scolding tone. She had heard it before, but it was still a little weird, considering.

"For the money."

"Sounds like Wolverton was looking for trouble."

"Some guys do. He always had me meet him at whatever property he was showing. I think the idea was to come as close as possible to getting caught. It got him off."

"How about you?"

"His tips got me off."

"I hope you can get by without his paydays."

"If he killed her. Maybe he didn't."

"Why would you think that?"

"Because she was an ex-hooker."

"Did she tell you that?"

"No, but I'm pretty sure."

"She had no record."

"Neither do I."

"Good point."

"You know any old timers? You know, cops who were plugged into things twenty years ago? I'll bet they would know if she was hooking. You guys always do."

"What makes you think she was?"

"Well, for one thing, she knew right away what I was doing. And she wanted to cut me some slack without making it obvious."

"So how does that affect who killed her?"

"Maybe it doesn't, but don't you always want to know as much as possible about the victim? And hookers can make enemies. I ought to know."

"I'll check it out. There's a retired detective I owe a call anyway."

Tillotson didn't sound enthusiastic, but so far she felt satisfied with the outcome of the call. She had tended their relationship, which helped keep her in business.

But then his tone changed.

"So what's this about Dawn and Gail?"

"What about Gail?" she said.

The words came out before she could stop them.

"Somebody clobbered her and stole her take for the day. Sounds like the same woman who attacked Dawn. The first question is, who is she? And the second question is, why did I hear about this third hand? And none of it from you?"

"Well, I didn't know about Gail. I did talk to Dawn. But I didn't think the bitch would be stupid enough to stay around and do it again. She must think hookers don't talk to anybody."

"Well, she's not completely wrong, is she?"

This was not going well.

"And I was also afraid you might decide that we're too much trouble."

"That could happen," he said, "but not the way you think. It could happen if you're not straight with us."

"Message received."

"Now, tell me about Dawn," he said.

"Some woman got in touch, said she wanted a date."

"Does that happen? Women clients?"

"I guess. Everybody who refers to me knows I don't do women or couples. They wouldn't even mention it if somebody asked. So what happened to Gail?"

"A woman said she was thinking of going into the business, wanted to hire Gail to talk about it."

"Was this at the Regal also?"

"Yeah. If you see or hear anything there, I want to know about it."

He hung up, leaving her to think. She didn't want to have another discussion like this with Tillotson. That meant getting rid of the cause of their conflict—the woman who thought mugging hookers was a path to career growth.

Tillotson wanted her to leave it to him, but if she handled it right, he would never know.

Diana didn't know how to find the woman, so she decided to let the woman find her. It was a matter of looking available. She started calling the people who referred men to her. Early the next afternoon a hotel bartender named Ron called back.

"I had this woman come in asking for you."

"Good."

"You know, this is weird," he said. "All this time you've been telling me, no women. What's different all of a sudden?"

"I can change my mind."

And change it back, she reminded herself.

"Whatever. Anyway, this woman asked for you. At least, that's what it sounded like. She didn't know you by name, but she's seen you someplace. I knew who she meant—blond, tan, cheekbones."

"Major nose?"

"I tell people it has character."

"Liar. Wait a minute. She's seen me? How could that be?"

"She said they're swingers."

It was possible. Diana sometimes went to couples parties with men who paid her to pose as a girlfriend. And some couples tried swinging but couldn't handle the emotional complications. If they still wanted variety, they called in the professionals.

So if this was the mugger, she was smart. She had come up with another plausible scenario for getting close to a hooker. As for how she really knew Diana, she had probably been staking motels out, looking for her next victim.

Ron read off a phone number. Diana took a handful of change and walked a half-mile to her favorite pay phone at the Shell station. The phone had an overhang to keep the sun and the rain away, and it was far enough from the traffic. She dropped coins and punched in the numbers. A woman answered. Diana gave her name and mentioned Ron.

"Did he tell you what we want?"

"Not in detail."

"I want to watch my husband with another woman."

"You only want to watch?"

"That's right."

"My hourly rate is two hundred, but I double it for a third person in the room. It doesn't matter if all you do watch. It's still double."

"That's fine."

"Can I talk to your husband? Make sure we're all on the same page?"

"I'm afraid he's at work."

Sure he is, Diana thought.

"Plus, this is a surprise for his birthday." The woman seemed to sense Diana's hesitation. "Maybe I should mention that we're good tippers. Especially if you can do it tonight."

They made a date for eight o'clock that evening at the Regal Motel.

The woman put on a good act. She didn't sound young enough or tough enough to make a wary hooker nervous.

At seven fifty-six Diana opened the door to the motel's office. The clerk looked up from his motorcycle magazine and told her that her date was in room 163. She went back outside and walked through the shadows to the main building. Guests preferred poor lighting at places like the Regal.

At one minute past eight she stood in front of the door. She had dressed down again, this time in jeans instead of the little denim skirt. She cupped a can of pepper spray in her right hand, and raised her other hand to knock.

Something cold and metallic touched the skin behind her left ear. Diana stifled an urge to flinch. Sudden moves were a bad idea when a gun was involved.

"Drop what's in your hand," said the voice that Diana had heard earlier on the phone.

The spray can made a soft clang on the blacktop—not enough noise to attract attention. People tended to mind their own business at the Regal, anyway.

"Go inside," said the woman. "It's open."

Diana turned the handle and pushed the door inward. She thought about slamming the door behind her, but then she would be trapped inside. Neither the door nor the wall of the building would stop a bullet.

"Have a seat."

Diana went to the bed on the right. As she turned to sit on the corner of the mattress, she got her first look at the other woman.

I know her, Diana thought.

She thought back to her date with Wolverton and the embarrassed look on the woman's face, as her husband stared into Diana's crotch.

Diana looked at the door.

"You'll never make it. Just sit."

Diana saw no alternative to obeying.

"I'm guessing you don't really go to swing parties."

"My husband always wanted to. He thought there would be lots of women like you. You're very pretty. He really should have looked at the rest of you. Not just—you know."

"I guess that's a compliment."

The woman sat on the other bed.

"I'm Grace."

Diana started to say, "Nice to meet you, Grace." Instead she told herself to get in the game. She had come prepared for a fight, but this situation felt like something else. She just didn't know what.

"Do we really need that?"

She nodded at the gun.

"That's to make sure you listen," said Grace, "while I tell you a story."

"Okay."

The woman said nothing for a while. She seemed to fear what would happen when she finished.

"About twenty years ago my husband and I went through a bad patch. I'm guessing you don't know much about marriage, but it happens. Probably more than it doesn't."

"That's what clients tell me."

Something about "building a rapport" flitted through Diana's mind. But was that good or bad? The term "Stockholm Syndrome" also came and went before she could grasp it.

"Maybe you know more than I thought. What do you think my husband did?"

"He probably went looking for someone like me."

Grace nodded her approval. The gun didn't waver.

"I knew exactly what he was doing. I'm the one who handles the money. It kept going missing, a few hundred at a time. I couldn't do much besides wait, so that's what I did. And after a while we worked things out, and the money stopped disappearing. We had put the whole situation behind us, or so I thought."

Grace paused for so long that Diana took another furtive look at the door.

"That was then. Just recently we started talking about downsizing to a condo. I thought it would be a good idea, eventually. But then my husband said he had found the perfect place. He insisted that we had to move immediately before someone beat us to it. I was willing to go along if I liked the new place. But we went to see it, and even without the entertainment…"

She gave Diana a smile that seemed very pleasant, considering.

" …I don't think I would have seen anything special about it. No one else was going to snap it up. I didn't have to do anything, though. A police detective came and told us that the deal was off. It seems that the realtor was dead. Murdered. I still didn't make the connection. I can't believe I was so blind.

"But the detective came back, and this time he wanted to talk to my husband alone. He thought he was being subtle, but he wasn't. He must not be very good at his job."

"Believe it or not, he is."

Grace ignored the comment. Diana wondered why she cared about defending Tillotson. She had other things to worry about.

"I said something about making coffee, and I listened behind the door. He asked my husband if he knew the woman who was killed. My husband asked why, and the detective said she was an ex-prostitute. And just like that, it all came together."

"The paper said she was having business problems," said Diana. "She was probably desperate enough to look up old clients. Maybe some of them were still feeling sentimental about her."

"And take a wild guess who was," said Grace.

"Sooner or later, Tillotson will figure it out."

"Figure what out?"

"That you killed her."

"Killed her?" The woman stared. "I didn't kill her. What on earth made you think I did?"

"Well, there's that." Diana nodded at the gun. "Somebody shot her."

"Well, I certainly didn't. It must have been that man they're looking for. The one whose bottom she thought was cute, for reasons that escape me."

"That was irony."

"So was my comment. No, I didn't shoot her."

Grace looked at Diana. Diana looked at the gun.

"I shot my husband."

"Oh."

Come on, Diana told herself. You can do better than that.

"They don't seem to have found him yet, but they will. I must be just about out of time."

"Maybe you have something better to spend it on than shooting me."

"Why would I want to shoot you?"

"Well, in that case," Diana said.

She stood to go. Grace gestured with the gun.

"I don't want to shoot you. But I will if you try to leave."

Diana sat.

"I'm serious," said Grace. "What could I have against you?"

"I'm the one who sent the detective back to you the second time."

"That hardly deserves killing. My goodness, this is your day for missing the point, isn't it?"

"I guess so. I'm not getting this. You don't want to shoot me. I like that part. But you don't want to let me go, either."

Even as Diana said the words, she began to understand. There weren't many possibilities left.

"No, you can't go," said Grace, "Not yet. I can't show that woman what she did to us, because she's dead. So that leaves you. I think you deserve to see…"

She looked around, as if this threadbare room held something that she had only seconds to find.

" …this—"

Grace put the gun barrel into her mouth. Diana closed her eyes and folded her arms over her chest. For a moment she felt like the smartest, toughest person on the planet. She had faced a gun, and now she was going to live. How many people could say that?

But the sound of the gunshot made her jerk, and contempt for her own cowardice scalded her.

Diana opened her eyes and found that she was still hugging herself. Grace lay on her back on the other bed. The bedspread and the wall behind her looked as if someone had spent hours painting them red and gray, but the intricate pattern had happened in an instant. Diana sat, unable to look away. She decided that fresh blood smelled like death, and that death made her want to vomit.

It only made sense.

Get up, she thought. Get out.

But she stayed. How could she give herself permission to go? The light switch was two steps away. She could at least darken the room and blot out the sight of the other bed.

But she didn't move.

Her hooker habits won in the end. She glanced at her watch, and saw that the time was eight fifty-nine. She had given Grace the full hour.

Hookers go, she thought. That's what we do.

Diana slid forward on the bedspread. Her legs seemed to work. She stood and walked toward the door. She must have opened it, because it was closing behind her.

As she started across the parking lot, her foot brushed something that rolled a couple of feet. She crouched to pick up her can of pepper spray.

She saw motion. Two feet in dark sneakers came at her fast. Only the white edges around the soles attracted her eye. The feet made no sound. If she hadn't glanced in the right direction, she would have missed everything.

She grasped the can but stayed low, as if she couldn't quite locate what she was looking for on the ground. In an instant the attacker came into range. Diana lunged sideways. With her left shoulder she hit the attacker just above the knees. The attacker's raised right arm was already on its way down. The blow went over

Diana, and something in the attacker's hand hit the ground with a metallic sound.

Diana thrust upward with her legs. With her left hand she grabbed whatever she could and flipped the attacker over her shoulder. All the squats and military presses she had done in the gym were paying off now.

The attacker landed hard. Diana's hand held the memory of a crotch like her own. The other woman lay flat on her back. She seemed too stunned to keep fighting, but Diana decided to make sure. She reached down and gave the attacker's face a short squirt of pepper spray.

The woman gasped.

For several moments Diana did nothing but breathe. Then she felt around with her foot, until she found the metal cylinder that the other woman had swung. It was a tire iron, or something else that was heavy enough to fracture a skull. Diana kicked it away.

She grabbed the woman's arm and started to drag her closer to the office, where there was light from the windows. The woman stayed limp.

"Walk or don't," said Diana. "I don't care if I scrape you all over the lot."

The woman found her feet and stumbled along with her.

"What's your name?" said Diana.

In the better light she could see a young bleached blonde in a dark sweatsuit.

"Fuck you," said the young woman.

"Okay, Fuck You, here's the deal. You're out of this town. As of right now."

"Or what? You'll call the cops? Whores don't call the cops."

"We do if it's good enough," said Diana. "And this is really good. Let me show you."

She twisted the young woman's right arm behind her back and marched her back to room 163. She opened the door and pushed the woman into the room.

"Can you see yet?"

Grace hadn't moved.

"Shit!"

The young blonde could see well enough through her watery eyes. She tried to back out of the room, but Diana blocked her.

"You either get lost right now," said Diana, "or I'll say you killed her. You'd better believe I can make it stick. Somebody besides me must have seen you hanging around. The cops will think you were waiting for her."

It was all bluff. Tillotson would know at a glance that Grace had shot herself, but Diana didn't plan on mentioning that.

The young woman flailed with her free arm. Diana thought she had made her point. She let go of the woman's wrist and stepped back. The other woman started running and disappeared around the corner of the building. Diana heard a poorly maintained engine roar in the rear parking lot. Tires shrieked, and a car careened onto the highway.

Diana didn't move. She had to call Tillotson, but it could wait a moment. She made herself look into the room.

"I'm sorry, Grace. For everything."

About as chilling a tale as ever we've read. Sylvia's boyfriend, Reginald, has screwed up again and desperately needs her to give him an alibi. But Sylvia has gotten very tired of Reginald and his problems.

KM Rockwood has worked as a laborer in a steel fabrication plant, operated a glass melter and related equipment in a fiberglass manufacturing facility, and supervised an inmate work crew in a large medium security state prison. Those jobs, as well as work as a special education teacher in county detention facilities, provide most of the background for novels and short stories.

Last Laugh

by KM Rockwood

The phone rang. The landline.

Sylvia looked at it, but she made no attempt to answer it. She took a sip of the black coffee from her mug and stared at the caller ID. The number glowed in the dim light.

Reginald. Who else would call at almost midnight on a Thursday?

Cheating bastard. Did he think she was a total fool?

The phone switched over to the answering machine. "Sylvia? Pick up! I know you're there. Why won't you answer?"

She tapped a cigarette out of the pack, lifted it to her lips, and pulled the ashtray closer to her. She flicked her lighter. But she didn't pick up the phone.

"You can't hide. I will find you." The line went dead.

KM Rockwood

Sylvia leaned back in her chair and took a long drag on the cigarette.

Across the room, in the depths of her purse, her cell phone began to chime. She ignored it.

Reginald couldn't know she was home. She could be anywhere.

Hers was a third floor apartment. The only windows visible from the street would be those in the living room, where she sat, and the small one over the sink in the kitchen.

The shades were up, but she hadn't turned on any lamps in the living room. Enough light came through the windows and from the bedroom that she could see reasonably. The overhead light in the kitchen was on, though. If Reginald came by and saw that, he might think she was there.

She got up and drained the mug, then refilled it with the remnants in the coffee pot. This looked like it was going to be a long night. Should she brew another pot?

No. She was jittery enough as it was. No need for more caffeine.

She should eat something. She opened the refrigerator. Not a whole lot of choices. She reached in and got out a thick wedge of cheese. A furry mold was growing on one end, but the rest of it would be all right. A block of six sharp steak knives sat on the counter. She pulled one out, cutting off the moldy part, and put the cheese and the knife on a cheese board. Rummaging in a cabinet filled with nearly empty boxes and unopened rolls of paper towels, she uncovered some crackers. They might be stale, but they'd be edible.

Sylvia switched off the kitchen light and carried her supper, such as it was, into the living room.

She grabbed a magazine and sat down again and flipped through the pages. In the dim light, she could see the pictures clearly enough. She could even make out the words, if she wanted to.

She didn't want to.

The cigarette burned down to the filter. She lit another one from it and inhaled the smoke deep into her lungs.

The doorbell buzzed. Well, Reginald couldn't get through the street door if she didn't push the button that opened it.

Unless someone else in the building let him through. Some people weren't careful with building security, like Sylvia was. And Reginald was a frequent visitor. His face would be familiar to some other residents of the building.

She put down the magazine and strained her ears. Sure enough, a few minutes later, footsteps thudded up the stairs and down the hallway outside her apartment, followed by a pounding on the door. Maybe if she didn't respond, he'd think she wasn't there and go away.

No such luck. "You've got to be in there, Sylvia. I was standing across the street when you switched off the kitchen light. What's up? Do you have another man in there with you?"

Sylvia clutched her coffee mug in one hand and pulled on the cigarette. What were the chances that he'd make enough noise to disturb the neighbors? And did she really care?

Bang! Bang! Bang! "I know you're in there. Do I have to wake up the whole building before you open the door?"

With a sigh, she went over and unlatched the door, standing in it so he would have to push his way past her if he wanted to come in.

He did, shoving her aside.

She closed the door after him and sat down again and switched on a lamp. She reached for the knife, cut a slice of cheese, and put it on a stale cracker. "Want some?"

Reginald stood over her, his hands on his hips. His usually pale face was flushed and his dark eyes were sharp and narrowed. "No."

"Okay." Sylvia put the whole thing in her mouth and chewed.

Neither one of them said anything else for what seemed like an eternity.

She cut another slice of cheese. "You're not gonna be any happier than I am if someone calls the police because of your noise."

He snorted. "Just make their job easier. They're probably looking for me anyhow."

"Oh? Why is that?"

"You've done it this time," Reginald said. "Olivia's disappeared. And the cops think I might have had something to do with it."

"Olivia?"

"Yes. Olivia. Don't pretend you don't know who I'm talking about. You called her and threatened her if she didn't stop seeing me." Reginald slipped off his jacket and dropped it on a chair.

"Oh, you mean Olivia, the little trust fund sweetie you've taken up with? All of twenty-two, isn't she? The one I wasn't supposed to find out about?"

"I didn't want to hurt you."

She didn't look at him, but Sylvia knew he'd put on his hangdog face. She'd had enough of that.

"I knew you'd be upset," he said. "So I didn't tell you. But she means nothing to me."

"Now there's a cliché if ever I heard one." Sylvia tapped the growing ash off the end of her cigarette.

"But it's *true*." He dropped his hands to his sides. "She has money to spend. And she's willing to spend it on me. So I let her. And I was pretty close to getting her to invest in my latest project."

Sylvia laughed. "You mean you told her you loved her. You had all kinds of plans for a business enterprise, if only you had the financial backing. She could come up with it, but you didn't deserve her."

"Something like that."

"And so she gave you some money, found an apartment for the both of you, and waited for you to move in."

"No." Reginald turned to look out the window at the darkened street below.

"Really?"

"She did get an apartment—she'd just moved to town and was staying in one of those extended stay hotels—but it was for *her*, not *us*."

Sylvia took a swig of her coffee. It was the bitter dregs. "Yeah, right. And she paid off a few people who were looking to collect on what you owed them. All very above board. And then, of course, you had this wonderful opportunity for her to invest her money…"

"She did lend me the money to pay off a few things. I admit I haven't been very smart about who I owed money to." Reginald stepped across the living room and picked up an almost full bottle of whiskey. "Look, I could use a drink. You want one?"

"No. I need a clear head. I have a lot of thinking to do." Sylvia thought about making a big deal about him helping himself to her whiskey, but decided it was too minor an issue to argue over. Besides, he'd given it to her.

"Ah, baby." Reginald grabbed a tumbler and filled it with the whiskey. He took a huge gulp before he continued. "What've you got to think about? I messed up. Again. I'm sorry. I'll make it up to you."

"How do you propose to do that?"

"You know. Follow through on our plans. Get married. Move to a new town. Start over." He cradled the half-empty glass in his hands.

Sylvia snorted. "Fat chance. I might move to a new town and start over. But it won't be with you."

"How could you say that? After all we've been through together?"

"That's why I can say it. I know you. What *did* happen to Olivia?"

"I don't know. She's just gone." Reginald took a smaller sip of the whiskey and frowned. "The police asked me about her, but they didn't have much, so they had to let me go. But they'll be back."

"With more evidence?"

Reginald shrugged. "Maybe."

"Could be she wised up." Sylvia took a final drag on the cigarette in her hand. "She could have decided to dump you and leave town. Like I'm going to do. Only maybe she figured it out quicker than I did."

"To tell the truth, I hope she did." Reginald stared at the liquid in the glass. "Solve a lot of problems if she turned up. But look, if they ask, I need you to tell the cops I've been staying here. Especially last night."

Sylvia raised her eyebrows. "And why would I do that?"

"So they don't think I kidnapped her or something."

"Why would they think that?"

"Because she's gone. Someone heard a scream from her apartment, but didn't see anything when he looked out in the hallway. "He called the cops and they found some blood on the carpet outside her door."

"Her blood?"

"They don't know yet. Or, at least, they're not telling me."

"You say she's a trust fund baby. All they have to do is contact the trust and find out where they're sending the money next month."

"I guess." Reginald shifted uncomfortably from one foot to the other.

Sylvia glanced at him, then laughed. "You've managed to get it sent to an account with your name on it, haven't you?"

"She's not a very good money manager. I was just going to help her. It seemed like a good idea at the time."

"And now that she's disappeared, it doesn't seem like it was so smart, right?"

He took a small sip from the glass and frowned. "This tastes funny."

"Always does, until it's been paid for. You brought me that bottle just last week. Remember? Charged on the girlfriend's credit card, I bet."

He lifted the glass and sniffed it. "You didn't put anything in it, did you?" he said, his voice rising.

"Don't be silly. Why would I do that?"

"You bitch! You're trying to poison me!" he shouted.

"Lower your voice. Would I do that in my own apartment?" She smiled as she firmly snuffed out the cigarette. "If I were going to kill you—and don't for a minute think the idea hasn't crossed my mind—it would be far away from anything that could be traced back to me."

He sniffed the glass.

"You're just not used to the good stuff," Sylvia said. "You drink so much rotgut that when you get a glass of decent whiskey, it tastes funny to you."

A banging came from the wall beyond the bedroom and bathroom.

Sylvia got up and closed the door. "See? You're disturbing the neighbors. They'll be calling the police after all."

Reginald swallowed hard. "Look," he said, sliding over toward the bedroom door. "I got to take a whiz."

"And see if I've got any pills in the medicine cabinet you can swipe? Oxies or something?" Sylvia planted herself firmly in front of the door. "I don't think so. Go take a whiz outside in the alley."

"But…" He reached past her, turned the knob, pushed the door open, and looked at the suitcase that lay open on the bed. "You're packing!"

"Of course I'm packing. Didn't I just tell you I'm leaving? Go someplace and start over."

"Yes, let's do that." Reginald took another sip of the whiskey and grimaced.

"Not us. Me."

"Aw, baby after all we've been through…"

"You'd better just go." Sylvia stood unmoving in front of the door.

He drew himself up and glared at her. "I know you. You'll come crawling back when I call. If I call."

"Dream on."

"What are you going to tell the police if they come around?" Reginald asked.

"Oh, I'll tell them you've been staying here, all right, if it means that much to you," Sylvia said, a smirk curling her lips. "But you know, Olivia's just going to turn up somewhere."

"Talk about clichés." He stepped across the room and put the glass down. "If I get in trouble over this, I'm not going down alone. I'll take you with me."

"And how do you propose to do that?"

"Olivia said you called her when you found out I'd been seeing her. And threatened her. She recorded it."

"I doubt that." Sylvia pulled the bedroom door shut behind her. "She's not smart enough. She was pretty snotty when I tried to reason with her. Laughed at me. Said you loved her. And she wasn't going to back off."

"I told you. I was just using her. You're the only one for me. I did it for us, baby. Get some money for us."

Sylvia laughed. "You think I'm gonna fall for that one more time?"

Reginald's nostrils flared. He reached behind him, grabbed the knife from the cheese board, and took a step toward her.

"Go ahead. Stab me. I'll get a good scream in first. The neighbors are already listening. They'll call the police. Try to get out of this one."

The knuckles clutching the knife turned white, but he stopped moving toward her.

"She'll turn up," Sylvia said again. "People like her can't stay hidden for long. And you can go turn the charm on her. Unless…" she threw back her head and gave another laugh. "Unless you've really killed her. Did you?"

An alarmed grimace flashed over Reginald's handsome features. "Of course not."

He turned abruptly, threw the knife on the floor, yanked open the door to the hallway and dashed out.

Sylvia went over to the window. After a few seconds, Reginald exited the building and hurried down the street toward the subway entrance.

He'd forgotten his jacket. It could just stay there when she left.

She waited a little while to make sure he wasn't coming back. Then she looked at the knife on the floor. It might have his fingerprints on it. She could pick it up by the tip, move it wherever she needed it.

In the kitchen, she pulled on a pair of thin rubber gloves and took another sharp knife from the set in the block. She carried it through the living room and bedroom, into the bathroom. She pulled back the shower curtain.

Olivia lay in the tub, trundled up in duct tape. Only her frightened eyes and her nose were visible above the layers of tape on her face.

The drugs must have finally worn off. Not surprising. She'd been lying there since early this morning.

Sylvia stood for a minute and looked at her. Tears cascaded down the girl's face, streaking her makeup. Snot bubbled out of her nostrils. Her designer jeans were wet around the crotch, and the room smelled faintly of urine.

Not exactly the pristinely beautiful trust fund heiress. If Reginald had seen her like this, he wouldn't have bothered to pursue her.

Sylvia hefted the knife. "I had to wait until you woke up."

She sat on the edge of the tub, twirling the knife in her fingers.

"You see, I want to be a lesson for you. A final lesson. If you do mess with another woman's man, don't be such a condescending bitch if she calls you about it."

Olivia's eyes opened wider and mewing sounds came from behind the duct tape.

"Now," Sylvia said. "Where shall we start?"

Lisa DeVoe appears to live a charmed life, complete with charming daughter and charming, successful husband, along with the requisite charming home in the suburbs. But one small misstep starts Lisa down a path, one that soon spirals out of control.

Margaret Lucke is a writer and editorial consultant in the San Francisco Bay Area. She has had over sixty stories published and a number of novels, including the forthcoming Snow Angel.

Femme Fatale

by Margaret Lucke

Tropical Sunset. Hot orange kissed with pink. Lisa could almost see the silhouettes of palm trees. She drew a thin line of color on the back of her hand.

Or how about Vintage Wine? Burgundy, ripe and luscious. She added a purplish stripe next to the orange.

Then her eye landed on Femme Fatale. She removed the cover, twisted the wand. Brilliant red. She drew a third line next to the others and giggled. This one, definitely. She'd never thought of herself as a femme fatale, but why not? Maybe it was time to shed her stodgy suburban-mom image.

Lisa capped the lipsticks and replaced two of them in the rack. Her fingers curled around Femme Fatale, hiding it in her palm. As she turned away from the cosmetics display, she slid her hand casually into the pocket on her cardigan. Femme Fatale snuggled into place alongside the bar of lilac soap, the little hand mirror, the irresistible earrings with the rhinestone cats.

"Mom!" The voice came from behind her.

Catching her breath, Lisa spun around. Katie was coming down the aisle, pushing a cart heaped with clothes.

"Hi, sweetheart," Lisa said, too brightly. "Find anything you like?"

"A whole bunch of stuff." Katie reached into the cart. "Look, isn't this cool?"

She held up a yellow top by its thin straps. If she were wearing it, it would reveal her shoulders, her midriff and Lord knew what else.

"I don't think so, honey. We're buying school clothes, remember?"

"I can wear this to school."

"That top is hardly suitable—"

"Mom, I'm in middle school now," Katie explained with exaggerated patience. "It's different there. People don't dress like fifth-grade babies."

"No, but they should dress like respectable young adults." Though Lisa found it hard to think of Katie, just turned twelve, as an adult.

"You said I could pick out my clothes myself. You didn't even want to come with me to the clothing department."

"I said you could choose things as long as they were reasonable."

"None of this stuff is expensive, Mom. Heck, nothing in this whole store is expensive. That's why they call it a discount store."

"Don't get mouthy with me, young lady. Reasonable means style as well as cost. Let's see what else you've got."

For the next ten minutes Katie wheedled, pleaded and sulked, while Lisa lectured and stood firm. They put back half of Katie's haul, but managed to agree on a skirt and three tops, none as skimpy as the yellow number.

Lisa paid for their purchases, and Katie wheeled the cart away from the checkout. The exit doors swung open, and they emerged safely into cold, bright November sunshine.

Yes! Lisa slipped her hand into her pocket, fingering the soap, the mirror, the earrings, the lipstick. Femme Fatale.

Always buy something before you leave the store, she thought. You look less suspicious.

Her treasures felt warm to her touch, as if they were glowing.

The black-and-gray cardboard box was hidden deep in the bedroom closet. Her treasure chest.

Lisa eased it from its place and carried it to the bed, glancing to make sure the door was closed. No one else was home; Warren wasn't due back from the office for another hour, and Katie had rushed off to study at her friend Janelle's house the minute they got home.

Still, better safe than sorry.

She lifted the lid and let her eyes feast on the delightful items jumbled within. Like the purple silk scarf that she would never dare to wear, but which felt so good when she rubbed it against her cheek. And the cut-glass bottle filled with a spicy-sweet perfume. And the Patty Grimes CD, its cover photo showing the country singer's flirtatious smile.

Simple pleasures. And, Lord knew, she enjoyed few enough pleasures these days. Surely she was entitled to one little treasure chest.

Every item she added to it filled a tiny part of the emptiness inside her, at least for a while. When something lost its magic, she tossed it out, so the treasure was constantly renewed.

She had started soon after Katie was born, taking baby things. Warren had insisted that she not return to work, and though Lisa claimed she didn't mind—real estate wasn't all that exciting anyway—it meant no extra cash for the little extravagances she wanted for her child. Every time she took something she swore she'd never do it again, but the more she got away with it, the deeper she got hooked. The objects themselves were a fringe benefit—what she really was taking was the high she felt, the sense of power, the fleeting moments when she felt truly alive.

Once, several years ago, she'd been caught sneaking out of a department store with a faux-pearl bracelet. She called Warren, who rushed to the store and talked the security chief out of pressing charges. When they got home, he hit her so hard that the bruise on her jaw showed for a week. She promised him she'd never take anything again, but the thrill proved too alluring to resist.

As Lisa tucked away her new prizes she was startled by a sound, a little click. She looked up quickly, holding her breath.

The door was still closed. She was just jumpy, a symptom of the delicious twinge of guilt she felt every time she took out her wonderful box.

She returned the box to its hiding place, then noticed she'd left the lipstick on the bed. It was a sign, she thought with a smile. Maybe it was time to set aside shame and fully enjoy her treasures.

———————

Lisa leaned toward her dressing-table mirror as if her reflection were a lover, and pursed her scarlet lips.

"Kiss me," she commanded. "I am the femme fatale, beautiful and sexy."

Her voice cracked on the last word. That would never do. Try again.

"Kiss me. I am irresistible and dangerous."

Ooh, much better. And she almost looked the part tonight. The new black dress set off her pale skin, and the sparkly pendant on its gold chain—her fifteenth anniversary gift from Warren—looked elegant in the deep V-neck. She tugged at the point of the V, hoping to create a little cleavage.

Femme fatale. She closed her eyes and entered a lavish ballroom where candles flickered and violins sang. She imagined herself accepting a glass of champagne from the Regency cavalier—no, the international master spy—no, the Oscar-winning superstar—

"Lisa!"

Warren's voice. Lisa snapped to attention. As he came into the bedroom, she turned toward him, primed for admiration.

"Chrissake, Lisa, aren't you ready yet? I told you it was important to get to the Addisons' party on time. I need to—" He stopped abruptly. "What the hell is that?"

"What?" She suddenly felt smaller.

"On your face." He rubbed a hand across his mouth as if brushing away something poisonous.

"Oh. A new lipstick. It's called Femme Fatale."

"Well, wipe it off. It makes you look like a slut."

"But—"

"Do it now, Lisa. We're running late."

She pulled a tissue from the box and pretended to dab at her lips. "I don't think it will come off. It's one of those long-lasting kinds."

"Shit. Well, we don't have time to worry with it. Just work extra hard tonight to make the right impression. Let's go."

Lisa watched until he had left the room. Then she dropped the lipstick into her black beaded party purse and scooted down the hall, tottering on her unaccustomed high heels.

She caught up with Warren at the front door. "Katie!" she called as she opened the coat closet door. "We're leaving now." She took out her suede jacket.

"Wait," Warren said. "You can't wear that. Don't you have something else?"

"Like what?"

"Something more—well, appropriate."

"What would you like better? My ski parka?"

"You don't need a coat. It's not cold."

"Warren, it's November."

Katie had come into the foyer and was watching them with that guarded expression she wore so often these days. "I know what you can wear, Mom. Just a minute." She dashed off and returned a moment later wrapped in a black shawl, its long fringe flying.

"What's that?" Lisa asked.

"It was Grandma's, remember? She gave it to me for playing dress-up when I was little."

Lisa threw the shawl around her shoulders. It felt like cashmere, warm and soft. Her fingers found a couple of small holes; apparently moths had liked it, too. That was probably why it had been handed down to Katie. With luck Warren wouldn't notice the flaws.

"Thank you, sweetheart. It will do nicely."

Warren opened the front door. "Lisa, let's go."

"Now listen, Katie," Lisa said, "the Addisons' phone number is posted on the fridge. Are you sure you'll be all right?"

"Quit worrying. You've left me home alone lots of times."

"Not for an entire evening like this."

"Mom, I am so past needing a babysitter. I can take care of myself."

"That's right, my girl's growing up." Warren put his arm around his daughter, but Katie quickly pulled away.

Katie tiptoed into the master bedroom. No one was home to hear her, but she made a habit of caution where her parents were concerned.

She was curious about that black-and-gray box. Her mom acted like it was some big secret.

Last week Katie had gone into her parents' room when the door was closed and seen the box on the bed. Mom flung a blanket over it and yelled at her for not knocking. Today she'd turned around on her way to Janelle's because she'd forgotten her math book. She opened the bedroom door to ask Mom where it was, and there was the box again. That reminded Katie she hadn't knocked, so she closed the door softly and left the house. She and Janelle had managed without the book.

It took her a few minutes to find the box buried in the closet. Her heart pounded as she dragged it into the light. What if opening it let loose something weird, like in that Pandora story they'd read in school? What if the box held mementos from some hidden life her mother never talked about—the blanket that had wrapped a baby she'd given away, or letters from a long-ago lover? What if it contained some kind of incriminating evidence against her dad?

She lifted the lid. What a disappointment. Nothing but junk. Well, not junk exactly, but a bunch of oddball things, and not very interesting ones. The purple scarf was kinda cool, but Patty Grimes? Katie wouldn't be caught dead listening to her. Maybe Mom had started Christmas shopping. But who would she give that awful CD to? And those silly cat earrings—Mom better not put them under the tree for her.

Katie returned the box to the closet, making sure it looked like it hadn't been touched.

───────

Wineglass in hand, Lisa scanned the Addisons' huge, crowded living room for Warren. He had stuck by her side for the first five minutes, introducing her to Josephine Addison, who was their hostess and his boss's wife, and fetching her glass of cabernet. After that, he abandoned her so he could find more important people to wheel and deal with. Or maybe he was campaigning for a promotion; he'd dropped hints about a vice president's slot that was opening up. Well, she certainly hoped he'd get it. They could use the extra money and maybe the boost to his ego would improve his constant mood of irritation.

Make a good impression, Warren had told her. She was willing to do that if it would help his chances, but she hadn't the least idea how to go about it. She didn't know any of these people, she wasn't good at small talk, these damn high heels were pinching her feet…

There he was, talking to a group of people across the room—a redhead who looked stunning in an emerald-green dress and a couple of men wearing expensive-looking suits. Warren must have been telling a joke, because suddenly they all laughed. The redhead playfully slapped his shoulder.

Lisa started to move in his direction, but couldn't make her way through a gaggle of people who were heatedly debating the merits of some high-flying tech stock. Turning to seek a different route, she bumped into a tuxedoed waiter and nearly knocked over his tray of miniature crab puffs. The hell with it. She set off in search of the bar.

She stepped into the powder room on her way down the hall to touch up her lipstick.

She found the bar in a room with an extravagant media center extending across one wall. What did you call a room like this? Family room, den? Those labels seemed too intimate for a house as grandiose as the Addisons'.

That room was congested too. Thirsty partygoers thronged around the drinks table, and the bartenders, in tuxes like the crab-puff man, looked harried. Lisa shifted her wineglass from hand to hand; this was going to take forever. Maybe she should order two glasses, set one in an out-of-the-way corner so she could come back for it later and avoid another tedious wait.

"Refill?" asked a voice at her elbow. Lisa turned gratefully, expecting another tuxedo. But the speaker was a silver-blond man in a dark blue blazer. "The bar line was taking forever, so I filched a bottle from the kitchen. I don't know what you're drinking, but this is a pretty good cabernet."

"Thank you. Cabernet is what I had before."

"I'm Greg Marsden, sales manager for the Addison Group," he told her as he poured. "We haven't met, have we? I'd remember someone like you. Are you a new hire? A client?"

"None of the above. My name's Lisa DeVoe." She sipped the wine. More than pretty good; it was excellent.

He frowned. "DeVoe? As in Warren DeVoe?"

Uh-oh. Something in his tone set off alarm bells. Was Greg a competitor for Warren's promotion? Or had Warren done something to damage his chances to move up?

"He's my husband. Why, is something wrong?"

"I'm just surprised. Warren's always—well, I never dreamed he had a wife."

Lisa's turn to frown. Instead, she hastily pasted on a smile. "Oh, he does. I'm living proof of that."

Greg smiled back, which crinkled the edges of his warm hazel eyes. "Clearly I was mistaken. With someone like you, I can't imagine why he'd—is he here? I haven't seen him tonight."

"He's stuck in the living room, talking to some people." Laughing with a redhead, she added to herself. She took a big gulp of the wine, leaving a slight smear of lipstick on the rim of the glass.

"Crowd's so big, he could be trapped there all evening," Greg said. "He'll probably faint from the heat. All these bodies, it's getting very warm in here."

"It certainly is," Lisa agreed.

"Why don't we go out on the terrace and catch some air? It's sheltered from the wind, and the stars are really brilliant tonight."

"Good idea." Those eyes are incredible, Lisa thought.

She shivered as Greg put his hand on her back to guide her.

"I'll bring the wine," he said.

———··———

Lisa set a platter of waffles on the breakfast table.

"How was the party last night?" Katie asked.

"Fine." Lisa licked her lips, savoring the memory of Greg's wine-flavored kiss.

"Just fine? What was it like?"

"Very crowded. The food was delicious. And you should see the Addisons' house, it's enormous."

Lisa kept her tone neutral, but she wanted to sing. If only she could wrap last night's party in silk and keep it in her treasure box. She couldn't help smiling as she thought of Greg's phone number, on a tiny scrap of paper hidden inside the cap of the Femme Fatale lipstick tube.

"Did Daddy have a good time? He seemed worried about this party."

"Oh, yes, everything went fine for him." When she and Greg had come back inside, Warren was standing near the buffet table with the redhead. She kept brushing Warren's lapel as if there were crumbs on it, although Lisa knew he was a tidy eater. Warren seemed unaware that Lisa had been gone for an hour.

"Good morning, ladies! See you later." Warren strode through the kitchen, pausing only to tousle Katie's hair. Katie didn't look up. With a grim expression, she buttered her waffle, scraping the knife across its surface long after the butter had melted.

"Wait, Warren. What about breakfast?" Lisa asked.

Warren grinned. "Don't have time. I'm joining the Addisons for their tailgate picnic, remember? Sure is lucky they had that extra ticket for the game."

How had she forgotten? All the way home last night, he had crowed about being offered the coveted ticket. He was certain it was a positive sign about his promotion.

When the sound of his car engine had died away, Lisa said as casually as she could, "Would you be all right here by yourself this afternoon? I thought I'd get an early start on Christmas shopping."

Katie pushed a bite of waffle around on her plate. "I was okay last night, wasn't I? Besides, I'm going over to Janelle's."

"That's good." Lisa ran to her bedroom and closed the door. Butterflies swooped and soared in her stomach as she dialed the phone.

Sneaking requires alertness, Lisa reminded herself as she pushed open the door of the Magnolia Inn.

She and Greg had been practicing the art of deception for four weeks now. The entire time, Lisa's heart had been beating wildly, from the thrill of Greg's embrace and from her fear that Warren would catch them.

Fortunately Greg's sales job kept him out of the office. Nearly every day he and Lisa were able to steal an hour for a cup of coffee or a glass of wine. On Wednesdays they had the whole afternoon in which to indulge in the pleasures of each other's company. And on Sundays—thank God the Addisons had taken such a shine to Warren, keeping him occupied with football tickets and rounds of golf.

She glanced around now to make sure she didn't see anyone she knew. Not much chance of that; the Magnolia Inn was located on a country road outside Glenwood, two towns away from home. But caution never hurt.

Lisa loved the inn—the Victorian porches and turrets, the antique furniture, the poinsettias and candles everywhere. She had come to think of the upstairs front guestroom as their own.

She slipped into the ladies room to refresh her lipstick. Warren might think Femme Fatale looked slutty, but Greg found the brilliant red sexy and alluring; he'd told her so. The face that smiled from the gilt-framed mirror looked younger, fresher, than it had a month ago. Falling in love must be good for the complexion.

When she emerged, she went past the stairs leading up to the guestrooms—that would come later—and entered the dining room. Greg was waiting at their usual table by the fireplace. He stood and greeted her with a kiss—a discreet kiss in deference to diners at nearby tables, but one that promised greater delights ahead.

"You look gorgeous," he said. He held her chair, a simple gesture that never failed to please her. Warren disdained such courtesies; at least he did when he was with her. But Josephine Addison, or the redhead from work—he probably behaved differently with them.

"Thank you," she said. "So do you."

Greg ordered a bottle of champagne, then presented Lisa with a slender box topped by a silver bow.

"What's this? Are we celebrating something?"

"Our anniversary. One month since the day we met. Open it."

Lisa unwrapped the gift. Nestled in tissue paper was a knife with a heart-shaped silver handle; in the center was a ruby-red stone that sparkled in the firelight.

"Greg, my God, this beautiful." She slid it from its velvet sheath, revealing a long thin blade.

"One of my accounts is an antiques store. The last time I went in, this was in the display case. It reminded me of that song you played the other day—'you cut the strings that bound my heart and set it free to love you.'" He sang the line in his rich baritone.

Lisa ran a finger along the flat of the blade. "I'll keep it forever."

"Careful," Greg warned. "It's sharp. Don't cut yourself."

"My mother's acting weird lately," Katie told Janelle as they sprawled on the couch in Janelle's family room, a bag of chips between them.

"Mine too," Janelle said between bites. "It's that change-of-life thing. She's totally bouncing off the walls."

"I don't think that's it," Katie said. "Your mom's older than mine. It's—I don't know. She's never home anymore. And she's got this box in the closet, it's full of dumb stuff but she hides it like it's some big secret."

"What kind of stuff?"

"Junk mostly. Like these." Katie brushed back her hair to show off the rhinestone cats dangling from her ears.

"Ooh, those are cool." Janelle reached to touch one.

"No, they're not." Katie slapped away her friend's hand. "Don't be a dork."

"Maybe it's Christmas presents."

"I can't believe she'd really give that crap to anyone. Hey, want to hear something really lame?" She grabbed her backpack from the floor and pulled out a CD case. "Let's put this on."

Janelle took it and frowned. "Patty Grimes? Isn't she like country or something?"

"Yeah, wait till you hear it. This one song about cutting heartstrings, it'll really make you laugh."

<hr />

Katie placed the cat earrings and the CD back into her mother's secret box. Oh, here was something she hadn't noticed before—a bottle of perfume. She spritzed some onto the inside of her wrist and inhaled the heady fragrance.

"Katie!"

She jumped. She'd thought she was alone in the house.

"Dad! What are you doing here? I mean, I thought you were playing golf with Mr. Addison."

"We skipped the nineteenth hole today."

"Aren't there eighteen holes on a golf course?"

Her father laughed. "The nineteenth hole is the clubhouse bar. Usually we have a couple of drinks after the game, but Mr. Addison's in-laws are in town, so he promised to get home early."

"Is he going to give you that job you want?"

"I hope so, sweetie. If nothing blows it for me, I've got a good shot." His arm encircled her shoulders. "What's all this?"

She twitched, trying to shake him off. She hated the creepy way he'd been acting lately—always staring at her and finding excuses to put his hands on her.

"Stuff Mom got. Christmas presents probably. I guess I shouldn't be peeking."

"Don't worry about it." Her father slid his fingers down her backbone. Katie stiffened. "Where is your mother, by the way?"

"Shopping. She'll be home soon." Katie tried to inch away, but he slipped his arm around her waist, pulling her closer. Her stomach clenched, and she jerked out of reach. "We better put this away. We don't want Mom knowing we spoiled the surprise."

She picked up the box but didn't move. She didn't want her father to know her mom's hiding place. Bad enough he'd seen the box.

"Your mother doesn't usually buy cheap stuff like this for Christmas gifts," he said. "I wonder…"

"What?" Katie said.

"Did you see her actually buy any of these things?"

"Of course not. I told you, they're for Christmas, they're secret. Why are you asking?"

"No reason, sweetie. Just speculating about how your mother acquired those things."

He turned and left the room. Katie felt faint with relief.

No time for waffles this Sunday. Lisa set muffins and juice on the breakfast table. Warren was going to a basketball game with Addison, thank God. Now if she could just talk Katie into spending the day at Janelle's.

"What are your plans for today, Lisa?" Warren asked as he spread his bran muffin with raspberry jam.

"I thought I'd head for the mall. Time's getting tight for Christmas shopping." She poured coffee into his cup. Every day, the lies got easier.

"Shopping," Warren echoed. "Katie, I want you to come with me today."

Katie looked up from buttering a chunk of cranberry-nut. "What?" For a second Lisa thought she saw fear in her daughter's eyes, but then Katie's face settled into its usual carefully composed blankness.

"You heard me," Warren said. "We'll spend some quality time."

Lisa nodded. "Great idea."

"I don't like basketball," Katie said stubbornly.

"You'll love it when you see a real team play. Someone cancelled, so Addison has a spare ticket. Can't miss this chance."

"But, Dad—"

"Whoa, look at the time." Warren gulped some coffee and stood up. "Get moving, Katie."

Ignoring her protests, he hustled her out of the house.

Yes! Lisa hurried to get ready.

She would wear the new red cashmere sweater. A real treasure—the most daring thing she'd ever taken. She'd put it on in the dressing room and worn it right out of the store under her zipped-up jacket. What a heart-pounding thrill that had been.

Red was Lisa's new favorite color, because Greg loved it so much. The sweater matched the Femme Fatale lipstick and the ruby stone of the knife, which she kept in her purse so she could reach in and touch it whenever she wanted to feel Greg near her.

She smoothed the sweater over her body. Soon Greg's hands would caress its softness, then slip underneath it to make her skin tingle, then strip it away and lower her naked onto the bed.

Greg was the biggest treasure of all.

Katie gripped the armrest as her father turned the corner and whipped the car into a U-turn. "Dad! What are you doing?"

"Waiting." He stopped at the curb but left the engine running. Their own house was clearly visible down the side street. The sky was low and gray.

"Waiting for what?"

"Your mother."

"You want her to come to the game, too?"

"We're not going to the game. Mr. Addison's in-laws are still in town; they're using his tickets."

One thing about grownups—they hardly ever made sense. "What are we doing then?"

"We're going to follow your mother to the mall."

"Why? To see what else she's buying for Christmas?"

"No, we're going to—Katie, I'm going to be frank. You're old enough to understand." He patted her knee, but only for a second. "I'm worried about her. Those things in that box, the ones you said were Christmas gifts? I don't think she bought them."

"What do you mean?"

"Do you know what shoplifting is?"

"Sure." Of course she knew. Janelle did it all the time, mostly candy from the drugstore. Katie tried it once, but she'd hated it. First she felt afraid, and then she felt guilty, and the two feelings had combined into a horrible sour mush in her stomach. When she ate the chocolate bar she'd taken, she almost barfed.

"I think that's how your mother got those items," Dad said.

"You mean she stole them? That's crazy."

"She's done it before. If she gets caught doing something illegal, she'll blow my chances for that promotion. I need to stop her, but I have to be certain. So we're going to follow her to the mall and see what she does."

Katie squirmed in her seat. That sour thing was starting in her stomach again. "Why do I have to come along?"

"Because it will be a good lesson for you. Besides, I might need another witness." He smiled at her. "You don't mind helping your dad, do you?"

This time her father's hand remained on her knee.

Katie eased her legs away and huddled against the car door. Down the street she saw her mother's Ford start to move, and she blinked back tears.

A moment later Mom rolled by on the street they were facing. She didn't seem to notice them.

Her dad shifted into drive. "Come on, Katie. Let's go catch her in the act."

Lisa felt like she was sailing on clouds—not the heavy dark ones overhead, but the puffy kind that angels sat on. Every turn of her tires was bringing her closer to Greg. The sky promised snow—how delicious it would be if they were snowbound at the inn. Not having to watch the time, not having any distraction from the delight of each other's company. She had no idea how she would explain her absence to Warren, but Greg would help her concoct a believable story.

Almost there. What a wonderful day. She couldn't help singing.

"Where the hell is she going?" Katie's father muttered as they sped along the Glenwood highway. "The turn for the mall was three miles back."

"There's lots of shopping centers, Dad." Katie stared out the side window, not wanting to look at him or at Mom's car up ahead. She felt as though the leaden grayness of the weather was pressing on her heart.

"Not many out this way. I can't imagine—wait, she's going left."

Past the town of Glenwood the road narrowed and houses gave way to forest. Her father slowed down, putting more distance between the two cars. He was right; there was no place to shop around here. Maybe Mom had spotted them and was leading Dad on a wild goose chase.

But as they rounded a corner, Mom's brake lights shone red. She swerved into a graveled area where several cars were parked by a big old house. A sign in the yard said MAGNOLIA INN.

Her father pulled to the shoulder of the road. As he cut the engine, a red convertible, some kind of sports car, sped past. It wheeled into the parking lot and stopped beside Mom's Ford.

Dad opened his door. "I'm going to find out what this is all about. Wait here."

Katie nodded, not daring to speak. When his face had that dark, hard look, it was best to be silent and invisible. She watched him cross the lawn toward the cars.

She gave him a moment's head start, then she followed.

Lisa's heart soared as Greg's Jaguar pulled up next to her. She flipped down the visor to expose the mirror and quickly applied more lipstick. Femme Fatale. Red, brilliant, magical.

"Kiss me," she whispered to her reflection. "I am irresistible."

Grabbing her pocketbook, she got out of the car and flung herself into Greg's waiting arms.

Electricity jolted through her body as they kissed. When he released her, she caught her breath, then reached her lips to his again. Who cared if someone was watching?

"Come on, love. Let's go inside." Greg was laughing, and she laughed too.

"Your face is smeared with red." She rubbed his mouth with a finger but the lipstick wouldn't come off.

"I like it that way." They started walking, arm in arm, toward the inn.

"Lisa!"

The voice was as sharp and startling as a gunshot.

She whirled around. "Warren! My God! What—"

"You slut! You whore!"

Warren slammed her with an open-handed blow. Lisa staggered backward, fell over a concrete planter, and landed in a heap on the winter-brown grass.

Head whirling, shoulder stinging with pain, she couldn't move. She didn't see Warren hit Greg. But she heard Greg's moan and the whoosh of his breath as it was pushed from his lungs.

She dragged herself to her feet and gasped at the sight before her.

Greg was sprawled face-up across the hood of his car. His face was red, only now the red was blood—blood that flowed from his nostrils, from his scalp, from a gash near his eye. The hood ornament, a leaping cat, had blood on its head and hair in its teeth; Greg must have fallen on it. Warren stood over him, pummeling Greg with blow after blow, even though Greg's body was limp.

Lisa screamed.

She screamed as she reached into her pocketbook and took out the knife with the heart-shaped handle and the ruby-red stone.

She screamed as she shook the knife free of its sheath and plunged it into Warren's back.

She screamed as she stabbed him again and again and again, until Warren slumped forward on top of Greg.

As the two bodies slid off the car and onto the ground, Lisa dropped the bloody knife and fell silent.

Yet she could still hear screaming. The high thin wail seemed to come from everywhere at once, as if it were part of the air. She inhaled the sound with each ragged breath.

"Mom! Mom! Mom!"

Feeling dizzy and sick, she turned and—oh God, Katie was running toward her.

Lisa rushed on wobbling legs to meet her daughter, to clutch her tight, to shield her from the terrible sight in the parking lot.

What have I done? Lisa thought. What have I done?

"Muh-muh-mom!" Katie's screams subsided into muffled sobs as she stumbled into Lisa's arms. "Wh-what's happening?"

"Katie! My baby! What are you doing here?"

"Dad saw your secret b-box. He th-thought you were s-s-stealing."

Lisa pulled Katie closer, wrapped her in her arms. Nothing made sense. The world was spinning crazily around them, a kaleidoscope of pain and blood.

"Box?" she whispered. "A secret?"

"In the c-closet. With all the little th-things."

Then she realized: "My treasure chest!"

"We f-followed you to c-catch you in the act. I'm s-sorry, Mom."

"It's not your fault, sweetheart. Everything will be all right." Lisa didn't believe the last statement, but she and Katie both needed to hear it said aloud.

People were spilling out of the inn onto the lawn, yelling, running toward them. She heard the wail of approaching sirens.

"Are they—dead?" Katie asked.

Lisa turned her eyes to the two men—the one she thought she loved and the one she had stopped loving long ago.

Greg was half-sitting, propped up against the tire of his car. Warren lay motionless; he looked like a pile of discarded clothing someone had dumped on the ground.

She fought tears as she put her arm around Katie's shoulders. Katie, her true treasure.

"I don't know, honey. I hope not."

Snowflakes swirled around them. A woman in a cop's uniform ushered them into the inn. It smelled of hot cider and a crackling wood fire. They sat on a bench in the entryway.

"What's going to happen now?" Katie asked.

"I don't know that either," Lisa said. "We'll hope for the best." If only she had the slightest clue what the best might be.

Katie nodded. "H-hope for the best."

Lisa pulled Katie's head to her shoulder and surrendered to the tears.

Everyone has a secret–said truism provided the genesis of our next story, from Bobbi A. Chukran—that and cats. Julia needs some time away from her husband and decides to spend a few days at the family cabin. Before long, the detective team of Lucas and Johnson enter the picture.

Ms. Chukran has written, as she puts it, everything under the sun, and then some. But it is the short story to which she is most drawn and is her favorite form. Several of her stories have appeared in anthologies from Darkhouse Books.

Cat's Outta the Bag

by Bobbi A. Chukran

Julia Morgan paced as the phone rang. It was critical to her plans that she talk to her sister. Finally, Jerri answered.

"Hey Sis, I'm just calling to let you know I won't be able to make it to lunch tomorrow. David and I had yet another argument and I'm going to take off a few days, go to the cabin with a new novel I just started. I need to clear my head. I can't be with him right now. He's driving me crazy."

"Is everything all right?" Jerri asked.

"Not really. We had a slight difference of opinion. He accused me of not being there for him--blah blah blah--whatever that means, and I accused him of screwing around with that blonde airhead he calls an assistant. Belinda Cooper."

Jerri's eyebrows lifted in surprise. "Whoa, sounds serious." She knew that her sister's marriage was in trouble, but had no idea it had gone this far.

"Yeah, tell me about it. Of course he denies it. Anyway, just wanted to let you know." Julia hesitated for a moment. "When I get back, I'm going to make some changes around here."

"Hey, listen. Maybe I'll take off, too, and meet you there," her sister suggested. "I'll bring Evan. She'd love to spend a weekend with her favorite aunt. Just us girls."

Julia was silent for a moment. "It sounds wonderful, but I need some time alone. And you have things to do. Any other time I'd love to see y'all. You understand, don't you?"

"Sure, if you insist." Jerri sighed. "Maybe next time. Is anybody else going to be around?"

Julia knew her sister's feelings were hurt, but she wasn't in the mood for a boisterous girl's weekend. "No, not really. There's a caretaker who looks after the cabins. He only comes by once in a while, leaves firewood outside, keeps the pond clean--that sort of thing. I'll be fine."

"If you're sure…"

"Of course I'm sure. Do me a favor, will you?" Julia asked.

"Anything. Just name it."

"I don't want David to know where I'm going. If he calls, which he probably won't, can you tell him I'm with you? I don't want him tracking me down this weekend. I need some time to think."

"I don't like lying to him," Jerri said. "But for you, I'll do it."

"Thanks, sis. Oh, and I'm taking Jasmine with me. He's always hated cats anyway. She'd never forgive me if I left her at home alone all weekend. No telling what would happen to her. I don't trust him anymore."

"Good plan," Jerri agreed. "I'm envious. Peace and quiet, a good book, a nice roaring fire, a bottle of wine, a secluded cabin and a ball of warm fur. Life isn't all bad, is it?"

Julia laughed. "No, not all bad. I'll call you when I get back home on Sunday night." She glanced at the calendar hanging on the pantry door. "I have a few appointments next week, or I'd stay longer."

"Well, have fun. Love you!"

"Love you, too. I'll call you when I get back home."

"You'd better," her sister said. "If you don't, I'll send the patrols out." Jerri disconnected. She couldn't help feeling that there was more to it, but she tried to mind her own business where her sister was concerned.

———————

Julia quickly finished packing, captured Jasmine and coaxed her into the carrier. She stopped by the kitchen to scribble a note, left it on the refrigerator, picked up a canvas bag of food and other supplies, hooked it over her shoulder, loaded it and the cat in the car and drove away. She sighed with relief. Downtown traffic wasn't too thick yet; she'd make good time and should reach the cabin by nightfall.

———————

Hours later, David Morgan slammed the door and frowned when he saw the note on the refrigerator. The least his wife could have done was text him to let him know she wouldn't be home. He hated not knowing where she was at all times. She spent way too much time at her sister's house, in his opinion. Now he'd have to deal with dinner on his own. Unless...

He grinned, then picked up the phone and punched a few buttons. "Hey, Belinda. How fast can you pack a bag? How about an impromptu weekend away? I'll pick you up in a couple of hours... Yeah, I know we didn't have plans, but something's come up. Let's just say that opportunity is knocking and we'd be fools not to answer it."

"Hey babe. Sounds good to me," Belinda Cooper, his blonde assistant, answered. "Give me an hour. But what about—you know who?"

"We've got plenty of time; I need to finish up a few things here first. She decided to go to her sister's for the weekend." David frowned. "I don't trust that witch, though. She's such a liar. I'll

201

check to make sure. I'd hate to run into her on the road somewhere. She's not the only one who can leave without warning for a fun weekend. We won't have to worry about that much longer, though."

"So you've decided to… uh, you know."

"Don't ask questions if you don't want the answers. And Sugar? Be sure to pack those little black things I love. You know the ones. It's chilly out there, so you might bring some warm clothes, too. How about wearing one of those tight sweaters I bought you? Yeah, I love the black cashmere. See you soon."

He hung up, deliberated for a moment then punched another number into the phone. "Hey, Jerri, is Julia there? Put her on the phone."

"Oh, hi David. Um, yeah, she's here, but she's in the shower right now. She had a headache and thought it might clear her head."

"Big plans for the weekend?" he asked.

She hesitated. "We're going to catch a movie and have some dinner a bit later. Evan's anxious to spend some time with her."

"I didn't realize she was going to be gone tonight. It's just a surprise, that's all."

"She just needed to take a few days off. We're going to do some shopping tomorrow, maybe visit a museum or two. She'll be back home Sunday night. That's all I know."

"I see."

"Should I have her call you when she gets out?" Jerri cringed as the words popped out of her mouth. She wasn't used to making up lies on the spot, and it made her nervous.

"Nah, I'll try again later," he said. "Y'all have a fun weekend. Tell her to stay as long as she needs to."

Jerri hung up the phone, letting out a breath. She'd almost blown it. She hoped it was worth all the subterfuge, and that Julia would have a relaxing weekend. Lord knows she wouldn't.

Julia stopped the car at the front door of the old cabin. She massaged her neck, realizing how much tension she'd built up on the drive there. She climbed out and immediately the cooler air blowing off the lake chilled her. The air smelled clean and fresh—a nice change from their stuffy Austin neighborhood full of roaring lawnmowers and leaf blowers.

The cabin was decorated in a rustic style, but with all the modern conveniences of home. It had belonged to her parents and although David had wanted to sell it, she was glad she'd convinced him to keep it. The building sat in the midst of an old oak forest only forty miles outside the city. They had only used it occasionally, but every time they visited there, some kind of argument started. A few times, Julia had snuck away to enjoy the peace of the natural setting where she could actually hear her own thoughts.

She grabbed the cat carrier, unlocked the front door and prepared for a nice quiet weekend. She hesitated, and then decided to bring in the bags with the cat food and her book after she'd had a chance to get a nice fire started.

She was happy to see that Matthew Waters, the caretaker, had left a tall stack of firewood beside the door. Nights at the cabin got chilly, and there was almost nothing she liked better than a roaring fire. She'd never been a Girl Scout type herself, and was an absolute klutz with matches and lighters. She was happy the wood-burning fireplace had an automatic natural gas starter valve. It didn't get better than that.

Julia stared into the flames. She couldn't believe that she'd dozed off. She took another sip of the champagne and smiled as the bubbles tickled her nose. She was glad she'd sprung for a case of the good stuff. And she didn't have to share it with anyone else if she didn't want to. She suddenly shivered and pulled the blanket up to her chin.

A small *click* came from behind her. She frowned, glanced around, surprised. It was only the cat. Jasmine had jumped from the hearth and was streaking down the hallway into the bedroom. Julia smiled then turned back to the fire. A large hand grabbed her by the hair and jerked her head back against the cushions of the sofa.

She shrieked and stared for a moment at the dark silhouette hovering over her. Then she smiled.

"Hello, Matthew. What took you so long?" she asked, reaching up and pulling him in for a kiss. "I was afraid you'd changed your mind." She nodded at the half-empty bottle. "I got a head start on the weekend."

"I wanted to make sure you were alone," he said.

"Well, it's just me and Jasmine. You know she adores you. She won't bother us."

"Great. I don't mind cats; you know that."

"I see you've been busy with the ax." Julia nodded towards the basket of kindling and logs he'd brought in earlier. "You're quite the brawny lumberjack, aren't you? Thanks for doing that."

He laughed. "No problem. You know how much I enjoy working out here in the country. And how much I enjoy the firelight against your naked skin."

She smiled and tilted her head back for another kiss.

He licked his lips. "Yum, champagne."

She nodded. "And there's plenty more where that came from, too. Enough to last the whole, long weekend."

He smiled. "Life doesn't get much better than this, does it?" He came around and sat down beside her and pulled the blanket around them both.

"Funny, that's what my sister said earlier today."

"Jerri's right about that." He reached across and pushed a strand of hair out of her eyes, as they sat back against the sofa, staring into the fire together.

David pulled the little red sports car up beside the cabin. The headlights illuminated another car in the driveway. He quickly cut the engine.

"Dammit, she's here."

"What?" Belinda had dozed off. She sat up and stared at the car in the driveway.

"My wife! Julia's here. That's her Volvo."

"What are we going to do now?" Belinda shrieked. "Let's just leave before she sees me. We can spend the weekend at my place."

David glanced over at Belinda. He was almost sorry he'd brought her along. She was a beautiful woman, and in that tight, black sweater she made his head spin. But sometimes she was a royal pain.

He drummed his fingers on the steering wheel, thinking. "Stay in the car! I'll deal with her."

"Can't I get out and stretch my legs or something?" she whined.

"STAY in the car! Do you hear me? I'm going to go see what's going on. Dammit, she's not supposed to be here!"

"Oh, all right!" Belinda pouted but sat back and stared out in the darkness. "Don't be long, it's damned spooky out here at night with all these weird trees."

He cursed again, took a flashlight out of the glove compartment then gently opened the car door, got out and crept up the path to the front of the cabin. Hesitating a moment, David tried the door and it swung open with a *creak*. He cringed, glanced back at the car then crept into the room.

Jasmine the cat sat beside the sofa. She blinked at him and her green eyes glowed in the dark. She arched her back, hissed and ran off into the kitchen.

David smelled lingering smoke, but the fire in the fireplace had burned completely out. It was dark in the living room, but with the flashlight he could see well enough.

There were two bodies sleeping peacefully on a rug by the hearth. It was obvious that both were naked, barely covered by a blanket. One was softly snoring. Three empty champagne bottles were lined up side-by-side on a nearby table.

For a moment, David stared and then rage took over. He hesitated then reached down to turn the valve key at the side of the fireplace to release the gas.

He heard a small noise behind him and he whirled around.

"Oh my god, are they dead?" Belinda whispered. "Who is that with her?"

"Shut up!" he ordered. "Keep your voice down! No, they aren't dead. It's the caretaker. I told you to stay in the car! What are you doing here?"

"I had to pee!" she said. "I couldn't hold it anymore. What are you doing?"

"Never mind. Just go, and hurry up." He pointed down a dark hallway. "No dawdling or primping, OK? I'm going to end this right now. This isn't what I planned, but when opportunity knocks, I gotta take advantage of it. This could work out great for us if we play our cards right."

Belinda stared at him for a moment then she realized what he planned to do. "I want no part in this." She quickly turned and trotted down the hall.

David turned his attentions to his wife. She looked so peaceful lying there. Julia was dead to the world, obviously sloshed on alcohol. He shook his head with disgust; she never could hold her liquor.

Belinda eventually came back, lugging a large, squirming white cat. Jasmine was not happy.

He stared at her. "What the hell are you doing with that cat?"

"I found her hiding in the bathroom. We can't leave her here."

"Put the damned cat down!" David whispered, as he crouched down and studied the valve key in the fireplace. "Go on, get out of here."

"What? No, we can't leave the cat! I won't let you kill this cat!" Belinda demanded. "I'll take it to my place, OK? I won't let you hurt it!"

"All right! We don't have time to dawdle around," he said. "Do something!"

She frantically glanced around, found the carrier and shoved the cat in headfirst. Jasmine yowled and scratched, but finally Belinda managed to get her caged. She flounced outside and David heard the car door slam.

He cringed at the noise, but still his wife didn't stir. He stared at her for a moment, reached down and gave the valve key a clockwise turn. He held his breath, heard the fatal hiss of gas then quickly escaped. He glanced backwards for a few seconds then smiled before firmly shutting the door behind him.

A couple of hours later, David was back home in Austin. Belinda had made a fuss when he mentioned that they were going straight back. She convinced him to stop outside of town for dinner, but he was too nervous to eat much. He rushed her through the meal and made a quick promise to see her at work on Monday. He said that they needed to take a break for a while, only until things died down. She reluctantly agreed. He raced to her condo, forced her out of the car then sped away. She barely had time to grab the cat carrier and her overnight bag out of the back seat.

———•——

Belinda couldn't sleep. She was tired and had a splitting head-ache. That damned cat had yowled all the way home on Friday night and had continued to cry almost all weekend. She was almost sorry they hadn't left it behind. When she had opened the carrier door, Jasmine flew out and raced down the hall, a white furry blur and hid in her closet. The next morning, Belinda woke up sneezing. Her eyes were red and itchy. She'd been awake most of the night, wondering what David did to his wife. She had an idea, although she didn't know exactly how he did it. She didn't care; didn't really want to know, but she'd obsessed about it the rest of the weekend.

She was angry but knew better than to argue with David. Whatever David did to his wife and her lover was on him. She wanted no part of it. Adultery was one thing; murder was another. She'd return the cat, find a new job and maybe even leave town. Put it all behind her. That would be best. First chance she had on Monday, she'd take Jasmine back where it belonged—to David. And she hoped the beast wouldn't destroy her entire wardrobe in the meantime.

———•——

Somebody was banging on the door and the doorbell was clanging. David groaned, then flopped over in bed—the bed he had slept in alone for the past three nights—then stared at the clock. It was early Monday morning—way too early for visitors. The doorbell rang again, and the knocking continued. "OK, I'm coming! Geez!" He peeled back the curtains in the bedroom and looked down at the street below. A police cruiser was parked by the curb. From his vantage point, he could see a man and a woman standing at his front door.

"Oh my god," he muttered, taking a deep breath. Take it easy, there's nothing to be afraid of. He pulled on his robe and stumbled down the stairs. He took a deep breath, and then opened the front door.

"Yes?"

"Mr. Morgan? Mr. David Morgan?"

"Yes, I'm David Morgan. What's this about?"

"I'm Detective Patrick Lucas and this is my partner Detective Marla Johnson. We have a few questions for your wife. Could we speak to her, please, Mr. Morgan?"

"My wife? She's not here right now."

"Do you know where she is?" Johnson added.

"Uh, she's at her sister's house. Or was. She's a bit late getting back. I expected her home last night, but she's frequently late. Why do you ask?"

"That's the thing; she's not at her sister's. Ms. Edwards called us because she's been trying to reach your wife. Apparently, she was supposed to check in last night, but when she didn't, the sister called us. She's very worried."

"Is that right? I don't know what to tell you. Last I heard, Julia was going to her sister's house. If she's not there, I have no idea where she could be. I'm sure her sister's worried about nothing. My wife frequently does things without my permission."

Detective Lucas's eyebrows went up. "I see. She didn't go to her sister's house. According to Ms. Edwards, your wife wanted some time alone, so she went to your cabin instead."

"So the little witch lied to me? Typical!"

The detectives said nothing.

David rubbed his hands over his eyes. "The cabin? Huh. Well, I suppose it's her right to do that. Just wish she'd invited me," he joked.

The detectives glanced at each other. "We've been trying to get ahold of her there, no luck yet."

"I'm not surprised; the cell phone service there is spotty at the best of times."

"How long's it been since you've been at your cabin, Mr. Morgan?" Detective Johnson asked.

"I haven't been there in at least a year. Why do you ask?"

Lucas shrugged. "Just routine questions, sir."

David gulped. "What's this really about? Have you actually… gone to the cabin? To see if she's there?"

"No, not yet. But we intend to."

Johnson glanced at Lucas then stepped forward. "Do you mind if we look around a bit?"

David hesitated for a moment. He could claim that they needed a search warrant. On the other hand, it might look better if he let them in. After all, he had nothing to hide there in the house. There were no clues and nothing to implicate him.

He shrugged. "Sure, why not? Come on in. Want some coffee? I was just having a bit of breakfast before going in to work."

"No, thanks. This won't take long."

Lucas quickly ran upstairs, and Johnson poked around downstairs, walked through the kitchen, opened the pantry door then glanced at the calendar on the pantry wall.

"I see that somebody's made a note on your calendar about a vet visit. Me, I love cats."

David nodded. "Oh yeah, that's for my wife's cat. She dotes on that little critter. Always taking it someplace or other. I can't stand them myself."

Detective Lucas nodded. "Yeah, that's what your wife's sister said."

"Oh, is that right?" David stared at the detective. "She needs to mind her own business."

"Hmm," Johnson looked up at him. "She also said that your wife would never go anywhere without her cat. Said she took it with her this weekend."

"No, she must have been mistaken. The cat ran away a month or so back. Julia was devastated when it happened."

Detective Lucas glanced at the calendar again.

"Uh, I guess she forgot to call the vet to cancel the appointment then. Or she forgot to cross it off the calendar."

"Of course," Detective Johnson said. "That explains it. I'm all the time forgettin' to change things on my calendar. Sometimes I don't know if I'm comin' or goin'."

David nodded. "If that's all, officers, I need to get to work this morning." He walked to the door and opened it.

"We'll be in touch."

David watched the detectives until they got in their car.

Detective Johnson stared back at the house, then down at her notes. She frowned.

Lucas grinned. "What's wrong? I know that look. There's something off, isn't there?"

"Yep," she agreed. "He sure was nervous. Had a whole lot of wrong answers, too."

Lucas nodded. "That he did."

Johnson twisted her mouth around. "The sister says Julia took the cat with her this weekend. She said she'd never leave the house for the whole weekend without that cat. And she never, ever lets it outside."

Lucas nodded. "Right. And we found two human bodies, deceased, but didn't find the cat. We found a canvas bag of cat food in the car and one empty can inside. But there was no cat—not at the cabin and not at the house."

"Which makes me wonder, where is the cat?" Detective Johnson asked. "I really want to know where that cat is!"

"So do I, pardner," Lucas agreed. "Let's go talk to the sister again. See if she knows anything else."

David had just sat down to eat a bite of breakfast when the doorbell rang again. He'd barely had time to dress and get coffee. He cursed, slammed up from the table and jerked the front door open.

Detectives Lucas and Johnson stood side by side on his front porch. A late model dark sedan sat in his driveway.

"Mind if we come in, Mr. Morgan?"

"Again? Weren't you just here an hour ago?"

"That we were," Lucas admitted. "We needed to exchange cars with a buddy. Check with your wife's sister again. Little bits of business like that."

Detective Johnson nodded. "Mr. Morgan, we have some news. We found your wife's car. It was up at your cabin. We'd better come in."

"All right! Come in. But make it snappy; I'm late for work as it is. So, you came back over here to tell me that you found her car?"

"Actually, we found more than that. We found your wife's car at your cabin. And we also found two deceased bodies there. We're sorry to tell you this, but one of them appears to be your wife."

David reeled backwards and fell down into a chair. "What?"

"Two bodies were found at your cabin. They seem to have died from inhalation of gas fumes."

"Gas fumes?"

Lucas nodded. "Yes, the gas valve on the fireplace was on."

David stared. "No. There's no way that could happen. Unless…"

"Where were you late Friday night?" Detective Lucas asked.

"I was at my office, working. My assistant can vouch for me." He let out a breath. "Did you ever talk to her? Just give her a call. Belinda Cooper. She's probably at the office already."

"We tried there; she didn't come in to work today. I'm sure we'll catch up with her eventually."

"There's still something that bothers me," Detective Johnson said. "Your wife's sister told us that Julia never goes anywhere without her cat, Jasmine. She claimed she took the cat with her. But we didn't find the cat at the cabin."

Lucas nodded. "Right. No sign of a cat anywhere there." He stared at David. "Well," he continued, "except for the cans of cat food in your wife's car."

"What?" David asked.

"She had some supplies in a canvas bag stowed in the back of her car. They were in a bag with a novel that she was reading."

"I told you that Jasmine went missing over a month ago."

Detective Lucas frowned. "We don't think so. We're figuring that she *must* have taken the cat with her. Why would she take food for a missing cat on a weekend rendezvous?"

Johnson added, "Not to mention the novel that she checked out of the library just two days ago in the same bag? You ask me, that's a strange thing to do if you don't have a cat with you."

"I don't know! What difference does a damned cat and a library book make?"

"Oh, I think it makes a lot of difference. Your wife's sister also told us about your wife's suspicions, about your late nights at the office with your blonde girlfriend and the affair that you two have been conducting."

"That's absurd!" David sputtered. "She doesn't know what she's talking about."

Detective Johnson looked up. "What was that?"

A cat yowled from the back porch. Then they heard keys rattling in the back door lock. Someone opened the door and called out. "Honey? Are you here? I saw the strange car in the driveway. Is the maid here on Mondays?" Belinda walked into the kitchen then froze when she saw Detective Johnson standing in the hallway. She quickly pulled the door closed behind her.

"Belinda!" David said. "Uh, I didn't expect you today."

"And who's this?" Detective Lucas asked.

Belinda stared at David then stepped forward. "Belinda Cooper. I'm Mr. Morgan's assistant."

"We've been trying to get in touch with you, Ms. Cooper."

"Oh, really?" She glanced at David but he wouldn't meet her eyes. "I've been… under the weather and haven't been answering my phone. I'm sorry. How can I help you?"

"Do you frequently use the door key to let yourself in here?"

She threw a glance at David then shrugged. "Sometimes I need to pick things up here, deliver paperwork, etc."

"I see," Detective Lucas said, making a note. "Awfully efficient of you."

Belinda scowled.

"Nice sweater," Detective Johnson said. "I do love me some cashmere. The black becomes you. Looks great with your blonde hair, too."

Belinda looked nervous. "Uh, thank you."

Detective Johnson's eyebrows went up. "But you know, it's a bitch to keep clean. Every little thing sticks to it. Dust, human hair, dandruff—and cat hair especially."

Belinda gulped. "That is true."

"You know, I got a white cat," Detective Johnson continued. "And I can't wear *anything* black. I would dearly love to, but I don't. It's just too much trouble to keep clean. What with a white cat around and all. It's hard enough keeping my work clothes clean."

David shot a glance at Belinda. Her black sweater was covered with white cat hair.

Suddenly, they heard an ear-piercing yowl from outside the door. Detective Johnson walked over and opened it. Jasmine sat in her carrier, howling at the top of her lungs.

"And who would this be?" the detective asked, staring at Belinda.

Belinda Cooper sighed. "Meet Jasmine. Julia Morgan's cat." Belinda blew out a breath then reached down and opened the door to the carrier. Jasmine sauntered out, stared at the detectives and then swirled around their legs.

"What a sweetie!" Johnson said. "But ugh, she sheds, doesn't she?"

"Cat's outta the bag with this case, I'm thinkin'," Detective Johnson said.

"Partner, when you're right; you're right."

He watched as David Morgan and Belinda Cooper were handcuffed and loaded into another car and driven away by two uniformed officers.

"Looks like we caught us another murderer this week."

"That we did."

"Although it seemed like child's play," Johnson admitted.

"How's that?"

She shrugged. "Way too easy. When Belinda Cooper started talking, that gal just could not shut up."

Lucas nodded. "She's a talker, that one."

"So, what do we do about the cat?" Lucas turned around and looked at Jasmine. She sat quietly in the carrier, purring, seeming to enjoy the conversation.

Detective Johnson picked at the white fuzz on her dark trousers. "I always have room for one more at my place, I'm thinkin'."

Her partner smirked. "You and your cats."

"So what? I like cats. But *Jasmine*? What a frou-frou name. Much too floral. I think I'll call her Lacey instead. She looks like a Lacey to me."

Lucas snorted. "Lacey? Tell me that's not frou-frou."

She stared at Jasmine. "Not *that* kind of Lacey. Like the cop Lacey. You know, on TV. OK, then. How about Cagney?"

He smiled. "Now you're talkin', pardner. That's a great name for a cop's cat. You can name the next one Lacey. How about that? Ready to roll?"

She nodded. "Yep. Head 'em up, move 'em out."

Alone in a foreign land, an immigrant bears the loneliness that accompanied him on his journey. But Kamal learns that there is something worse than being alone – being found by someone from his past.

Rosemary McCracken lives in Toronto and writes the Pat Tierney mysteries, the first of which, Safe Harbor, was a finalist for Britain's Debut Dagger. Jack Batten, The Toronto Star's crime fiction reviewer, calls Pat "a hugely attractive sleuth figure."

This story was previously published in 2003, in Mother Margaret and the Rhinoceros Café from Kaleidoscope Books.

Crazy

By Rosemary McCracken

"Kamal!"

Not him. Kamal cursed silently and spilled a pile of salt on the sidewalk of the shopping plaza. Tightening his grip on the bag, he kept his eyes on the salt crystals as he spread them in arcs over the ice-covered pavement.

"How you been, Kamal? Long time since I see you."

Kamal looked up. Pawel had a big, goofy grin on his face. *The same grin that he always had.*

"Okay," Kamal muttered, wishing that he could disappear. He thought he had shaken Pawel when he'd left the garden center in September. What was he doing in this part of Toronto?

"Me, I move to this neighborhood one month ago. Job not far away. Girlfriend and me, we rent nice apartment. Just other side of 401 highway."

215

Terrific. He would be bumping into Pawel all the time.

"Hey, we go for drink, Kamal. Past nine now. You must finish soon. We have drink and talk about old times, eh?"

"Late. Must get home."

"Come on, Kamal. We have drink, just small one."

As he locked up the maintenance room behind Centennial Bakery, Kamal considered heading for home through the streets behind the plaza. But Pawel knew where he worked. It would be better to have a coffee with him, get away as soon as he could and, hopefully, that would be the end of it.

Pawel was waiting in front of the plaza and led Kamal across the street. They entered a doorway under a yellow sign with the words, Restaurant Bar, in black letters. Inside, the air was warm and smoky, and stank of grease. Kamal blinked. He stood in a small vestibule connecting two rooms. The room to his right was filled with tables with blue-checked cloths; about half the tables were occupied. Pawel took the left doorway into a dimly lit room. A woman's voice poured out of speakers set high on a side wall. A sad, caressing voice accompanied by a tinkle of piano keys. She was singing something about being crazy.

Pawel pulled a chair out from a corner table. "Sit, Kamal. We have drink."

Kamal sat down, keeping on his padded jacket. He looked around the room nervously.

"Some place, eh?" Pawel leaned back in his chair. "Come here last Saturday with Jola."

"Jola?"

"Girlfriend. Live music here on Saturday night."

Kamal shrugged.

A waitress appeared at their table. She wore a short, red skirt and a black sweater. Kamal took a quick look at the cleavage displayed by the low neckline. "What're you guys havin'?" she asked, flicking back her mane of chestnut hair.

"Golden," Pawel said. "That okay, Kamal?"

Kamal had no idea what Golden was. "I not…"

"My treat, Kamal. I buy you drink."

"Two Molson Goldens coming right up," the waitress said.

Kamal turned to her. "That song," he said, taking another look at her white breasts and neck. "What is that song?"

"On the jukebox? That's an oldie. Patsy Cline singing *Crazy*."

Kamal wondered if he should know who Patsy Cline was. There was still so much he had to learn about America.

"So, how you been, Kamal?" Pawel asked when the waitress had gone.

Kamal tensed and remained silent. *What was he doing in this smoky room with this guy who asks so many questions?* He didn't trust anyone who asked a lot of questions. Back in Iraq, Saddam Hussein's men were always asking questions.

"You leave Country Gardens awful sudden," Pawel said. "One day, you there no more. Last day I see you was day you cut your hand."

"I get new job."

"Ahhh. At shopping plaza."

Two glass mugs arrived at the table. Golden meant beer, Kamal realized, looking at the glass of liquid in front of him. The color was beautiful, a golden amber. He suddenly felt thirsty. He wanted to pick up the mug and pour the liquid down his throat. *Don't be stupid, Kamal. The Quran forbids alcohol.* If he picked up this mug it would be the first step into sin. The Crazy Lady's voice filled the room again. *What is she singing? Something about feeling lonely.*

Pawel poured half the contents of his mug down his throat and wiped his mouth with the back of his hand.

"You like your new job, Kamal? You big boss at shopping plaza?" Pawel grinned. "I bet you make lots of money there."

"Part-time job only." Kamal's friend, Saad, had found him work at the plaza when the garden center laid off its summer help. But he was still living in the shadows.

"Where you live, Kamal?"

He wasn't going to tell Pawel that the apartment he shared with Saad was less than a mile away. "Other side of city," he said. "Near airport."

"Mario say you go to Dr. Edno when you cut your hand."

"So? I cut hand pruning roses. I get stitches."

"Dr. Edno, he fix up workers with no papers. He take cash and he keep his mouth shut."

"Maybe. I not know." Kamal could feel Pawel's pale green eyes boring into him. He kept his own eyes on the mug on the table.

"Country Gardens give job to workers with no papers. Pay them cash."

"Yeah?" Kamal licked his dry lips. The beer looked inviting. He could almost feel the golden liquid sliding down his throat, filling him with sunshine.

"If government find out, Country Gardens' owners must pay big fine. Workers in even more trouble. Have to go back to their country. Me, I not have that problem. I got contacts, good contacts. Immigration not bother me."

Kamal reached out and wrapped his hand around the mug. The glass was cold but he could feel the golden sunshine seeping into his hand. Sunshine that burned like ice.

Pawel drained his mug and laughed. "Drink up, Kamal. What the matter with you? I already finish." He waved at the waitress. "Where you from, Kamal? I forget."

"Iraq." Kamal remembered Pawel telling him that he came from Poland.

"Iraq. Saddam Hussein, that maniac, running Iraq. I think you not want go back there. Americans gonna bomb hell outta Iraq."

The summer before, Kamal had been visiting Saad in Toronto when Saddam invaded Kuwait. "You cannot get on that plane," Saad told him the night before his return flight. "You spoke out against Saddam. Now he is making his big push, and he will crush dissenters like ants under his feet."

Kamal did not show up for his flight the next day. Now it was January and the United States was demanding that Saddam pull out of Kuwait. Pawel was right. He could not go back.

He took the mug by its handle and raised it to his lips. His nostrils twitched. The beer had a strong, yeasty smell. He parted his lips and poured liquid into his mouth. It tasted bitter. He gulped down several mouthfuls and set the mug back on the table. His stomach churned. He sat up straight, willing his guts to hold still. He felt warmth rise from his belly and sweat break out on his neck and face. He had tasted the forbidden.

The Crazy Lady, Patsy Somebody, started to sing again. Her voice wrapped itself around his mind.

The waitress arrived with two more mugs. Pawel held one up, as if to make a toast.

Kamal picked up his mug again. But his hand was shaking so much that beer spilled onto the tabletop.

"Hey, what you doing, Kamal, wasting good beer?" Pawel cried.

Kamal pulled his wallet out of his jacket pocket. "How much this Golden?"

"My treat, Kamal. I buy you drink."

Kamal placed a five-dollar bill on the table. "Gotta go."

"Kamal, listen—"

"Getting late." Kamal darted to the door and tripped on the mat at the entrance.

Outside, he broke into a run. He ran two blocks, then turned in behind a convenience store and rested his forehead against the cold brick wall. He cursed himself. He had done the forbidden. He had lost control and succumbed to temptation. He had polluted his body and his soul.

And he had Pawel to worry about.

"Kamal, we meet again. Two times in one week."

For the past three days, Kamal had been looking for another job. A job where Pawel would not find him. He had scanned the ads in the *Toronto Star*, but he knew that these jobs were not for illegals. Saad had told him that he would ask around but, so far, he had not come up with anything.

He wanted to ignore Pawel. Finish up his work and head back to the apartment.

"A drink tonight, Kamal? I have time for one drink with you. You almost finish here, I think."

What if he refused? But the fear of being deported sent Kamal's mind racing. Pawel suspected he was working illegally. He could go to the authorities and tell them where to find him. Kamal would be on the next plane to Iraq.

The bar was crowded that evening. The tables were filled with men and women unwinding after a week of work.

"Friday night, lots of people," Pawel said as they squeezed into chairs at an empty table near the back door.

Friday. Kamal should have been at the mosque but he had completely forgotten. *He'd fallen that low.*

"Hi, guys," the red-skirted waitress sang out. "What'll it be tonight?"

"Molson Canadian." Pawel winked at Kamal. "Canadian like you, eh, Kamal?" "Golden," Kamal said.

"So, Kamal, you got yourself sorted out?" Pawel asked when the beer arrived.

The back of Kamal's neck tingled. "What you mean?"

"You have no papers when you work at Country Gardens."

"Why you say that?"

"Worker who go to Dr. Edno have no papers. Everybody know that. You have no papers then and I think that you have no papers now."

Kamal took a sip of his Golden, then downed half the liquid in the glass.

"You know what they do to people they catch working with no papers. I think you not want to go back to Iraq. But listen, Kamal." Pawel gripped his arm. "Jola got cousin who help friends. You understand?"

Kamal felt warmth rising from his stomach. Suddenly, he felt very warm all over and he considered removing his jacket. *No, he would leave soon.* He tried to think of something to convince Pawel that he wasn't an illegal, but with the laughter and music around him, and the beer sending waves of heat through his body, his brain was not working properly.

"You think 'bout what I say, Kamal."

What is he talking about?

"Bit expensive but worth it. No more need to hide." Pawel glanced at his wrist watch. "How 'bout I meet you here on Monday, Kamal? Same time. I bring Jola's cousin with me. He make you deal you can't refuse."

Kamal's brain cleared. So that was it; Pawel wanted money. He wanted Kamal to pay him to keep quiet. But if he gave Pawel money, he would be admitting he was an illegal. He would never be free of him.

Pawel rose, clapped him on the shoulder and threw a ten-dollar bill and a loonie on the table.

"My treat, Kamal. I see you here Monday night. What time you finish work? Nine? I meet you here nine o'clock."

Fear clutched Kamal's belly. This cousin of Jola's was from Immigration. He was paying Pawel to turn him in.

Pawel went out the back door, and Kamal dashed after him.

Outside, he found himself in a narrow alley behind the building. He reached into his jacket pocket and took out his Swiss Army knife. He opened the knife and held it behind his back. "Pawel!" he called. "Wait."

Pawel turned. "What the matter, Kamal? You not look so hot. Go home."

"This deal you talk about…"

"I forget. I have something for you." Pawel took his wallet out of his jacket pocket and searched through it. "Jola write list for you. Monday, you bring everything on list."

Kamal stepped behind him. He held his breath and summoned all his strength. With his left arm, he reached under Pawel's chin and pulled his head backwards. With his right hand, he plunged the knife deep into the side of Pawel's neck. Pawel lurched forward, making a gasping sound. Kamal raised his hands over his head into a fist and brought it down as hard as he could on the back of Pawel's head. Pawel crumpled on the pavement in front of him.

Kamal looked around. The alley was deserted. He pulled the knife from Pawel's neck and wiped it with a tissue. His jacket was covered with blood. He touched his face; it felt sticky.

A window in the bar opened and Kamal stepped into the shadows. He waited several minutes, but nobody came out of the building. Inside, the Crazy Lady started to sing.

How long before the police arrive? How long before the waitress tells them that Pawel was not alone?

Pawel's wallet! If his wallet is missing, it could be a long time before the police identify his body.

Kamal found the wallet on the pavement and picked it up.

He crept along the side of the building and ran across the street. If he kept to the back streets, away from heavy traffic, he would reach the apartment building about 15 minutes. He would throw his jacket into the dumpster and wash up in the laundry room in the basement. Tomorrow, he would leave Toronto. He would head for somewhere far away. Calgary, maybe.

He paused to catch his breath, leaning against a cold brick wall. He remembered the wallet in his hand and opened it.

Not much cash, thirty dollars. A folded paper slipped from between the bills and fell to the ground. Kamal scooped it up and opened it.

Recent color photo, two inches by two inches.

Place of birth

Date of birth

Color of eyes

So Jola's cousin could make papers for him!

A tear ran down Kamal's cheek and he squeezed his eyes shut. He slumped against the wall and dropped the paper.

He wept while the Crazy Lady sang in his head.

The author tells us that our next story began with a writing prompt: a man wakes up in a alley. What resulted was tight, tasty tale of noir.

Jan Christensen has published over seventy short stories, most of them crime fiction. Her stories about Artie, a burglar with a weakness for beautiful women with peculiar problems, are featured in Artie Crimes, available from Untreed Reads Almost as an afterthought, she mentions she has had nine novels published, as well.

Family and Friends

by Jan Christensen

Alex had been so busy throwing up at the other end of the alley, he didn't learn about the murder until the next morning when the cops rousted him.

One kicked him, and the other hauled him up by the scruff of his neck.

"Wha?" he asked, shaking off the one holding his neck. "Whadda you want?"

"You here all night?" asked the pretty one. Alex had always thought of this cop as pretty. He had curly dark hair, bright blue eyes, and a tiny mouth. Kind of short for a cop, Alex thought, but he made up for it by acting tough. Thus the kick. Alex rubbed his hip, and glared at Officer Pretty, then looked at Officer Henry who, although tough, seemed to have some humanity which went beyond what most people thought cops had.

"Guess so," Alex answered, rubbing his eyes now. "Where am I? You got anything to drink?" He made his voice sound hopeful, although the idea of booze made his head hurt and his stomach twist.

Officer Pretty shook his head. "Don't be stupid. You hear anything, see anything?"

"Like what? All I see is the dumpster and you two clowns." He squinted toward the other end of the alley and saw some commotion down there. "What's going on?" His head cleared, but his stomach lurched more than ever. He doubled over and retched, making both officers jump out of his way. Wouldn't want to get their shiny shoes all messed up, he realized dimly. What was wrong with him? He must have eaten something rotten last night.

"A girl was killed in this alley," Officer Pretty said. "What do you know about that?"

Alex stood up straight and willed his stomach to behave. "What girl?" he asked, and began to tremble.

"ID says she's Jane McGregor," Officer Henry said.

"Jen?" Alex whispered, and his knees buckled so that he sat down hard. The air whooshed out of him, and he retched again, dry heaves. Tears sprang to his eyes. "Jen," he moaned.

"You knew her?" Officer Henry said sharply.

Alex looked up at the two cops, hating them. They were supposed to serve and protect. Why hadn't they protected Jen?

"No," Alex said. "Never heard of her." He stood up carefully, holding onto the brick wall, glaring at the police.

Officer Pretty actually took a step backwards. "What's wrong with you?" he asked.

"I'm sick," Alex said. "Rather obvious if you look at the clues."

"Hung over, or still drunk, you mean." Officer Pretty sneered, but he kept his distance.

"Sick," Alex whispered. *Sick and couldn't keep watch.* Oh, Jen.

"I think you'd better come down to the station with us," Officer Henry said. He looked thoughtful, and Alex realized he should pull himself together. Fast. But Jen was dead. How could he pull himself together?

They put him in a room with a table and four chairs, everything plastic, scratched and ugly.

He rubbed his face, feeling his rough beard. He needed a shave, a shower, a meal, and something cold to drink.

They brought him hot coffee. He glared at it and them. They sat, Officer Pretty facing him, Officer Henry to Pretty's left.

"Take us, step by step, through your evening," Henry demanded.

"Last night?"

They both nodded.

"I did my usual rounds. You can ask. Ended up at Louie's, had one of his fried shrimp plates. Felt sick after I ate it, and went out into the alley to have a cigarette and try to calm my stomach down. You got a cigarette?"

They both shook their heads.

"What kind of cops are you?" he asked, not expecting an answer. "I didn't do anything else last night. Never saw the girl. Didn't hear anything. Must have passed out."

His stomach rumbled. He still felt queasy, but hungry, as well.

Henry said, "Never saw you passed out in an alley before." They'd questioned him on the street several times since he'd come to town about six months ago, but they'd never taken him to the station before. He made sure he always stunk of booze, wobbled when he walked, and slurred his words.

Alex gave Henry a look. "Not my usual style," he said with as much dignity as he could muster.

Officer Pretty sniggered. "You don't have any style. You know more than you're telling. I want to know what it is." He pounded his fist on the table.

Alex waved his hand at him, knocking over the coffee which splashed across the table toward the cops. Pretty jumped up. Henry, off to the side enough to avoid the flood, gave Alex an appraising look.

"Come on, Alex," he said. "Whatever it is, we're gonna find out soon enough."

Office Pretty slammed out of the room and returned with some paper towels. "Let's just lock him up for public drunkenness and talk to him later when he's sober."

A knock on the door interrupted them, and Henry answered it. He held a muffled conversation with someone, then came back in, looking peeved.

"Your lawyer has arrived. He wants to talk to you before you say anything more to us."

Alex felt as surprised as the two cops. He shrugged, trying to look nonchalant. As if his lawyer always showed up in the nick of time.

Marcus stood in the doorway, filling it with his bulk. Alex couldn't help the shock that ripped through him, so he was glad the coppers were looking at Marcus instead of him.

"Gentlemen," Marcus said, his voice the same as Alex remembered—smooth as one-hundred-year-old Scotch. His beefy hand held a tooled leather briefcase, and Alex could smell his expensive aftershave from where he sat. Marcus stepped into the room, filling it, it seemed, to capacity. The two cops sidled out, closing the door.

Marcus hefted his briefcase onto the table and sat down, his legs spread wide, his face a mask. His gray suit was impeccably tailored to his frame, and Alex noticed the silk tie had tiny Porsches all over it, all different colors.

"How you doing?" Marcus asked and pulled out a pack of some kind of foreign cigarettes Alex had never seen before. Holding them out, Marcus studied Alex while he took one. The gold lighter seemed to appear like magic in Marcus's hand, he quickly lit both cigarettes, and then took a long pull on his own.

Smooth as ever, Alex thought. "I've been better," he said. "You haven't changed."

Marcus studied Alex a moment. "You have. You sick? Or have you been playing your part as the town drunk too well?"

Alex sat up straighter. "What do you know about it?" His tone was sharp.

Marcus sighed. "You may have given up on me, my friend, but I never gave up on you."

Alex didn't know whether to laugh or to cry. He remembered the times he'd felt a presence, someone following him and had dismissed it as paranoia. He should have known. "You've been watching. All along. Then why couldn't you save Jen? Why? Or were you the one who killed her?" Tears came, and he brushed them away angrily.

Marcus looked away. "I would never hurt a hair on her head. I tried to prevent it. I really, really tried. They were determined, Alex. They had the advantage of picking the time and the place. And your getting sick last night was a distraction."

The tears stopped as quickly as they'd come. "What do you mean?"

Marcus turned his gaze back to Alex and studied him a moment. "My man got so busy wondering if he should do something about you, he took his eyes away from Jennifer. Just for a moment. Which, of course, was all they needed. I loved her, too, you know."

Alex knew that. He'd always known that.

"We have to decide what to do next," Marcus said. "I need to know, honestly, Alex, whether you were drunk last night. Whether you've actually been drunk when my men have thought you were only acting."

Shaking his head, Alex stubbed out his cigarette. "It must have been the shrimp last night. I should know better than to eat at Louie's place, but I was hungry."

"You've eaten there before. No problem."

Alex stared at him. "Poisoned? I guess anything's possible." He felt sick again, and tired. So tired.

"All right. I believe you. Now we've got to get you out of here. We have work to do." Marcus stood up, grabbed his briefcase and strode to the door, opening it wide. "My client has nothing more to say to you," he said as he closed the door behind him. "Therefore you can release …"

Alex put his head in his hands and concentrated on not crying, not thinking about Jen, not thinking at all until he was out of here. He knew Marcus already had a plan.

The limo idled near the front entrance when Alex finally walked out of the police station. He made himself saunter to it calmly, leaving the chauffeur time to get out and open the door. He slipped into its cool interior, which smelled of leather, gin and fine cigars, almost masking his own body odor.

Marcus gave the driver no instructions, and Alex didn't care much where they were going. Depression settled inside of him. He knew he wanted revenge, but after that? After that, it wouldn't matter what happened to him.

Jen had been the bright, shining light of his childhood. Three years older than he, she'd tried to protect him from their father's drunken rages and their mother's sometimes savage beatings. Both parents left Jen alone. She was golden, and they seemed almost afraid of her. People like them didn't have beautiful children like Jen. But Alex was ordinary enough, and all their rage against life they took out on him. If Jen was around, she stood between Alex and whichever parent was harassing him.

Of course he adored her.

When she turned eighteen, she had one boyfriend after another. Alex and Marcus, his best friend, didn't pay too much attention. They simply did what most fifteen-year-old boys did—as little schoolwork as possible, as much stuff as they could get away with without the law coming down on them, and a lot of panting after one girl one week, and another the next.

Later their world came crashing down.

The limo pulled up in front of the largest apartment complex in the small town of Madison. The driver opened the door, and Marcus led the way inside. They took an elevator to the sixth floor, then entered an apartment with a small foyer which led into a huge living room. The far wall was all glass. On the right was a large fireplace, and opposite that a portable bar. The room was furnished entirely in black and white. Even the carpet was black with white swirls. White sofa and chairs, black-legged glass tables, and black, Oriental side pieces.

"Took two apartments and knocked out some walls," Marcus explained. "Wasn't going to buy a house in this Podunk town."

"Of course not," Alex murmured.

"I expect you want a shower more than anything." Marcus led the way down a long hallway to a bathroom with a sunken tub and a shower large enough to hold a dance. Black and white towels fluffed from all the racks, and Alex counted four kinds of soaps, three types of shampoo, and several different types of razors and shaving creams. A large terrycloth robe hung on a hook on the door.

"Help yourself. I've sent Raul for some clothes from your place."

"How will he get in?" Alex asked without thinking.

Marcus just looked at him, shook his head, and left the bathroom.

He tried not to think as he luxuriated in the shower. But Jen was never far away in his thoughts, and since he'd been keeping watch over her for the past six months, he couldn't stop himself now. He tried to remember the good times.

Those hadn't started until he graduated from high school and moved out of his parents' house. By then, Jen was working as a secretary in the city, and Alex moved there to be near her. He'd even found an apartment in the building where she lived. It helped that Marcus's father hired Alex as a salesman in one of his few legitimate businesses—dry walling. Marcus had gone on to college, and they saw each other infrequently for the next few years. Alex became a good salesman and could save some money while still having a good time. He talked to Jen every day, either in person or on the phone.

Their parents died, their mother first—Alex always thought she died of meanness—and their father next. Jen and Alex went dutifully to the funerals, but regret for what might have been far outweighed grief. They were surprised when they learned their father had insurance and they received a few thousand dollars each.

After Marcus finished law school, he went to work for his father also. Alex never knew exactly what he did every day, but he knew it wasn't legal, and sometimes he worried about his friend.

When Marcus and Jen met again after several years, Alex could feel the electricity between them. Marcus now dressed and acted like a man of substance. He was confident, almost arrogant.

Alex couldn't sort out his feelings about Jen and Marcus as they began dating. He loved them both. He worried about Marcus getting into trouble because of the life he'd chosen, but Alex figured Marcus could take care of himself. But he began to worry about Jen being pulled into that life. When she met Marcus's father, Antonio, she told Alex how charming he was. Alex had known Antonio almost all his life, and he had to think a bit about how meeting him for the first time would be, especially for a young woman. Antonio had always seemed interested in Alex, asking him questions about school and sports, encouraging Marcus to have Alex over for dinner and to swim in their pool. Alex guessed Antonio had a dark side, but he never saw it. He could only like and admire the man.

When the words "marriage" and "Marcus" were first uttered in the same sentence by Jen one evening during a quiet dinner with only the two of them at her place, Alex knew with sudden clarity that he felt violently opposed. He stood up so quickly, his legs banged into the table, making the wine glasses overturn.

"You can't! You know what he is!"

Jen's beautiful eyes widened with surprise. "He's your best friend!" She set the wine glasses upright and stared at her brother while mopping up the dregs with her napkin.

"That's different. You're my sister. I forbid it!"

Jen gave him a long look. At least she didn't laugh. "I didn't think you'd object—"

"Not object! Who wants his sister to marry a gangster?"

"But we don't think of Marcus that way."

"That's what he is, though." Alex began to pace the small dining room. "And you're all I have." His voice sounded strangled, and a sob escaped his lips. He sank back into the chair. "Promise me you'll wait. Don't rush into this. Give it a year, at least, maybe two. See if you still feel the same. See if Marcus still feels the same."

Jen frowned. "He loves me. I love him. That will never change, Alex." She stood up to clear the table.

He grabbed her hand. "Promise me. At least a year."

"If it means so much to you, I promise."

Oh, Jen, Alex thought as he stepped out of the shower and toweled off. He slipped into the robe and walked back to the living room. Marcus was on the phone, his face red with anger and his voice raised to a shout.

Then he lowered it, sounding ominous. "I know you ordered it, old man. And I'll never forgive you. Never." He slammed the phone closed, saw Alex standing there, and attempted a smile. He couldn't make it, though.

"Have a nice shower?"

"Wonderful," Alex said and plopped himself down on a sofa. "What happens next?" He realized he didn't care.

"We find you another job, in another city. Far away from here. And I find the scumbags who… who hurt Jen. They're walking dead men right now."

"Your father's not going to like that."

Marcus sat down opposite Alex and frowned. "He's a walking dead man, himself."

Alex gasped. "Marcus. You can't. You know what will happen to you."

"What does it matter? I'd just as soon be dead myself."

Alex had no answer for that. He felt the same way.

A knock on the door. Marcus stood up to answer it. As he opened it, it seemed as if a dozen cops came barging in. One wrestled Marcus to the floor and cuffed him. Officer Pretty approached Alex. "You gonna give me any trouble?"

"Not me," Alex said. He allowed the cop to cuff him, and everyone marched to the elevator. Marcus looked furious, but he didn't say a word.

They were put into separate cars and then separate interview rooms.

"You knew Ms. McGregor, real name Jennifer Mastern pretty well after all," Officer Henry said to Alex after they were all settled into chairs once again.

An overwhelming feeling of grief shook Alex from head to foot. He bowed his head, not wanting to look at the implacable faces of the two cops.

"She was your sister," Officer Pretty spat out.

Alex looked up at last. "How did you find out?"

Officer Henry shifted in his chair. "Anonymous tip," he muttered.

"Ah," Alex said, and then nothing more, even though they hammered at him for over an hour. No Marcus to rescue him this time.

But another lawyer showed up. Alex assumed he was one of Antonio's. There was an arraignment, bail was set and paid by the lawyer, and Alex, still wearing the white, fluffy robe and feeling ridiculous, was driven out of town to the city. There they put him in a room in an apartment building, brought him some clothes, food and cigarettes, but no booze, and left him with one goon who sat in the kitchen playing solitaire and listening to Italian opera on the radio, his gun showing from beneath his jacket every time he shifted in his chair.

"What's gonna happen next?" Alex asked, lighting a cigarette. Hunger came and went, and right now it was gone, baby, gone.

The goon gave him a look and dealt another hand.

"A man of few words, huh?" Alex said and blew some smoke in the guy's face. He didn't react. "What's your name?"

"Leon. What do you care?"

"Well, for one thing, it's nicer than thinking of you as 'the goon' all the time."

Again, no reaction. "So, tell me, Leon, you have a girlfriend, a wife, a sister?"

Leon looked at him with more interest. "All the above," he said. "Why?"

"You know what happened to my sister?" Alex asked.

Leon shrugged. "Haven't got a clue." He put the ace of spades above the other cards on the table.

"Your boss killed her!" Alex shouted. He jumped up and grabbed Leon by the collar.

Meaty hands easily tore Alex's away, and a gun suddenly appeared in Leon's right fist.

"Easy. Easy now," Leon said softly. "My orders are to take you out if you cause any trouble."

"Well, why don't you do that? I caused some trouble, didn't I? Go ahead and shoot me. You people have already murdered the only person in my life who was any good. Any good at all."

Alex sank back down into the chair and began to cry. Great, gulping sobs tore out of him. "Do me a favor and shoot," he managed to get out, and then cried even harder. He was aware that Leon had sat back down and put the gun away. Dealt another hand of solitaire.

Finally the crying wore down, and then stopped. Exhausted, Alex stumbled to the living room couch, stretched out, and fell asleep in seconds.

He woke to the smell of bacon frying. Disoriented, he looked around, remembered where he was, and buried his face in his pillow. After a few minutes, he swung his legs to the floor and stood up. His legs were shaky, and he stumbled around until he located the bathroom.

In the kitchen he found Leon making breakfast. Bacon, eggs, english muffins, hot strong coffee, and orange juice. Alex sat down heavily and drank the full mug of coffee Leon handed him. Leon watched him, his face impassive, then turned to put the food on a plate he gave Alex without comment.

"You get any sleep?" Alex asked as he shoved some eggs into his mouth.

"Enough," Leon answered, then sat down with his own meal and began to eat.

"What time is it?"

"Nine or so."

"I don't understand why I'm not dead, too," Alex said. Took a bite of bacon.

"Look," Leon said, "all I know is that for some reason the Boss trusts you not to talk. He mentioned the word 'honorable.' But he wants to give you some time to think. To realize that retaliation would be extremely dangerous. He's worried about Marcus, and he doesn't think it's a good idea right now for the two of you to be together."

"The anonymous tip," Alex said and pushed his plate away. "Very clever."

He drank the orange juice then walked haltingly back to the living room couch and stretched out. More clear-headed than he'd been since he woke up in the alley, he thought about what had happened.

So trite, so predicable—Jen found Marcus with another woman. Alex and Jen walked into their favorite bar and found Marcus and Ivy in a clinch hot enough to singe the tablecloth. They were sitting on the same bench at a booth in the back, and Alex's first thought was how stupid Marcus was being, doing such a thing in the bar where the three of them hung out.

Marcus saw them first and jerked away from Ivy. When Ivy saw Jen, she smirked and languidly rose from the bench, traced a finger across Marcus's lips and left without a word.

"How could you?" Jen asked, her voice strained.

"Jen, let me explain." Marcus tried to get out of the booth, but his bulk was a problem. Alex also noticed the napkin held carefully in front of Marcus's fly when he finally did stand in front of them.

After all, Ivy was beautiful. And sexy. It would take a few minutes to recover from such a kiss.

"She… she practically attacked me," Marcus said. Alex had never seen him plead before, never seen him so discomposed.

"And you fended her off so well," Jen said, her voice dripping sarcasm. She turned with a flourish and walked to the front of the bar, Alex and Marcus following.

Marcus caught up with her and grabbed her elbow, trying to turn her around.

"Take your hands off me." This time she did raise her voice, and people turned to stare.

"Jen, please," Marcus said, but she walked out the door and toward Alex's car without saying another word.

Marcus still followed, but did nothing further as Alex and Jen climbed into the car and drove off. Alex saw him through the rearview mirror, standing in the parking lot, a little-lost-boy look on his face.

Alex didn't try to talk to Jen on the way home. He knew she needed to cool off. At their apartment building, he asked if she wanted to come to his place for a drink.

She nodded, and they said nothing more until they were settled in his living room, both with their favorite drinks.

"He probably told you the truth, Jen. Ivy probably came to the booth, made him scoot over, and then kissed him."

Jen glared at him. "He wasn't pushing her away, was he, when we showed up?"

"Honestly? No. But Jen, you have to understand guys. It's hard to resist when something like that happens. I'm positive it wouldn't have gone any further. He loves you."

"Alex," she said, her voice weary, "I saw the napkin. I can't trust him. You know, I never have, totally. He's too smooth. He likes women too much. He'll get bored with me someday, and I'll end up sitting home alone. It's better this way." Then she began to cry, softly.

She broke off with Marcus the next day, over the telephone. Soon after, accidents began to happen to her. The scariest was when the apartment elevator crashed to the basement. Fortunately, the cable didn't break until it was near the ground floor, so it didn't pick up much momentum.

Jen left in the middle of the night, after that. She didn't even tell Alex where she was going, but he guessed it would be to Madison, a small town downstate. They'd had an aunt there long ago who had been kind to them when they visited for a week once.

He found her there even though she'd changed her name and dyed her hair. But he didn't approach her. He understood she wanted to be alone, or she would have told him where she was going.

He quit his job and lived off his savings. Jen found another job in Madison, and with nothing to do all day, Alex began to haunt the bars. But he never drank at them. He was afraid to, afraid that he'd get drunk and not be able to keep watch. Instead he'd order drinks, take them to the men's room with him and flush them, or spill them on the floor under the bar, or pour some into the guy's glass next to him. It was funny to see the expressions on people's faces when the taste of their drinks changed halfway through, but no one ever said anything.

Jen had always taken care of him. Now it was his turn. He didn't really know if Marcus was responsible for the accidents, but he decided it best to assume so. Either Marcus or his father—what difference did it make which one?

In only two months he began to feel that someone else watched Jen as well, but he could never be sure, and he never recognized anyone he'd ever seen associated with Marcus or Antonio. He debated telling Jen about the others, but what could she do? She could go somewhere else, but they were bound to find her again.

Anguished and torn, Alex had kept watch. And now it was over. He'd been too sick to prevent it, and he wished he'd been with her, and if Jen had to die, he would have gladly died with her.

All that was left was to kill Antonio. A hollow laugh escaped him. Yeah, that was going to happen. He'd probably never see Marcus or Antonio again.

At the thought of Marcus, he groaned. He had nothing left— no sister, no best friend.

The apartment door crashed open, and another of Antonio's goons stood there, gun drawn. He stepped into the room, and Alex sat up straight on the couch and watched as Antonio walked in.

Antonio looked bad—real bad. He needed a shave. His eyes were bloodshot, and his mouth and chin sagged. His gray hair, usually so impeccably combed, stood up in odd places, as if he'd been running his hand through it. His wore a wrinkled blue suit, and there was a spot of dirt on his left shoe.

"Leon?" shouted the goon.

Leon came into the living room as another man in the hired-help team surrounding Antonio closed the door behind them.

Great, Alex thought. *Antonio plus three lunkheads.*

"Alex," Antonio said. He just stood there a moment, looking a bit lost. He ran his hand through his hair and sighed. "Marcus is dead." Then he collapsed into the nearest chair and put his head in his hands.

"What? How?"

Things began to gray around Alex. He clutched at the edges of the couch so he wouldn't topple over. Jen *and* Marcus gone. He had no one left alive now.

Antonio looked up and stared at Alex. "He tried to attack me. Of course, he was taken out."

"Of course," Alex said softly. Then he jumped up and shouted, "You son of a bitch!"

"It's all your fault, you know," Antonio said, ignoring Alex's outburst. "If it hadn't been for his friendship with you, he never would have fallen in love with Jennifer. And he'd still be alive."

"You twisted jerk!" Alex stood rooted to the floor. He knew if he moved toward Antonio he was a dead man. "If you'd left Jen alone after she broke off with Marcus, they'd both be alive."

"I couldn't," Antonio said. "She knew too much. Marcus had a loose mouth while in the sheets."

"She never would have told anyone anything."

Antonio's mouth twisted into a sarcastic grin. "Of course she would have. All it would have taken was some federal agent appealing to her sense of honor, duty, patriotism, whatever, and she would have talked. Wouldn't she?"

"I don't know," Alex said softly. He sank down onto the couch. "I don't know. I suppose you're here to kill me now."

"No. No, I'm sick and tired of killing. I've always trusted you, Alex. In some ways, more than I trusted Marcus. *You* always knew how to keep your mouth shut. I came here to offer you a job. I figure you have nothing to lose now. I figure you might like to make some real money."

"I want you dead!" Alex said. "You'll never be able to trust me."

"If you give me your word you won't attempt to kill me, I'll believe you, Alex."

But Alex saw the truth in Antonio's eyes. He wanted Alex to kill him. He couldn't kill himself—it wouldn't be right. But if after awhile he and Alex were alone someday, and Alex killed Antonio, or they killed each other, neither would have to live with the pain they were now feeling.

Alex didn't want Antonio released from the pain he was feeling. He did want that release for himself though.

It surprised him—how fast he could still move. He'd grabbed Leon's gun and almost fired at Antonio before the other goons reacted and began shooting. As he fell, he saw Leon take a hit in the forehead from the crossfire. No more opera or solitaire for Leon, he thought just as he went down himself. He was glad it was over. Maybe he'd be with Jen again. But if not, anything was better than living without her, without hope. His only wish was for Antonio to live a long, unhappy life.

He relaxed into the carpet and let go. He floated, all tension gone from his body, and then from his life. *Was that Jen, off in the distance?*

We move now to a different kind of alley, a bowling alley. Jack Murphy wants to know who used a bowling trophy to kill Joey, his long-time friend and bowling companion. Jack's no PI – he's a laid off shop mechanic, his investigative credentials are his fists, his nosy nature, and a certain ability to pick locks.

Diane A. Hadac also writes as Philomena Benedetto, and in 2014 under that name won third place in the Arizona Mystery Writers Short Story Contest.

Kegler Killer

by Diane A. Hadac

Siren screaming, the ambulance skidded to a stop somewhere on my street. Its seesaw sound was common in this rundown ethnic neighborhood occupied by scores of old-timers—somebody was always being bundled off to a hospital or a morgue.

Sitting at the kitchen table, morning coffee in hand, I ignored the commotion and concentrated on reading the "Help Wanted" ads. Caught in a layoff on Friday, me and my shop cronies decided to bar-hop our worries away. The weekend had dissolved into one long blur; the only focal point remaining was a hell of a pounding headache.

Later in the day, I learned that I would've recognized the body on the stretcher if I'd been more inquisitive. It was my longtime friend, Joey Hackman. As he slumbered peacefully, somebody beat his brains out with one of the marble and metal bowling trophies displayed in his room on a homemade wall shelf. Ironic—killed with a cherished keepsake.

Working the night shift screws up your social life, so I hadn't seen much of Joey during the last six months.

I learned of the tragedy from the person who'd found his body, Mrs. Scamenti, his next-door neighbor. During the two years since his parents had passed away, the elderly widow had treated Joey, an "only child," like a beloved son.

She flagged me down from her front porch as I was returning from the grocery store. Pale and shaken, tiny hands wringing absently, she related the morning's events in a halting, anguished voice.

Joey hadn't shown up for work today and didn't phone to report his absence. I knew, as did Mrs. Scamenti, that only something serious would keep Joey away from his job without first notifying the proper people.

Human Resources had called his house about ten in the morning, receiving no answer. Next, they called Mrs. Scamenti, Joey's designated contact in an emergency.

Mrs. Scamenti had also tried phoning him without success; then she went to his house and knocked, noticing his car was parked out front. When he didn't respond, she assumed he was ill, and she used the spare key he'd provided for just such a crisis to let herself in.

Because the thief had struck while the occupant was home, the officers responding to her 911 call cataloged the crime as an amateur job. Joey must have turned over in his sleep, startling the crook in mid-search. There was no sign of a struggle; but, in addition to the gash in his skull, Joey's right hand—his bowling mitt—had been mangled. Although the murder weapon wasn't found on the premises, the hole in the trophy lineup spoke for itself. Joey's wallet was empty; a good bet that the culprit was an addict needing drug money.

As she finished her story, Mrs. Scamenti began to sob, wiping wet eyes with the back of her hands. I embraced her in fatherly fashion and escorted her into the house, staying until her composure returned. Then, after phoning a friend on the police force, I headed for the morgue. Since Joey was an orphan with no "next of kin," I was going to shoulder responsibility for his funeral.

Bureaucratic red tape stalled my plans, and the sight of his badly beaten corpse made me promise retribution. I was no PI; my only credentials were my fists, my nosy nature, and a certain ability to pick locks, which came in handy when I misplaced my keys after a night of heavy partying. Momentarily jobless, I'd have enough time to tackle the task.

Joey was twenty-eight, average height; a thin, quiet guy with glasses the thickness of early Coke bottles. He was eight years younger than me, and I thought of him as the little brother I never had. There weren't many kids his age on the block when we were growing up, so he sort of became my "shadow." I bowled in three leagues a week back then and introduced Joey to the game by taking him with me to Saturday morning practice. From the start, he was a natural.

Bowling, or Kegling, the old term that Joey preferred as he matured, became his one big love. All his free time was devoted to the game. He strove to raise his average high enough to qualify for the pro tour. Most of his leisure time during the last few years had been spent caring for his elderly parents, putting his career plans on hold. But that didn't deter him. He felt bowling was one sport in which age was secondary to skill.

I figured the Strike Spot was a good place to begin my private investigation. It was the alley where Joey had bowled on Friday nights with his team, the Three Hundreds; and it was the place where most of the town punks hung out playing video games. I also knew the lane mechanic, Maxie Corgan, who'd be able to give me the lowdown on most of the locals. Maxie understood Joey's desire to become a champion. In his younger days, he'd tried and failed to make the pro circuit.

When I walked in, Maxie's wiry frame was lounging against the counter; he wore a baggy faded-blue uniform with a name patch hanging by a thread above the shirt pocket. I'd lay odds it was the same outfit he wore years ago when I bowled there regularly. Maxie turned his grizzled head to the glass door as its metal edge scraped open and I called out a greeting. A smile rearranged the lines in his thin, usually expressionless face, and he extended a hand.

"Jack Murphy, you old son-of-a-gun! Where you been hiding?"

"Here and there." I grasped his outstretched hand and got right to the point: "Did you hear about Joey Hackman?"

He said no, so I filled him in.

"What's this world coming to?" he said afterwards, shaking his head ruefully. "Joey, of all people—such a nice guy."

"None better. Honest, decent, and a real sportsman."

"You and him go back a long time," Maxie added with gruff compassion.

I nodded. "Let's talk, Max."

We headed for a bar booth. Drinks were gratis because I was with Maxie and leagues weren't rolling yet. I had a 7 and 7 and Maxie had a VO.

"What're you after?" he asked, downing the shot.

"I'm gonna find the bastard that killed Joey."

If Maxie seemed surprised, he didn't show it. He simply waited patiently for me to continue.

"The cops think the murderer's male, probably a junkie. They claim women shy away from committing violent, bloody crimes. Whether or not that's true, I'd like to start my search here. This place was Joey's second home; and characters fitting the cops' profile haunt the joint, too. Any possibilities over there?" I pointed across the bar's plate glass window to the arcade on the opposite side where four guys hunched over a Video Mania machine while a fifth worked the controls.

Maxie focused his gaze on the group. "Maybe. They're punks who hang out here after school and on weekends, smoke pot in their cars at night and throw fast-food wrappers all over the parking lot."

"Joey have run-ins with any of them?"

"You know better than that," Max chided. "Joey got along with everybody. Some of these kids hung around just to study his technique. They'd check the board for his Friday night scores and shoot him a 'high five' when he shot a good series."

"Are you saying they kept tabs on him?"

"Sort of," said Maxie, slowly. "But that don't make them killers. Maybe they thought Joey'd be a celebrity someday, and they should get acquainted early."

Max ordered another VO and I continued to nurse my 7 and 7, dismissing a fleeting thought of him protecting someone.

Drinks in hand, we studied the Video Maniacs in silence.

Finally, he spoke as if to himself, "You know, I almost forgot about that."

"What?"

"See that guy alone there, playing Space Combat?"

I surveyed the direction he indicated and saw a slim six-footer in a silver-studded black leather motorcycle jacket, viciously manipulating the machine's controls. His straight, shoulder-length black hair whipped angrily from side to side with each jolting movement.

"His name's Rick Grover," Max explained, "and we've had some trouble with him—just turned twenty-one—can't hold a job for more than a month—drinks too much and harasses women at the bar. He's been warned that he'll be kicked out of here for good if he keeps it up. A few weeks ago, Grover made some smutty remarks to Monica Johnson, Joey's friend."

"What started it?

"Nothing particular. Grover decided to make a nuisance of himself when Joey went for fresh drinks, but Joey got back in time to catch him in the act. He grabbed Grover by the shirt front and said, 'Leave the lady alone; she didn't come here to be insulted by you.' The punk was too drunk to do anything else, so he started with the foul language, and a couple of guys from Joey's team slid off their stools. George, the bartender, stepped in before fists started flying and told Grover to shut his mouth or get out. The bar got real quiet and everybody held their ground; then Grover spit on the floor and staggered out, cussing all the way."

"Were Monica and Joey more than friends?"

"No. She bowls here on a Friday night ladies' league. Her and Joey liked to discuss the game, that's all."

"Thanks, Maxie. It's a start."

I got up and ambled over to the Space Combat machine, watching the action for a few minutes. When he'd lost the game, I said, "You Rick Grover?"

He replied insolently with a phrase I hadn't heard in years: "What's it to you? You a cop?"

The old blood pressure escalated a notch, but I controlled myself. "All I want is some information. I'm Joey Hackman's friend, and I heard the two of you exchanged hot words a few weeks ago."

He lounged against the machine on one elbow. "So? It ain't none of your business, is it?"

My patience drained away like water on a downhill slope. "I'm making it my business. Joey's dead and he was a friend of mine. I want to know why somebody hated him so much they had to kill him."

"Let the cops figure it out. I don't have to tell you nothin'. Now get outa here. You ruin my concentration."

The bastard booted me in the shin as he turned back to the machine. I cracked him sideways across the face in return; the sharp sound attracting attention.

Grover retaliated with a roundhouse which I easily blocked, knocking him off balance. He fell on his can stunned for a second, causing the Video Maniacs to snicker. I headed for the door before I completely lost my temper and buried his face in the video screen.

"I'll get you for this, you son of a bitch," he yelled after me.

Out of the corner of my eye, I caught Jake, the owner, hotfooting over to check out the commotion. I pointed at Grover and said: "Sore loser."

By now, it was after six. I picked up a burger and fries to eat at home with an Old Style.

Towards eight, I called Frankie Conti, an old tech school buddy of mine, and one of Joey's teammates. I asked him if he'd heard about the murder. He hadn't, and was stunned by the news. Said he'd let the other guys know, and that I should come over and fill him in on the details.

I said I'd be there in twenty minutes.

We sat in his family room, each with a Heineken. I related the whole story with the Bears game muted on TV in the background.

Frankie ran a hand through his curly black hair and said, "I'll be damned. Who would want to hurt Joey, anyway?"

"That's what I want to know. And why would a thief smash his bowling hand?"

I asked Frankie if he knew about any trouble between Joey and some of the kids that hung out at the bowling alley. To avoid interrupting his train of thought, I purposely left out the Grover incident that Maxie told me about.

Frankie scratched the back of his head and considered the question thoughtfully. "No trouble that I know of. Most of the kids, even the tough types, had respect for Joey's talent. He'd throw a couple of lines with those who were interested in improving their game and he'd pick up the tab."

"I hope the freebies didn't give these guys the idea that Joey was in the chips."

Frankie replied slowly, "I suppose it's a possibility."

I downed a slug of beer, then mentioned the Grover altercations, both Joey's and mine; and asked Frankie what he knew about Monica Johnson's relationship with Joey.

Frankie recalled the episode between Grover, Monica and Joey, but attributed it to the fact that Grover couldn't hold his liquor. He also claimed that there was no romance between Monica and Joey. They were just friends who enjoyed sharing a drink once in a while.

"Grover wasn't interested in her, was he?"

"I doubt it. He goes for the flashy type, and that's not Monica."

Frankie got us each another beer and I asked how the team was doing.

"We squeezed into first place last Friday, but we'll drop without Joey."

"I thought you guys were on top from the start?"

"For the last three years, but not this season. Even Joey was averaging only 182 the first few weeks. That would be great for anybody else, but it was at least ten pins under average for Joey."

"What happened?"

"We got into a slump. Jake's son, Andy, joined the league for the first time this year with his own squad—four guys that the NFL would enjoy signing as tackles—all in their early twenties and terrific bowlers. Of course, Andy was always top-notch. It helps when your father owns the bowling alley and you practice free."

"I remember watching Andy bowl in those Saturday morning junior leagues. He definitely had talent."

"And his old man does everything to promote it. Wants him on the pro tour eventually. It would be good publicity for the Strike Spot and papa would enjoy seeing his boy in the limelight. The only problem is I don't think Andy has the temperament.

"Take last week—position night. We were the last group to finish and the game was tight. Andy and his team created a commotion every time our guys were on the approaches—talking too loud, laughing too loud. We asked them to keep it down, but they kept goofing around. Finally, win or lose came down to the anchors, Andy and Joey. Andy threw two strikes and seven in the tenth. Joey had to strike out to get us the game because he was down a few pins from Andy in the ninth. He got the double, then buried the third for a turkey, clinching our first place lead. Andy's team didn't say as much as 'good game' to us. Just packed up their gear and headed for the bar. Our group stayed at the lanes talking till the place was almost empty. Suddenly, somebody yells out, 'Hey, Three Hundreds!' Naturally, we turned to see who's calling, and there's Andy shooting the moon at us through the bar window.

"We were pissed, to say the least, especially after their behavior during the last game. Joey told Jake afterward that if Andy or his team ever again displayed unsportsmanlike conduct during a league game, he'd report them to the American Bowling Congress. An unfavorable ruling on that charge could suspend them indefinitely from competition in any ABC sanctioned league or tournament."

"Joey issued a tough warning, but it sounds like they deserved it."

Frankie nodded agreement. "Jake was angry with Andy—the Strike Spot is an ABC house—and promised to personally reprimand him and his team."

"This all happened last Friday? I was talking to Maxie today, and he didn't mention it."

"He was sick Friday night. The part-time kid filled in."

Frankie and I talked a while longer, then I left for home.

———————

Tuesday morning about ten a.m., the doorbell rang. It was Jerry Kruger, a homicide detective, and sometime drinking buddy of mine.

I asked what brought him by so early in the day. A look of discomfort passed over his usually cheerful, chubby face, and he declined the seat I offered.

"Can't stay long, Jack, so I'll get right to the point. I know you're sore about Joey, but you can't play detective and beat up innocent citizens."

"What're you talking about?"

He explained that Rick Grover went to the station with his parents and complained about the crack I gave him. From what Jerry said, they made it sound a lot worse. Jerry finished with, "You're lucky they're not pressing charges."

"Pressing charges!" I roared. "I was defending myself! Grover kicked me. Want to see my shin? I gave him one slap, no matter what they said. Besides he's twenty-one—legally an adult. I could have done a lot worse."

Jerry raised a restraining hand. "Take it easy! I know all about this guy's reputation, but I still have to warn you to lay off the punks. That's our territory."

I was steaming. "Only if they lay off me. What do you want me to do? Wait 'til you guys haul one of them in so the court can slap him on the wrist and let him go?"

"I don't need this from you, Murphy," he barked. "Joey was my friend, too."

I jammed a fist into my palm. "Yeah, I know. Sorry."

"Forget it," he grunted, then added: "There's something else, Jack. Joey left a will."

"So?"

"He never mentioned it to you?"

"No, why should he?"

"Because you're the beneficiary. The house and insurance are yours."

I was so stunned, I couldn't think of anything to say.

Kruger shifted his weight uncomfortably from one foot to the other and said slowly, "Unfortunately, this throws a whole new light on the situation, Jack. You profited from his death."

"But I didn't know about the will. If I had to guess, I'd say he'd leave everything to a home for retired keglers, if there is such a place."

"I'm sorry, Jack, but you'll have to come downtown and answer some questions."

Kruger was just doing his job, but when I left the station, I felt foul. The cops figured Joey was killed Sunday morning, but they were waiting for the autopsy report. The fact that my co-workers could give me an alibi for the entire weekend made me feel worse. I didn't like having to explain my movements on the night my best friend was murdered. I parked in a forest preserve to think things over. Then I headed for the Strike Spot to talk with Maxie.

By now it was early evening, and the place was packed with leagues in full swing. My old pal was propped against the front counter staring at the floor, a stubby cigarette dangling from his lips.

"Don't you ever work?" I teased as I approached.

His head swung up, a rough grin angling off the corner of his thin mouth. "The part-timer's on tonight. After so many years here, seems like I come back whether I'm working or not."

I clapped him on the back. "Good, or I'd be drinking alone. C'mon, I'm buying."

We took a window booth in the bar with a view of the alleys. Maxie got his usual VO and I ordered my 7 and 7.

"Is that Andy on Sixteen?" I asked, nodding toward the lane.

"Yep. First season he's brought a team here, but he's sure making up for lost time. They shoot Tuesdays, Thursdays and Fridays; cornered first place all three nights until Joey's group jelled last Friday."

"So Frankie Conti mentioned. He told me about another incident involving Andy and his team, too."

Maxie wagged his head in disgust. "Heard about it yesterday after you left. I was off Friday night. Showing his backside like that. Never thought Andy was such a sorehead."

"I wanna talk to him when he's finished bowling."

"You're barking up the wrong tree, Jack. Andy may be spoiled, but he doesn't have to kill for money. Jake gives him all he wants."

"I still wanna talk to him." My stomach rumbled in protest as I drained my 7 and 7, reminding me that I hadn't eaten anything since breakfast. I told Maxie I'd get a bite in the snack shop, and then wait for Andy.

His expression implied I was way off base, but I needed to cover every angle.

———••———

After wolfing down an Italian beef, I stopped at the arcade. Some of yesterday's crowd was there, but Rick Grover wasn't in sight.

One of the Video Maniacs broke away to join me. "Aren't you the guy who nailed Grover yesterday?" he asked eagerly. "Not many people'll tangle with him, but he sure had it coming. We saw the cheap shot he pulled on you." He flicked his foot to mimic a kick, then stuck out a hand saying, "I'm Eddie Darrell. Maxie mentioned you were a friend of Joey Hackman. Sometimes us guys bowled with Joey. We know he didn't have any family, but we wanted to tell his friends that we thought he was cool, and whoever bumped him off oughta fry."

"If I have anything to do with it, they will," I assured grimly.

We maintained a moment of silence, the assorted beeps and whirrs from the video machines issuing a sort of high-tech dirge.

Finally, I said, "Do you know Andy Cermak, Jake's son?"

"Yeah, but not well."

"Were you here when he pulled that 'about face' on Joey's team?"

"No, but I heard about it. Andy thinks because his father owns this place, he's a cut above everybody else. He hates losing, too. Course he's good. He don't lose too often."

One of Darrell's friends signaled him to return, so he cut the conversation and took off.

Andy's team won three games that night, ensuring their first place lead on Tuesday. He was in a cheerful mood when I corralled him in the bar after his dad sounded his 645 series over the loudspeaker.

"Good shooting," I congratulated, taking the stool next to him. He was downing Michelob like soda pop; his team fanned out along the rail in the opposite direction.

"Thanks," he replied, sweat trickling down his florid, beefy face. He mopped his forehead with his beer napkin and peered closer at me.

"I remember you," he said finally. "You're Joey Hackman's friend. Sorry to hear about him. I feel kinda rotten losing my temper with his team like I did a few nights ago. You probably heard about it."

I shrugged. "We all do things we wish we hadn't sometimes. I hear your team's cookin' this season."

"Yeah. It's the first time we're bowling here. Didn't want to be considered a show off just because it's my dad's house. Then I figured, what the hell, if anybody should be here, it should be me and my team. My dad runs a straight place. We don't get no special favors. If we do good, it's because we are good."

No false modesty here, I thought. I was about to ask a few more questions when I spied Maxie threading his way through the crowd. I waved, and Andy turned his attention back to his buddies.

As Maxie wedged in next to me, one of the league bowlers tapped him on the shoulder, complaining drunkenly that the alleys were poorly maintained. He insisted that his team and the opposing team had gotten fast racks and greasy return balls all night; a combination that makes good bowling impossible.

"Yeah, yeah; I'll take care of it," Maxie pacified.

Then he muttered to me: "These guys have a few drinks too many and the first thing they do is blame their bad games on the alleys. The ball triggers the rack when it hits the backboard. It ain't gonna stop pin action by coming down any faster unless somebody stands back there and presses the manual switch. And these alleys are oiled according to ABC specs, so the return balls can't be as greasy as he says. Complaints! The only team that doesn't gripe about the lanes is Andy's and that's because he knows the business. Sometimes I think I should retire!"

I gave him a sympathetic shoulder pat and caught the bartender's eye. We got our old standbys.

Maxie nursed his for a change and said, "Find out anything new?"

"Not much."

We killed some time discussing my job situation, had a few more drinks and then I left.

The lights were out on the side of the lot where I'd parked my car. While fumbling for my keys in the darkness, I was tackled from behind. As I lurched around, a solid right jammed into my jaw, knocking me backwards, but not down.

"I said I'd get even," a voice hissed.

"Grover," I shouted. "Don't be an idiot. I'm a street fighter and I'm not drunk."

"Prove it, gramps," he taunted, swinging wildly.

I flattened him with a left.

"Look, punk," I thundered as he struggled to get up. "Take some lessons before you pick on someone my age and size. And if you really think you're so tough, don't run to mommy, daddy and the cops tomorrow morning."

I don't think he understood much of what I said because he kept shaking his head, trying to recover the few wits he possessed. I massaged my jaw and squelched an urge to clobber him one more time before I left.

Driving home more disgusted than angry, and thinking about the events of the evening, I tried to sort through the information I'd obtained so far. Grover was the revengeful type if I went by tonight's sneak attack. Andy Cermak seemed destined for a successful professional career, but his temper needed shackling or the pressure would ruin him. Eddie Darrell's show of sympathy could be faked; after all, he hung around with a pretty rough crowd.

An idea unraveled from this tangled thread of details. I spent all of Wednesday morning and afternoon rounding up more information, and all of Wednesday night sorting it out.

Although Frankie had insisted that Joey and Monica were just casual friends, I located her phone number and called her anyway, explaining who I was and what I was trying to do. She expressed sympathy over Joey, but could supply no new leads. Her description of the Grover incident matched Frankie's.

On Thursday evening, after one last phone call, I returned to the Strike Spot. When Andy had finished bowling, I asked to speak with him privately for a few minutes. He was sore because his team had lost two games, but he said he'd meet me on alley one after a trip to the locker room. The lane's distance from the counter and bar would offer some privacy. I sat down on the seat closest to the side aisle. Andy appeared about ten minutes later in a fresh shirt with his hair slicked back.

"What's up?" he asked as he approached.

"It's about Joey Hackman."

Annoyance flickered across his face. "I said before that I was sorry to hear about him."

"I know," I replied slowly. "There aren't many guys here that could offer you such strong competition."

"I thrive on competition," he spat out belligerently. "Now what did you want to see me about? I'm in a hurry."

I gave him a long, hard look. "I did some investigating. Seems like your dad's place is the only bowling alley you're welcome at anymore. None of the other houses would tolerate the conduct of you and your team."

"Who the fuck do you think you are, checking up on us?" he shouted, edging closer, fists closed.

I got up and faced him. "When your best friend's murdered, you take action."

"Are you accusing me of killing Joey?"

"You got it, shithead. You killed Joey before he could bring your team before the ABC's Legal Committee. Isn't it funny, when Maxie's not working the machinery, all the alleys except yours operate fast and greasy? You claim to thrive on competition, but you have to ensure an edge. How much of your old man's money are you paying the part-timer to give the other teams trouble?"

Andy didn't waste time with words. He was a big guy, and the punch he threw would have dropped me for sure if I wasn't keeping an eye on his hands while I talked. I ducked, tripped him, and pinned him to the floor in a full nelson.

He started yelping, "Let go of me, you son of a bitch."

The bar crowd filtered out to see what was going on.

I increased the pressure on Andy's arms and out-shouted him: "Showing disrespect for the game was one of the few things that could make Joey mad. He got wise to your gimmick and was determined to turn you into the ABC. Their ruling could bar you from the top-notch tournaments. Joey's sense of sportsmanship jeopardized your chance at a professional career, so you killed him, using the robbery to divert suspicion—but his smashed hand gave you away—"

"You'll never prove it," he screamed.

"That's where you're wrong, punk. I picked the lock on your car's trunk tonight. How come you never bothered to wipe out the dried blood after you dumped Joey's trophy?"

By now, Jerry Kruger, who I'd phoned earlier, and Jake Cermak had pushed to the front of the crowd.

I released Andy and he scrambled to his feet.

"Pa," he pleaded, scurrying to a sad-eyed Jake. "Don't believe any of this."

In official tones, Jerry advised Andy of his rights.

I made arrangements to have Joey buried on Saturday. Frankie and his teammates came to the church. They sent a stand-up cross of blue and white carnations. Maxie, Mrs. Scamenti, Jerry Kruger and Monica Johnson were there, too. Mrs. Scamenti sent a casket spray of deep red roses. Even the Video Maniacs came—wearing suits that made them look like respectable citizens. Later, Maxie and I placed the cross and roses on Joey's grave.

We left something else, too. A new bowling pin. We figured he'd like that.

Hell hath no fury like a woman scorned, and Nick is about to learn the frightful truth of that adage. Author Patricia Dusenbury tells us this story was born of a cross-country road trip, and the time it provided crafting plots of revenger – strictly fictional, of course.

A recovering economist, Ms Dusenbury's newest novel, A House of Her Own, completes an award-winning trilogy. When not devising fiendish felonies, she tends her garden in San Francisco.

Nor Death Will Us Part

by Patricia Dusenbury

Nick had vacillated between Cinzano's, checkered tablecloths and candles in wine bottles, and the more upscale Traviata. He'd decided on Cinzano's because they'd gone there on their first date. Jen liked it when he was sentimental.

The hostess led them to a corner table and placed a single rose on the table. "Happy anniversary."

"But how?" Jen's eyes sparkled.

"I told them when I made the reservations."

The waiter brought their wine, and Nick raised his glass. "To the six months we've had together." He'd considered saying something about the lifetime to come but decided that was premature. He hadn't asked Jen to marry him—not yet.

They ordered the same meals they'd ordered on their first date and stole little tastes from each other's plate. The evening was perfect until a loudmouthed couple sat down at the next table.

"That's three in less than a year," the woman said. "It's a serial killer."

"It's probably her ex-husband. The paper said she was divorced."

"Nope. Serial killer. Every victim was an attractive young woman who lived alone. Serial killers are losers who always go after pretty young women." Her tone became ominous. "One night, she comes home, and he's waiting for her. She doesn't have a chance."

"You've been reading too many trashy novels."

"Says the man who reads nothing but the sports page. Take a look at the front page some day. See what's happening in the world."

Nick glared at them, and they lowered their voices, but the damage had been done.

"It really is a serial killer," Jen whispered. "Whitney is dating a police detective, and that's what he said. He made her get new deadbolts for her doors. She says I ought to get some."

"Okay, I'll call a locksmith. Tomorrow. Tonight you won't be alone."

"No, I won't." She smiled.

"Let's talk about happier things. Like me. I'm the happiest man in the world thanks to you."

"I bet you say that to all the girls. You have a reputation, you know."

"I won't lie, Jen. You're not the first woman in my life, but I promise, you're the last."

They shared a kiss across the table, and the evening was back on track. It stayed there until Nick's phone signaled a message.

"Go ahead," Jen said. "I know you financial types are always on call, and I want to visit the ladies' room."

He watched her thread her way between the tables; the loudmouthed guy was watching too. Nick bet every man in the restaurant envied him. *Eat your hearts out, fellas; she's mine.*

The message was from Bill. "Melissa said to ask about BPP. Said you'd made a killing. Buy???"

Nick deleted the text, but he couldn't get rid of the knot in his stomach. Melissa was a vindictive bitch. She'd just ruined his romantic evening with Jen. If she wanted to, she could ruin his life.

When Jen came back, Nick tried to act as if everything was fine, but he couldn't stop thinking about the implied threat in Bill's message. He pushed his food around his plate, pretending that his appetite hadn't disappeared, until the waiter finally cleared the table.

"There's a special dessert waiting at my place," Jen said.

Nick cleared his throat. "That text was business, Jenny. I have to follow up. Tonight, I'm afraid."

"You've been distracted ever since you read it." Jen pouted. "It was Melissa Arnold, wasn't it? She's still bothering you, isn't she? Why don't you just fire her?"

"It wasn't Melissa, and I can't fire her. She's the best analyst in the office." He looked deep into Jen's eyes. "On a personal level, Melissa is ancient history. You are the woman I love. Today, tomorrow, and forever."

"I love you, too."

"I wish it weren't necessary, but I have to stop by the office. I'll put you in a cab."

"I don't want to go home alone. There's a serial killer on the loose. Whitney said he knocks his victims unconscious and cuts their tongues off. They drown in their own blood." She shuddered. "That is so gruesome. Can't your business wait until tomorrow?"

"I wish it could, but I won't be long. Promise. I've been waiting all week." Nick put his hand on Jen's. He hated making her unhappy, but he wouldn't be able to think about anything else until he'd had it out with Melissa. "Finance is international, and I have to be on 24–7. The Japanese stock market just opened."

"If you absolutely have to go, let me come with you."

"Jen, for Christ's sake. There's nothing to worry about." Nothing for her to worry about. He had to worry about Melissa ruining his reputation. He'd lose this job and never be able to get another. He could go to jail.

"Hey, man, you don't have to yell." It was the male half of the couple who had annoyed him earlier.

"Let's go." Nick took Jen's arm and hurried her out of the restaurant. If he'd stayed, he would have punched the jerk in the nose.

"You don't have to drag me." Jen's lip trembled as if she was about to cry.

Nick slowed his pace, but he was still fuming when he put her in a cab. "I'll make it up to you later." He slammed the door and walked back to his car.

Melissa lived downtown in one of the new high-rise condos. Why, Nick couldn't imagine. He didn't like being downtown after office hours, and he was damned unhappy about going back now. He didn't deserve this crap. He hadn't done anything that everyone else didn't do.

He'd bought a thousand shares of BPP for a client and a thousand shares for his personal account. The price doubled in six months, but there were rumors, so he sold half of each holding. The SEC announced an investigation the next day and BPP tanked. He'd sold the rest fast enough to clear a profit, although a smaller one. A minor adjustment put the proceeds from the first sale in his account and the proceeds from the second sale in the client's account.

My client was happy, damn it. I saved his ass. Lots of people lost money on BPP.

He told himself that Melissa couldn't turn him in without implicating herself. Those sales were a year ago. Why bring it up now? Their week in Tortola—she'd known damn well where the money came from. Didn't that make her a co-conspirator?

Rather than park at Melissa's building, where someone might see him and tell Jen, Nick found a space in the public lot next door. He waited until no one was around before getting out of his car and hurrying over to the entrance. The doorman was nowhere to be seen. Nick blessed good luck, punched in the security code, and took the elevator to the fifth floor.

Melissa wasn't home. At least, she wasn't answering her door-bell. A call to her cell went straight to voice mail. Frustrated, he kicked the door. Still no response, and if the neighbor across the hall had heard anything, he wasn't investigating.

"Bitch." Nick gave Melissa's door another kick, this one hard enough to do some damage, and walked away. He took the elevator to the basement, in case the doorman had returned to his post, and exited through the garage.

Back in his car, he texted Melissa, "Heard from Bill. WTF Can't we behave like adults?"

It was a dumb question. Melissa wasn't capable of acting like an adult. The night they broke up, she'd thrown a tantrum, along with anything of his she could pick up. He'd tried to break it gently.

"You're not meeting my needs," he'd told her. "I think we should try some time apart."

The words were barely out before Melissa jumped down his throat. "'You're not meeting my needs.' That's jackass speak for 'I'm cheating on you and pretending that it's your fault.' Who is she, Nick?"

The discussion had gone downhill from there, in part, because she was right about another woman. He'd met Jen and fallen deeply, truly in love for the first time in his life. There had been other women, lots of them, but no one had connected with the man he really was. Until Jen.

Who was at her place, waiting for him.

He detoured by the liquor store. A bottle of bubbly would help restore everyone's good mood—God knows he could use it. He bypassed the cheap stuff and picked up a bottle of Babineaux Brut.

"Candy's dandy, but liquor's quicker." It was the guy behind him in the checkout line.

"She's a little ticked off tonight; I'd better get both." Nick grabbed a box of chocolate truffles from a display next to the checkout. French champagne and fancy chocolates, Jen would love it.

"If Mama ain't happy, ain't no-one happy," his new best friend said. "Hell hath no fury." The guy was a fountain of clichés and already trashed without the six-pack he was about to buy, but he had a point.

"They get mad and torture you for the fun of it," Nick said. Thinking of Melissa made him angry all over again. He had to drive around another twenty minutes, talking himself down, before he was ready to go over to Jen's.

The first thing he noticed was the outside light, which should have been on but wasn't. Then he noticed that no lights were on, period. The units on either side were brightly lit. Jen must have blown a circuit. *All the circuits?*

That didn't seem likely. Maybe she was so spooked about this serial killer that she decided not to go home until she knew he'd be there. Thinking that this evening couldn't go much further wrong, Nick hurried up the walk, key in hand.

Jen's front door stood slightly ajar. He pushed it open and saw light coming from the kitchen.

"Jen? Is everything okay?" Something slammed. The back door? "Jen? Where are you?" He ran down the hall.

She lay face-up on the kitchen floor. A puddle of blood surrounded her head; more poured from her mouth.

"Jen! No! Oh my God, no!" He knelt beside her. Did he hear a faint gurgle? Was she still alive and struggling to breathe?

Nick had been a lifeguard. Reaching into her mouth to clear her airways was a reflex. He felt the stub where her tongue had been, and his stomach heaved. Fighting back nausea, he rolled her over and started artificial respiration. When he pressed down, blood gushed from her mouth.

"Help," he cried. "Someone help. Call an ambulance." He remembered his cell phone, took it out, and dialed 911.

The ambulance came quickly. At least that's what they told him later. To Nick, it seemed like an eternity before the EMTs rushed in.

"Her tongue," he said.

"Stand back. Let us do our job." An EMT shoved a metal tube down Jen's throat. Another attached her to an IV bag. Someone yelled, "Get a stretcher in here STAT. Tell the hospital we're on our way, and tell the cops we have another one."

"It's the serial killer, isn't it?" Nick said. "She was afraid, and I made her go home alone. Oh my God, it's my fault."

He followed them to the ambulance and watched in mute horror as they loaded her stretcher. When he tried to climb in, he was told, no room, and when he persisted, get the hell out of our way. A police officer materialized at his side, a woman who asked him to stay and answer a few questions.

"It won't take long," she said. "The detectives are on their way."

"I want to go to the hospital. I can't leave her alone."

"She's not alone, and there's nothing you can do for her that the doctors can't do better. The detectives will drop you at the hospital—after you talk"

"I love her. I want to be with her."

"Right now, the best thing you can do is help us catch the SOB who attacked her." She gestured toward the bag Nick had dropped when he saw Jen. "What's that?"

The bottle had broken. Clear bubbly liquid flowed across and around Jen's blood. Blood was everywhere. Sticky, metallic-smelling, bright red blood covered the floor and splattered the cabinets. It was on him—his shoes, his clothes, his hands. Nick began to sob.

Jen died on the way to the hospital. The enormity of her death left no room for any other thought or emotion. Nick answered the police detectives' questions, accompanied them to headquarters, and was arrested and charged with her murder. None of it penetrated the fog of his grief.

At his trial, the loudmouth couple from the restaurant, the taxi driver, and the guy from the liquor store all testified. Nick was taken aback by their hostility. He prayed that Jen had not died mad at him. The only bright spot was the police detective who described Jen's murder as an attempted copycat crime. The real serial killer abused his victims after he cut out their tongues; this had not happened to Jen. Knowing he had saved her from that last horror gave Nick a bit of solace.

He was found guilty and sentenced to twenty years in prison.

Two weeks after Nick's conviction, a man named Arthur Gault was apprehended while attacking a young woman. The police discovered a tongue collection in Gault's home. None matched Jen's DNA.

Gault was sentenced to life in prison, but it would be a short sentence. He'd been diagnosed with lung cancer. Two years and four months later, he succumbed. On his deathbed, he confessed to several murders other than those for which he'd been convicted. One was Jen's. Her tongue wasn't in his collection because he'd dropped it while running away after "her jerk of a boyfriend" walked in the front door.

The Innocence Team took up Nick's case. Nick, who had been a passive observer at his own trial, now wanted desperately to be released. No one asked why. Wasn't it a given that no man wanted to live behind bars? And for a crime he didn't commit?

Nick was exonerated, free to resume his old life, but the things he used to care about—a nice car, living in the right neighborhood, going to clubs and restaurants—no longer mattered. His time in prison had left him with an appreciation of simple pleasures.

He had also come to appreciate Melissa's part in Jen's death. Others had played small and unwitting roles in the tragedy. Bill sent the text, the guy in the liquor store delayed him, but Melissa had started it. Arthur Gault had been crazy, and he'd died in prison; Melissa had been sane and malicious—she'd actually testified against him at his trial—and she'd gotten away with it.

Nick moved to a smaller city two hours away and looked for a job that would give him access to government databases. The county tax office hired him. The work was not demanding, and on most days, he'd finished his assigned tasks by lunch. That left the afternoon free to search the Internet. Soon he had the information he needed.

When D-day finally came, Nick woke well before the alarm.

He lay in bed until the crack in his drapes lightened with the sunrise. Then he sat up and rotated his shoulders to loosen his tense muscles. Of course he was nervous, that was to be expected, but he was also resolute. And he'd learned from experience.

The first time all the pieces had fallen into place, he'd left after lunch and been caught in a miles-long traffic jam. A semi carrying something hazardous had overturned on the interstate. He'd sat for hours and then arrived too late. Today, he was leaving as soon as the morning rush hour cleared.

Life being what it is, Nick encountered no delays. He was hours early. He'd planned for that eventuality and spent the time at the movies in a multiplex not far from Melissa's new home.

She had done well since Jen died. She'd switched firms and been made a broker. She still owned the condo downtown but rented it out. Her current address was a single-family home in one of the city's best neighborhoods. Melissa couldn't have afforded it herself, but she'd married a lawyer, a partner in one of the city's largest firms. The house they owned jointly was estimated by a real estate database to be worth over a million dollars. It also backed up to a public park.

Tracking Melissa had been simple; gathering information about her husband's schedule had been more challenging. Hacking the law firms internal system proved impossible, at least for Nick. However, he was able to access court records. Most of Mr. Melissa's cases were local, but every now and then, he worked on a case being tried elsewhere. He was in New York today, Melissa would be returning home alone.

The final challenge is using the knife. Nick has practiced on a beef tongue purchased from an ethnic market and knows that the knife in his glove compartment is more than sharp enough. Having the will is the only question. But when he reminds himself how Melissa's vindictiveness led to Jen's death, Nick knows he can do it.

He also knows they'll catch him. He'll probably get the death penalty this time. That's okay. Jen is waiting.

Hack taxi drivers are ingrained in our national psyche, and are, themselves custodians of a heritage, the capable stranger coming to the rescue, that stretches back as long as stories have been told.

J.J. Lamb has recently discovered that it's been difficult to sneak in a short story because of the success of a series of novels he co-authors with spouse, Bette Golden Lamb, the latest of which, Bone Crack, was released in April of this year. White Knight previously appeared in Over My Dead Body in 2012.

White Knight

by J.J. Lamb

It's the creeps in this business who really get to you. I mean, there's one helluva lot of people in this crazy world who should never, ever be given the opportunity to ride in the back of a taxicab.

Not that the three-year-old Chrysler minivan I wheel around is a limo, or anything close to it, but after twenty-some years as an independent cabbie, I sure wish I could afford to be choosey about who I cart around.

Take the night before last, for instance.

It was one of those slow nights, mid-week. Nothing moving, no excitement. Maybe the weather was a little too nice for people to be cooped up in a cab. Happens that way in San Francisco sometimes. If you're the romantic type, you'd call it a lovers' night.

So, me and some of the other cabbies get into a discussion at the St. Francis Hotel taxi stand about, what else, chicks. Mainly, we're talkin' about whether a guy should take advantage when a chick's defenses are down, like her getting fired from her job, or seeing her fiancé stepping out with another good-looking female, or any number of things.

I argue my head off that it ain't the gentlemanly thing to do. I say those are times when a chick needs a shoulder to cry on, someone to talk to. Last thing she needs or wants is some horny bastard tryin' to get into her panties.

Get it when and where you can, is the consensus of my cabbie cohorts.

We bat the subject back and forth. I can't seem to get through to these knuckleheads that being a good guy now and then can't hurt, may even have a payoff down the road. Like, what goes around comes around, you know?

But I can't make my point; a minority of one

"Never happen, putz," yells this big Russian mafia-type who drives for one of the multi-cab franchises. "I got twenty bucks here that says if the opportunity comes your way, you'll jump."

"Jump it, or hump it," laughs another jerk.

Now I'm pissed. I climb back into my cab, give them a very firm digital salute, and hit the road.

I check out a few other hotels, see nothin's happenin' downtown. So I decide to cruise some of the fancier apartments and co-ops on Nob Hill, in Pacific Heights, and down along the Marina. Never know when someone'll decide to take off for a late dinner or hit a club or two.

I'm on the prowl no more than 15-20 minutes when I see this twenties-something- dressed-for-action dude standing curbside under the awning of one of the classier Marina co-ops. He's giving his watch a no-nonsense frown, which I take to mean he's probably called for a town car that's failed his get-here-now test.

I do a slow drive-by and get what I'm hoping for—a whistle and wave-over. As I pull up, I'm thinkin' he's got to be in a hurry to get someplace, which usually means a bigger tip.

"Downtown?" I ask.

"Pacific Heights." He gives me an address.

"Running late?" I say.

"Not at all," says he.

Disappointing. But a fare's a fare.

Since there's no hurry, I start to make with the usual cabbie small talk—the Giants, the Forty-Niners, the weather, the stock market, city politics, whatever. But a glance in the mirror tells me this guy's already deep into one of those fancy smart phones—BlackBerry, BlueBerry, StrawBerry. Whatever.

I think he's probably about to call whoever he's going to meet, chick or dude, but the flip-open never goes to his ear. His thumbs are all over the tiny keyboard, a skill I've yet to get the hang of.

So maybe it's not a late date. I've been wrong before. Part of the fun of jockeying a cab is creating scenarios about where people may be going and what they might do when they get there. Had a writer as a fare once who told me it's the "what ifs" that make life fun, interesting. I been keepin' track; think he's right.

What isn't fun are traffic snafus, like one I spot in the making just as we're about to cross Lombard and I see it's too late to take evasive action. Some doofus with out-of-state plates tries to make a U-ie across three lanes of green-to-go, oncoming traffic. He gets spun one way by a Bimmer, spun back around by a pickup, and all three end up blocking the whole damn intersection.

"Can't get through here," I toss over my shoulder.

"What?"

He's seen nothin', his eyes still on his smart phone, thumbs busier than cliff swallows building mud nests. Or maybe he's getting a head start on tomorrow's stock market. Who knows?

"Gotta go another way," I say.

"Whatever."

By now there's a couple of cars stacked up on my back bumper, but with a little yelling and a lot of arm waving, we retreat to the intersection behind us and it's off onto another cross street.

I pull up in front of the address he gave me, which turns out to be one of those very elegant stone mansions in Pacific Heights, with a view out across The Bay that adds at least a couple million bucks to any real estate listing. I reach over to drop the flag, knowing it's taken me about twice the time it should have.

He taps my shoulder, a little harder than necessary. "Hold it. I'll be right out."

I can dig the waiting 'cause it's almost pure profit. I'm beginning to wonder, though, what this guy's up to. I know if it'd been me on the way to do the town with a hot date, I'd have been out and about hours earlier.

Fifteen minutes or so later, I'm wondering whether I've been stiffed. Can't even go knock on the door 'cause he was buzzed through a tall, heavy-duty, wrought iron gate, then he disappeared down a curved flagstone walk.

I decide to give him another ten minutes, which turns out to be a good thing. I see him comin' up to the gate with this very lovely chick on his arm, a chick like you've never seen before. Well, like I've not seen before in my forty-eight years.

I'm in such a hurry to get around to the other side of the cab, so I can hold the door open for her—them—that I almost lose the driver's door to a passing, horn-honkin', big-as-a-tank SUV. I let it pass 'cause I mainly want to get a better look-see at this gorgeous creature I'm about chauffeur someplace; hell, anyplace.

She's all smiles and wearing one of those lacey summer shawls over bare shoulders that rise out of a scoop-neck silk blouse that sings with a swirling pattern of so many colors I can't count 'em all. A black, flowing skirt swishes with every step; a hem of uneven, upside-down spearheads bounces around her knees to set off smoothly curved calves. I'm in love.

Then she gives me this really extra nice smile, which turns off quick like when the dude steps around her and jumps into the rear of the cab first, leavin' her standing at the curb, surrounded by the delicate aroma of very expensive perfume.

Now you can bet I want to say something smartass to the dude, but I just stand there and wait until she's settled in her seat before I slide the door closed. She stares straight ahead, lips an unwavering horizontal line, hands atop one another in her lap, and a big, fat solitaire on her left ring finger, bouncin' back every street light in sight.

"SoMa!" the dude orders when I'm back behind the wheel, then barks the name of a club like he's making a side bet that I've never heard of the South-of-Market place. My nod calls his bluff. Not only do I know how to find this dive, I also know it's no place he should be takin' this fine-lookin' lady, with her shoulder-length auburn hair and sparkling green eyes, fiancée or no fiancée.

As soon as I'm rollin' again, I check the mirror: her statue-like expression hasn't changed one bit; he's back to manipulating the damn smart phone, and the two of them are sittin' about as far away from one another as they can get. This is startin' out to be one weirdo evening.

When we get to the club, he commands—not asks—me to wait. The still-running meter prevents a nasty response. I cool my heels and walk across the street to grab a couple of chicken tacos from a Mexican café I try to hit whenever I'm in the neighborhood.

No more than thirty minutes later the dude's out of the dump, the chick's trailing two or three paces behind. He stands by the cab, doing the impatient thing with his foot while I skip around to open the back door for them. Same deal: he gets in, she follows. I get a nose impression that in the short time they were inside, he was hitting the booze pretty hard.

The seating arrangement in the back seat is just as sad as before.

After this non-starter, he directs me to one of the classier clubs, but pulls the same in-and-out-like-a-rabbit routine. Or maybe he's one of those hyper types who can't sit still or hang around any one place for more than a few minutes. The only advantage for me, other than the climbing numbers on the meter, is that by this time, with so much getting in and out of my cab, I've established that the chick is wearing absolutely nothing under the scoop-neck but her, which is a very enjoyable distraction.

Does she know I'm doing a look-see each time? Of course she does. No matter how discreet a guy tries to be, the chick always knows.

It's really getting to me that with each club, he leaves her farther and farther behind, both going in and coming out. At one exclusive jazz joint, he's so far ahead of her that the doorman almost refuses her entrance, thinkin' maybe she doesn't have an escort. I want to go over and tell the jerk that this definitely isn't the kinda lady-of-the-night he's being paid to keep out.

After our fifth stop, it's quite obvious the dude's not doing much inside each club except slammin' down a quick drink or two. But not the chick. Her walk and talk says she may not have had more than a sip of wine the entire evening—not a hair out of place, not a wrinkle or spot on her clothes to be seen anywhere.

Just to keep things straight between me and the dude, I remind him that the meter's been running all this time and the total's well into three figures—without the decimal point. He glares at me, belches, pulls a Franklin from his wallet, and tosses the bill onto the front seat.

To my surprise, there's a change in the cab entry routine this time—he steps aside and makes a grandiose sweep of his arm to usher her into the back seat ahead of him. As she dips to enter, providing me with another heart-stopping view, he brings his other hand up and gives her a hefty goose.

She's lets out a little yelp and blushes all the way deep down into the blouse.

"Stop that!" she says over her shoulder.

"Stop that?" he repeats. "Don't start giving orders, babe, not if you want my Daddy to save your Daddy's financial ass by buying into his loser company."

The dude gives me this silly grin, crawls in, and this time he sits next to her, actually, almost on top of her. Again, she sits with both hands in her lap, her expression almost as blank as the first time she got into my minivan … but it seems to me there may be a touch of anger showing in her eyes, at the corners of her mouth.

We do two more clubs and by this time the dude is really swacked, unable to walk a straight line, but still manages to stay a few paces ahead of her. It would have been funny and a good tale to retell at the taxi stand if I hadn't been so completely taken with this chick—like some damn teenager instead of a guy old enough to be her daddy, the real kind, not the sugar kind.

There I am waitin' like a lonely puppy to see her again when she exits what I hope is the last club of the evening, arms swinging at her sides, a big grin pasted across her face.

Oh, ho! What's this?

Next comes the dude, followed closely by a gent I take to be the manager, who's yapping away a mile a minute.

I can't catch all of it, but the club guy is saying somethin' about "... do not allow that sort of thing on our dance floor."

Then I see the chick is doing the big blush again, but the grin remains, maybe even gets a little bigger. And I notice her blouse and skirt are a bit askew.

She climbs into the back real quick like, but not before the dude goes a lot farther with his manual explorations, rearranging her skirt even more, and getting a firm "Stop that!" again for his ungentlemanly actions.

I know I shouldn't, but I'm beginnin' to take all this real personal. But I still got enough sense to know not to stick my nose in where it's not invited. And then there's the fact the chick seems to have things pretty much under control. Why should I risk having them end their evening in some other joker's cab?

I'm thinkin' it's past time to take the chick home, but the dude lays the name of a private club on me even though it's well past two. Then all hell breaks loose in the back of the cab. Because I'm yellin' at some yo-yo who just cut me off at the traffic light, I miss the first part of the boy-girl scuffle.

Next thing I know, I hear this blood-curdling screech from the chick and a big grunt from the dude. The mirror reveals that the expensive multi-colored blouse is now down around the chick's waist and the dude's hands are all over her breasts. She lets him have it with her handbag, but it doesn't slow him one bit.

I stomp on the brakes, curse an imaginary stray dog, and the dude goes *kerplunk* onto the floorboards. The chick grabs the door handle, then realizes she's not exactly dressed for a sidewalk stroll. She collapses into a curled-up heap in a corner of the back seat and starts crying.

Now I gotta say, I can't stand to see a female cry, of any age or description. Just plain gets me right in the mid-section. And whenever there's something I can do about it, I do it. This time I whip the cab around the corner, into an alley, and come to a slow, coasting stop.

When I look in the back, the dude is trying to both untangle himself from the floorboards and make a clumsy hand exploration up her very long legs.

I'm expecting her to give him a bash in the head with her purse again, but apparently she's had it. I hear a long sigh from one of them, then she leans back and just sits there, hands in her lap, crying.

For me, it's now or never.

I drop the flag on the meter, pull in my gut, and climb out of the cab. The dude is back on the floorboards when I slide open the back door, clamp onto one of his $500-loafer-clad feet, and drag his ass out onto the asphalt. I'm expecting some kind of verbal abuse, but he doesn't move and no sounds escape his pouty lips.

Fair play says one really shouldn't take advantage of a helpless drunk, but this dude has made me forget all the niceties. I grab him by his linen lapels, lift him a couple of feet off the ground, and toss him onto a stack of stuffed plastic garbage bags outside the back door of a Chinese restaurant.

As he lands, I see something I didn't see before—there's an oval pearly thingy sticking out of the left side of his neck. A trickle of blood trails down inside his shirt collar.

Shit! What the hell have I gone and done now?

I look behind me. The chick is watchin', but not reactin' as I might have expected. Without looking down at her hand, she pulls the engagement ring off her finger and zips it into her small black satin purse.

You can be damn sure I have questions, and it must have shown on my face.

"I told Daddy I was never going to marry that man," she whispers. "He should have listened to me."

I step over to the garbage heap, take hold of the pearly thing, and pull a long hat pin from the dude's neck. After I get back into the cab, I drive around for a while to give the chick time to put her clothes back in order and collect her thoughts; not once do I look into the rearview mirror. Really!

On the far side of the Broadway tunnel, I hear a soft "thank you."

I pull over to the curb, look back at her, and ask, "Home?"

A nod and a dab at the tears that continue to flow.

"Need a coffee first, or something else?"

"No, thank you."

"Want to sit up front?" I ask.

"Do you think he's dead?"

"Very."

"Good," she whispers. She slides across the seat, opens the curbside door, gets out, and comes up front to sit with me. Before I can get the cab rolling again, she has her head buried in my shoulder, soaking everything with her non-stop tears.

I slip my arm around her shoulders, strictly for her comfort of course, and take off for Pacific Heights. She makes no move to suggest I should keep both hands on the wheel. In some ways it makes me feel like a protective brother, but there are other feelings that have nothing to do with brotherly love.

I'm feeling better when we get to her place—she seems to be pretty much herself again. But I'm also sad at the prospect of having to take my arm from around her firm, young body. The tears have stopped and she even manages a small smile or two at some of my not-so-funny comments about other drivers and the state of the world in general.

It takes everything I've got to remember my manners and not get in a good solid squeeze as I take away my arm. I get out, go around, and open the door for her; she holds out her hand for me to take

I start to sweat a little because she holds onto my hand as I walk her up to that big iron gate, and she continues to hold on as

273

she punches in the security code. Then she gently tugs me down the flagstone walkway to a massive, carved front door.

Before doin' something stupid like tryin' to give her a kiss, I try to gently pull my hand from hers so I can get back to my cab, remember who I am, and forget about her. But she won't let go.

Next thing I know, she's takin' me through the front door, across the marble floor of a foyer that's almost as big as my apartment, and up a *Gone-With-the-Wind*-like staircase. At the top of the stairs, she gives me the sweetest smile I've ever seen and plants a great big kiss right where a kiss should be planted.

I would describe her room, if I could remember it. When I get back to my cab, I feel in my pocket and the hatpin is gone.

The next night I feel an obligation to go look for the big Russian. When I find him in the St. Francis cab line, as expected, I give him a crisp, new Jackson.

"Oh, ho!" he says. "Tell me who, my little friend."

I wiggle an index finger in front of his nose and say, "No way!"

"Hah! Then I suppose I'll *never* find out who left you *that*, or why." He points to a brand new yellow Camry hybrid parked at the far end of the cab line, a big red ribbon tied around one windshield wiper.

I walk over to take a look, see an envelope stuck under the other windshield wiper blade with my name on it. Inside is the title, a temporary registration slip in my name, and a note that reads:

"Just between the two of us!"

I look up and give the Russian a big, self-satisfied grin.

Would that there were an establishment like The Blue Lady, for to step through its doors would be as passing through the portals of a time machine to a bygone age, one of swank, and discrete nightclubs, and beautiful women in beaded gowns.

Author JoAnne Lucas, no stranger to readers of Darkhouse Books anthologies, steps out of her cozy comfort range with this story. We believe our readers will agree Ms Lucas should step out more often. A shorter version of this story appeared in the print anthology, Dime, in 2004.

One for My Baby

by JoAnne Lucas

"Hi Boss. Would you see that if a guy checking us out is still hanging around back there?" The young gal who works as a hatcheck girl held open the club's door for me. "You can't miss him, he's really mean looking. Gave me the creeps," she said.

I picked up the long skirt of my dress to miss hitting the stair step with it and looked over my shoulder. Street traffic on Perrin was settling down to its slower pace before the evening festivities kicked it back into high gear. There were few pedestrians and none that showed any interest our way.

I shrugged it off. "As long as it's not Old Man Trouble hanging around, it's nothing to worry about."

Maybe I should have kept quiet about trouble. Like a dog at dinnertime, the mention of his name would send him running home to mama. Most people talk a lot about trouble, say it comes in threes. Could be, but most people just don't know what trouble is. Like being born in the steel mill city of Fontana, California, also known as Fontucky because of the many who moved west to work in the steel mill came from Kentucky. Or Felony Flats with crime being the way of life. Heck, Al Capone's house still stood there, all fenced off on a large empty lot. Take your choice on the names, it's been called worse. It was a rough, brawling place, and living there was miserable. Even the weather was brutal with the hot Santa Ana winds fiercely blowing hard hitting sand in from the Mohave Desert. God, I hated that town.

The steel mill closed a few years after I was born and Dad was out of a job he'd had forever. The town was full of the suddenly unemployed. Mom took off for parts unknown and Dad took to drinking his evenings away. Understandable, 'cept evenings came earlier and earlier for him. They eventually started whenever he could grab a bottle and drink it without spilling half the contents.

So my older sister and I grew up in a drunken lout's household (Trouble #1), she got married and moved out of town and I got into real trouble at fourteen (Trouble #2), then I ran away forever at fifteen (Trouble #3).

I ditched the bad memories and followed Maggie the hatcheck girl to her station, where I handed her my vintage 1930's silver fox coat. Damned thing was older than Maggie and me combined and I loved it. Wearing it made me feel like a movie star.

Immediately, pride of place chased the rest of my glooms away as I noted the number of discreet reserved notices already on the tables in the main dining room. This was my club and it was perfect. One of the most important accomplishments of my life. I breathed in my satisfaction and got to work.

In the midst of our regular opening operations for the Blue Lady Lounge I snagged the right shoulder of my beaded gown against a coat hook while checking out the ladies lounge. A thread that wove sequins and loops of beads over all the soft and clinging blue jersey material broke. This, after the piano player had turned up too drunk to play and the chef threatened to quit again – just normal problems that precede regular Saturday night business at Fresno's hottest place to be.

Watching all those old B movies when I was growing up, made me want to be in a swanky club too. I used to dream just how it was going to be. My dreams were all I owned those days and I vowed that someday I would open The Blue Lady. My club was a classy number in living color, complete right down to cigarette girls with their fishnet stockings and the merchandise trays that hung around their necks, and the young flower girls in sweet, full skirted dresses selling corsages and boutonnieres out of their baskets. Both sidelines were lucrative as well as decorative.

Happiness for me is when an SRO crowd packs the lounge and a line is stretched outside, all waiting for a table, and preferably one that rings the dance floor and bandstand. I've hired six to eight older college kids costumed as glamour gals with upswept hairdos, tuxedoed gentlemen, and gangsters with their molls. The kids are seated throughout the club to encourage the customers to give free rein to their fantasies and come dressed like-wise. Encouraging and playing to the public's fantasies rakes is a better pay-off than simply watering the whiskey.

The pissed piano player was quickly dealt with and I sent counter threats back to the chef. He periodically needed large jolts of indignation to bring out his best cooking, and it *was* the best in town. That left me holding up the broken thread on my gown to stop the run of beads until I could fix it properly. It made it so that I couldn't pin on my corsage.

Bill Reynolds, a young pre-med student in a tux, helped me. He was one of the regular Friday and Saturday night crew. "Did you see where both the mayor and the D.A. have reserved tables?" he asked. "Man-oh-man, are we going to have fun tonight! We've got a pool going that says the mayor shows up as a gangster this time. Want in?"

"I'll pass," I said and thought again what a nice kid he was. The new piano player was warming up with 'One For My Baby' and played well enough that he would be able to sell it to the crowd later. The corsage was being taken care of and I figured after I fixed the gown, I would have maybe a half hour to myself in my office before I made an appearance on the floor. Yeah, I'm part of the program. The customers expect to see me and schmooze a bit, maybe send over a round of drinks on the house or a bottle of champagne.

I smiled down at young Bill's blond head bent close to me in order to scrutinize the corsage pin as he worried it through wired stems and the gown's material. "Thanks for giving me a hand here, Bill."

"Hey, no problem." He finished the job and straightened up. "Can't have our Blue Lady running around without her signature gardenias." He gave me a grin and patted my shoulder.

"Well, now, ain't that charmin'," said a gravelly voice I had hoped to forget. "He's a little young for you, Lizzie."

This was trouble, as in Fontana Trouble #1, and probably Maggie's creepy stranger.

"Hullo, Mitch," I said.

"Surprised to see me, doll?"

"It's been a while."

"Yeah, it has." He gave me a slow once over. "You still look great, baby"

He didn't, just fatter and older, but mean as ever as he moved in close and grabbed my upper arm hard in a cruel grip. He smelled bad, too – concentrated Mitch. "Me and you need to go somewheres quiet and have us a little talk," he said, "catch up on old times."

Bill tried to intervene, but Mitch let go of my arm to punch him in the stomach while he sapped him with his other hand. The poor kid crumpled to the floor.

Obviously proud of his work, Mitch leered back at me. "You want to talk now, or maybe I should work your hero over some more? How 'bout I re-arrange his nose so he don't look so pretty?"

I suppressed a shudder and looked bored instead. "Don't you ever get tired of suckering kids in so you can play with your sap? It doesn't matter whether we talk here or not, but first you leave that on the bar."

Mitch opened his fist to show his buddy sap secured around his wrist and finger. "Sure, baby, just as soon as you drop your bag."

I moved to place my silver satin evening purse on the bar, but Mitch intercepted it and fingered the contents through the fabric.

"Still carrying that little purse gun? Worthless piece of shit." He shook his head. "Always told you that thing can't do any damage. Know what I mean?"

"Depends on what you're aiming for," I said. "What is it you want?"

"Well, now." Mitch dropped the sap with the purse so he could make an expansive gesture. "I want what's owed me. The last time I saw you, you was holding two grand for me. Next I hear you blew out of Wichita without a good-by." He waggled a fat finger at me. "That wasn't nice. Took me a while to track you down after I got out, but I figure two thou plus sixteen years' interest just about makes me and you equal partners in this sweet little place."

"You're crazy!"

He back-handed me and I staggered only a couple of steps. *Whoa, Trouble #2. I'd forgotten how Mitch likes to get physical. But he's losing his touch*, I thought and quickly felt my face for damage control. The bar's back mirror showed his ring had missed connecting. A little ice for the swelling and a lot of make-up would cover the redness, but I would have to play this carefully so there wouldn't be a repeat scene.

From nearby where he could keep an eye on Mitch, my manager Hal Weever and a couple of his waiters rushed over, all eager and pumped. I put up my hand to stop them. "Just trying out some material for a show. Need to get the kinks ironed out," I said and waved them off. The waiters left, but Hal stayed close. I turned to Mitch, "Leave your guns with the sap and we'll talk in my office."

Mitch sneered as he pulled out an old Colt .38 and placed it on the bar.

"I said *all* your guns."

He shrugged and added an automatic. I knew he carried a switch blade and possibly another piece in an ankle holster, but I let him think he got away with it.

I turned to my manager and gestured to the items on the bar and to Bill Reynolds on the floor who was beginning to come around.

"Take care of things."

"Always," Hal said. His soft southern accent and manner made it a personal promise. We'd been together for years and he's always been loyal and dependable. I knew the kid would be in good hands.

I headed for my office, not looking to see if Mitch followed.

Of course he did.

Once inside he closed the door and hit the lock. "Hold it, babe. You stay right there where I can watch you. Don't try nuthin' cute and keep away from any drawers."

I looked at him over my shoulder and noted he was getting a little excited. Total dominance after putting down some sassy resistance was Mitch's big turn-on.

"You want a drink?"

"Yeah, a drink would be good," he allowed and followed me over to the little mirrored bar.

Still holding up the gown's broken thread, I awkwardly poured him a generous double whiskey, and for me, a brandy in my best crystal goblets.

"Very fancy." He lifted his drink. "Here's to old times."

"If you say so."

"I do." He clinked his glass against mine, tossed down the drink, and motioned for me to do the same. I took a sip of the Courvoisier and inwardly fumed. Old times my hind foot. Years ago I was still a young kid, too scared of him to do other than be his little personal slave. Thank God he got busted for using his sap too vigorously in an alley fight. An old federal warrant turned up when he was arrested and he got seven to twelve at Leavenworth, while I got the hell out of Kansas and never looked back.

No, this isn't at all like old times and to show it I deliberately strolled over to the music console while he was pouring himself another double.

"Hey! Did I tell you you could move? Get away from there—Now!"

I gave him another long look, sauntered toward my desk and stopped in front of it. I faced him and leaned slightly back against the desk while I sipped my drink. Mitch's eyes were all over me like hungry mosquitoes and I let them feast.

He gulped more whiskey. "You've really done good for yourself, Lizzie. Very swanky. You always did have class, even as a punk kid. Yeah, I'm gonna like it here just fine."

Right, like I'm going to let that happen. I set my brandy snifter down and reached back across the desk for the red enameled cigarette box. He threw his empty glass right past my head and it smashed against the wall behind me with the melodic tinkle only a Baccarat crystal can make while dying.

"You need me to teach you again how it goes? You don't touch nuthin' 'til I check things out! And put your hands on top of the desk where I can see 'em."

Oh, yeah, he was coming along nicely. I gave him a sly "make me" smile, straightened up, and pulled down hard and slow on the broken thread. Crystalline beads started a waterfall from my shoulder, rippled in a race across the bodice of my gown, and sensually rained from the nipple of one breast.

Mitch's breath came heavy as he watched the domino effect. I groped for the office door release hidden under the desk's lip while I leisurely rolled my shoulders and upper body to make the run of beads wantonly drip from the other breast.

He wet his lips.

As he had demanded, I now made a big show of placing my hands flat on the desk top, a little behind me so my bust jutted up like an offering.

"Is this what you wanted?" I asked in a husky voice.

He was on me like a dog on a leg, smashing kisses against my face, and holding my upper arms pinned to my sides in his rough embrace. "Oh, yeah, baby. I've been wanting this for years." He pulled me completely upright so he could grind his groin hard against me. Then he yanked my head back by grabbing a handful of hair and twisting it in his fist. "You miss me, babe?" he demanded, his sour whiskey breath right in my face. "Tell me how much you want me."

"Mitch," I breathed an invitation in his ear and nipped the lobe.

He plunged his tongue into my mouth. I moaned and sucked it while I held him tight at his waist against me.

He growled, groaned, and after two muffled popping sounds jerked stiffly before collapsing to the floor. Trouble #3, but not mine this time.

I wiped his spittle from my face with the back of my hand and watched him die. Hal Weever kept his eyes on Mitch and held my little purse gun at the ready. It wasn't necessary. His two shots to the back of Mitch's head had done the trick. Yeah, double tap.

Hal set the gun on my desk. "Always said this was a nice little piece." He bent over the corpse and started to empty Mitch's pockets. "Yep," he continued, "no noise, no fuss, and no exploded brains to clean off the wall." He looked up at me and winked.

I tossed him a smile, reached for my brandy and drank the rest.

Then I stared at the wall for a long time.

"How's the Reynolds kid doing?" I asked.

"Bill? I looked him over. He'll be okay, just a little shook up. Like you said, I told him the guy was an out of work actor who auditioned for the role a little too vigorously and we decided not to use him."

I nodded my compliments on his good work. Then I crossed the room to the safe, counted out two thousand dollars in hundreds, and handed it to Hal. "When you dump him, leave this stuffed in his mouth." As I walked by the corpse I gave it a hard kick. I always pay my debts.

After Hal supervised the body removal and cleanup process, I changed my gown and let him zip me up. His hands lingered on my shoulders. "You know, Liz," he drawled, "I could almost feel sorry for that poor dead slob. If he knew you for so long, how come he didn't know you'd kill to protect what's yours?"

"I didn't have much back then," I answered.

"Yeah, but, still. Everyone knows the Blue Lady's your baby and you wouldn't let anyone hurt it."

Wrong, I thought and moved away. The Blue Lady's not my baby... Bill Reynolds was.

Warren Bull's second appearance in this anthology relates an encounter between two people and a beagle on a lonely highway an hour outside Wichita on Christmas Day.

When writing, Mr. Bull looks for settings and situations where his protagonist has nowhere else to turn.

A Christmas Journey

by Warren Bull

It was the coldest Christmas Day I could remember. The morning had started with a temperature of two degrees above zero and nose-dived faster than my bank account during the holidays. I was driving toward Wichita in a minivan modified into a delivery vehicle when I saw a young man standing by the side of the road. He had a backpack on, the tall kind you use when you hike the Appalachian Trail. He held a basset hound in his arms. He didn't try to thumb a ride.

I was early with the delivery. When I finished I could head home. But still… There was something about the fellow. Traffic was so sparse it was almost nonexistent. It was easy to swing around, head in the opposite direction and pass him in the other lane. I could see no other vehicles or people anywhere in any direction. I came back around slowly a third time. I pulled off the road and rolled my window down. Biting cold wind streamed into the van, stinging all my exposed skin. At least I had my leather driving gloves on. The young man hurried over.

"Do you have a ride coming?" I asked.

"No." he answered.

"You weren't hitchhiking," I said.

"No. I hear it's dangerous," he said.

"It can be. Exposure to weather this cold is absolutely dangerous. Were you waiting for some poor slob to stop? You know, somebody so unimportant he has to work on Christmas?"

He shrugged. "I guess so."

"I guess I'm that guy," I said.

The young man looked through the window at me and at the empty back seat. The rear of the van had been closed off behind the back seats to form a place for cargo. It had no windows.

"It's wise to check me out. I'm sure you'd feel more comfortable about getting in if the van had a family inside or a couple of women. You can wait for somebody like that or you can ride with me. Decide quickly because I'm not waiting much longer with the window open. It's cold. It would be just you and your dog, me and the man riding in the cargo bed."

He looked like someone had smacked him between the eyes with a claw hammer. Then the ends of his lips moved up. He smiled.

"You had me going there, mister."

"Sorry," I said. "That was probably in poor taste on Christmas Day. I'm hauling a load toward Wichita. Do you want to hop in?"

"Okay," said the man. "I'm aiming for my home town, Waterloo. It's just forty miles from Wichita." He put the dog down and slipped off his backpack.

"You can put the dog and your stuff in the back seat," I said. "You sit next to me. I'm not comfortable with a stranger sitting behind me."

He loaded his pack and the dog into the back seat. Then he opened the passenger side door. As he slid in, I got a better view of his face, I thought he might be in his mid-twenties. The coat he had on could have been a Salvation Army store special, much too thin and worn for this temperature.

"I'm Tom," I said, putting my hand out toward him. We shook hands.

"I'm Gary," he said. "And your friend in the back seat?" I asked.

"That's Muffin," he said, buckling his seat belt.

"Nice to meet the two of you," I said. I checked the mirrors, put the vehicle in drive and drove down the road.

"Can I ask why you were carrying Muffin?" I inquired.

"Day like this her feet get cold when she walks," Gary said.

"I thought that might be it," I said. "It's a good thing for a man to take care of his pets. It speaks well of him."

Gary didn't answer. I drove in silence for about twenty minutes or so.

"You're probably too polite to ask," I said, "but you might be wondering why a man approaching retirement age would be making a delivery on Christmas. There are plenty of younger men who could have driven. Some of them would have been happy to. See, I'm in the transportation business. I was a laborer, a mechanic and a wheelman before I became warehouse manager. Lots of younger men who work there are faster and stronger than me. A few think they're smarter than I am. They might even be right. I know a couple of them want my job."

Gary nodded.

"I'm not quite ready to retire," I said. "I used to say I was a pencil pusher, but now I'm more of a keyboard pounder. It's the best job I ever had. No heavy lifting. No dangerous roads or dark alleys. I just have to stop the loaders from killing the drivers and the drivers from killing the mechanics. The loaders and the mechanics get along great. They both hate the drivers. So when I get a chance to please the boss, I take it. The cargo was elusive. We didn't locate it until just before the holiday. And the loading, wow."

I shook my head before continuing. "The boss didn't want the customer to get what she ordered after the holiday season was over. So I offered to drive. The boss was very happy."

I looked over at Gary. He didn't say a word.

"That's my excuse for being here. What yours?"

I'm going to see my mama," he said

"Are you moving back to be with her?" I asked. "I mean you've got your dog and lots of stuff in the pack. You wouldn't need all that for a short visit. It seems to me you're moving somewhere. But, uh, let me know if I'm being too nosy. Sometimes I talk too much."

"No problem. Fact is, I don't know if she'll let me move in," said Gary. "She practically kicked me out. I deserved it. Been gone a couple of years. She don't exactly know I'm coming."

"Well, Christmas is a good time of year to try to reconnect with family," I said.

He nodded but did not respond. More miles passed quietly. I was thinking about turning on the radio to see if I could listen to a football game or Christmas music. Then I noticed Gary inspecting the inside of the van as if he were about to make an offer to buy it.

"Is there something on your mind?" I asked.

"I wish I could come home with something to show that I did something good while I was gone," said Gary. "I left home with nothing but the clothes on my back. I'm coming home with Muffin and a pack full of work clothes and boots."

"That's more than you left with," I said.

"It's not much," said Gary.

We travelled for another long stretch of time without any more conversation. Gary's legs began to twitch. He kept his head still while he looked at me out of the corner of his eyes.

"I bet you carry real valuable stuff," he said.

"Not this trip," I said. "This one has strictly sentimental value. It wouldn't be worth much to anybody except the customer. But on other trips I do."

He withdrew into his thoughts. I didn't like the tone of his question or the direction of his thinking. I could imagine the gears in his brain meshing: Isolated road. No witnesses. Cargo important enough to deliver on Christmas Day. Vehicle to use to go home. Then sell it. Or burn it. Few police working through the holidays. They'd be tired. Transport company with few workers for nearly the whole coming week. Older driver. Balding. Fat. Out of shape. Talks too much.

Gary unbuckled his seat belt. "Tom, I need to get something out of my pack and to piss. Can you pull over?"

"Sorry, Gary, but picking up you and Muffin put me a little behind schedule. I have to keep going," I said. I put more pressure on the gas pedal. We sped up.

"There's a gas station up ahead," I said. "It's close. I could use the bathroom too. You'll like this place. Because it's open every holiday, folks with no place in particular to go stop by. The people there know me well. I could top off the tank while you use the facilities. I can introduce you around. It's well lighted and I won't have to worry about anybody messing with the van."

"No need for that," said Gary. "I can hold it till Wichita. Let me just reach into my backpack."

He turned around. He leaned over the back of the seat. I stomped on the brake pedal. The brakes squealed and the van bucked like a bronco. My seatbelt held me from hitting the steering wheel. Muffin and the backpack flew a short distance into the back of the front seats before falling to the floor. Muffin yelped. Gary was not as lucky. He slammed into the roof and dashboard. Then he slid down.

"Ow! Why'd you do that?" asked Gary.

"Because you were going for something sharp or something with bullets in it," I said. I let off the brake pedal and stepped on the gas.

"Buckle up," I said. "If the cargo was damaged, I'm going to be very unhappy with you. You are one lousy liar. You'd pee outside when the wind is blowing and the temperature's likely to freeze the piss before it hits the ground rather than wait for a warm, clean bathroom? Then you don't need to pee at all until Wichita? No way. If you want to fight me over the van, just let me know. I will pull off and oblige. Just give me your mother's address first so I know where to send your junk. I'm old. I'm fat. I'm bald. And I've been in at least ten times as many fights as you have. I have dirty tricks you've never even dreamed about. I'll hurt you so bad your grandmother won't be able to get out of her bed for a month. After that I will kill you."

Gary awkwardly pulled himself into his seat and buckled in.

"I ought to kick you out of this van and drive off with Muffin and your stuff," I said.

"Sorry," said Gary. "Sorry. Please don't. It was a really dumb idea. I see that now."

"I pick you up out of the bitter cold and this is how you thank me?" I asked.

"I'm stupid," said Gary. "I'm just stupid. I pulled that kind of crap back home. Mama was right to kick me out."

"Look, Gary, just because you get an idea doesn't mean you have to act on it," I said.

"The way you talk, you must have gotten schooling," said Gary. "I didn't."

"I didn't graduate from high school," I said. "I thought I already knew everything important. I didn't of course. Now I read a lot. When I'm around someone who's educated, I listen. You could do that."

"I don't read fast," said Gary.

"Who said anything about fast?" I asked. "Can you read?"

"Yeah."

"That's what matters," I said. "When you get an idea you imagine how it could go well. Do you then stop and think about what could go badly?"

"Not so much," said Gary.

"You might try that," I said. "How does it go when you jump in without thinking about the consequences?"

"It goes piss poor," said Gary.

"If something is really good it will probably wait around," I said. "When someone tells me I have to decide right this very second, I always decide to decline. If a man or a woman doesn't give you time to think, that is a very good reason to think long and hard."

Gary nodded

"Have you ever killed a person?" I asked.

"Jeez, no," said Gary. "No," said Gary. "I would have…"

"You would have what?" I asked. "You're not Bruce Lee. Have you been trained in how to disable a man without killing him?"

"No," said Gary. "I didn't think that far ahead. Probably you would have killed me."

"You would have put the burden of killing another human being on my soul," I said. "That's not a kind thing to do to someone trying to help you out. Your mother would be devastated. Who knows what would have happened to Muffin."

Gary cowered in silence mile after mile.

I spoke again. "So, what's your plan for meeting your mama?"

"I don't… I don't know."

"Well," I said, "Given how well it goes when you don't think it out, maybe you should make some sort of plan."

"Yeah," said Gary. "How do I do that?"

"Where do you think you will see her?" I asked.

"She'll be working at Janos as a waitress," said Gary. "She works every holiday because that's when she gets big tips. The restaurant stays open way late."

"Good," I said. "That's information to use in planning. So you and Muffin enter the restaurant. Then what?"

"They don't mind if dogs wait inside out of the weather while their owners eat," said Gary. "I'd introduce her to the people. Pretty much everybody there likes dogs."

"Sounds like a homey place," I said. "You park Muffin. Then what's next?"

"Maybe I could. I don't know," said Gary.

"Will it be busy?" I asked.

"It's always busy," said Gary.

"Will the owner be there?" I asked.

"Yep," said Gary. "He always comes in and works on holidays."

"That's good to know," I said.

Gary straightened himself in his seat.

"How about asking the owner if you can bus tables or wash dishes or do whatever needs to be done?" I asked.

"Ask him to hire me?" said Gary. "'Cause he always says 'no.'"

"You don't ask for anything," I said. "You offer to help for free. He might offer you a job later if you show him how much you work without griping or goofing off. Strictly volunteer. If he offers you money, decline."

"What?" asked Gary.

That certainly got his attention.

"Decline the first two times," I said. I put up two fingers. "You don't want charity. You want work. Stick around as long as your mother does. Help clean up after they close. It might not get you a job, but it will help your mother out. Also, it's easier to talk when your hands are busy."

He looked out of the side window. "Hey, we're almost at Waterloo. Wichita is back behind us."

"It's only forty miles or so," I said. Gary told me how to get to the restaurant. He unloaded Muffin and his backpack. "I don't know how to thank you," said Gary. "Will I ever see you again?"

"I know where you live," I said. "I wouldn't be surprised if we bump into each other some time."

After I dropped off Gary, my GPS led me to what appeared to be the only occupied house in a new development. A Toyota Camry sat at the front curb. I called the phone number I had written down. "Special delivery," I said. "Please open the garage door."

The door rose. No light came on. I could see the garage was empty. The walls were not finished on the inside, but the interior was totally enclosed. I drove the van in. The door closed behind me. I walked to the back of the van and opened the door to the cargo bed.

"Is that him?" came a woman's voice. I saw her standing by the door into the house. She was bundled up in winter clothing so I couldn't see much of her. She wore sunglasses but I see that both eyes had been blackened. Her face showed swelling and redness.

I climbed in the cargo bed. The man looked up at me from the floor. He was restrained in chains according to U.S. Marshal Department standards. Transporting feisty prisoners is a big part of their jobs. Why reinvent the manacle? He was gagged based on my twenty years of experience.

"I'm sorry about slamming on the breaks during your ride," I said. "It was unavoidable. Come with me." He didn't get up to move. I grabbed the collar of his coat and dragged him to the open tailgate.

He groaned.

The woman walked over, took off her sunglasses and stared at him. The expression on her battered face was bleaker than the weather outside.

The man whimpered. I looked at the woman.

"Merry Christmas," I said. "After he beat on you, he went to ground. He wasn't easy to find. However, as you requested, I brought your ex-husband to you for the holidays."

We conclude our anthology with a story that casts a spell of words that conjure up the wharves and mysterious streets of Hong Kong shortly after the end of World War II.

When talking of his story, Kenneth Gwin says it is about the tone of black and white mysteries, urban shadows, and whatever waits in the dark. The title came to him from a distant realm found in dreams, and he wrote the story to help find his own Kowloon Princess. Mr. Gwin is a visual artist living in San Francisco.

The Kowloon Princess

by Kenneth Gwin

Aboard the 8,000-ton freighter, S.S. Leftson, on the South China Sea, in the summer of 1949:

His eyes were barely open. He was not sure what woke him up. Maybe the constant rumble deep within the freighter had altered slightly, the low pitch varying imperceptibly as the ship labored against an errant swell. Maybe this was just enough to shake him from his nap, or maybe he just woke up on his own. If he had a dream, it had vanished in a flash.

The slow realization that his eyes were open meant he really had been sound asleep. Dead asleep. There was a half-empty cup of coffee on the table in front of him, his motionless thumb looped through the handle. He looked across the galley.

The cook politely ignored him, leaving him to his business.

Startled upright, he grabbed his cap and headed out on deck. Shading his eyes with the palm of his hand, he squinted through the shock of afternoon sunlight. Hurriedly, he grabbed the rail, ran up to the bridge, his boots pounding away on the metal treads.

Through the bank of windows, the coastline was clearly visible rising in a panorama of ragged peaks. A scattering of sharply drawn islands could be seen off the starboard bow. In a convergence of vessels, there were freighters, tankers, and countless coastal junks spread out across the open waters. Landfall was closing in.

"Everything is in order, sir." The mate stood firm, both hands on the wheel. "We should be at anchor before sunset. Everything's running smoothly."

Captain Flannery moved to stand next to the engine telegraph. Both men looked toward their destination. There was a wordless acknowledgment as the two felt the ship beneath them drawn inevitably toward the land.

After eight long years, Hong Kong lay straight ahead.

———

The streets were busy with nighttime activity. Only the bobbing of Simms' white Panama among the dark-haired masses led him through the confusion as the older and much shorter man showed the way. The captain, dressed in rumpled civvies, followed the best he could.

"Whoa! Look at that!" Simms pointed ahead toward the snake that was slithering down the pavement, while smiling excitedly and shaking his fist. "I just love this fucking town."

"That's a cobra!" Flannery cautioned, backing away. "What the hell are they doing with a snake like that in the middle of the street?" He knew China could offer the unexpected often found in foreign ways. Through the lights and noise it all looked like a sideshow complete with freaks and smoke.

"They say it's medicine." Simms pointed toward the cages that lined the curb. Snakes and vipers of varying sorts were displayed in a range of colors, bands, and stripes. "They milk the venom. You haven't seen this? They say it cures diseases."

A man wielding a thin pole continued to guide the large cobra with smooth quick gestures, leading it in circles around a well-lit area in the street. Waves of people moved around this strangely dancing pair. Free of the meddling pole for a moment, the snake raised itself up as if on cue, flaring its cowl with an ominous hissing sound. With obvious excitement, the audience oohed and aahed, jabbering away in Chinese. Surely the threat from the snake was real. But just as real, this whole performance was an irresistible flame to this swarm of people on a crowded street.

"There's nothing like it!" Simms motioned in approval. "Something new here every day. You don't see stuff like this back in the States."

Flannery was still wary. "No. Not a chance. We've got turtles and frogs in Chinatown, but no snakes. We don't let snakes on board, especially the human ones if we can help it."

"Keep it that way." Simm's tone was more serious. "You don't need snakes in your life. And there is more than one kind of snake here in Hong Kong, so watch your step. I'd be wary. I'd look at any snake as a sign. There's shady business with immigrants and Chinese gangs here. They sometimes bite." Despite Simms' age and short and stocky stature, he led the way with brisk agility.

"So where's the office?"

"I wasn't sure you could find it with things the way they are. There's so much change. It's difficult to stay abreast. Everything's so fast now that the Japs are gone. Even I get turned around. We first set it up in the old location, but had to move recently because of all the new construction. The building next door was under repair. The street was torn up. Dust and dirt was everywhere; it messed up our equipment. I couldn't keep my desk clean and my coffee cup was always full of crap."

The old man slipped between a crowd of pedestrians, leading the way through cluttered streets, ignoring curbs and sidewalks as he zigged and zagged at a healthy trot.

"It's not that much further," Simms reassured, starting to show signs of perspiration. "And try to keep up."

Crossing Nathan Road, Flannery once again recognized landmarks and buildings, and the bustle of cars and buses. He was led down a quiet lane off a side street. Pungent smells of cooking and smoke filled the air. They paused briefly in the light of an open doorway to watch a man squatting on the floor of a tiny workshop. With the simplest of tools he appeared to be in the business of metal casting. There was a primitive gas furnace on a stack of bricks, sand molds, and what looked to be a number of finned metal disks piled on rough wooden shelves. Flannery wondered for a moment what this man was making. Then he understood: water pump impellers, for small motors or irrigation. "Clever."

"This is the definition of cottage industry," Simms said. "They seem to work all night." He continued to lead the way.

The narrow alley was like a fun house of wood-framed balconies with banners, wires, and clotheslines strung overhead. The discordant staccato of Chinese chatter surrounded them as they walked along a row of storefronts packed together, side by side.

They stopped in front of a closed door. Across the street, a middle-aged man with a Charlie Chan mustache, dressed in neat but baggy clothes, was closing up shop for the day. He looked at them with suspicion as he turned off the lights and locked the door behind him. They watched in silence as the man scurried away into the night.

"Doesn't seem too pleased about something," Flannery said.

"Don't worry about him. He's friendly enough, once you get to know him.

"World Wide Travel" was painted in block letters across the window next to the door. The shades were pulled down behind the glass. Simms spoke in a low voice as he opened the door into his office. "Step inside. We've done wonders here with nothing."

The room was spare and clean. There was a blonde oak desk and two padded chairs. A desk lamp cast a circle of warm yellow light that filled up most of the space. The only other furniture was a file cabinet in one corner; a single wall calendar with a photograph of palm trees was the only decoration.

"I'm sure there's more here than meets the eye," Flannery noted, indicating the door leading to another room.

"What would you expect? We're in a certain business." Simms gestured as he sat down behind the desk. "Have a seat. I'd offer you a drink, but I try not to have that stuff around." He gave a guilty shrug. Removing his hat, he placed it on the edge of the desk

"I'll manage." Flannery sat down across from Simms.

"Good. I wanted to see you before morning and things got busy—all the business of managing a ship in port and all." Palms down, he leaned back in his chair. "This project will require continuous vigilance by a good many people over time."

Flannery was rightfully suspicious of what they might want of him now.

"Should I be armed?" He figured the answer might give him a clue as to what this assignment might be.

"Probably not. Perhaps on some other occasion it might be required. Just don't get caught with a weapon. This is not America."

Glancing around, Flannery noticed an ashtray on a stand beside him. "Do you mind if I smoke?"

Simms shrugged again. "Be my guest, though it's a habit we do not share." He rubbed the smooth top of his head and waited until Flannery had run through the ritual of lighting a cigarette and closing his lighter with a snap. He continued: "The British have been forced to alter certain things in their relationship with the local Chinese. Things are different now. There's a bit more bureaucracy and a bit less control. But they still share many common goals here, as do we in this important matter."

Flannery listened.

"People are living on rooftops, makeshift camps in the foothills, on any kind of boat that will stay afloat in the harbor. Naturally, every resource is stressed with the thousands of refugees flooding in across the border every week. Here in Hong Kong there is both hope and desperation."

"That's what I understand." Flannery continued to listen.

"The Communists have all but taken over the mainland. The British have done well to stabilize the situation here, but we have Communists in the government hiding in plain sight, in the schools, everywhere. We have gangsters—opium, murder, organized crime. Bad guys. But with a firm resolve against these kinds of forces,

Special Operations believes this town could be the Mother Lode, the Goose That Laid the Golden Egg to change the eastern world."

"Hong Kong?"

"Yes." He paused. "You seem surprised."

"So what am I supposed to do?"

"You have official access to the harbor. Simple. You have a ship. And you have additional eyes that we might use."

"I see." Flannery waited, cautious and suspicious.

"My dear friend Christopher, we are about to witness a great changing sea. Let me explain."

———

Flannery stood in the dark on Shanghai Street. Through a dusty window he could see faint glimpses of tables and boxes, walls lined with jars and tins. They could be tea or spices, maybe medicinal herbs. He couldn't tell. There used to be another business here, one he knew quite well. But it was gone and so was she. His feelings sank with the realization. What had happened here under the Japanese? He knew things were brutal. But where could she be?

The streets were nearly empty. Rattling and clanging noises echoed off the nearby buildings. A few lights along the street provided scant illumination. There was not much else that he could see. He was tired. He needed a drink. He knew bad things had happened here during the war. He didn't want to hear of any more.

If he remembered correctly, there used to be a bar nearby that catered to the Aussies, the Brits, and Americans. Mostly the Aussies, but he could make do. A drink would be nice. They might even have good bourbon.

It was a short walk. He was in luck. The bar was still there. Perhaps it would improve his mood. There was a welcoming light over the door and faint music could be heard as he approached the entrance. The inside was dark, familiar. It had that certain smell. He could hear the music more clearly. Frank Sinatra's *But Beautiful* drifted softly through the room. It seemed unreal. Songs like that gave him the sense he'd walked into a movie, or onto some grand stage that was bigger than life.

He took a stool at the bar away from the door, passing a lone drinker who turned to give him an indifferent look displaying neither friendliness nor disapproval. He placed a Zippo and a pack of Luckies on the heavily varnished top. The bartender slid an ashtray his way, took his order, poured him a generous shot and left him alone to enjoy his drink.

Captain Christopher Flannery looked around the room.

Two men were in deep conversation at the far end of the bar. They had the look of colonial British. A man and a woman sat at a table in the corner. Something about their clothes said they were probably Americans. They never looked up.

There was another couple sitting at a nearby table. The woman was Chinese and chatted away comfortably to her man while he sat listening attentively to every word she said. She was lovely. Very. His fear of loss and emptiness was creeping in.

Flannery sipped his drink. It might have helped. The pleasant sharpness of the whiskey bit his lip. He watched the Chinese woman, trying not to stare. His mind wandered off.

The music continued.

I'd Like To Get You On A Slow Boat To China began to play. He had to smile. He'd just gotten off a slow boat to China. Dry humor and irony seemed to follow him everywhere. He'd spent the better part of his life on a slow boat going somewhere, just to end up here.

Somehow his glass had emptied. The bartender poured another. Flannery's mind drifted off again.

He tried to remember her face. There were no pictures of her that he could pull out of his pocket to prove that she was real, only memories that lingered just beyond his reach.

The song continued. He let his mind wander, following the words. The song was about being somewhere and with someone special. He liked the song. He looked around. Nobody seemed to be paying attention to the music, not even the guy he'd passed coming in.

The Chinese woman continued to chat with the man at the table.

He was thinking; they didn't even look alike. There was nothing similar in their manners. But there was something in this woman that brought her image back to him. He continued to watch. What was it then about her? He could not say.

She caught him looking.

He turned away.

She continued chatting, perhaps with even more assurance knowing she had another man under her spell.

He hesitated to look directly at her. It wasn't the hair. This woman had a cascade of silky black flowing like water off her shoulders. The Josephine he remembered had worn her hair with tight bits of wave tied back in a bun against her slender neck. Perhaps it was the roundness of her face, the unquestioning look in her eyes that never seemed to blink. He could catch some flicker of recollection, some hint he could almost see. What was it then? The image that came into focus quickly faded, then was lost.

It had been a long time. Was she even alive? Was she dead? The thought grabbed him by the throat.

The war had separated everybody, bringing with it grief and loss. Where was she now? Was she still in Hong Kong? Or had she escaped to somewhere else? These were questions he could not answer. He'd had no chance to seek her out.

When *Stardust* started playing, he had to leave. Still, he was the captain; the launch would have waited all night.

Morning came down hard. Sleeping less and not sleeping well had taken its toll.

The steward knocked on Flannery's cabin door before sunrise, announced that hot coffee, toast and scrambled eggs were ready in the mess. The coffee worked like a Brillo pad, scrubbing out a spot inside his brain where he could slowly put his thoughts in order. Eating breakfast gave him a moment to recover some sense of equilibrium before the real business of Hong Kong came alive.

Shortly after dawn he ordered the crew to pull anchor and the ship was nudged gently into a waiting berth. Shouting deck hands fired up the winches, manned the booms and were soon unloading crates, bundles and boxes to an army of dockworkers armed with push carts, wagons and trucks. A flotilla of sampans bobbed precariously off the stern. Full sacks of foodstuffs and household goods were lowered in nets from number four hold. It took medicines and spices, lumber, heavy equipment, and tools of all kinds to feed Hong Kong. And Hong Kong was hungry day and night.

Flannery stood in his khakis, watched the docks from the flying bridge, thinking of Josephine and everything Simms had said.

That afternoon he took the Star Ferry. Simms had told him Winston Fong, the antique dealer, was the man to see.

He boarded the lower deck, choosing to mingle freely with the crowds. At just over six feet tall and fitted out in a crisply pressed jacket and trousers, he wasn't even trying to blend in. He simply liked the view so near the water. It gave him a chance to see other ships, boats and junks pass close above him, see and hear the sounds of Victoria Harbor slowly gliding by. It was also nice to have someone else bear the responsibility for a vessel's safe voyage.

On the island, he followed the crowd through the gates of the terminal. He hailed a taxi waiting at the curb. It was only a short ride, but he cut it shorter, instructing the driver to let him off on Queen's Road Central at the base of Ladder Street in front of a building latticed in bamboo scaffolding several stories high. Here he climbed the last few flights up to Hollywood Road. He was told that Winston Fong's shop was on the right, just down from Man Mo Temple.

It was a narrow shop, cluttered to the ceilings with bronze figures, objects and vases of indeterminate age turned black and brown and muddy green by the passage of time and the constant work of the elements. Rows of glass shelves displayed precious little bottles and boxes made of porcelain, glass and horn bill. The aisles were lined with intricate carvings in jade, stone, earthenware and age-yellowed ivory.

The captain stopped in front of a small figure placed on one of the shelves.

A Chinese man approached. At nearly the same height, he stood eye to eye with Flannery, was solidly built and immaculately dressed in a well-made summer-weight suit. "I see this has caught your eye. You have excellent taste." He spoke the most perfect King's English. "It's a beautiful piece depicting one of the followers of Buddha."

"I'm sorry. I wouldn't know. But it is very interesting."

The man picked up the statue, turned it lovingly in his hands, offering Flannery a better opportunity for inspection.

"Do you know how old it is?" the captain asked.

"Of course. You understand there are many forgeries on the market. There are so many clever artists busy at deception. As the owner of this shop, one must be careful with verification. It takes an experienced eye to know the difference. But this is from the fourteenth century. Exquisite. It is one of several I have here in the shop."

"It's very nice. But I doubt it would survive long on a ship."

"You have no home in which to place it?"

"I have a place to stay when I'm not at sea. It's at White Point. It's near Los Angeles, but I can still see the ocean from my front door. Have you been to America?"

"Yes. Several times. But that was before the unfortunate occupation by the Japanese."

"I see." There wasn't much Flannery could add to this and chose not to question any further. "I was told to see a man named Winston Fong by a Mr. Simms. I am Captain Christopher Flannery. I have a ship berthed in the harbor."

"Ah, I am Winston Fong. You are in the shipping business. Out of the United States." He gestured toward the back of the shop where another, similarly well-dressed Chinese man was sitting at a desk. This man stood up and walked toward the entrance. "I am in the business of trade—shipping and receiving as well. Let us take a moment to talk. I have many friends beyond the borders, on land, and on the waters. I might be of assistance in your journey. And you may be helpful to mine."

Flannery was led to the back of the shop and offered a chair next to the now vacant desk.

"Please be seated. We should all be comfortable."

They both sat down at the desk.

Flannery could recognize fine craftsmanship and commented on the smooth rosewood construction while caressing the desktop gently with his hand.

"Yes, it is beautiful; however it is not antique, but a perfect example of the Art Deco style. These date only from the nineteen thirties." Winston also indicated the polished metal desk lamp: "I found this at the same time. Even as a dealer in antiquities, one should not exist solely for the past."

"Handsome. Is this nickel plated?" Flannery was intrigued by the warm metallic sheen.

"Ah, very discerning. Actually, this is machined from solid Monel. A beautiful metal. Quite rare. Not Chinese. These are actually American and of the very highest quality. The set was made for an executive in the aeronautics industry. The purchaser believes he possesses the only such one in existence. But, of course, the artist made two of everything." Winston's expression displayed calm self-satisfaction and a bit of the cat that ate the canary. "It is good to have alliances abroad to alert one to good fortune and rare opportunities. It's a minor deception. But who is to know?"

"I see."

A momentary cloud came over Winston's face. "Hiding treasures such as these required considerable resources and ingenuity during the occupation." He paused for a moment, moved to change the course of conversation: "Do you know what you are looking for, Captain Flannery? Mr. Simms and I have recently established an agreeable understanding."

"Not exactly. But I've been given guidelines and general directions."

"Perhaps an overview of the state of affairs might explain to you how the game is played." Winston leaned forward. He placed his palms together and rested his elbows on the desk. "You are familiar with Hong Kong?"

"Yes. From before the war."

"That is good. Perhaps then you know something of the spirit of the people here. There are traditions that are not beneficial to the new sense of order. There is opium to waste the mind and subvert the energies required for progress. There is the tradition of crime. And there are political influences from the mainland that seek to undermine the great strides that are moving us forward. The totalitarian machine that has taken over the mainland has chased the weak and corrupt forces of opposition to the island of Formosa. The Kuomintang have no place else to run. We, on the other hand, are not fleeing or running from anyone. In Hong Kong there is great opportunity. There is mass migration with these changing times, and profit to be made in the movement of people and goods and manufacturing." He paused. "And with profit often comes corruption."

Flannery was silent.

"Hong Kong must be rebuilt to honor the spirit of the people here. While there are those driven by self-interest or seduced by rhetoric shouted from the mainland, we have a city to rebuild. The British have been both instrumental and complicit in the trade of opium and corruption. This has existed for generations. It has been the basis of their power. But they too have much to gain in these modern times. It is a benefit to many. Things change, as you will see."

"And what part do we play here?" Flannery finally asked. "The Americans."

"There are various ways. We have many powerful enemies. Local crime brings fear and violence, drugs and prostitution. Still, there are many friends in our endeavor. We seek to build an army. But this is a quiet war we fight." Winston paused. "Are you familiar with the outlying islands, Captain Flannery?"

"Somewhat."

"There is movement there, the smuggling of drugs and stolen goods—even precious antiquities such as those you see here—

under the cover of native fishing. On the island of Cheung Chau, on the beach beyond the village, there have been exchanges, even items awaiting export, hidden in the most obvious of places—the pirate's cave near the south end of the island, for example. What is not consumed in Hong Kong must find a market elsewhere. Do you want more of these poisons and illicit goods to find their way to America?"

"Of course not."

"You should be watchful then. Every ship may be unwitting transport."

"We keep an eye out. I hear there is also theft of goods that land here, missing shipments, false papers, outright piracy off the docks."

"Yes, it goes both ways. The police can only see and hear so much. But the exporting of vice can reap great profits. Containing this flow could act to discourage, weaken the disease that festers here. America may serve as an example of enterprise beyond crime and the threat of Communism. You can be a partner in this fight."

"Is there anything specific I should be aware of?"

"Ah, yes. Quite so. Egg jars shipped by rail from Fanling will be waiting on your dock."

———————

Outside, Flannery turned away to the right, wandering aimlessly through narrow streets, alleys and lanes so dense with activity they seemed more like caves. Stalls, busy with commerce, were filled with beads, cottons and dry goods offered for sale. There were scarves and lace, an endless array of women's clothing, cheongsam, slippers, and western-style pajamas made of the finest of silks.

Somehow he had wandered in circles, ending up on Tai Ping Shan Street. There he watched a man refinishing furniture and wooden screens, scraping away worn varnish and lacquer with only a sharpened piece of metal for a tool.

As Flannery worked his way downhill, the lights were coming on in the city. The hive of activity that was Hong Kong faded slowly into darkness and glowing points of light.

He took the ferry back to the Kowloon side, watched lamp-lit junks glide across the black lake of the harbor while holding a carefully wrapped bundle nestled in his lap.

By nine the next morning, the day was already heating up. Deckhands had cleaned the holds a second time and greased and oiled the machinery.

There was great discussion on the docks as goods were being staged for loading. Busy clerks with clipboards pointed out items, checked lists and goods received-for-shipment. Local officials directed traffic though warehouses piled high with merchandise. There were bundles wrapped and stuffed with straw, barrels and bags waiting on pallets.

Flannery kept watch as he'd been told. His crew was alerted. The winch operators knew their business.

Shortly after eleven, three inconspicuous crates of egg jars were wheeled out onto the docks. The first load was stored safely, placed below decks without incident. As planned, a purposeful miscue by one winch operator sent the second load spilling, the whole affair sliding off the board to tumble back to the docks. One corner hit hard on a bollard. The crate broke open. One cracked egg jar rolled out.

"Good shot," Flannery mumbled to himself. "Look inside!" he shouted. "Check for damage!"

"Pick it up!" The bosun gathered his men.

A scrambling of hands rushed in to assist. The broken jar fell apart, its strange cargo spilling onto the planks.

"Those aren't eggs," someone pointed out.

"What do you see?" Flannery called down.

"Looks like carved ivory. Pretty fancy stuff, if you ask me. And a lot more expensive than eggs."

The captain was satisfied with foiling a plot. Easy enough. He knew Winston Fong would be satisfied too, since these goods might have been his at one point. "Well, this will take them awhile.

The local officials will have more than enough to sort through this afternoon."

───────────

It was late in the day, but he made it back again, through the streets, looking for the shop that used to be. Change was everywhere. Some internal guidance led the way.

Through the same dusty window he could see the same boxes and jars and painted tins he'd seen the night before. The shop was open. He went inside, inquiring about the business from before the war. What had happened? Where did they go?

The owner, a gaunt man speaking very little English explained: "Old man died. They gone. Move. They go away." A look of incomprehension blanketed his face.

"What do you mean, go away?"

"Gone." The man gestured waving, brushing the inquiry away. "They gone."

"Gone?" Flannery stood in the shop, helpless to communicate the sense of loss.

"Long time."

"Long time? Where did they go?"

The man seemed to listen, trying to understand, remembering something long forgotten. He went to a row of cabinets lining the back wall, pulled open one drawer, a second one. He mumbled to himself, shuffled through some papers. He pulled out a card. He held it out.

There was an address.

There was hope, but still no promise.

───────────

The clutter of Temple Street was disorienting. Push carts, food stands, every manner of commerce shouted for attention.

He followed a lean young man through the crowds. As if by magic, this man navigated a nearly straight course through all the noise and confusion. Although dressed in nondescript clothing—pale shirt, loose pants and soft canvas shoes—he possessed some air, some noble bearing others sensed that cleared an open pathway for him.

Flannery was intrigued. Perhaps there was something more to learn here.

He soon found the building from the address printed on the card. The rush of humanity pressed against him as he stood before it on the pavement. On a sign across the bricks, Chinese characters were outlined in gold. A sign in English, painted just below, announced: "Jewel of the Orient Trading."

That was the name. There was still hope. Perhaps her father had died, or something else happened that forced them to move.

Tentatively, he went inside.

An older woman looked up from her task. She turned her eyes to a younger woman standing toward the back.

He first noticed how small and thin she looked, a few strands of grey. But there was a flash of the person he used to know.

The woman placed the package she was holding on a nearby table. It seemed to take forever for her to speak, as if English was unfamiliar to her, or time had momentarily come to rest.

"Christopher. You are alive. More now than just a dream."

"Hello, Princess. You promised me dinner. If you don't have other plans."

About This Book

The typeface in this book is 11.5 Garamond and Helvetica (for the headings). It was laid out using Adobe InDesign software and converted to PDF for uploading to the printing facility.

About Darkhouse Books

Darkhouse Books is dedicated to publishing entertaining fiction, primarily in the mystery and science fiction field. Darkhouse Books is located in Niles, California, an inadvertently-preserved, 120 year old, one-sided, railtown, forty miles from San Francisco. Further information may be obtained by visiting our website at www.darkhousebooks.com.

Made in the USA
Middletown, DE
23 May 2016